The Tree Goddess

The Tree Goddess

The Mapleview Series – Book 2

Tom Raimbault

Published 2015 by Creativia

Book design by Creativia (www.creativia.org)

Cover art by http://www.thecovercollection.com/

Dedications

To Bear (my wife) and my two daughters, Megan and Lauren.

To my Mother and Father.

And to my Grandmother who enjoys my writings. I hope she likes this one, too!

Preface

The light of a candle flickers, bobs and sways throughout the hours in a darkened, old house. Perhaps it sits at a dusty table in an attic or some corner of the basement. At the table, nothing more than a pen scribbles on sheets of paper by a seemingly unguided force.

This is the sight you might expect to see at some haunted house in the darkest hours of night. And this is the time of night when the material was written for this novel. 2:30 in the morning, I would sometimes joke with myself and wonder if I wrote as if something from the coffin, dead. Yes, arising during the witching hour can certainly lead one to feel drained of all life; especially as the day progresses long into the afternoon hours. But those many hours alone in the dark of night had proven to be the most precious moments of creativity.

Looking back at the entire growth of The Tree Goddess, I believe the initial spark that put the story in motion took place while my wife, kids and I were packing up boxes to move into a new residence. At the time, my 9 year old daughter (oldest) was cautioned of a box of fragile centerpieces that I claimed to be expensive antiques. Only being silly with the child, in truth, the items were cheap and could easily be replaced. Challenged by my daughter that the claim was fiction, the stories I made up for each item were enough to draw laughter from the wife and kids.

Writing off and on for a number of years, a website was created to showcase my short stories and unusual essays. Halloween week had always been a special celebration on the site as it featured spooky, Halloween-related material. And in the spring of 2009, the plan was to make Halloween really special with some fantastic, original material. The stories that were centered on the box of fragile items which entertained my wife and kids while moving were planned to be developed into detailed writings. Spending some weeks, 5 short stories were written. Upon their completion, I realized that they were all related. In fact, with only a few alterations, the same characters could have appeared throughout.

But writing a novel is no easy task! The Tree Goddess had been written not once, not twice, but three times! After my second try, it was realized that I needed to further develop the craft of storytelling. Since I had done much technical writing in my job, the first two drafts of the Tree Goddess were nothing more than technical papers with logical presentations that attempted to describe the bizarre and supernatural happenings of Mapleview.

My story book, Freaked out Horror was the training ground where I created a collection of strange and morbid tales and then added a macabre tone, something which I had never done before. It was written after my 2nd attempt of writing the Tree Goddess. Satisfied with what I had written, I was confident that the 3rd attempt of the Tree Goddess would prove successful. Now, in 2010, the novel is complete and ready to be released. I thoroughly enjoyed writing it and I hope you enjoy the completed product.

But there is one thing that I need to call to the reader's attention. Being that there are four disappearances in the fictional town of Mapleview, I found it necessary to divide the book into four parts. It's only right to venture into each character's past and reveal the events which led to another disappearance in Mapleview. As you read part one, the story will unfold with

Mary, who purchases the historic Trivelli house from her aunt and has some bizarre experiences. Towards the end of part one, we witness the first disappearance of Mapleview. But then part two will venture 10 years into a new character's past. Towards the end, that character's decade will track back into the running story of the book so that we resume where part one had left off. Had I not partitioned the novel this way, it would have been confusing for the reader. And had I given a proper, sequential three decades of the events in Mapleview, the work would have been extremely boring and lengthy. Presenting it as four parts is best.

Recently, I took a family vacation to the Black Hills of South Dakota. During this trip, I was fascinated with not only the mountainous, western landscapes that were highlighted by pines; but also the history of the area. Towards the end of my stay, I was very, much aware that the Black Hills region was victim to General Custer's invasion and then a gold rush which further contributed to the interesting history of the area. And there were so many antique buildings, mining shacks and caves; each with stories of their own. One could become an expert of local history just by living there.

Returning home to polish my final draft of the Tree Goddess, I soon realized that there are history buffs who know many details of our nation's history. I thought of this while noticing that the story goes into great lengths, describing the setting of the novel along with the region's history. Wolves populate the dense forests, and of course, tribes of Native Americans had populated fictional Mapleview, long before the town was established in 1830.

But it's important to know that Mapleview is fictional! Don't bother trying to solve exactly where in America Mapleview is located. The very fact that Mapleview was founded in 1830 might lead an expert to pinpoint an area in this country that was settled in during that timeframe. And then one might conclude that dense forests shouldn't be located in a particular area, or that wolves are not indigenous to a certain imagined part of the country. Again, Mapleview is fictional; and so are the accounts of its history.

I hope you enjoy this novel. And to all my readers who have read my daily edits all of these years: this book contains the material that was originally supposed to run on Halloween week of 2009.

Tom Raimbault
Frankfort, Illinois
July 16, 2010

Prelude:
Painting on a Bottle of Wine

On a Saturday, mid-October night a beautiful woman accompanied the man she had been falling in love with to his duplex condo in the rural town of Robin Creek. It was about an hour drive from Mapleview.

It was a typical night out, absolutely wonderful as the hours flew by like minutes. Many have experienced the blissful moments of falling in love, when we desire to spend every waking second with that special someone. During this moment, Dana hated the idea of going home for the evening to endure the absence of this wonderful man for the week. He had business matters that needed attention on Sunday, and most likely would not see Dana until Friday. Perhaps it wouldn't hurt to go back to his place, let him crack open a bottle of wine and spend some more wonderful time together. It was, after all, what had been suggested.

A peculiar painting, somewhat comical and somewhat grotesque, was displayed on a bottle of red wine. It was one of those inexpensive wines that one might find on sale at a discount store. Perhaps to give it more appeal, the bottle was indicated as special, limited-edition for Halloween. The orange background along with jack-o-lanterns suggested a spooky, autumn theme.

But the subject of the painting was silly! It was nothing more than a half-tree, half-human creature that was recognizably female with firm, shapely thighs; large breasts and woman-like arms.

The bottle sat on a coffee table in a candlelit living room and enjoyed on that Saturday, mid-October night.

"Hey, I actually know the guy who did the painting for this bottle."

Dana was used to his wild stories, created just to amuse her, and at first assumed this was one of them.

"No seriously! And the artwork is really no laughing matter. The actual story behind the painting was gruesome enough, and because the vineyard wanted to release a limited Halloween edition, they figured it would be the perfect artwork."

Dana looked at the picture on the bottle and was a bit confused. "I don't get it. When I think of Halloween; I think of ghosts, witches or vampires; not a half woman, half tree thing." But as the conversation continued, it was pointed out that the vineyard added a couple of jack-o-lanterns on the picture and highlighted the Halloween tone with an orange background. The story behind the painting made it worthy to be Halloween material.

Dana drew closer and took another sip of her wine. "Okay, so what's the story behind the painting?"

"Well, it all started with a mysterious disappearance that took place in the town of Mapleview."

The very mention of Mapleview perked Dana's interest, "The Mapleview disappearances? I remember those from the news."

Part One:
The Mausoleum

Chapter 1

You pass through them while driving on vacation; the peaceful, historic towns surrounded by miles of forests, lakes, mountains and untouched wilderness. And yet some of them appear to be thriving communities complete with every convenience and luxury one would expect to find in the city or suburbs. Such towns have been known to generate income from a yearly flow of tourists. Or they can be occupied by individuals such as artists, writers or people who travel much in their jobs. This is the sort of town Mapleview is.

Founded in the early 1800s, it offers a place for people to get away from it all and finally live in an area that values peace, quiet and communion with nature. But there's an unknown, dark side to that wonderful town where most people would only dream of living. Some attribute it to a mysterious sentience that blankets the town in a wilderness deep in unknown history. Some explain that the legendary Trivelli house continues to curse the area since the well known tragedy that took place in the 1830s. Other residents adopt a more sensible theory and state that many of the people in that town are simply crazy.

There's a private section of forest near the Hidden Lake Forest Preserve in Mapleview that has been owned by the Trivelli family since 1832. One must travel uphill on a half-block driveway to get to the historical house. The house overlooks the actual lake that is in Hidden Lake Forest Preserve, and has become an icon to residents of Mapleview who gaze up to the old house on the hill. As mentioned before, the house has a terrible legend that really seems to be fed by those who continue to tell the story.

Although the story in this book is focused on the time when Mary owned the Trivelli house, it is probably best to give a very, brief account of the last person's experiences who resided there, just to understand what Mary had walked into.

It was two years before the sale of the legendary, historic house of Mapleview, and two years before the series of mysterious disappearances. Terri was the last tenant of Loraine Trivelli. Loraine inherited the historic house that had been passed down for generations.

Terri drove on a Saturday morning through the heavily forested highways with nothing but miles of wilderness and seclusion to surround her. Finally reaching Mapleview Road, she soon found the oversized, historic house and ascended the half-block driveway where Loraine Trivelli had greeted her.

Loraine was a friendly, older woman; perhaps in her early 60s with an air of grace and of following all things that were proper. She led Terri into the home and provided a tour of the place which most people only dream of.

"It's a house that was built in the 1830s and has been passed down through the generations. As you can see it's fully furnished, many of the pieces antiques. If you decide to stay, I only ask that you make no changes to the decorating and structure as this is a historic landmark to the town of Mapleview."

It was a beautiful home in a quiet town, and just the place for Terri to rediscover her talent for art. How could she turn down such a place?

"So what brings you to Mapleview, if you don't mind me asking?" Loraine was always curious of her potential tenants.

"I'm an artist, just looking for a quiet place and some inspiration." Peace and quiet was something that Terri most certainly needed, considering the stress and near nervous breakdown experienced at the company just outside of Chicago that specialized in biomedical manufacturing. The wiry-thin, middle-aged blonde who served as a punching bag to management and the FDA alike could no longer take the damage. Threats of being fired because of production mishaps, and threats of heavy fines from the FDA inspectors were squeezing the very life out of her. There was no reason to stay as she had other talents and plenty of finances saved up. Many people left the company under similar circumstances. It was just Terri's turn.

"Oh, I get plenty of artists and writers who stay here for a year or more so they can complete a work." It seemed to Loraine that her historic house was the ideal place for people like Terri to live, offering peace and quiet in the communion of nature.

But then Terri hinted towards a question, hoping not to offend Loraine. "It's so nice here and peaceful. I couldn't imagine anyone wanting to leave after a year or so."

Loraine wasn't going to take Terri's curiosity personal. Although she desired to keep renters for longer periods, the legend and stigmatism of the house eventually pushed tenants away. She was lucky to have a renter like Terri who needed a quiet place to stay. Loraine very calmly speculated, "Oh, I suppose people want to move on. Not much happens here in Mapleview. I'm sure after a couple of years; you might want a new environment for inspiration as well."

Again, the historic house was beautiful and sat in a quiet town. It was just the place for Terri to rediscover her talent for art. How could she turn down such a place? The rental agreement was filled out that very day.

* * *

Certainly not expecting inspiration to immediately hit her, Terri spent some time getting acquainted with the historic house and the small, charming town of Mapleview. As a gentle reminder to creativity's subconscious, Terri did set up her oil canvass in the living room, just in front of the old piano with antique vase seated on top. The vase was certainly in need of fresh flowers, and her oil canvass was in need of inspiration.

The Trivelli house overlooks the Hidden Lake Forest Preserve and backs into a narrow, wooded path that descends to the bottom of the forest. Returning from her first nature hike one morning, Terri took sight of the historic house from a distance and realized that it had been built on throughout the 150 years or more since its original construction. She could see the very center of the building which revealed the possible appearance of the home as it would have looked in the 1830s. That was the moment of initial inspiration. The canvass was brought outside, some distance from the house, and the brush strokes began to take form.

The exclusive colors were blue and light-gray, ignoring the lush greens and browns of the forest world. Terri was unable to create a clear, discernable image of the house and attributed the stymie to the fact that she was painting the building as it looked 150 or more years ago. The end product was eerie, dark-toned and suggested a haunted environment. Maybe the inspiration was a bad idea. Terri decided to bring the painting inside and work on it after dinner that night. But the house, itself, seemed to welcome the painting. It almost complimented Terri and congratulated her on the fine work!

Terri became obsessed with the imagined presence that adored her artwork. It was necessary to personify the presence that was drawn as tall and dark, wearing a suit and seated at the piano bench. Just like the painting of the house, his face was made barely discernable; but there were subtle characteristics of being handsome.

One could almost consider Terri's art as a medium that attempted to understand the paranormal presence in the home.

All paintings created after the attempted personification became increasingly horrific; which illustrated various rooms with walls to include bodies trapped behind them, along with ghostly people who pounded to escape.

Terri suffered from a lack of sleep, lost her appetite and remained obsessed with the horrific paintings. The final two were much too disturbing to mention; but it can be said that they reflected her pain and loss of life that had been brought on by the legendary, historic house. With her realization, she escaped and never returned to the town of Mapleview.

As for Loraine Trivelli, it was just one of many tenants lost. For years she rented the house out to people, needing a quiet place to do their art or write their novels. These were usually people from out of state and unaware of the terrible legend of the Trivelli house. After some time, these renters would become outraged that they rented a stigmatized property and terminated their rental agreement with Loraine.

Upon inheriting the home to herself at the death of her father, Loraine thought that using the house as a pricey rental property would be an excellent source of income. But since the renters were far and few between, the house was more of a burden, so she decided to sell.

* * *

Loraine's niece, Mary, heard word of her aunt's plan to sell and immediately offered to purchase before it went on the market. She cashed in on some investments and paid for the house in full, as she did not want to lose the home she always wanted since a little girl. This, of course, disappointed the local Realtors who had already been talking to Loraine.

Mary didn't care about the legend of the house. It was a beautiful, historic house and the perfect place to enjoy her soon-to-be husband and raise a family. Her wedding was two months away and she and her fiancé, Daren, decided that taking up residence in Mapleview would be a great idea. Daren traveled the country; demonstrating innovative, new medical equipment and could set up residence anywhere. His job only required quick access to the airport. Mary planned on getting her old job back at the flower shop in town.

"Are you sure you're going to be happy here?" Loraine and her niece, Mary, came back to the Trivelli house after their closing in town. Mary now had full-ownership, and Loraine accompanied her niece back to her new home just to make sure she was happy. The house was fully furnished with beautiful, antique furniture that had been accumulated in the Trivelli family for over 150 years. It was a sweet deal for Mary; simply buy the house, settle in and get married.

"Why wouldn't I be happy here? This has been my house ever since I could remember. I've always wanted this house."

"Well, it's stigmatized and might have some sort of curse. I'm actually glad to get it off my hands."

"It's a legend! And really it shouldn't be a legend. It was just a tragic accident!" For years, Mary believed her aunt had a neurotic obsession with the supposed curse of what was now Mary's beautiful home. And the last thing she wanted to hear on the day of the closing was that her dream home had such a stigmatism.

But Loraine continued, feeling she needed to set her niece straight of the supposed legend of the Trivelli House. "Just a legend? I'm well aware of the legend. Grandma and Grandpa Trivelli built this house and lived here when Mapleview was just a half-block of stores about a mile away from here."

Considering that people of previous generations had married at 18 (or younger) and immediately had children, it was very possible to have five generations within a span of 100 years. For that matter, a long list of "greats" could prefix Grandma and Grandpa which could be redundant when mentioning them. To remedy this, Loraine, and anyone else who spoke of the tragedy, simply called the original owners of the Trivelli house from 1830, Grandma and Grandpa Trivelli.

Aunt Loraine continued her story to Mary, "One winter, Grandpa came down with a life-threatening flu and was in bed with a very, high fever. Grandma went outside to get some firewood and according to Grandpa, his wife's voice could be heard, screaming, buried beneath the noise of a wild pack of wolves. In his words, they dragged her off into the woods! Grandpa was too weak and sick to get out of bed; so sick, in fact, that it wasn't until early spring when he reported the disappearance of his wife to police.

And I'm sure the Mapleview police were just as slip-shoddy with their investigations, then, as they are now. According to their daughter who was young then, but sleeping during the supposed night that her mother was dragged off by wolves, her father was a binge drinker and had seasonal depressions. She said he would become violent and beat his wife in the night. I don't think wolves dragged Grandma Trivelli off as the legend claims; nor do I think that Grandpa was in bed with a fever.

According to their daughter, earlier that day, her father came home smelling of booze and started a huge fight with his wife. Then he went down into the basement to get an axe. When he came upstairs, he proceeded to chop up the kitchen stove into tiny pieces while laughing. It was the most God-awful sight. And when there was nothing left, he looked at his wife and said he had an early Christmas present while raising the axe and implying she was next. But it was all in good fun for Grandpa Trivelli. The surprise was he had a brand, new stove for his terrified wife. Imagine chopping up a stove while laughing, just to surprise the one you love with a new one. And imagine doing all of that while deathly ill with the flu. Their daughter said she heard plenty of fighting and beatings on the night that her mother was supposedly dragged off by wolves."

Mary was amazed and further convinced that her neurotic aunt grew steadily worse as the years progressed. For someone who wasn't alive when these supposed events took place, she knew everything!

Aunt Loraine was completely absorbed in discovering family history and continued with the knowledge she had. "I believe Grandma Trivelli was murdered in this house because of a generational curse that was put on the women in this family. I've been researching the history of this curse, but it seems that many of the women in our family die horrific deaths throughout the centuries. And the husbands are all heavy drinkers... *borderline psychotic...*"

Mary could tell what was coming next. She was going to get "the talk" about marrying Daren. It was almost as if her aunt's voice had increased a notch in volume to make a point.

"It's why I have never been married. Are you sure that Daren is the right man for you? Seems like a nice man but..."

Mary quickly cut her off. "He's fine Aunt Loraine! And yes, I'm sure I'm doing the right thing. I don't build my life around legends and family curses while dwelling in what happened before I was born."

"Well, I suppose you're right. I just want to make sure you're happy and want to clear my conscience of selling you a place that I feel is stigmatized. But as long as you are okay with it; welcome back home Mary."

One might think that Aunt Loraine is as Mary believes: obsessed to the point of neurosis and eagerly misconstruing of vague facts to mold reality. But in Aunt Loraine's mind, she firmly believed that there was something wrong with that house and simply needed to clear her conscience of selling it to her niece.

* * *

Mary sat out on the deck that overlooked the lake that night while talking to her fiancé on the phone. "It's so quiet here. You're going to love it. Daren I can't wait until you spend a night. It's the perfect house and town for us. You're still coming out here this weekend, right?" It was then that Mary noticed that Daren was not himself and finally voiced her concern, "What's wrong? I can tell something is wrong?"

Daren finally broke the bad news to Mary. "Well, they're sending me out to Missouri, tomorrow, to demo a unit at a weekend convention. I'm not going to be able to come out this weekend. I'm sorry."

Needless to say, Mary was disappointed but remained understanding. It was, after all, Daren's job that made it possible to live in the beautiful, historic house and live in the town of Mapleview.

There was much to do in the new house. Although fully furnished and in livable condition, it was necessary to sort through her smaller, personal belongings; put clothes away; and of course, stock up on food. When Daren finally moved in, the same would need to be done with his personal items. And of course she would be confronted with the challenge of explaining that not everything needed to come with him!

It's an interesting house when considering the construction. The initial building was a small dwelling for Mary's grandparents (from the 1830s), but had been added on throughout the 150-some years while owned by the family. Several additions along with modernized utilities helped the home grow into a rather large, historical house. And one of those modernized utilities that Mary looked forward to was the shower. She recalled enjoying it while staying at the house during her teen years.

Mary finally stepped into the shower after her long, exhausting day. The shower was a drug for Mary that cleared her mind of everything, placing her mind at ease. She forgot about wolves dragging her grandmother into the forest. She forgot about husbands chopping up furniture in the house and murdering their wives. And she somehow found herself to be understanding that Daren had an important job which required his presence over the weekend.

Two hours into her night's rest, Mary was startled awake by a vivid and terrifying dream. Holding out her hands in defense; one was grabbed, held down on a table and quickly chopped off, yielding startling pain. Now awake, Mary could hear a violent storm outside while she quickly turned the light on to examine her hand, thinking she had injured it while sleeping. No injuries were noticed and it moved fine. Perhaps she bumped it on the nightstand in her sleep.

Mary turned the light back off and laid in bed while listening to the storm. A woman must learn to hide like a frightened, little girl when trapped by an angered man. All her days and nights should be spent attentive to his moods and hoping that this morning, this afternoon or this evening won't be a sudden metamorphosis into an evil monster. And now he was coming for her, up the stairs, to punish panic-stricken Mary who could not escape.

But Mary did nothing wrong! How could this man be angry with her?

That's the point: such a man has no rationale for his change of mood!

"*Crash!*" It was a starling noise downstairs that forced Mary to spring from her bed. It was best for her to hide! He was really angry this time and was prepared to hurt her. As Mary hid and crouched in the dark closet, a flood of speculations entered her mind. Most disturbing was the realization that when he finally found the intimidated, little girl; the punishment would be far harsher. Hiding was forbidden, and so was protecting the face or other parts of the body during beatings.

Light: Mary needed to quickly flash on one of the lights. That would pull her out of whatever hallucination she was having. It must have been some half-awake / half-dreaming thing. There was no one living with her, and as a grown woman, she wasn't about to hide from any man who intended to punish her. A sobering flood of light and a few gentle smacks on the face pulled Mary out of the trance. But she still had the crashing noise downstairs to investigate. Hopefully a tree branch didn't blow through the window.

Once downstairs, Mary found everything completely intact and undisturbed. But she wasn't about to go down into the basement at night. As Mary recalled, the basement was very scary for her when she visited the house as a little girl. She would wait until morning to go down and investigate.

Perhaps she could have called Daren before going back to sleep. Mary was certainly in need of the welcome sound of his voice after the startling dream and sudden, unexplained hallucination of an angry man coming to deliver punishment. But what was this? Daren did not answer his phone. Where was he on that late, Thursday night that was now Friday morning? It was 1:20am on her clock which meant it would be 12:20am where he lived. Daren didn't have to leave for the airport until 8:00am that morning. At least that was what he told her on the phone when breaking the bad news about Missouri.

She called his cell phone, but Daren still did not answer. She texted him. "Hello???? Where are you?????"

But there was no reply.

Attempting to call her fiancé certainly did help her forget about the frightening episode as she was now worried about Daren. Did he get in an accident? Was he out on a date with some woman? Now all she could do was lay awake and wonder why her fiancé wasn't answering his phone. She called two more times throughout the night but could not reach him. She finally fell asleep around 4:30am.

Mary awoke the following morning with nauseating adrenaline, wondering if Daren was okay. She called his home and cell, but there was no answer. Where was he? She heard of this phenomenon before; a significant other moves away which spells the end of what appeared to be a beautiful love. Still, she had to give him the benefit of the doubt. There had to be a reasonable explanation for Daren being unreachable. But was he hurt?

Since it was now morning, Mary felt safe to go downstairs in the basement and investigate anything broken. She was now fully convinced that the loud crash was only part of last night's hallucination. But still, it was best to ensure that all was well. If you've ever been in a basement of an old home, it's unlike the ones we see in modern dwellings. And really the basement of Mary's historic dream-home was not a basement at all. It was a cellar that provided just enough headroom to walk around in and seemed to be made for storage only. The floor was a collection of large, flat rocks joined together with cement. Although a crudely-finished area, the cellar did have 2 rooms that, as Mary remembered, were an old tool room and a canned goods room.

As a little girl, Mary hated venturing past the cistern and deeper into the cellar where those two rooms were. And in the musty, dimly-lit place where she stood now; Mary still hated the idea, especially after the strange feelings of last night.

She gazed into the canned goods room and took notice of all the mason jars and antique cans of vegetables that were perhaps 50 or more years old. And there, on one of the shelves, sat the oversized mason jar of some dark, oily liquid that had been there ever since she could remember. As a child, she and her brother and sister often dared one another to open the jar, and drink some of the liquid. No one was brave enough to open it. But the jar sat there and looked just as nauseating as ever. Now that Mary owned the house, she was going to throw all this stuff out, including the oversized jar of dark, oily liquid.

She gazed into the tool room, an area that had always intrigued Mary. The room contained a collection of antique tools that probably should have been sitting in a historical museum as many of them looked to be pre-20th century. Supposedly, Grandpa Trivelli built that tool room, the old bench, and stored his own tools in there. She walked in and studied the collection of antique equipment and took notice of a very, old axe that was hung on the wall along with shovels and hammers. Mary laughed to herself and spoke out loud. "Is this the axe that chopped up the stove?"

And then she needed to explore the texture of the old workbench that her grandfather built. She ran her fingers across the dusty, old wood while realizing it would be necessary to wash her hands. That bench was dirty and had decades, nearly two centuries of dirt and grease on it. But running her fingers on the bench was not enough. She was compelled to study the workbench, examine any damage; hammer marks, or even gash marks from an axe. Then right at the edge of the bench she found an old gash that certainly resembled an axe blade. She was going to reach for the axe on the wall to compare the length of the cut against the blade, but heard the tool room door close behind her which shut her in the small, dark room.

That wasn't an event Mary was welcome to at the moment. It brought her back to her childhood fears of being alone in that room. To make matters worse, the sounds of feet could be heard scuffing across the floor on the other side of the door. Fortunately the door didn't lock (why would it?) and Mary ran out of the room and back upstairs. She needed to get out of the house for a while and get her mind off things.

* * *

Mary spent the morning in town at the flower shop, visiting her old boss and friend who had agreed to hire her when she moved back to Mapleview. They went over some of the details of the new job which was very much like the old one, but had a few changes. Then they had lunch together and Mary agreed to start work on Monday morning.

Her friend, and soon-to-be-boss, Shelly, was amazed with the fact that Mary had purchased the legendary Trivelli house and was living in it. "Your aunt just could not keep renters in that house. I guess the last woman who lived there quit a very, stressful management job at a biomedical manufacturing company. She moved out here and hoped to resume her long, lost love of art. But she wasn't able to paint because of how disturbing the house was."

Mary wanted to know more. "Did you know her? How did you find this out?"

But then just like all the gossip and legends passed down about her home, Shelly could only speak of the hearsay as it applied to the desperate artist who was staying at the Trivelli house, and how the curse affected her painting.

Mary continued to listen to Shelly's wild gossip about the Trivelli house (now Mary's house) while drinking her iced tea. She was very tired from the rough night which surely caused her mind to float back to the basement in the canned goods room. Mary looked at her glass of nearly finished iced tea and imagined that the dark, oily liquid was in that glass. Is that what was in the oversized Mason jar; tea from the 1950's? The thought of drinking the nauseating liquid made it difficult to finish her beverage.

Mary finally spoke up, "You know Shelly, I'm glad I bought that house. I'm going to up and remove any item that was connected to any legend that house might have. Today I was downstairs in the basement and realized that there are probably canned goods from over a hundred years ago down there. Throw that stuff out, you know? Donate those old tools to the historical museum or something. I'm going to end the legend of that house. And if I need to get the place blessed, I will do it."

Shelly just drank her coffee and listened to her friend. If Mary really thought she could do it, then more power to her.

* * *

Nightmares are a very strange phenomenon as they happen during the first few hours of sleep. Experts tell us that everyone has horrific nightmares during the first half of the night; but because we are in a deep, paralyzed state we forget them. And it's a good thing we do because nightmares can be traumatic. But if you've ever woken up in the middle of one, then you realize how senseless and pointless one is, despite how traumatized you may be.

It started as a simple dream in the early hours of sleeping. Mary was sitting in the living room where she suddenly became aware of Daren standing on the roof of the house. He pushed a wire down the chimney and through the fireplace while calling out to her in an eerie voice. *"Mary? Mary? I have a surprise for you, Mary."*

Mary watched as the wire came out of the fireplace, drawing closer to her. For the life of her, she did not want to make contact with that wire. Drawing back towards the piano, Mary suddenly heard bloodcurdling screams from within the antique vase. It was screams of a woman pleading for mercy and begging for help. What was in that vase? Mary just had to look. But overpowering fear of seeing the unknown woke her up.

Mary just had to reach her fiancé, Daren! It was now Saturday morning at 1:14am and he was most definitely at whatever destination he needed to be and sleeping. But just as usual, there was no answer from his cell phone. Mary was tired of leaving voice messages and bouncing from anger to worry. Perhaps a call to Daren's mother in the morning would answer all the burning questions. All she could do, now, was lie in bed and concentrate on falling asleep.

There was no need to fret or worry. Grandma Trivelli would watch over the young woman and see to it that all was well. Mary did, after all, have the shrunken corpse of her grandmother proudly displayed on the piano, in a glass case filled with lamp oil. She looked like a miniaturized Sleeping Beauty, just resting on the piano with a fresh cut rose laid over the glass case. Mary would often sit at the piano and play for her dear grandmother who just floated ever so lifeless in over a century of preservation.

Although Grandma Trivelli enjoyed Mary's musical performances, the ultimate reverence would be to undo the rubber stopper of the glass case and taste some of the fluids. Mary drew near to the transparent, miniaturized coffin and breathed deep the smell of antique death. That's when she sat up in bed, startled from another bizarre dream.

Mary couldn't take much more of these horrific dreams. And where did such a ridiculous concept of a glass coffin come from? Perhaps it was on the day of Daren's, father's funeral.

Chapter 2

It was like any normal funeral as a crowd of somber faces circled his final resting place to bid farewell. Holy water was sprinkled and roses were placed on the casket by a teary-eyed wife. Her 28-year-old son, Daren, along with other 2 sons, Eric and Anthony, did their best to comfort Mom. Accompanying Daren was his fiancée, Mary, who was saddened that her future father-in-law would not see his grandchildren.

Just as any funeral, the priest made the closing prayer, "Oh God, by your mercy rest is given to the souls of the faithful, be please to bless this grave."

He was young, only in his late 50s. Yet there was nothing out-of-the-ordinary about his death other than a sudden heart attack. It's the cold shock that life throws at us. One day everything is fine, and the next day someone is gone.

"Eternal rest: grant unto him, oh Lord."

"And let perpetual light shine upon him."

Daren's father would be placed in the family mausoleum containing his grandfather, grandmother, two uncles and their wives. But there was something peculiar about the mausoleum that Daren and his two brothers would discuss later that day during the luncheon. Daren had only visited the mausoleum as a young boy to see his grandfather, and the experience was very odd.

"So are you going to visit Dad in his new place?" Daren spoke up later that afternoon at the luncheon. He was the oldest brother and wondered if the other two had ever gone into the mausoleum.

Anthony answered, "Sure, why not?"

Daren sighed, "Well, I suppose I better make a habit of it. I mean, what's the difference? We looked at him all morning during the funeral. Why not next month, next year and the years to come?" Daren was speaking of a controversial method that the older generation of the family practiced, allowing mourners to see the body of the deceased whenever desired. Unlike most mausoleums, this one had crypts that opened which allowed one to gaze in a glass tank filled with formaldehyde containing the body of the deceased relative. The formaldehyde preserved the body so it looked exactly the same as the day of the funeral.

Daren's brother, Eric, did once go to the mausoleum and provided an account of his experience. "It's weird; I went one Sunday afternoon with Mom and Dad to visit Grandpa. Dad pulled out the drawer, and we all looked. You know how the mortician is supposed to glue the eyes shut along with the mouth, nose, ears and stuff? Well, I guess one of his eyes wasn't fully glued during the process. Or maybe the liquid they put in the tank ate away at the glue. I don't know; but his eye was open! It just kind of looked at you as you stood there, gazing at a body that's been dead over 25 years."

Mary was doing everything in her power to be well-mannered and understanding of the three brothers who lost their father. But the conversation was a bit disturbing, especially just moments before eating. The look of disgust could be seen on her face, and Daren put his arm around his fiancée's shoulders while proceeding to speak. He intended to steer the conversation in a different direction. "I don't know; whoever thought of that idea was twisted. Let's vow not to do that when we die and just have a normal burial so our kids can visit us with the memories of when we were alive. I mean who is going to visit that mausoleum once we are all gone? That's the trouble with graves and mausoleums; no one visits you generations later. Why go through so much effort for an elaborate grave, mausoleum or whatever?"

Mary was growing impatient, "Daren?"

"What, it's true! And I don't know about everyone else, but I'm in the mood for some more wine." Mary watched in silence as her fiancé finished off his 2nd glass of wine before going up to the bar for his 3rd. "You want anything else, Babe?"

Mary shook her head, no. Daren had promised her to cut down on his drinking. When they were first dating, Daren was a heavy drinker and nearly lost Mary with his fits of anger and near-violent behavior. He admitted that he could do without the booze in his life, but wasn't about to jump on the wagon. As he saw it, there was no reason not to have a beer or some wine during a social occasion. But a 3rd glass of wine was pushing it in Mary's eyes. He did recently lose his father, so she wasn't going to say anything, especially in front of his family.

Daren returned with his 3rd glass of wine and spoke with excitement. "I looked at the bottle. It says Charles Shaw 2002. That's 3 years old, now!"

"It's still good wine", said Eric.

Daren sat back with his already quarter-finished glass of Charles Shaw Shiraz from 2002. It was apparent that he was loosening up and under the influence of a heavy wine buzz. "Yeah, but it would be so cool if we could find something 25, 30, or even 50 years ago. Wouldn't that be worth trying?"

Now Daren's brother, Anthony, was well educated on the finer things in life and did much reading on the culinary arts and matters pertaining to wine. He saw the suggestion as a cue to showcase his knowledge, "You know, I recently read an article that reported some of the greatest wine connoisseurs who compared those upscale wines to some of the more modest ones we get at places like Trader Joe's. They all came to the conclusion that the wines from those places were just as good, if not, better. It isn't a terrible thing to enjoy something simple."

Daren finished his glass of Shiraz. Mary patted him on the back and silently whispered, "I think you've had enough."

She was right, but Daren continued the conversation and proceeded to drive in his point about aged wines. "Oh, I agree with you and totally believe that these wines are just as good as the upscale stuff out there. But I'm not talking I need an expensive wine. I'm talking about drinking aged wine. Consider this: Suppose I go up to the bar and purchase some bottle from 1901. Obviously we are all going to be very intrigued and eager to open it and try it. Imagine the thrill of drinking something made not from the turn of this century, but the turn of the previous century."

Anthony and Eric agreed that it would be quite an experience, and the three brothers began to seriously discuss how to go about obtaining old wines. At least Mary's fiancé had steered the conversation from viewing preserved bodies behind glass to a more appropriate dinner conversation. By then the soup and salad had arrived, but Mary found it difficult to eat the cherry tomatoes.

* * *

"So are you and your brothers going to start collecting wine and drinking it?" It was Saturday evening. Daren and Mary were driving back to their residences in Flagstaff, Arizona. The funeral was held in Phoenix and Mary couldn't wait to get home. She spent the past 3 days at her fiancé's, mother's house and under sad circumstances, seriously needing alone time to decompress and prepare for work on Monday.

Daren replied, "I don't know; we just want to try an aged bottle of wine. I never had that before, have you?"

"No; I have no desire to drink something over 50 years old."

"Well why not?"

Mary was in no mood to explain how senseless it was to drink antique wine that may very well be bad. But she was concerned about her fiancé possibly relapsing into a bad habit of heavy drinking. "I just don't, Daren! And you know I hope you're careful. I don't mind you having a glass of wine with your brothers, but I know you can get carried away."

Daren realized Mary's concern, and held his fiancé's hand. "I won't start drinking again; I promise you." He kissed her hand which seemed to tone down the mood for the remainder of the ride home. And that was the only thing Mary had witnessed of Daren and his sudden interest with aged wine, which profoundly affected him some time later.

* * *

Nearly 8 weeks passed since the funeral. After doing some research and meeting various wine experts, Daren and his brothers managed to obtain a very promising bottle from 1861!

There are a few things, among others, that are important to know when scouting out old wines. The first thing that one needs to be aware is that purchasing old wines has a risk factor. What are the chances that buying something from the 1950s or 1930s is found to be bad once it is opened and tried? Contrary to popular belief; simple, old wines are not in the millions of dollars, but generally run around $100 per bottle. However, it would remain disappointing to purchase such a wine, only to discover that it has turned into vinegar.

One needs to be aware of something called ulage, which is the amount of air between the cork and the wine in the bottle neck. The more ulage, the more chance the wine has oxidized and gone bad.

It just so happened that the bottle of wine that Daren and his two brothers obtained for $120, dated 1861, did not have an excessive amount of ulage and was rated to be a safe risk. And so the three brothers sat in Daren's backyard around the resin table one early, Saturday evening with the bottle from 1861. They simply admired what they had in their possession.

Daren appeared to be expanding on his point made weeks ago while the three initially decided to seek out an old wine. "Do you realize this wine was made before we were even born; before our parents were born; before our grandparents were even born? I mean the vineyard that this wine came from may very well not even be around anymore. The people who made this wine are long gone."

Anthony added some insight from his collection of knowledge of fine wines. "I've heard that drinking an old wine is like making love to an old lady. It can be done; you just need some imagination and an open mind."

Eric brought everyone back down to Earth. "What are we waiting for? Crack that bottle open and let's drink up!"

Daren opened the bottle of wine as his brother suggested and showed everyone that the cork had not been deteriorated in over a century while the wine was sealed in the bottle. As mentioned before, this was a very good sign that the wine had not been oxidized and gone bad. He then poured half a glass for everyone. All three brothers sat looking at the wine in their glasses and smelling the aroma.

Eric dove right in by taking a good sip. "Mmmmm... Not bad! Not bad at all!

Daren looked at Anthony and repeated the Life cereal commercial, indicating it was safe to try. "He likes it; hey Mikey!"

The other two both took their sips. Daren immediately set the glass down with tongue sticking out, "What are you talking about? It's so strong and pungent!"

Anthony came to the rescue, "Now, now: you're rushing into it. When making love to an old lady you need to be slow and gradual. Go get us a block of cheese so we can clear our pallets. This wine is fine; you're just not drinking it right."

Eric finished his glass by the time Daren left for the block of cheese and a knife. He was ready for more, but realized he should let his two brothers catch up, first. Upon Daren's return, the three brothers ate some cheese and proceeded to slowly drink the wine while appreciating the flavors that had been preserved for nearly 150 years. Of course one shouldn't put a bottle of wine like this in the refrigerator to drink more next week! So the three finished the bottle while engaging in discussions of what happened in the year 1861 or around that time. They were quite impressed with themselves for enjoying something from so long ago. They cracked open a second a bottle of wine, no more than two years old, and continued to drink with a never ending quest for the ultimate wine buzz. But anyone who truly loves wine understands that such a desire of vineyard-induced euphoria is paradoxical in nature. Too much of a buzz is not a good thing and can ruin the pleasant, short-lived experience. Two bottles were plenty. And beside that point, people needed to drive home. It's always a good thing to consider other motorists and other people's loved ones!

After some time, the intoxicating buzz wore off as the now groggy bothers engaged in more sobering conversation, initiated by Daren. "Well, are we going tomorrow?"

"To the mausoleum with Mom?" asked Anthony.

"We did, after all, promise her. I guess she wants to make sure they entombed Dad properly." Daren wanted to appear mindful of doing the right thing, but secretly dreaded going alone with his mother. The mausoleum disturbed him and he imagined the effect to be reduced if surrounded by more company. With tomorrow being Sunday, and the fact that the Eric and Anthony lived near Daren, there was no excuse not to go. It would only require about a 2-hour drive down to Phoenix.

* * *

Daren hadn't been to the family mausoleum since he was young boy, and was a bit apprehensive as going there would most surely guarantee a look at family members who had been deceased for a quarter-of-a-century or more. His youngest brother, Eric, seemed to enjoy the mausoleum as if it was entertainment. While approaching the building the following morning, he kept whispering to Daren, "Dude, you gotta see it! We gotta take out Grandpa's crypt and look at his opened eye! It'll freak you out!"

Daren was doing his best to maintain composure. He wasn't exactly easy with viewing his deceased father now encapsulated in a glass tank of formaldehyde, and he wanted to tell his brother to shut up. But at the same time, Mother could not be agitated in this delicate moment. Such is one of the challenges we need to experience in life.

The door was opened, and immediately the overpowering odor of formaldehyde could be smelled. Mother looked horrified, "Oh my God! Did one of the tanks break open? Is it Dad?" She immediately entered the building and could see that the chemical seeped through the bottom of the east wall, which was evidenced by the stains on the floor. "Did they break a tank when entombing your father?" Mother's eyes became glassy.

Which deceased relative was most important to the family at that moment? Was it the uncles, or Grandpa? Not likely as the family was mourning the recent loss of the father. They immediately opened his crypt and were relieved that he was still intact.

"I bet it's the next drawer over! I bet it's Grandpa!" Eric appeared ecstatic at the notion that his grandfather's crypt needed to be opened in which he could see the eye peering at everyone.

"Relax Eric!" Daren sternly looked at his brother and motioned his face at their mother who had eyes filled with tears. It was apparent that removable, glass tanks were not the ideal resting place for loved ones to visit while mourning. Seeing a loved one go to the grave, in a sense, brings closure to surviving family members, allowing them to begin the mourning process. But father wasn't buried, and mother was, once again, looking at his lifeless body floating in a tank of formaldehyde. Such a moment needed to be experienced carefully, and Mother needed time to visit her husband before closing the crypt and checking the others for cracked glass.

After some time, Father's crypt was closed and the family began the investigation of which tank was cracked and leaking formaldehyde.

"Let's open Grandpa's first! I know it's his!" Sensing Eric's increasing impatience, it was mutually decided to open the suggested crypt. And just as expected, his glass tank had been cracked at the bottom near the right hand, allowing all the formaldehyde to leak out. And yes, his opened eye peered at those who stood over his glass tank. The chemical mess was nothing short of a disaster, and the cemetery would have much explaining to do. To make matters worse, Grandpa's hand was beginning to decompose. In fact, it looked like it had been decomposing for some time. This suggested the possibility that the glass tank had cracked long before the cemetery put Father's body in the crypt.

Mother was outraged. "You mean to tell me they knew about this and ignored it?"

There's a thing about drinking aged wine. For some, it may trigger a morbid lust for days long past. If only it was possible to drink deeply the past and savor every memory. Perhaps Daren's experience of drinking aged wine stirred a curiosity while he observed some of the decomposing matter mixed with fluid near the crack of the tank leak out on his hand. It was preserved life, encased in glass and very possible to stir the essence of memories forgotten a quarter of a century ago. Daren licked the fluid from his hands which brought morbid numbness to his lips and tongue. It also yielded both his brothers to outburst in nauseous disbelief!

The act itself must have defied every bit of logic, along with all that Daren believed in. He had a dream later that night in which he was reminded of his experience at the family mausoleum and the secret pleasure of tasting his decomposing grandfather mixed with formaldehyde. He suddenly found himself contemplating this necrophagous addiction and wondered if there was a way to create a wine made from a decomposing corpse. Could he collect several bodies of his own and let them rot in such a way that his grandfather did?

Consequently, Daren developed the part time career as a serial killer. This, of course, was only in his dream. He collected several bodies, preserved them in tanks of wine and then stored them in his tool shed.

When satisfied he had enough bodies to age, he ended the part time career, but speculated that someone might find his collection. At this point, Daren fell into a deeper sleep and forgot he was only dreaming.

As luck would have it, his neighbor asked Daren if he could take the keys to the house and check on it regularly while gone on vacation for a week. What better place to bury a collection of bodies than in a neighbor's home, who would least expect them to be there!

Since the house to be watched was on a slab, Daren spent the week taking apart his neighbor's kitchen cabinets, jackhammering the floor under the sink, digging a deep hole, and ultimately burying his collection of wine-preserved bodies under the kitchen sink. He filled up the hole, re-cemented and re-assembled his neighbor's cabinets. It looked as if nothing had ever happened. However, upon returning, Daren's neighbors did ask if there had been some construction in the neighborhood while they were gone. Throughout the jack hammering, there was much dust which Daren neglected to remove.

A couple years passed, and Daren's neighbor had not discovered the collection of bodies under the sink. Eventually, Daren was asked to watch the neighbor's home, again. Daren was so clever as to implement a concrete door under the kitchen cabinets. And in those couple years of living with wine-preserved corpses, Daren's neighbor was clueless of the door. Now on vacation, it was the perfect opportunity for Daren to check on his bodies.

But to his horror, it was discovered that the cases encapsulating the wine-preserved corpses had fully cracked and shattered underground. What could have done this? There were no reports of earthquake activity in the area. Such a waste; the bodies were rotting which provided a feast for a colony of bugs and maggots. The sight disturbed Daren very much as he began to screamed bloody murder.

Unfortunately, the kitchen window and curtains remained carelessly open, which invited one of the neighbors from down the street to investigate the chaos. Everything was exposed and the police were quickly summoned.

If you've ever awoken in the middle of such a circumstance, wishing the events of your bad dream weren't true, then you can imagine the relief Daren experienced, finding himself lying in a bed drenched in sweat. It was a rather bizarre 48 hours, some of the events never disclosed to his precious fiancée, Mary.

Chapter 3

Mary awoke Saturday morning after an evening of nightmares. Despite the small interruptions during the night, she felt rested and in a more positive frame of mind. It was a beautiful day which called for opening the windows and allowing the woodsy air to circulate. Mary passed the antique vase that sat on the piano and remembered the nightmare she had overnight. Really it was a beautiful vase, probably 200 years old, and would look so nice if she put some fresh-cut flowers in it. Mary decided she would correct anything causing stress or anxiety in her life by replacing it with something that was positive. If a vase caused a nightmare, she would clean it and put fresh flowers in it. She would sell all those old tools in the cellar and get rid of the bench her Grandpa made. And if her soon-to-be husband was causing stress in her life, she would break the engagement off.

Mary picked up the beautiful, antique vase and noticed it hadn't been cleaned in a while. For most homes across America; the vase is a very, much misunderstood piece of decorating. The average person sees a vase as being a practical item and will not display one unless it involves flowers or some kind of floral arrangement. To most, the idea of collecting vases is ridiculous, especially if one is not fond of small knick-knacks or centerpieces.

But for centuries, the vase has been proudly displayed in homes, stores and offices throughout the world. And there still is a population of people in America who admire the vase and proudly display them in the home. If you are such a person, you realize that it is not only a beautiful piece of decoration, but a secret place to hide things.

Do you have spare keys you don't want laying around? Hide them in that vase. Want to hide jewelry or money away from possible burglars or visitors who may have sticky fingers? Hide these things way at the bottom of your vase. Secret love letters you don't want someone to find? Hide them away in the vase.

Mary looked down at the bottom and noticed something that appeared to be stuck. Maybe it was some old, dried up flowers. She brought the vase over to the sink and rinsed it out; hoping to dislodge whatever was at the bottom. The stubborn item remained

Suddenly the phone rang and Mary ran over to answer it. The caller ID said something about a rehabilitation center. But it was from Arizona, the state where Daren still lived.

Mary answered, "Hello?"

"Mary?" It was Daren!

"Daren, where are you? Where have you been?" Needless to say, Mary was expecting a good explanation!

"Mary? I've decided I need to be honest with you. I want honesty in our relationship and marriage, and keeping this a secret from you is wrong. Besides, it's not working keeping it a secret." When someone begins a conversation this way it's a little strange and one can interpret that he or she is being prepared to hear something disturbing.

"What is it Daren?"

"Mary, I was randomly picked for the company drug screen last week, and they found cocaine in me. I did a lot the night before without knowing I would be called down the following morning for the test. In order to keep my job, I have to do a mandatory, three-week, inpatient treatment program. If you were trying to reach me yesterday, I've been in the rehab center. They weren't even going to let me call until I explained to my councilor that you didn't know and was probably worried.

I hope you're not mad Mary."

Mary was speechless upon finding out her soon-to-be husband had a cocaine addiction. Not that a cocaine addiction would be an indicator of problems in a marriage along with possible violence and abuse down the road! But would you want to marry someone like that, especially after he was trying to keep it a secret?

"Daren, I don't know what to say! You know, you told me you had kicked your drinking habit and promised to stay clean. Now I find out you were using cocaine? Call me when you get out!" Mary slammed down the phone. Maybe her aunt was correct in hinting that Daren wasn't right for her.

Now where was she before answering the phone and finding the truth about her husband-to-be? Frazzled and much disappointed, Mary needed to focus on the moment. Just minutes ago, she was in a fantastic mood and... oh, there was something at the bottom of that vase, and it was of most importance that she learn of the secret. Using the vase as an object to become absorbed in the moment, she truly believed that any discovery pertaining to it would make things clear. It was as if her life depended on it.

Grabbing a yardstick, she picked and picked until finally dislodging. Whatever it was, the vase rattled when shook.— evidence of a hard object or perhaps... *antique jewelry?* The vase was brought over to the sofa and turned up-side-down.

Out slid the skeletal remains of a human hand, wearing a woman's wedding ring! Was it a souvenir kept by her Grandpa Trivelli? Or perhaps he tormented his wife with the knowledge that her hand was hiding somewhere in the house? Whatever the reason, the decomposed flesh apparently served as glue that bonded the skeletal hand to the bottom of the vase for many decades.

Mary stood frozen in disbelief, waiting to take her next breath. If her aunt didn't get the message across, then her Grandmother did! The dream of having her hand chopped off and the need to look for axe marks on the workbench made sense to Mary, now. And this was the fear of gazing into the unknown bottom of the vase in that dream.

* * *

Now this incident in Mapleview could very well have served as a marker for Detective Tom Morehausen and his partner Larry Copperwright. Prior to this day, the detectives of the Mapleview Police department simply investigated fatal traffic accidents, theft, or an occasional drug ring. It was a fork in the road for Detective Tom that could have pointed the direction of his much deserved retirement, or the beginning of a rash of mysterious disappearance in Mapleview. He had been on the force many years, and the common belief throughout the department was that he would soon retire.

Finding the skeletal remains of a human hand in the Trivelli mansion had, more-or-less, solved a nearly 175-year-old mystery of what happened that terrible winter. The explanation given for the disappearance of Grandma Trivelli was an attack by a pack of wolves. Now the possibility was open that Grandpa Trivelli had murdered her. And since the people involved in the incident were longtime dead, the finding in the vase was a cause for celebration at the Mapleview Police Department. Detectives Tom and Larry were thrown a party. And as a subtle coax to finally retire, Detective Tom was given a trophy for solving the 175-year-old case.

But Detective Tom merely brought the trophy in his office, and proudly displayed it at his desk. He raised a cup of coffee in toast to himself, "Here's to many more!" Little did the seasoned detective know that he was about to get more than bargained for.

But on this day, being the initial discovery in the vase, he stood before Mary with his partner, offering comfort and asking casual questions of what she knew. Again, the incident would have taken place nearly 175 years ago, and there was no one to prosecute, only to bring closure to the Trivelli family and the town of Mapleview that spoke of the legend.

Detective Tom asked, "So you actually bought this house from your aunt?"

"Yes, and I'm going to clean it up! I'm going to end the legend and stigmatism that this house had for years!" Mary was still shook up over the discovery. Really she had been through much in the past 48 hours and this was the final straw.

Detective Tom sensed the anxiety in the woman and offered some idle conversation to put Mary at ease. "Well, let me tell you what you do with the vase. I'm sure you don't want it anymore, right?"

Mary provided a blank stare.

Detective Tom continued, "On the other side of Sillmac, just down Route 4, there's that touristy part of town. You know where I'm talking about, right?"

"Oh yeah, I've been there—lot's of restaurants and shops."

"Well here's what you do, Mary. Take a day, drive out past Sillmac, and sell the vase to the World's Strangest Collection of Antique Vases. It's a small museum. I think it's wedged in between a coffee shop and popcorn store. People all over the country sell vases that have (or had) unusual discoveries to the museum. It's an antique, so you'll probably make money. Then take that cash, buy yourself a nice lunch, browse the shops in town and get your mind off what happened."

Detective Larry added his input, "But don't travel Route 4 at night!"

Detective Tom continued, "Yeah, stay off Route 4 after sundown. There's some weird activity going on there in the late night hours. You should be fine before 9:00pm."

* * *

Mary's mother and father lived in Florida, enjoying their golden years. And both Mary's siblings had settled down in New York City as they each pursued successful careers. Although this was a family matter, the last person Mary would have wanted to call was her Aunt Loraine. Recall that it was Loraine who insisted that Grandma Trivelli had been murdered in that house. In Mary's determination of enjoying her new home, and ridding the house of the stigmatism and legend, calling Aunt Loraine was like crawling back, defeated—admitting that the crazy, old woman was right. Being she was the only family member in Mapleview, and not to mention was so attached to family history, it was only right to inform Aunt Loraine of the recent discovery.

"You mean to tell me that the vase contained her severed hand all those decades?" Needless to say, Aunt Loraine was engrossed by every detail. She rushed over to Mary's house and closely examined the centerpiece. "Why, I can see some of the dried up decomposed matter at the bottle of the vase! I'm surprised the Mapleview Police didn't take this with her hand! What about the wedding ring? Did they take that?"

"It was pretty much stuck on the bone of her finger, Aunt Loraine! I wasn't about to take it off. I didn't even touch the hand."

Aunt Loraine walked over to the piano and set the vase back down, as if it should have continued to be proudly displayed in the living room. "It was your Grandma Trivelli! She was warning you about Daren! I know she was!"

"Aunt Loraine! Stop it!" Although realizing the crazy, old lady was probably right, Mary wasn't prepared to disclose her recent knowledge of Daren's cocaine addiction. "Alright, so Grandma was murdered in this house; so what? What does it have to do with me? If anything, I took the first step in exposing the truth about this house and have begun cleaning it up. And you know what? I'm getting rid of all that junk downstairs. I'm throwing out all the canned vegetables from the 1950; I'm throwing out the huge jar of whatever that oily stuff is; and I'm selling all those antique tools in the basement."

Aunt Loraine appeared very disappointed. "Well if it suits you; it's your house."

Mary could not understand her aunt. She originally desired to rid herself of owning the Trivelli house, but was now heartbroken over Mary's attempt to discard the decades of garbage and any items associated with supposed curses. It was as if the very stigmatism of the house was Aunt Loraine's purpose in life. Even stranger, the woman stormed out of the house, appearing to be deeply hurt.

Finally alone, Mary called her mother to inform her of the discovery. Over an hour of conversation with Mom was just the thing that Mary needed. But at some point, Mom was growing impatient with her daughter's vague explanations of Daren's absence.

Mary sighed while holding her eyelids shut. "Daren called me from a drug rehab in Arizona this morning. He was given a random drug screen, and they found cocaine in him."

Mom gasped, "You've got to be kidding me! Are you serious? Well at least you found this out, now."

Unsure of how to handle her recent knowledge, Mary didn't want to disclose the fact to family just yet. She had yet to consider forgiving Daren. But as far as Mom was concerned, the engagement was off as she asked the question, "What about the house? What are you going to do, now?"

* * *

Seriously needing to get away, Mary thought about Detective Tom's suggestion of trekking just past Sillmac to sell the vase. Carefully placing it in a box with crumpled up newspaper, the vase could no longer be proudly displayed on the piano. The trunk of her car was a better place. The next stop was either the museum or an antique dealer.

But what fun would it be to go alone? Perhaps her friend, Shelly, would have been open to a Sunday out. Mary called her friend (and soon-to-be-boss) who owned the flower shop. "Shelly? Hi, it's Mary. Do you have a minute? You're not going to believe what happened to me this morning!"

* * *

And so the two head off to the other side of Sillmac, Sunday morning, down Route 4 with Grandma Trivelli's vase in the trunk. Mary and Shelly's friendship began in 5th grade as "best friends", which only lasted a couple of weeks as girls that age change best friends like yesterday's socks. But the bond was strong through high school; through college while attending, together; and while Mary worked at Shelly's flower shop some years ago. Of course Mary didn't major in floral arrangements and taking customers' credit card numbers! The job was only temporary. She moved when an opportunity in Flagstaff allowed the pursuit of her intended career, which led to meeting Daren.

Mary had been to the touristy section on the other side of Sillmac on a few occasions. In fact, both women had been there; but neither remembered seeing the World's Strangest Collection of Antique Vases. It was just as Detective Tom Morehausen said, "Wedged in between a coffee shop and popcorn store". From the moment one walks in the scent of musty, old carpeting can be smelled. Many get the impression that at one time, the small attraction was to be a museum of oddities and strange facts. But somehow, the owners received numerous donations of unwanted vases, which resulted in changing the name to "The World's Strangest Collection of Antique Vases".

During the owner's initial evaluation of the vase, Mary was hit with the realization that the centerpiece was an antique. And being that it was about to be sold to a small museum of oddities, perhaps she wasn't about receive top dollar for the family possession. Maybe it was better to seek out an antique dealer who was knowledgeable of valuables. But before doing so, Mary was curious of what the owner of the museum had to say.

The owner asked, "What's the story behind this vase?"

"Well, it's from the Trivelli house in Mapleview…"

He interrupted Mary, "The Trivelli house?" Everyone in the area was familiar with the legendary Trivelli House. And such an item originating from the home was very exciting for the museum owner. "How did you get this?"

"Well, I'm a member of the family who just recently purchased the home, and I'm trying to get rid of some things." Suddenly, it occurred to Mary that a detailed account of her experience with the vase was necessary. The discovery of Grandma Trivelli's skeletal hand would certainly set the record straight of the 1830s legend. Perhaps it was best not to sell the vase to the museum. Then again, the newspapers would jump all over the story once the Mapleview Police announced the discovery of the skeletal hand. Why not make it a good story? Perhaps it would promise more money for the vase.

Mary continued, "Well, I'm sure you are aware of the legend of the Trivelli house. Supposedly my grandmother was tragically carried off by a hungry pack of wolves."

"Yes, uh-huh… I know all about the legend."

"Well, as of yesterday, the Mapleview Police closed the mystery with the recent discovery of my grandmother's skeletal hand that was found at the bottom of this vase."

"Good Heavens!"

Mary continued, "This means that the original legend is not true. Apparently, she had been murdered in that house by my grandfather, who reported to police that she was carried off by wolves."

Mary did a fine job of captivating the owner of the museum with the recent news of the Trivelli house. But she hoped he would offer an equally captivating offer for the vase. It did, after all, originate from one of the greatest legends in the area. Mary and Shelly stood in silence, implying that the ball was now in the owner's court to make an offer.

The owner of the shop closely examined the vase, "Well, antique-wise, the vase would be worth $675; but because of the discovery and legend, I'll offer you $700."

Mary could have sold the vase at an antique dealer which gave her the advantage to negotiate with the owner of the museum. He most likely desired the vase for his collection. But just how much profit did the museum make each year? The waters needed testing as Mary replied, "Oh, come on! This vase is at least 200 years old, maybe more! It came from a legendary, historical house and it had my grandmother's hand in it! I guess if doesn't mean much to you; there are other antique dealers back in Mapleview..." She turned to walk away.

"Wait! 750! I'll give you $750 for the vase, and that's my final offer!"

Seriously, how many visitors did the museum get each year? Were tourists really into this stuff? Why not demand more? Mary sharply replied back,"$800!"

But the owner was persistent, "$775! Lady, I can't go much higher! This is a small museum in a small, unheard of town!"

Apparently at his breaking point, Mary decided to give in at his final price; under one, small condition. "Okay, $775. But I want something else for that price."

The man was growing irate, "Well, what is then?"

"My friend and I want free admission into your museum, just to see what this place is about."

The man placed his hand to his mouth and stroked his shadowy beard as if contemplating. "You want me to waive the $10 admission for both of you?"

Mary nodded.

"Well okay; it's a deal."

For such a small space and an odd business, the World's Strangest Collection of Antique Vases certainly had much to view. The entire gallery was a hallway that mazed from the entrance to the exit and contained numerous contributions and stories from around the country. Many of the contributors claimed their vases to be haunted. One of them contained a hand gun at the bottom that supposedly murdered the mayor of a small town in Nebraska.

An ancient, Egyptian vase, donated by the Dobsmoore family in South Dakota, immediately captured Mary's attention. It contained a most unwanted artifact from an antique trunk that had sat in a basement for decades. On the placard it was described that Richard Dobsmoore accompanied his professor on an archaeological dig in Egypt. He was tragically killed during the visit and his belongings were sent home to family in South Dakota. Since his mother was uneasy with Egyptian decorating after the tragic death of her son, she put the vase in a trunk and kept it sealed up in the cellar until family members, generations later, went through the trunk.

At the bottom of a vase was an Egyptian ankh wrapped up in several handkerchiefs. The family thought the finding to be really cool, until the letter from Richard Dobsmoore's professor was read. The professor apologized and said that his tent had been robbed when he was not there. He claimed the thieves had murdered Richard Dobsmoore and took an ankh that had been excavated during a dig. He felt responsible for Richard's death because of a curse that the ankh supposedly had, "Whoever wrongfully acquired the ancient item would certainly die a horrific death." Unbeknown to the professor, Richard was the one who stole the artifact from the professor, and put it in the vase that he purchased from a shop. Apparently a very, real curse; the family wanted nothing to do with the vase or the hidden item that now both sit with the collection in the museum.

Another antique vase from the late-1700s was boasted to sit on one of the shelves in the study of George Washington. Mary wasn't sure if she believed the story; but it was entertaining, leading her to wonder if some of the contributors fabricated the supposed facts.

The art and texture of the vase was beautiful and must have been very expensive. But inside the vase was a strange letter from a woman by the name of Madam Sinclair Oveaut. The placard below the vase told the story of whispering gossip, barely heard by those close to George Washington, of how strange it was that he had tea with Madam Sinclair Oveaut every other Tuesday in his east garden. The visits lasted about 4 months. Was this a mistress of his? The east garden was isolated and hidden from most people. And the nature of Madam Sinclair Oveaut's visits was never understood until the letter was found 200 years later in George Washington's study at the bottom of a vase. The letter discussed a colony of witches that was soon to arrive in America, and the wishes that Madam Sinclair Oveaut had that they would be protected from the public.

How about you? Do you believe the story?

After the entertaining tour and $775 richer, Mary spent the remainder of the morning with her friend, browsing the shops and storefronts. Mary treated herself to some new summer wear, and purchased a few novels at one of the small book stores. And of course she treated herself and friend to a nice lunch at one of the upscale seafood houses. At some point through all the conversation and memories of younger days, Mary realized that the whole day was made possible by poor Grandma Trivelli. She was in a better place and probably resting easier, now that the truth was known.

* * *

"You know Shelly; I just remembered something that the detective said yesterday." The two women were driving home in the early afternoon after their big lunch. They were stuffed from crab cakes, lobster, shrimp and fried calamari as an appetizer. As Mary's brain had finally relaxed after some seriously-needed idle-time, she began to recall small details of the past few days that were odd.

Shelly replied, "What's that, Mary?"

"The detective who suggested that I sell the vase at the museum, warned me about Route 4. He said something about not traveling at night. What did he mean by that?"

"He did? Oh, he's talking about some incidents on the highway late at night. I guess motorists are chased by people flashing their high beam lights. No one's been raped or anything. It's just scary and the reports concern police.

Chapter 4

Being the forgiving woman that she is, Mary reconciled with her fiancé upon his release from rehab. A couple months and many talks of advice from family later, Mary experienced the day she had waited for her entire life. The two celebrated their honeymoon in Cancun, Mexico and settled into Mary's dream home in the beautiful town of Mapleview. The first few weeks of marital bliss were wonderful—as they are for everyone. And although the honeymoon ended, Mary felt she had a wonderful marriage with her husband, Daren.

* * *

It was a Sunday midmorning after church as Mary finished her homemade marinade for the meat to be barbequed. Such is the many joys of a marriage when a husband and wife can enjoy a private barbeque on a quiet Sunday. She gazed out the window and took notice of Daren doing some activity behind a row of bushes that edged the property's perimeter. It was difficult to see behind the bushes; but it appeared he had a collection of shovels, a sledge hammer, some wooden stakes and a tape measure in his hand while measuring the ground. What on Earth could he have been doing?

She quietly approached her husband who was now actively engaged in driving a corner stake in the ground. "Hi!"

"Hey…" From the tone of his voice, the man did not want to be interrupted.

"What's up?" Mary remained friendly but deliberately showed curiosity.

"Oh, not much; how about you?"

This game of avoidance had gone far enough. Daren most-surely knew why she was there from the beginning. But incase it wasn't apparent, she sternly asked, "*Daren? What are you doing?*"

Daren finally put the hammer down, "Oh, I was thinking we don't have a mausoleum on our property."

"Excuse me?" Mary thought she understood her husband, but just needed to confirm that Daren was, in fact, constructing a mausoleum in their backyard.

"I'm building a mausoleum. We don't have one, and every historic house isn't complete without a mausoleum."

Mary was hoping there to be humor or some sort of punch line. "Daren, since when? What are you talking about? You can't be serious!"

"Well sure I'm serious. Don't you want a family mausoleum?"

"No Daren! I don't want a mausoleum in my backyard! The backyard looks fine without one!"

Daren threw the sledge hammer down and kicked over the half-driven corner stake in a fit-of-rage. "Fine! That's just fine! Now I know how things are going to be! I need to ask you per-mission (emphasized facetiously with wide, open eyes) if I want to do something. You know, it's my house too!" And at that state-ment, he stormed back into the house and sat down in front of the TV, holding the remote control in a means to rule the world.

Mary stood in disbelief, studying the aftermath of the bizarre behavior of her husband. Was she being unfair? Every means to consider the house a community possession was done on Mary's part. But realistically, it was her house. And the state she lived in legally saw the premarital acquisition of property as solely hers. Unfair-or-not, Mary wouldn't allow the construction of a mausoleum in her backyard, especially while trying to end the stigmatism and reputation that the Trivelli house had.

She, once again, carefully approached her husband who sat at the couch, grasping the remote like a dog that protects a bone. Mary had no idea her husband had such a passion for watching fishing shows. "Daren, don't you think you're overreacting?"

"Forget about it, Mary! It's done! I won't construct a family mausoleum."

"Don't you want to talk about it?"

"What's there to talk about? You won't let me build something. I know where I stand, now."

At a loss of words, the only thing Mary could say, "Well, are you going to leave all your tools out there?" Daren sat motionless, staring at a fishing expert who taught the world the best means of catching a northern pike. From what Mary knew of her husband, Daren hadn't gone fishing a day in his life.

And that's how the day remained on a Sunday that was supposed to be the happily married couple's private, little barbeque. Daren sat motionless in front of the TV, and Mary sat outside under her favorite tree, reading one of the novels she purchased in the touristy section of Sillmac.

Later that afternoon, she fired up the grill; cooked the meat; had a couple margaritas while preparing the rest of dinner; and then summoned the angry man to eat. "If you want, dinner's ready."

The two sat at the table, Daren staring down at his plate while eating, and Mary wearing a shit-eating grin of disbelief at her husband. "Okay Daren, don't you think this has gone far enough? I mean you're having a major meltdown over something as stupid as a mausoleum in the backyard."

He looked up, sighed and then calmly explained the importance of his mausoleum dream. "Look, owning a mausoleum in the backyard shows dedication to the family and fidelity to a marriage. I don't know about you, but I love this house. I never want to move. And when I die, I want to stay here while the house is passed down in our family from generation to generation. I want our names to be engraved on the mausoleum."

Although beautifully stated, Mary wasn't convinced that his dream was such a good idea. "I'm very glad to hear that you love this house, Daren. I love this house too; I've wanted it since I was a little girl. But have you considered that our children may not want this house? And there's something else, Daren. Since I've moved in, I have worked very hard in trying to end the reputation of this house. I'm tired of people thinking it's haunted and cursed. A mausoleum will only add to the rumors. So no; your answer is no. You cannot build that in our backyard."

He sighed and went back to silently eating.

"And Daren? You need to put those tools away. It's supposed to rain tonight, and I don't think you want your tape measure and shovels getting rusty."

* * *

Gone for a week to demo new, medical equipment; Daren returned home, Saturday, in a much, better mood. It was as if the disagreement hadn't occurred 6 days earlier. And in Mary's belief, her husband's dream of a mausoleum was now behind him. Their post-honeymoon bliss resumed.

But bliss was interrupted with a long-distant phone call that Saturday night. It was Mary's sister-in-law who lived in New York City with very, bad news that her husband (Mary's brother) had been involved in a serious car crash. He was floating in and out of consciousness, near a coma. Doctors were unsure if the man would recover. In apprehension that her brother was going to die, Mary immediately booked the next flight to New York City to possibly be with him in his last moments alive. Daren was unable to join his wife as he had a medical convention to attend in California the following week. He brought Mary to the airport early Sunday morning, and saw her off with a loving embrace and wishes that her brother's condition improved.

It was Sunday evening while Daren sat in the living room, watching the local news. The anchor woman wore a confounded look, "A Mapleview man will be receiving heavy fines, and is being ordered to tear down a 600 foot radio tower that he installed in his backyard while his wife was out of town. Beverly Noidlar was shocked to discover the tower had been constructed in her backyard. Her husband, Fred, claims he had it built for recreation and sport, saying he only wanted to have a beer at 600 feet while overlooking the forests and wildlife of Mapleview. Officials say that if anything, a permit had not been acquired for the addition to the property; and even more, a commercialized tower is a violation of zoning ordinance in the residential area. It's unclear if the man will receive fines from the FAA as well."

That's when Daren realized that his wife's absence was the perfect opportunity to construct his mausoleum in the backyard. Although he needed to be in California for the week, Daren could easily hire a contractor for top dollar to build the mausoleum. Such a project could take time if done in the standard way. But since Daren had money, a highly generous incentive would ensure the completion before Mary came home.

Chapter 5

It was Wednesday afternoon while Daren sat alone in his hotel room. The medical convention in California had ended, and Daren rewarded himself with his 4th beer in the past half hour. Back at home, Mary wouldn't allow more than two beers as it would be considered a violation of his promise to cut back drinking. Fortunately for Daren, he traveled in his job which enabled him to drink as he pleased. At least he was only drinking beer!

The contractor who worked feverishly on the mausoleum back in Mapleview provided an update, reporting that it would soon be complete the following day. And Daren lay back in bed in a sudden guilt of reasoning. Perhaps it wasn't such a good idea to have the building constructed. But it was behind the bushes, near the perimeter of the property and out of view. About the size of two ordinary tool sheds, the roof allowed only enough room to stand up which, as Daren imagined, would be just below the top line of the bushes. Still, perhaps Mary would be angry.

Just then, his cell phone rang. "Hello?"

It was Mary. "Hi Sweetie! Whacha doin'?"

"Hey babe! I just came back to my room. The convention is over and I'm flying back home tomorrow."

"Oh good! I miss you and can't wait to see you!" Now at this point, it would be worth mentioning that Mary's, brother's condition had stabilized and he was now fully conscious. Although the incident gave the family quite a fright, Mary and her two siblings were now enjoying each other's company while catching up on events since Mary's wedding with Daren.

Mary had a younger cousin named Kelly, whose mother died from cancer when Kelly was only 10. Since Kelly was without a father, Mary's sister was so kind as to foster the young girl who obviously became an integral member of the family. Although not a problem child, Kelly always had and continued to appear "misguided and misunderstood". She had no consistent man in her life; but Kelly was a beautifully attractive, 22-year-old woman with the perfect figure to turn many a head. She worked at a gentlemen's club as an exotic, non-nude dancer. Although the money was nice, Kelly felt that she was rated as average and not destined to last in the business.

It was a yearning she had to get out and experience something other than the life she'd known since entering adulthood. Per Mary's suggestion, Kelly developed in recent days a desire to move to Mapleview and explore a different life. Although not a favorite establishment for Mary, Mapleview had the Hotlicks Sports bar and Grill that featured young waitresses who wore tight shorts and sleeveless halter tops. Aware of her cousin's livelihood, Mary suggested that in the small town environment, Kelly might become a star and earn decent tips since Hotlicks girls are very popular in Mapleview. Within a few days, the brief suggestion planted a seed in Kelly's mind that quickly grew into a strong desire to live in Mapleview. But how could she land a job at Hotlicks and establish a residence in a small town hundreds of miles away?

It was the phone call to Daren on Wednesday afternoon that Mary intended to find a means for her cousin. "Hey, do you remember my younger cousin, Kelly, who stood up in our wedding?"

"Kelly? Yeah; why?"

"Well, she needs a change of pace and she wants to move out to Mapleview. I'm sure you know Kelly works at a gentlemen's club. I thought she'd be perfect over at Hotlicks."

"Hotlicks? She wants to be a Hotlicks girl?" Daren halfheartedly giggled at the thought of women out of state desiring employment at the Mapleview sports bar and grill.

Mary continued, "I thought it would be good for her. But I want to ask you something. Our house is big with a few open bedrooms. Would you mind if Kelly came back home with me and lived with us for a short while until she finds a job and establishes residence?"

There was a long pause. Under normal circumstances, Daren might have asked his wife if there was a vacancy sign over the door of their house. But this was a perfect opportunity to negotiate the existence of the mausoleum with his wife. Of course Daren wouldn't mention the mausoleum over the phone. He would wait until his wife came home with Kelly, and allow her to discover the building. "Sure she can! It's always nice to extend a helping hand. When are you two coming home?"

"Friday afternoon. Oh, thank you Daren! This is very nice of you!"

Daren might have given the automated "no problem" reply, but there was something waiting at home for Mary that would make up for the inconvenience of a temporary, live-in guest.

* * *

Friday afternoon came along, and Daren picked up his wife and Kelly from the airport. Of course Kelly only brought two suitcases containing a small wardrobe and necessities. Once a permanent residence was found, Kelly would go through the process of long distance moving—an event that no one looks forward to.

Greeting her husband with a kiss, Mary missed Daren and was extra kind to show appreciation for his generosity. And Daren, too, was extra nice. He inquired of the status of his brother-in-law. He spoke of Kelly's opportunity to land a job at Hotlicks Sports Bar and Grill. And he excitedly suggested to his wife, "What do you say we pick up dinner at Big Boy's Beef and Ribs? I didn't do any shopping, and I'm sure you and Kelly are pretty hungry. After dinner, you can whip up your famous margaritas. We can sit outside on the deck and start the weekend off right." Mary, of course, accepted the suggestion.

He was so helpful, offering to carry Kelly's suitcases up the stairs of the Trivelli house. He gave the young girl a personal tour of the 3 bedrooms, each one boasting a panoramic view of the deep, summer woods. Her favorite view, as Daren suggested, should be the guiding force that chose her room. And he sat with Mary and Kelly at the kitchen table, excitedly eating his ribs with fries, actively engaged in the conversation.

It wasn't until near the end of dinner that Mary suspected her husband to be guilty of something. Did he have a fling out in California? Maybe he did more cocaine while she was gone? What possibly could Daren have done that forced him to cover guilt with overdone kindness?

Mary whipped up her margaritas in the blender. Outside, Daren eagerly awaited his wife and the guest while slamming two beers from the cooler. Already, he was holding his third as if it was only his first. It was going to be a challenging moment in their marriage. Daren needed all the help he could get!

A midsummer evening on the backyard deck, the three of them sat while overlooking the woods. The sun in the horizon glistened through the trees. Song birds and robins of the woods sang their goodnight song, accompanied by the mellow chorus of crickets and frogs. And out of the corner of her eye, Mary spotted something unusual behind the bushes, near the perimeter of the property and seemingly out of view. "What... *is*...

that?" She stood up, set her glass on the table and placed her fingers over her agape mouth. "Tell me you didn't! You didn't! Oh my Gosh, you did! *I can't believe you!* **I can't believe you!**"

Pretending to interpret his wife's reaction as pleasant excitement, Daren smiled while taking another sip of his beer. "You like it? I thought I'd surprise you while you were gone. See, it doesn't look so bad."

Mary stormed across the deck and slammed the screen door behind her. "I cannot believe you! Ugh! How did I get myself in this mess?"

Daren re-assuredly smiled at Kelly and followed his wife inside. Did Kelly come to the right place? She stood up to investigate whatever had caused Mary to be angry. All she could see was the roof of a small building beneath the top line of some bushes. To Kelly, it looked as though a small storage building or tool shed had been built. Apparently, Mary didn't want this; but Daren took it upon himself to build it while she was gone.

Apparently, Mary really didn't want this building as the sound of violent arguing could be heard inside. Daren shouted of how important it was and then he lowered his voice to a barely, audible grunt.

It was followed by the shrilling voice of Mary who screamed, "*I owe you?* That's your rationale? I knew you were up to something, but I had no idea you had built the mausoleum (which I told you not to build) while I was gone!"

A mausoleum? Within seconds, Kelly watched as Mary stormed out of the screen door, across the deck and down the stairs to the ground level. Daren followed behind, which turned into a train as curious Kelly hesitated behind like a sluggish caboose.

New in construction; the building emulated the old-style, small, family mausoleum that was complete with textured, slab-stone walls; a locked, iron door and the family name above the entry. Kelly had never seen her cousin with such a red face and eyes of destructive fire. The anger settled into silent rage. Kelly could see Mary sinking the difficult emotions that were unable to process at the moment.

But Daren didn't understand. He set his hand on the wife's shoulder, now relieved that she was calming down. "There; see, it's not so bad."

"Don't touch me, Daren!" Mary hated his deliberate misinterpretations of her feelings.

* * *

As the days passed, Kelly expected to see Daren banished from the Trivelli house. But he remained, and the marriage between Daren and Mary resumed, almost as if Mary forgot the mausoleum.

Everyone has experienced the transition from joblessness to employment. It's the period when all one can do is wait patiently for the word of an interview while sitting idle, coping with the existence of being unproductive. Kelly had no choice during this time but to go for her morning runs; have breakfast and coffee; maintain her social network on Facebook and stay up-to-date on her favorite TV shows. Mary worked full time at the flower shop; but throughout the week, Daren had a few days of down time while waiting for the next biomedical demonstration. This, of course, meant that Daren and Kelly lived those hours alone and under the same roof.

Initially maintaining to stay out of the man's way, Kelly did her best to be little of a bother as possible. But it soon became a speculation that perhaps in her youthful attractiveness, Kelly was the forbidden candy now prancing about the house. If only she could have had eyes behind the back of her head, she might have caught sight of his watching and fantasizing that quickly looked away as Kelly turned around from the strange feeling.

Kelly was full aware that she lived with Mary and her husband for free. And she was welcome to eat as she pleased. Although the arrangement was only temporary, most people would grow uneasy living with a freeloader. But Daren was most generous and regularly invited her to help herself at home.

One day, while Kelly made a turkey on rye sandwich for lunch, Daren closely passed behind. She knew his hand was supposed to lightly graze the cheek of her butt. And in the way she was dressed with daisy-duke shorts and a sleeveless top, Kelly knew the man couldn't help his lustful desires. But contact hadn't been made with the firm bubble. Perhaps he momentarily lost touch with his bold nature. But as Kelly reached for a bag of chips; Daren once again passed closely behind. This time he placed his hot hands on her exposed shoulders in a motion of politely passing by, "Excuse me…"

Kelly closed her eyes, bit her lip and deeply inhaled. The touch was well received.

But the days of subliminal foreplay were interrupted when Kelly finally received word of starting her career at Hotlicks Sports Bar and Grill. She was unlike many of the girls who worked there, and unlike many of the girls who competed for the 3 openings. Kelly was their first choice, and management was most eager for the aspiring Hotlicks girl to begin.

The good news called for a celebration back at the Trivelli house as Mary made Cajun-style shrimp on the barbie and a double, strong batch of her famous margarita blend. The three of them sat out on the deck after dinner. It was Kelly's last weekend before beginning employment at Hotlicks. Daren wouldn't dare lay a hand on the young girl now, not in front of his wife. And it was good that Kelly finally started work. In her perception, the unmentionable game between her and Daren was getting a little out of control.

While sitting outside, Daren mentioned to his wife, "Oh; just so you know, next week when I'm gone, a contractor will be coming here to install air conditioning in the mausoleum."

Mary took a savoring sip of her margarita. "Air conditioning? Why do you need air conditioning in a mausoleum? Are you moving out and planning on living in your little club house, outside?"

Kelly laughed.

"No, it just needs air conditioning. It might get hot in there during the summer months and rot whoever is in there? Did you want to rot in the summer heat?"

Mary had no answer to the question, but did offer a suggestion. "Daren, do you know what we should do with the mausoleum? We should grow ivy on top and around the building. Cover that blasted thing up so I don't have to look at it!"

Chapter 6

Not far from the Trivelli house is the entryway to the Hidden Lake Forest Preserve, a popular section of woods in Mapleview. The actual Hidden Lake is only a couple hundred feet from Mary's house. But the actual entryway to the woods is about a 20 minute hike from the lake. Really the forest preserve is closed after sunset, but the parking lot is like a small wayside off the highway that late night motorists have been known to park and rest. Police simply patrol the area for any suspicious activity, and aren't terribly concerned if a car happens to be parked in the lot late at night.

A serious endeavor of starving and frustrated artist, Steve Coldsworth, was to see one of his nature landscapes accepted by a vineyard and ultimately displayed on a bottle of wine. One of the problems that prospective vineyards had with his art was the nature of his paintings. They featured nude women standing in the midst of nature settings. Most vineyards that received unsolicited samples of his art felt that it would drown out the very essence of what their wines were about. But Steve's art was purely driven by freely expressing that which was in his heart. I suppose one could say that Steve had an obsession with nudity.

Driving along the stretch of highway; passing the legendary Trivelli house where Daren, Mary and Kelly slept; Steve Coldsworth continued until reaching the entryway of the Hidden Lake Forest Preserve. Overwhelmed with discouraging feelings of another possible rejection, Steve was in need of exhilaration and an experience that would jolt his mind back to that of confidence.

On that particular night, Steve ran out to the middle of the woods, stripped naked and ran throughout the forest while experiencing darkness and the fragility of exposing his humanity to the unknown. He imagined the slithery creatures hiding under forest vegetation that could bite him. He realized the possibility that an animal could attack him. But these were all feelings that Steve needed to experience so he could begin working on his next painting that he hoped would be used for special, Halloween-edition bottles of wine.

The experience was soon ended upon reaching a clearing of the forest where he took sight of a very, large, old tree. It looked so peculiar, standing out there and surrounded by tall weeds. Steve carefully drew closer to the tree with the sensation of stupidity, as he was naked, but gazed in awe at the sight of the tree that remained some distance in front of him.

A jolting experience out in the woods is often interpreted by Steve as the highlight of his visit. He originally ventured into the forest with the intention of experiencing his fragility in darkness. But the tree was rapidly becoming the purpose of tonight. In Steve's mind, he could see the tree as a half-human creature, exhibiting limbs and a human head—sort of like a mythological beast. And through his art, Steve could produce such a painting that might be grotesque enough to be used as Halloween art.

And this was the vision that took place on a warm, summer night and not far from the Trivelli house. Steve shut himself in that night to begin his masterpiece to be titled, The Tree Goddess. By dawn, the magnificent painting of a tree and landscape that he remembered had been completed. But this was only the beginning of his work. The arms, legs and head of the beast needed to be found and added.

* * *

It only requires the contents of 5 tea bags to be emptied into the espresso filter basket. Add the appropriate amount of water, and within minutes a thick brew comes trickling out. If the blend of tea contains orange pekoe, the dark liquid soon turns to a bright orange when allowed to cool. Steve brewed the concoction and gulped it down in the early morning hours. Desiring not to throw his sleep off schedule, he planned on remaining awake during the day and retiring in the early evening. And it was necessary to brew another concoction around midmorning as he began to feel sleepy. Familiar with the "boomerang effect", Steve was aware that no more than two cups should be drunk. The effect, hours later, could be unpredictable; which he would soon be reminded later that evening.

Skipping lunch and doing chores throughout the day, he felt a ravenous hunger around 6:00 that evening. The perfect remedy and wrap-up for a day lasting more that 24 hours would be some of those famous hot wings down at Hotlicks Sports Bar and Grill, washed down with a couple of beers.

Kelly approached her customer, Steve. "Hi, welcome to Hotlicks. Are you alone tonight? Can I start you off with a drink? We have many domestic and import bottled beers."

The young waitress, Kelly, had the perfect arms for Steve's Tree Goddess painting. They would look so beautiful on the tree; so long and slender, yet muscular with perfectly unblemished skin. Steve examined her arms so intently, beginning with her shoulders, all the way down to her finger tips. They were perfect!

"Sir?"

He quickly looked at the waitress's face for the first time as she nervously smiled. Kelly caught much attention from the male patrons during her first week on the job, but no one had examined her arms so eagerly. "Oh, gimme a Bud Lite."

"Sure thing. I'll bring that out and you can take a look at the menu. We have the best hot wings with a variety of sauces."

Steve probably should have stayed at home, ordered a pizza and retired early that evening. The lack of sleep brought on the peculiar sensation of being isolated and removed from the bar as-if watching the activities on a movie screen. The sensation evolved into receiving moving images, almost like powerful daydreams that could be seen in front of him. Is that what his espressed tea was going to do to him? Known to be unpredictable, hours later, this time it would appear that he was on some sort of post-Lipton quasi-LSD-trip.

Studying Kelly from a distance, a high-definition, panoramic vision materialized of the waitress sleeping soundly in the night. In her dream, the young woman ventured through a storage closet that ended up behind her bedroom wall. There, a peep hole could be found where Kelly looked through and excitedly watched herself undress.

"There you go sir. Have you decided what to order?"

Steve was pulled out of the strange vision at the presence of Kelly, who placed his bottle of Bud Lite on the table. But in the unusual frame of mind, combined with a need to explore the new addition to the Tree Goddess painting, Steve rose from his seat and immediately placed his hands on Kelly's shoulders while rubbing and caressing them. "You have such beautiful arms; they're perfect!"

The startled Hotlicks girl didn't know how to react, but stepped back, obviously uncomfortable with the strange customer's physical assault. Steve followed her retreat and firmly caressed her arms to feel the silky, soft skin and thin, yet muscular construction. He knew exactly how to make her arms on his painting. She screamed and further backed into the corner, nearly knocking into a table. But Steve was right there, exploring every inch of her arms.

Within seconds, a bouncer came to the rescue and pushed Steve off the waitress. "Hey, hey what's going on here? You keep your hands off the girls! And I'm going to ask you to leave!"

"But I didn't finish my…"

The bouncer forcefully grabbed Steve, dragged him over to the cashier and made him pay for his beer that was opened, but untouched. Then he pushed the troublesome patron out the front door and into the parking lot. "I don't want to see you here again! You come back and I'll call the cops!"

And so was Kelly's first encounter with a dangerous customer. Even as an exotic dancer back in New York she had never been attacked by a patron. But as security explained, some of the men who entered Hotlicks were dangerous and quickly labeled unworthy to visit the establishment. Steve would never be allowed to return.

* * *

Perhaps Daren had come to his senses and realized that whatever game existed between him and Kelly was dangerous. The only thing that changed in Kelly's life was the fact that she awoke around noon. Coming home at 2:00 in the morning, she didn't fall asleep until an hour later. But there would have been plenty of time for Daren to resume his subliminal pursuit with Kelly as she went downstairs for afternoon breakfast. On the days that Daren was home, she encountered the man as the two continued to exist alone. Mary wouldn't come home until 4-ish; but no further attempts of fondling and touch were made.

Much to Kelly's disappointment, the town of Mapleview lacked a wide selection of men to choose from. In fact; most, if not all, of the men who visited Hotlicks were really quite trashy. Kelly was accustomed to high-class patrons and business men who visited the gentlemen's club back in New York. But these sorts of men did not visit Hotlicks in Mapleview. If there were any such men in the town, they were happily married and devoted to a career and family, not visiting Hotlicks. They were men very, much like Daren who Mary was most fortunate to have.

Late at night, Kelly often lay awake in bed, all the while imagining Daren on the other side of the door with a burning desire to knock. It was so real! Why didn't he knock? So she wore a see-through nightgown on an evening of overpowering fantasy, and carefully approached the door. Her fingers touched the knob as she felt his on the other side. It would only take a careful opening of the door, pretending to need the bathroom. The soft light would shine through the nightgown and expose Kelly's beckoning nipples and the curvature of her back & buttocks. Unable to resist, Daren would finally seize the young girl to use and abuse in overpowering lust. But Kelly had cold feet. Perhaps the plan was all wrong. The door was never opened.

Days later, Kelly made a strange discovery in the corner of the bedroom wall near a row of shelves. Really the warped, dark trim between the antique walls appeared to already contain the formation of a small, natural hole. But it looked as though someone had carefully widened this hole as a means to see inside her bedroom. But where was the observation post? She knocked on the wall, taking notice that there was a space behind it. Exiting her room and exploring her way down the hall, Kelly opened the linen closet to discover a removable panel in the back that provided access to a storage space. But the space remained empty as she walked sideways between the dimly-lit, cobweb strewn area until reaching a crack of light in the wall. She peeked through the small hole which yielded a full view of her own bedroom. Everything could be seen, including her dresser, her bed and the very walk-in closet where she stood naked to dress. Mary would be the least-likely suspect of Kelly's invasion of privacy. Daren had been watching the young girl in her most private moments!

On the day of her discovery, Daren was out of town. This gave Kelly some time to evaluate the finding which; through a few nights of serving the watchful eyes of horny, male customers at Hotlicks; evolved into a mischievous plan. Not a word was mentioned to Mary. And not a clue of her awareness was spilled to Daren of the peep hole.

Kelly awoke at noon, on a day that Daren was home, and did her usual routine in the shower. But on this day, she returned to the bedroom with a small bucket of water, shaving cream and a razor. The bathrobe was removed which exposed her fully-naked body—an appetizer for the peeping eye.

She turned side-to-side, examining herself in the mirror and then studied her most private possession. Then she sat on the bed with the bucket of water on the floor and lathered her pubic region with shaving cream. Daren was going to be treated to a private show of the young girl shaving!

She performed the display as to be the most beautiful thing he had ever seen. Kelly could hear the rapidly-beating heart through the wall, along with barely controllable breathing. How many guys were treated to such delicate sight of a young girl doing this? Many men had probably gawked at her in the sports bar, but Daren got to see what they could have only dreamed of.

Chapter 7

Science has disproved it time and time again. There is no correlation between a rise in crime and violence, rise in birth rates or rise in visits to the hospitals during times of the full moon. And yet many law enforcement officials and staff at emergency rooms are in tune with those times of lunar peak. People are crazy during the full moon, and there are plenty who take notice of this.

Just ask Aunt Loraine who visited Mary and Kelly on a hot, summer afternoon in August. Daren was flying back from Detroit after a biomedical convention. And before warning the young, Hotlicks girl of the full moon, Aunt Loraine commented on the mausoleum that now sat in Mary's backyard. "Your Grandpa Trivelli always wanted a mausoleum in this backyard. But Grandma Trivelli wouldn't allow it!"

Poor Mary could only sigh and imperceptibly shake her head in disbelief.

Then Aunt Loraine warned Kelly of a possible danger in the evening. "And do be careful at the establishment of ill repute, tonight! It's a full moon and lots of crazy things happen then. And I'm sure Hotlicks is just the sort of place where the activities of Sodom and Gomorrah are resurrected. Are you sure about working at Hotlicks? It seems like a nice place, but..."

"She's fine, Aunt Loraine!" As always, Mary found it necessary to cut off the crazy, old lady in her irrational attacks of whatever the obsession was of the moment. Kelly saw it to be the perfect opportunity to excuse herself and head off to work.

It must have been close to 100 degrees outside! It was going to be a hot time in the old town that night for sure! For the heavily forested region of Mapleview, the heat was an unusual phenomenon. To make matters worse, Kelly was without air conditioning in the inexpensive car purchased for temporary use while becoming established in Mapleview. She couldn't wait to get in the bar and grill where, on a day like that one, the air conditioning would run.

But although Hotlicks Sports Bar and Grill had the air conditioning running full blast, the heat seemed to pour in through the walls, the windows and any time a patron entered. And what a wild night it was! Kelly had never seen the likes of it before as customers demanded more and more beer! There was shouting, fighting and plenty of ass-grabbing in between! Aunt Loraine must have been right. The full moon on a hot night would bring the worst out of everyone.

1:00, the last patron had left, arguing he wanted one more drink. But town ordinances for serving alcohol were to be strictly followed, and closing time at Hotlicks was 1:00. This rule not only gave employees time to clean up, but allowed an hour for the parking lot to clear and a chance for the popular Hotlicks girls to safely step outside to their vehicles.

The unbearable summer heat had eased, but it was still humid and uncomfortably warm. Traveling with her windows wide open provided Kelly some relief. Perhaps the hours of craziness, the sticky humidity and the weeks of games back at the Trivelli house mixed with the full moon and caused Kelly to pull over at the Hidden Lake Forest Preserve, where she hesitated before following through with a crazy idea. Remaining in the car, Kelly's shirt was lifted off; her bra was removed; and shorts along with panties were pulled down. The only articles of remaining clothing were her shoes that were needed for driving, of course.

Completely naked, she turned the opposite direction from home and drove the lonely, forested highway that was illuminated by the light of the full moon. The breeze blew freely against her bare skin, yielding the sense of ultimate freedom. And then a car approached in the opposite lane with its brights on. What if the occupants of that vehicle saw the naked Hotlicks girl and turned around for a chase? Fortunately, this did not happen. But it changed the mood into panic for Kelly as she wondered, "What am I doing?"

The forested road offered shoulders on both sides. Trembling with racing heart racing, Kelly immediately pulled over and quickly stepped into her shorts. The panties were neglected for the sake of speed and so was the bra as both undergarments were thrown out the window. The white t-shirt was pulled on, and Kelly made a u-turn to head home. Passing the entryway of the Hidden Lake Forest Preserve, she continued along until finally reaching the half-block, uphill driveway of the historic house.

She was greeted by the unexpected presence of Daren, who smiled with a bottle of beer in his hand. Approaching her car as Kelly exited; he was in the mood for small talk while drawing close. "Unusual weather here in Mapleview, huh?"

Kelly agreed, "Oh Yeah! It was so hot today! And the bar was roasting."

There was something locking of Daren's stance, almost as-if he had the power of holding the young girl captive. And he smiled with a frightening glint in his eyes, suggesting that tonight was the night he had been waiting for. Taking a guzzle from the half-finished bottle, the will of his invitation could be felt before speaking. "Come here, I want to show you something." Daren motioned the young girl to follow as he walked off the driveway and towards the backyard.

Kelly worried that it might look odd to resist his invitation. Although she suddenly didn't trust the man, he was Mary's husband, and he did allow her to live there. Feeling she had no choice, Kelly trailed behind, wondering what might be so important for Daren to show her.

The mausoleum? What did he have to show her about the building? They stood at the entrance as Daren pulled the keys out of his pocket. "Here that? That's the new air conditioning." He was proud of the new addition to the building. And Kelly couldn't believe that Daren had unlocked and opened the thick, iron door. No one, outside of Daren and the contractor, had ever seen the inside of that building, including Mary. He placed his hot hand on Kelly's sticky, sweaty shoulder. "Come on in; it's nice and cool in here."

It was just like any small family mausoleum, except it lacked decaying occupants. A lightly-stained, wooden bench was mounted to the center floor; two dimly-lit sconces affixed to the rear-wall; and empty but closed crypts took up the sidewalls of the building. "Ah, air conditioning! Feels good, huh?" Daren swigged the remains of his beer, set the bottle in the corner and closed the iron door.

Kelly didn't know what to say. He acted like his mausoleum was the greatest thing ever while appearing to believe that it was the only place to stay cool. She reminded Daren that the house, inside, was just as cool. "Well, when I was home earlier today, Mary had the central air on. The house should be comfortable."

"Oh yeah; she's still got the air on. But maybe it's a little cooler in here. Maybe it's just the thing you need to cool down after a long, hot day." His eyes darted at her chest as Kelly realized that coming in from the hot, humid air brought on an immediate chill in the air-conditioned mausoleum. Within less than a minute, her skin was cold with goose bumps. It was then apparent as to why Kelly had been brought inside Daren's club house.

There wasn't much room to back up. The young girl had no choice but to receive a sloppy, wet kiss from Mary's husband. He was such a good looking man with thick, muscular frame. The weeks of fantasy and the sexy taste of beer on his breath left Kelly enchanted as she pulled herself in. Clothes were removed from the naughty girl who neglected to wear undergarments. She was lifted up with legs wrapped around his waist. Kelly's head hit the ceiling a few times; then after a few minutes, her back rest upon the icy wall of crypts. Finally, she was laid on the wooden bench where she slid back and forth until the moment had ended. All of this was done while Mary slept soundly in her bed.

Chapter 8

Just as expected, the nightly encounters would continue in the mausoleum. Many evenings, Kelly stepped outside in the August air, curious if Mary's husband waited. Sure enough, he stood at the iron door with the mischievous, guilty look in his eyes. Other times she was disappointed to learn that Daren was out of town. The nights of his absence were unbearable as Kelly lay tossing and turning in bed, worrying if he brought another woman back to his hotel room for a fling. And of course there were nights when Daren chose the company of his wife over the mistress. It brought on mixed feelings of jealousy, guilt and anxiety. Did Mary feel her cousin's kiss through Daren? Did she sense the man fantasizing of the young girl while they made love?

Kelly attempted to convince herself that this new, steamy, summer affair was all wrong. But the reasoning was soon drowned by her realization that the sexual encounters were much needed, both physically and emotionally. Moving to Mapleview was a bit of cultural shock, and Kelly was in serious need of companionship. There wasn't much to choose from in the small, rural town; but she wasn't about to live a life a celibacy. And really she wasn't ready for serious relationship. That's why a dirt bag like Daren was perfect for her. Oh, he was kind and appeared interested in the personal life of Kelly. But

Kelly knew men, and Daren was no different. Only a dirt bag would cheat on a wonderful wife like Mary.

It was the thoughts of Mary that occasionally grounded the young girl and choked her uncontrollable desires for Daren. Mary truly was a wonderful person. She was beautiful, kind, generous, well-mannered and patient. She had a special gift for easy conversation. She calmly listened without reservations or preconceptions, and spoke in such a calming, re-assuring manner. There was a light that shone from Mary; she truly was special. How could Kelly have become involved in such a betrayal of an angel on Earth?

Then her desires for Daren would return as she could not refuse such fantastic sex. In turn, the guilt for betraying Mary would eat away at her soul. Each time she turned back to desire, the guilt became stronger. Then one September night during the ride home from work, both desire and guilt were equal. They were like two horses with parallel strength, pulling Kelly's mind in opposite directions. She would go mad if continuing this lifestyle. That night she had to break the cycle and immediately avoid the mausoleum.

Up the half-block driveway on a cool, September night; Kelly walked right up the house and up to her room. For sure, Daren was waiting and probably disappointed that his concubine would not join him for the night. But enough was enough. Kelly had to take the first step in gaining control of her life.

Nothing was initially said the following afternoon when Kelly went downstairs for breakfast. Daren sat at the sofa, watching TV, appearing unaffected by last night's change of plans. But there was something dark that overshadowed the man as he remained speechless with somber, pale face. While Kelly ate her bowl of cereal, Daren slowly and calmly entered the kitchen with eyes locked on the young girl. "I'm going out of town for about a week."

She could see how skilled the man was in camouflaging his possible, violent anger. The spoon was set down and Kelly sighed, "Daren, I can't do this anymore. I just can't."

His eyes burned red with fury, but he produced a mask of understanding sadness. "Okay…"

Then he turned, walked away and ascended the flight of stairs. Just as Kelly could feel Daren's hidden lust weeks ago, she could now feel his subliminal outrage which frightened her beyond belief. It would only be a matter of time before she learned of the monster that awaited her. It was time to leave the Trivelli house! She had the money saved up. An apartment could be obtained in Mapleview in less than a week. She could even sleep on the floor without a bed until she either purchased one or moved her own into town from New York.

After a few days of arising early and scouting Mapleview for an apartment, Kelly managed to locate a 1st floor unit in a complex located in town. Living there would require another 10 minutes of travel from work; but the time had come to establish herself in Mapleview.

* * *

"Moving out? This week? Why in such a hurry?" Mary was baffled at the sudden announcement that her cousin was leaving. With only the baggage she brought with, Kelly had no furniture or bed. If the young girl didn't have the family reputation of being "misguided and misunderstood", Mary might have thought that Daren had something to with it. Maybe Kelly was simply moving in with a newfound boyfriend. Or maybe she needed the privacy for drugs or sex. Her cousin was a grown woman, and Mary wasn't about to hold her back. She watched as Kelly left on a late, Wednesday afternoon for work with baggage in her hands. The Trivelli house would now only have two occupants.

* * *

If you happen to commute the same route to work, then perhaps you've found yourself reflecting of thoughts from the previous day and the day before that. This phenomenon might be done on an isolated road in the early morning or late evening hours. Although they might not be the exact same thoughts, or the same topic for that matter, the spark of neurons seem to be affected in such a way that the daydreams, speculations and ponderings are related. If time were an illusion, then that lonely stretch of road would be a timeless realm where one returns to a private story book, read again and again, under different frames of mind.

Kelly was not a deeply, intellectual person that involved herself in mind-altering, philosophical thoughts. As far as she was concerned; the dark, lonely, wooded highway that she traveled home each night was the same. But she did pay attention to the change of weather. Only weeks ago, she was faced with the unbearable, August heat. Now in Early September, she drove home with the windows partially cracked; passing the entrance to the Hidden Lake Forest Preserve; passing the half-mile driveway to the Trivelli house; and into town where her apartment complex was located. But every night was a personal trial with imagined, un-seeable judge and jurors who probed Kelly of the affair with Daren. Would she ever find peace? And did she truly learn her lesson? And although Kelly was the one on trial, she couldn't help but wonder how in the world Mary could live with a man like Daren. Did she see the frightening side of Daren and his potential to become a monster? To intensify these late night, private trials into anxiety; the presence of a pick-up truck tailed Kelly some distance down the highway before turning right. It annoyed the Hotlicks girl. It was like clockwork: the aggressive vehicle was part of the nightly ride home and seemed to push her faster along the road. Kelly seemed to forget the vehicle once out of sight, but then strongly wished there was a way to avoid it upon suddenly appearing during her ride home.

Kelly was called into the manager's office of Hotlicks on a Friday night, a half-hour before leaving. Keep in mind that the bar and grill closes at 1:00, and the parking lot is expected to clear within the hour. This provided the ability for the Hotlicks girls to safely exit the building and walk to their cars.

Bouncer Carl sat in one of the chairs and immediately informed Kelly of a threat to her safety. "Kelly, we noticed a vehicle parked out in the lot, long after everyone had left. Don and I went up to the driver to advise him to leave. And then I noticed it was the same guy who grabbed you that one night. You know, feeling your arms? I pretended not to recognize him and was like, 'Can I help you?' He said he was waiting for one of the girls to get off work, waiting for Liz."

Liz was Kelly's stage name. In an effort to protect the Hotlicks girls, none of their badges displayed real names. Carl advised Kelly to be cautious while driving home. Then he provided his cell phone number in case she felt in danger. It's funny to think of how unprofessionally the incident had been handled by an establishment that valued safety of the girls. Carl never recorded the name of Steve Coldsworth, who paid for his unfinished beer on the night of Kelly's assault with a debit card. He never called the Mapleview Police to report a motorist that was loitering in the parking lot of Hotlicks after hours. And he never gave Kelly so much of a description of the vehicle, only to be careful. To make matters worse, the big-headed bouncer who prided himself in being aggressive and strong, never recorded a license plate number or a description of the vehicle. Exactly how safe was it for a Hotlicks girl to work at the bar and grill?

Spooked over the discovery and realization that her attacker had intentions of stalking, Kelly kept watchful eye on the rearview mirror. The timing was so unwelcome, being that she now lived alone. Kelly would soon find out that tonight's trial called forth a witness who had sat in the back row, ignored, during her nightly reflections of summer mistakes. The same, red pick-up truck that trailed her night after night was parked some distance down the lonely stretch of road. As Kelly passed, its lights turned on and soon pulled out behind her. Was this the explanation as to why Kelly was trailed by the vehicle each night? To further prove this possible theory, she referenced a mental note that was made the previous evening of where the pick-up truck turned. Last night, it made a right on Lint Road, and Kelly assumed that was the direction of nightly commute for the driver. But tonight, it did not turn right on Lint Road. It continued, almost suggesting that a stalker was gradually tracking her route home each night. Much to her unwise relief, the pick-up truck turned left on Vine Road, which left Kelly alone for the remainder of her ride home.

As a 22-year-old Hotlicks girl, and previous exotic dancer at a gentlemen's club, Kelly had pretty much seen it all. She knew men, knew their stupidities and realized that there are two kinds of men in this world. The first type of man is the common sort that Kelly was exposed to night after night: stupid, jerky, immature and in pursuit of only one thing. The second sort of man is stupid and immature, but in a different sort of way. He appears quiet, creepy and somewhat dangerous. He actually plots of ways to get what he wants—sitting in the parking lot of Hotlicks after hours in hopes to stalk the girl he is obsessed with. He might get the nerve to touch her in personal places while in the bar, and dreams of discovering where she lives so his staking fantasies can become a reality. Fortunately, security is aware of this type of man and they have protocols in place to protect the girls who work there.

However dangerous, this second sort of man is just as stupid as the first. No man would be that clever to engage in such a diabolical scheme that would take nights to track a girl's route home, no matter how desperate. And the only way such a scheme could begin is if an obsessed man hid in the woods behind the parking lot of Hotlicks to note what car Kelly entered and what direction she drove once leaving. And really, the only reason she was alarmed at the sight of the pick-up truck was because of the incident Carl had advised her of.

The following night was a cold one, in the mid 50's with a light drizzle in the air. Kelly, once again, left the bar and grill under the same protocol: with coworkers escorted by bouncers. But the predictable presence of the pick-up truck was causing her to be concerned. And as she pulled out of the parking lot, the light drizzle turned into a shower which forced Kelly to engage the windshield wipers. Rain trickled on the glass, and vents were turned on high to reduce condensation. This extra noise and energy only agitated Kelly into a deeper anxiety as she anticipated another encounter with the pick-up truck.

This was crazy! Kelly needed to gain control of her conscience that synergized the guilt of the affair, and the guilt of playing with men at the bar to get tips. Most women would love to have the body that Kelly had along with the power to excite men at her presence. It was this gift of beauty that enabled her to have the title of Hotlicks girl and show some leg for tips. She only needed to be friendly and flirtatious with her customers. If a group of guys started the night off with a pitcher of beer, she would immediately acknowledge that this was a cool thing and then smile at the guy who seemed to be the "group leader". Men are so easy! Show a little leg, show a little interest and flash a smile; they'll be eating out of your hand in no time. Patrons of these sports bars and grills that feature young girls in tight shorts and halter tops might argue that checking out the waitress is not what it's all about. These men might argue that they go there to be with friends, have beer & hot wings, and watch the game. So why don't they have old grandmas working at these places? Would such sport bars be as popular then?

Although a very exciting lifestyle at Hotlicks, Kelly drove alone that rainy night, realizing that she wasn't always in to her job. Now don't think for one second that Kelly didn't enjoy the life of men worshipping her and giving her tips simply for the beauty she possessed. But there were nights that Kelly wished it wasn't necessary to prance about partially naked while flirting with horny men, especially the downright creepy ones. And when they were tanked up on beer, they could become worse. That's probably what happened to the customer who attacked her in the bar on an early-summer evening...

...and may have possibly sat in the pick-up truck parked on the side of the road where she passed! If you've ever come close to getting into an accident or saw the flash of police headlights in your rearview mirror, then you would recognize the intense adrenaline that overcame Kelly as the headlights turned on and the pick-up truck quickly pulled out to follow her. Although unreal to Kelly, it added to her belief that someone was, in fact, slowly stalking and tracking her route home each night. She passed Lint Road and Vine Road; all the while the big, red pick-up truck closely following behind with the heat of the headlights reflecting off the rearview mirror.

Then it made it right-turn onto an unknown road that, as far as Kelly knew, led to an old church. She was, once again, alone. It just had to be coincidence!

Chapter 9

There are many strange qualities pertaining to the seemingly quiet and peaceful town of Mapleview. As an onlooker or a passerby on vacation, the area is beautiful, serene and a place one only dreams of living. But the residents know of the urban legends, the most famous being connected to the Trivelli house. And there's more, a lot more, as residents can feel a certain energy that blankets the town of unexplained happenings. Something occurred in that area hundreds of years ago, long before Mapleview was established and the great Trivelli house had been built.

Exactly one week after Kelly's manager and bouncer informed her of the stalker who waited in the parking lot, Mary watched the early-morning news that reported a horrific story. Live helicopter footage revealed images of a tragic mishap, overnight. Fortunately, it didn't involve Kelly, who had yet to visit Mary since moving out. But the event was associated with the mysterious Route 4 that Detective Tom Morehausen had spoken of.

Route 4: a 10.6 mile stretch of highway between the towns of Sillmac and Mapleview. Although not entirely true, the highway has the reputation of being a region with poor, if any, cell phone reception. It's not until a motorist is near Mapleview or Sillmac that cellular service is restored. The road is lonely late at night with deep wilderness on both sides. And if it weren't for the occasional highway lights that were recently installed for safety, the partially illuminated stretch of road would be pitch black. It's the perfect setting for any woman who is concerned of her safety during a late night drive. Should headlights that suddenly appear in the rearview mirror and crazed drivers who glare into the window be reason for alarm?

It was a Friday night and two young men sat in an apartment in search of the ultimate night out. Surrounded by a bombardment of adult entertainment, it could quickly be concluded that Mark and Dave were frustrated individuals. Neither was capable of maintaining a long-term relationship with the opposite sex. And to make matters worse, both had started the weekend broke with nothing to do on a Friday night.

Dave sighed, "Dude, I'm sick of looking at this stuff. You know, it's the weekend and we're sitting here wishing we had some action."

Mark came up with a great plan for the evening. It was based on information he heard earlier in the week of a game played on Route 4. Most of the participants who engaged in this activity believed that female motorists drove the highway late at night with the sole intention of being stalked and pursued on the road. These women were believed to be lonely housewives or unsatisfied in their relationships. The 10.6 miles of lonely, dark highway was an abandon of a woman's inhibitions. She could be chased, symbolically assaulted and then make it to safety by either of the towns separated by the 10.6 mile stretch of highway.

There's no denying that young men are highly motivated to participate in any activities that remotely resemble the seduction, attack or assault of a woman. And to come to the defense of men who may play such a game, many (not all) women do have fantasies of coercion. The chase game on Route 4 appeared to be a harmless outlet of frustration and need for coercion alike.

Dave wasn't sure about this game. "Dude, it's a total bust! All some woman needs to do is get your license plate number and call the police once her cell starts working. Besides, a cell phone might not work, but On Star will!"

Mark's argument was that not everyone had On Star. And he insisted it was no crime for simply looking at a motorist on the highway. In his words, "So we were driving down Route 4 and like the way some chick looked. So what? We can't go to jail for that!"

In their friendship, one might have noticed that Dave was the more sensible person. A sensible person might ask, "What if a woman was simply driving the stretch of dark highway for the sake of commuting home or traveling on vacation?" To Dave, it sounded like this game was a fantasy, and may very well have taken place in the minds of those pursuing the women on Route 4.

But Mark was persistent. "Come on, man! Aren't you sick of merely looking at stuff online or going to strip clubs? Don't you want excitement? Don't you want to play a wild game with an un-expecting woman out there? Besides, they like that stuff! Women get off on being stalked and chased by guys out on the road. The worst thing that could happen is a neglected house-wife will be out and in search of a thrill, and we give her a run for her money. Don't you get it? Why else would she be driving that road late at night?"

Dave remained motionless with a blank look, unsure if the suggested activity was really a safe form of entertainment. It seemed harmless, and Mark's argument was a reasonable one. After several more seconds of deliberation, he agreed to try the game out.

The two drove down the lonely stretch of highway with Mark driving. He was nearly psychotic with a crazed look, heavily breathing and red face that indicated a surge in blood pressure. Needless to say, he was most eager to encounter a vehicle containing a lonely, female driver.

Dave's mind was racing, too, but in different way. Was this really a good idea? Was there any possible chance to convince his friend to back out? He suggested that the road was so desolate that they might not encounter anyone.

But Mark remained positive and tried to reassure his friend that the patience would pay off. "I'm telling you man, women come out here because they know about the game that's played. Why else would some chick come out on a lonely, dark road at night? We'll find one!"

Shortly after Mark provided the reassuring words, the two spotted a set of tail lights some distance down the dark road. Mark sped up with the roaring engine that growled like an animal on the prowl. In less than a minute, their rapid approach of the vehicle revealed a mini van.

Mark was excited, "Ooooo! A minivan! It's probably some soccer mom. Let's check who is driving." Although Route 4 was a lonely stretch of road, it was a two-lane highway (in both directions) with shoulders wide enough for passing. The potential vehicle to assault was traveling in the right lane, so Mark moved into the left lane and slightly increased speed in hopes to catch a glimpse of the driver. He was delighted to see it was a woman. "Oooooo, a blond! She looks cute." He pointed out that the woman was alone and immediately theorized she was eager to play the chase game on Route 4.

Apparently aware of the car next to her, and the sensation of someone watching, she faced left to see who was there. That's when the excitement began with Mark giving obscene, tasteless gestures. The woman immediately faced forward.

"Ha-ha! She likes it! I can see it in her eyes!"

Mark slowed down to pull behind the mini van; then he moved to the right shoulder and sped up. He wanted to get another view of his victim through the passenger side of her vehicle. Once in sight, Mark continuously glared as if his eyes could penetrate the glass and into the passenger seat of the mini van.

Her face remained forward as she appeared to increase speed. Dave concluded that she didn't enjoy the circumstance, and he imagined the woman was desperate to get past the lonely stretch of dark highway to a safer area. "Alright man, that's enough. I don't think she likes this! She looks scared."

But Mark was persistent and wanted to continue this game of his. "What do you mean enough? This hasn't gone nearly far enough! And even if she doesn't like it here, I guarantee she's gonna think about it and wish for more while she's at home! Let's give her more!"

Seeing that the minivan increased velocity, Mark moved back into the lane and turned on his brights. "Turn those babies on and let that sweet thing know we're on her!" He was becoming increasingly excited. And just as Dave suspected, this chase game appeared to take place in Mark's mind. But maybe it really was fun. Dave was someone willing to try anything once, and he felt he should make the most of this bizarre experience as he abandoned inhibitions and joined the pleasure of frantic pursuit.

Dave joined in the madness, "She probably adjusted her rearview mirror so the light is on her thighs!"

Mark laughed, "Totally man! I'm telling you, women love this stuff!"

In crazed spontaneity, Mark tore off his shirt and ordered Dave to do the same.

"What? What are you doing?" Dave didn't think the game would involve removing his clothes.

"Come on man! Just take it off! Let her see what we really want!"

And so the vehicle pulled into the left lane with an opened throttle of the roaring engine. Their flabby man-boobs and beer bellies jiggled down the highway. All the while, Mark and Dave were excited and hoped to get the woman in the minivan aroused.

Mark honked and the woman driver turned to look. They signaled the woman to pull over while making more obscene gestures. But there was no display of arousal on the woman's part as she simply looked forward and continued to travel.

"Ha ha ha! Yeah, you know you want it, Baby!" Mark reached under his seat and gave Dave a rope. "Here, hang this out the window and start whipping her van with it! Just do it!"

Dave laughed and rolled down the window, all the while under the new perception that this was a good time. He whipped the hood of the minivan, yielding a look of concern and disbelief from the female driver. "Yeah, you like that don't you? I bet you want me to tie you up with this and spank that sweet, little ass of yours!"

Mark slowed down and switched lanes so that the car was, once again, traveling on the right shoulder. It was now his turn to have fun with the object of pursued entertainment "We're almost at the end of Route 4! I want to make this a good one! Here, hold the wheel and keep your foot on the accelerator."

"What the...? What are you nuts?" Dave held the wheel and maintained the speed as Mark extended half of his body out the window. Mark pulled down his pants which followed all sorts of obscene activities that could be considered a visual assault.

Suddenly, the two vehicles side-swiped. Dave wasn't sure if it was careless steering on his part or if the woman had enough and decided to issue a warning. But the vehicles swiped which rammed Mark and Dave off the road, causing the car to roll over several times before hitting a tree. Since they were clowning around, sticking a rope out the window and doing obscene gestures of visual assault, neither was wearing a seatbelt. And in a blink of an eye, the two had been ejected from the vehicle where vertigo had catapulted them into the temporary realm of "life-before-your-eyes".

Dave was seriously injured, possibly paralyzed, as he struggled to evaluate the surroundings. At the moment, the only thing he could move was his neck and head. From what he could see, Mark appeared to be either dead or unconscious. And in the distance, the woman in the minivan could be seen backing up on Route 4, where she soon exited the vehicle to hike down where her two assaulters lay. Just moments ago Dave was tormenting the woman out on the road, and now she was coming down to help. Her good nature and heroism was remarkable!

The woman knelt down besides Mark, and laid a monster-like hand with sharp claws on his neck. If Mark was unconscious, he definitely pulled out while he quivered and squealed in pain from the flesh being torn off as if one pulled the meat from a turkey carcass. The woman had huge, sharp, monster-like teeth as she took a bite out of the flesh and began to chew with Mark's blood dripping down her chin.

She took another bite and seemed to marvel at how good Mark tasted. Then she pulled the cell phone out of her pocket and began to dial. So much for cell phones not working on Route 4! "Hi honey; sorry I'm late. I was held up at work, but I got us dinner. Bring the kids and meet me at the end of Route 4… mmm-hmmm… yep, two of them. And hurry before the other one gets cold… okay, love ya…"

Dave watched in horror as she put the phone back in her pocket and proceeded to rip off more flesh as Mark screamed and convulsed in agonizing pain.

* * *

Mary watched the news anchor report the tragic discovery on the road. "Mapleview police made a very gruesome discovery early this morning. The remains of two motorists that appeared to be ejected near the end of Route 4 in an overnight accident were found lying on the side of the road. The unidentified motorists were apparently devoured by a pack of wolves before being discovered by authorities. It's unclear if the driver simply fell asleep or if there was another vehicle involved."

* * *

12 hours later, shortly before heading to work for Saturday night, Kelly watched the news. The story had evolved and was soon overshadowed by a discovery made during the incident investigation.

The news anchor reported, "During a public statement earlier today, Mapleview's Detective Tom Morehausen warns that the game is over, after what appears to be a tragic ending of a chase in the early-morning hours on Route 4."

The TV switched to the public statement made by the Mapleview detective. "No woman should have to be concerned of her safety when traveling roads near the community late at night. It's been a lonely and often unpatrolled area in the evening hours, but local and county police will be in the area from now on. Harassing any motorist is considered aggressive driving and such people will be prosecuted if found."

Did this game explain Kelly's encounters with the red pickup truck each night? She didn't travel Route 4 on the way home, but it was a possibility. Why would players of the chase game limit their pursuits to Route 4? There were plenty of other dark roads late at night that surrounded the town of Mapleview.

Chapter 10

Hotlicks is located at the very edge of Mapleview and only a block from where Route 4 begins its stretch to the neighboring town of Sillmac. Being that the gruesome discovery was some half-mile down the road from the popular bar and grill, Mapleview Police asked Hotlicks to step up security and observe any suspicious activity from customers.

Initially, the group of early-twenties girls who served as flirtatious waitresses found Carl's announcement of "stepped-up security" to be the most absurd thing ever heard. Whispering and giggles in the corner questioned the bouncer's reasoning. Why in the word would he step up security for a pack of wolves that devoured two injured motorists? The young girls lived in a world where the news was truthful and shed light onto the events of local and world affairs. As far as they were concerned, the discovery was a freak-accident that could only be blamed on the natural phenomenon of famished wolves that devoured a helpless meal. And although police didn't know the real truth behind that early Saturday morning discovery, the fact remained that someone had rammed into the car belonging to Mark Cornblack and drove off. The public announcement of the game on Route 4 was only a response to satisfy residents of Mapleview and neighboring communities. And it was intended to bring a sense of closure to the tragic finding. If one took the time to carefully evaluate, the supposed game on Route 4 did not supply a good explanation for what was found in the early morning hours. There had to be a vehicle out there with paint and dents originating from Mark Cornblack's car. Needless to say, the owner of that vehicle would have much explaining to do.

Tricia, the bar tender of Hotlicks, is a woman who knows much about the town of Mapleview. And while listening to Kelly relay the common belief, in partial laughter, that Carl was a useless bouncer who would report any suspicious wolves to authorities; the slightly older bartender reminded the young Hotlicks girl that someone in a white vehicle had actually observed the victims' last moments alive. Hopefully Kelly would understand that this was the meaning of "stepped up security". As Tricia continued to explain, people needed to be on heightened alert for any unusual discussions, unexplained injuries or even a dented vehicle with the paint from Mark Cornblack's car.

And there was more that the seemingly carefree Kelly needed to be aware of. Tricia continued, "Look, I know you haven't lived here all that long, but a lot of weird stuff happens here. The discovery of early this morning was just one of them. There's some kind of spirit or negative energy that hovers over Mapleview. Supposedly, something really bad happened in the area hundreds of years ago."

Kelly interrupted, "The wolves carrying off Grandma Trivelli? That legend was disproved. My cousin bought that house and found my grandmother's hand in a vase. She was killed by her husband. I actually lived in the Trivelli house for a while."

"Did you? Well I saw the news and am very well aware that the Mapleview Police solved one of the oldest murders in this town. But that's not what I was about to tell you. Something happened here hundreds of years before the Trivelli house even stood. The region was populated by several tribes of Native Americans; and at some point, a huge massacre took place between one tribe and another. It wasn't a war; it was an evil murder to appease the wrong set of gods, or whatever. There's an evil spirit or vibe that remains hundreds of years later. Some say it feels as though an un-rested presence watches us while planning more vengeance.

People see things out there—strange animals, unrecognized spirits. Others become possessed.

You lived at the Trivelli house?"

For a moment, Kelly was mesmerized by Tricia's revelation. "Yeah, I lived there while waiting to work here. And you know that was the weirdest story I ever heard. Is all that true?"

"It's supposed to be. Now, I'm sure much of it is exaggerated and urban legend, but you really need to take care of yourself out there. I mean, when you lived at the Trivelli house with your cousin, didn't you notice something odd about the walls?"

Kelly thought for a second. Outside of the peep hole, nothing unusual stood out. "No; what's wrong with the walls?"

"I guess the woman who owned the house rented it out."

Again, Kelly interrupted. "Loraine Trivelli; that's my aunt."

"Well, she rented it out to people, and one of the tenants swore that the walls changed colors. They sent paranormal investigators in there who concluded that no consistent color could be seen on the walls and ceiling. If you looked away, the color would change!"

As far as Kelly recalled, nothing unusual was noticed about the paint while living there. "Hmm; I'll have check that out the next time I visit."

Just then, a loud, unfamiliar alarm could be heard from Kelly's cell phone. She quickly pulled it from her pocket and discovered that neglecting to charge the device for two nights in a row resulted in weak batteries. She quickly powered it down in case needed on the ride home.

* * *

It was a cold, near-autumn night with a light, misty rain. Kelly drove home with the heat and defoggers on high. Perhaps it was best to dress for cooler weather now that summer had ended. Perhaps it was best that she take care of herself in many different ways, such as keeping her cell phone charged and paying attention to strange phenomenon that could be dangerous. These were the things that Kelly thought of during her late night cruise home. But what did Tricia mean of people "seeing things" like strange animals and unrecognized spirits? Kelly would soon find out in a chilling moment of terror on that dark, isolated road.

It was human in form, wearing the skins of animals and stood a height much taller than people, perhaps 10 feet. Its face was fierce and grotesque with features that of an animal. Kelly didn't know who it was or what; but it stood in the middle of the road as she approached and chucked a long object, almost like a spear, at the driver-side tire of her car. The tire went flat as evidenced by the "flub, flub, flub, flub" of the road. Then the creature ran back into the forest before Kelly would run into it.

Instinctively, she coasted to the side of the road. But the thought of the strange creature on the road suggested that if Kelly exited the vehicle, another encounter would be experienced. Maybe it was best to travel the shoulder with hazards on for about a mile before getting out.

It suddenly became difficult to maneuver and steer. Did Kelly blow another front tire? How far could she travel like this? Kelly was in need of help and she reached for her cell phone.

"What a great time to be low on batteries!" She powered up the device; heard the trademarked jingle as it booted; and then read the disheartening message, "Recharge Batteries, Powering Down!" On a cold, rainy, dark, isolated road with two flat tires and a frightening creature somewhere in the woods, Kelly was without a phone!

If only someone could have driven by and saw her in trouble, that person might have stopped to help. And although accepting help from a stranger might open the possibility to danger, it was the lesser of two evils in comparison to being alone with whatever had whipped the spear at her car.

Just then, a set of headlights could be seen rapidly approaching from behind. As the vehicle drew closer, Kelly's anxiety spiked upon recognizing a red pick up truck that pulled over to the shoulder and slowly followed behind. This was not the help she wished for! And instinct told the young girl not to let the mysterious driver come close. She continued to slowly travel the shoulder with difficulty maneuvering and the red pick up truck flashing it's brights from behind. And in a moment of unbelievable irony, Kelly would discover that the phrase, "when it rains, it pours" could be taken literally. It became impossible to drive as she suspected one of her rear tires had deflated. And the rain came down harder than ever before!

Chapter 11

Early Sunday morning, Mary was startled awake by a rapid pounding at the door which immediately brought anxiety and concerns for her husband's safety. She often wondered if while traveling in his job Daren would become injured, be involved in an accident or—worse—killed in a plane crash. Mary nervously dashed down the stairs and to the door where the terrible certainty of an officer-of-the-law stood.

"Yes?" Her face froze, waiting for terrible news.

Although it was relieving to hear that the news didn't involve Daren, the sickening anxiety shifted to Mary's cousin. The officer spoke of an abandoned Chevy Cavalier with 3 deflated tires that was parked on the shoulder some ways down the highway. Since Kelly's license plates and owner registration listed the Trivelli house as the residence, the officer was there to inform her of the vehicle impoundment. Apparently, Kelly had yet to change the address after moving. Mary now had to explain that her cousin no longer lived there. In Mary's world, Kelly was in trouble and missing.

No answer to Kelly's cell phone was a very bad sign. But was the young girl simply ignoring Mary? The last time seen was the day she moved out. But why hadn't Kelly contacted Mary, since? The reputation of being "misguided and misunderstood" filled the mysterious gaps, only bringing speculation back to that of horror. Mary fought her instincts and wouldn't dare allow the materialization of the most obvious thought.

When it comes to missing adults, Mapleview follows state laws that are fuzzy and unclear. As unfair as it may seem, a legal adult has the freedom to suddenly leave home and start a new life. Only in evidence of foul play is it necessary to actively investigate the disappearance of an adult. Fortunately, the town of Mapleview had Detective Tom Morehausen who was full aware that the missing Hotlicks girl was not yet considered foul play. But he became actively engaged in the casual Sunday morning investigation, collecting pieces of information and noting how eerie the Chevy Cavalier looked with 3 deflated tires. Detective Tom was well aware that something happened in the late night hours. It would only take time to uncover evidence of foul play, forcing the Mapleview Police Department to open a serious investigation. In his lengthy career, Detective Tom had witnessed chases gone cold, simply because facts weren't obtained earlier. He refused to see that happen now that he was the lead detective on the force.

Waiting patiently until Hotlicks opened for lunch, Detective Tom finally had the opportunity to request viewing video of the premises and parking lot of the previous evening. He wanted anything unusual on tape; such as customers who were drawn to Kelly, lengthy stares from patrons or even a vehicle that may have followed the Chevy Cavalier out of the parking lot.

As seen on video, at exactly 1:11am, the parking lot was seemingly void of any patrons' vehicles as Hotlicks had closed for the night. Emerging from the forest behind the lot, an individual dressed in dark clothes with a baseball cap and sunglasses quickly approached Kelly's car. Spending less than 10 seconds at each tire, the mysterious suspect removed a tool from his or her pocket and did something undetectable by the camera. Apparently, the individual sensed being discovered, perhaps a noise, and neglected to sabotage the 4th tire of Kelly's car. Whoever it was quickly ran back into the forest. The last time Kelly was officially seen was 2:07am as she entered the Chevy Cavalier with partially deflated driver-side tire, as seen on the video.

Detective Tom was well aware of what the mysterious suspect had done to Kelly's tires. But he was amazed with the fine precision and perfect timing. It is possible to slowly deflate a tire by barely loosening the valve of a tire's core stem. Only a 360 degree turn, provided by a valve stem wrench, would ensure a gradual deflation. Back at the vehicle impound, Detective Tom (and now Detective Larry) inspected the tires. Sure enough, the valve cores of the three tires had been barely loosened.

* * *

By the time Daren returned in the late afternoon from a weekend convention in Alabama, the disappearance evolved into a serious investigation that certainly appeared to have involved foul play. Kelly's new apartment had been located and entered by the Mapleview Police for examination. And upon noticing that the young girl had no furniture or no bed—only a modest collection of clothes and small items scattered on the floor—Detective Tom stood back and made his initial assessment. "She was running away from something."

"What makes you say that?" asked Detective Larry. Detective Larry, had worked the force a number of years, himself. But he was younger than his partner and valued the knowledge and experience provided by his senior.

Detective Tom was eager to share his intuitive knowledge for detective work. "Larry, for weeks she was living at the fully furnished Trivelli house with Mary and suddenly moved into an apartment with no bed. Why would she do that?"

Detective Larry tested his partner's theory with other possible scenarios. "Overstayed her welcome? Maybe there was tension between her and Mary?"

But Detective Tom's argument was persistent. "Larry, when we visited Mary back in the spring, she was engaged. Remember that? What's to say that her new husband didn't have something going on with this girl?"

Being the next logical step, the two detectives paid the Trivelli house a visit.

This was an afternoon that Daren would find himself in boiling, hot water. For starters, Aunt Loraine greeted the man as he entered the house with baggage in hand. Before the loving husband could embrace his worried wife and offer emotional support, Aunt Loraine simply asked, "Back from your trip from Alabama?" Nothing outside of that question was said. But she maintained a tone of suspicion on the man, almost implying that he had something to do with Kelly's disappearance.

Adding heat to the situation, the hot water would soon boil as Detectives Tom and Larry drove up to the house. The three of them; Mary, Aunt Loraine and Daren; walked outside on a cloudy, brisk, September afternoon to greet the Mapleview detectives.

After brief greetings, Detective Tom changed his mood to that of a grave tone. "Alright, I'm leading this investigation and we suspect foul play. And just to make sure we've covered all possibilities, I want to look around and ask a few questions. Fair enough?"

Mary was most open and welcoming to the detectives as being hospitable and generous was part of her nature. She had nothing to hide; only wanted answers. But Daren secretly dreaded the investigation of Kelly's bedroom as he dreaded the discovery of the peep hole. This would surely make him a prime suspect.

Divide and conquer: that seemed to be the reasonable approach of the pair of detectives. Mary and Daren sat downstairs in the living room while Detective Tom investigated the bedrooms upstairs. Aunt Loraine sat outside in the unmarked police car while answering the questions of Detective Larry.

Of course Aunt Loraine was more than happy to share her wealth of knowledge. "If you ask me, I think that Daren had something to do with her disappearance. I've warned my niece about him! Seems like a nice man, but... Well, he's a binge drinker and borderline psychotic. And just like Grandpa Trivelli, Daren desired to build a mausoleum in this backyard. And look! He did it!" She extended her aged, bony arm and finger to the newly constructed building.

"He recently built that mausoleum, Loraine?"

"Why yes! He built it this summer."

"Is there anyone in it?"

"Well no one has died, recently, but I suppose... Oh good Heavens! You don't think?" Aunt Loraine raised her hands to her mouth—the famous overwhelmed Trivelli expression that the women in the family, including Mary, used for many generations.

Moments later, Aunt Loraine rotated locations with her niece so that Mary now sat in the unmarked police car with Detective Larry.

Mary did her best to provide any and all information along with shared observations that she found peculiar and odd. "Kelly announced to me one afternoon that she found an apartment and was moving out that day. She lugged two suitcases out the door with only a short goodbye. Something told me that it would be my last time ever seeing her. Why didn't I stop her? Why didn't I check on her to see how she was doing? I only explained her leaving with the belief that Kelly was the problem child of the family." Poor Mary wiped the tears from her face while secretly blaming herself for the disappearance of Kelly. In her mind, she was the one who brought Kelly to Mapleview. She was responsible for her safety. Instead, Mary let the young girl walk off without offering persuasion to stay.

Detective Larry did his best to be empathetic while offering sympathy. But he was curious of information that Loraine Trivelli provided. "One other question I have for you; did your husband build that mausoleum?"

Mary exhaled in annoyance, "Yes..."

"Is there anyone in there?"

"No, he built it for us and our kids so that we could always live here, forever. His family has a history of mausoleums and I guess he wanted to continue the tradition."

Just then, Detective Tom walked up to the car. For some reason, this was the cue to end the questionings with Mary. The two exited the vehicle and Mary was instructed to wait in the house while the two detectives discussed findings in private. Daren had yet to be interviewed.

The three of them; Mary, Aunt Loraine and Daren; remained motionless in the living room and in silence. The husband and wife sat on sofa, holding hands; while Aunt Loraine sat in the old, rocking chair with eyes fixed to the floor. The silence was broke with the entrance of both detectives.

Detective Tom announced while entering, "Okay, we're almost done here. One final thing: you've recently built a new mausoleum on the property, and it's to my understanding that no one, living or dead, should be in there." Detective Tom then looked directly at Daren. "Sir, would you mind unlocking that door and letting us check it out?"

Daren looked bewildered. "You want to investigate the inside of the family mausoleum?"

Mary exhaled loudly. "It's fine Daren! Under the circumstances, I think you could let the detectives in. I don't think it would be considered sacrilegious."

Detective Tom sensed the sudden hesitation to unlock the door. "Should I get a search warrant? You've been cooperative up until now. What's the problem?"

"No, I'll open it. It's not a problem. Forgive me; the mausoleum has a sacred value. But my wife is right. Under the circumstances, the door should be unlocked for you."

Aunt Loraine nearly jumped out of her seat, eager to witness the incriminating discovery made in that building. But she was quickly brought back to her seat by Detective Larry who announced, "Ladies, Detective Tom wants to ask Daren some questions, so we're going to ask that you remain inside and in your seats."

Detective Tom stepped outside with Daren and stopped at the front porch. Reaching inside his jacket pocket, he quickly looked up at the suspect, "Do you mind if I have a smoke?"

"No, not at all; feel free."

"So when did you build this mausoleum of yours?" The two walked over to the building.

"Early in the summer."

"Yeah? It looks nice. It's not every day someone builds something like this on private property. What gives?"

Building a mausoleum is something a family man does. Daren wasted not a minute explaining this. "Well, I'm a family man, and I believe that owning a mausoleum in the backyard shows dedication to the family and fidelity to a marriage."

But it was only show for Detective Tom. "Oh yeah? Nice touch."

Then Detective Tom noticed the equipment outside the building. "Is that air conditioning?"

Daren proudly nodded, reached into his pocket for the keys and then unlocked the thick, iron door that squeaked when opened.

"Jeez; you better get that fixed, Daren!" The detective took a deep drag from his cigarette and extinguished it on the wet grass. "Don't want to smoke in your family mausoleum." He entered the building and immediately took notice of about a dozen cases of wine that were stacked up against the far wall, just beneath the two sconces.

"You drink a lot of wine, Daren?"

"Yeah, I like wine."

"It's one hell of a place to keep it. And these are the crypts? Is there anything in here that you want to tell me about, anything that might affect our investigation?" Already, detective Tom was carefully examining the mechanics of sealing. Simple crypt locks held the covers in place that could easily be removed. Under normal circumstances, he would feel disrespectful with no regard to one's resting in peace. But the crypts were supposed to be unoccupied, and the detective had an undying devotion to seeking justice for those who may have been wronged.

Perhaps the suspect didn't hear Detective Tom, so the question was asked again. "Daren, anything you might want to tell me about the insides of these crypts?"

Daren reassured the detective, "No, nothing illegal in there."

"Very well; why don't you have a seat on your bench and I'll check these out. Nothing personal; just detective work."

Detective Tom carefully unsealed each crypt and examined the insides under the illumination of his Bic lighter. It was the last crypt on the left-hand wall, nearest the door where Detective Tom noticed that the drawer was heavier than the others. His face grew pale, expecting to make a terrible discovery. But the discovery was unlike anything he expected. The drawer contained two large coolers filled with ice and plenty of beer!

Although relieved the discovery wasn't a body, the sight was surprising." Let me guess, Daren. This is going to be your final resting place?"

Detective Tom closed the drawer, sealed the crypt and then sat down on the bench next to Daren. "So why in hell do you have beer in there? That's kind of strange! Can't you keep it in the refrigerator or in your basement?"

Of course Daren was embarrassed. "Well, my wife doesn't like it when I drink too much beer. But I like beer and enjoy a few cold ones at night."

"So you come outside to your mausoleum, crack open your tomb and crack open a cold one? That's freakin' sick!" Detective Tom gave Daren a moment to comment, but the suspect remained silent.

"Alright, I'm going to ask you something and I want you to be completely honest with me. That girl that was living here: were you fooling around with her?"

Sitting on the very bench where Kelly laid many a night, Daren answered a firm, "No!"

"You sure? You absolutely positive?"

Daren reassured the detective, "Absolutely positive; I wouldn't do something like that."

Well Daren, I hope you're telling me the truth. There's going to be a serious investigation into the disappearance of Kelly; and if someone mentions that you and her had a thing going on, you will become a prime suspect. For now, you're off the hook. Let's just hope it stays that way."

And with that, Detective Tom rose from the bench and walked out of the mausoleum. Daren automatically followed behind, and locked his sacred mausoleum for the night.

But the Mapleview Detective left the husband and wife on what was a very, strange note for Mary. Detective Tom bid them good evening and then suggested to Daren that he relax and, "have a cold one" while motioning towards the mausoleum.

The wife looked in confusion at the husband who only shrugged his shoulders in a look of dramatic confusion.

Part Two:
The Thing in the Crawlspace

Chapter 12

Turn left onto Creek Highway, just before the main road of Mapleview opens into Route 4. Slightly past Hotlicks Sports Bar and Grill, the road borders what could be considered the very edge of the town of Mapleview. Creek Highway runs about 7 miles of open forested road before connecting with the interstate roadways. But there is no need to venture that far. And there's no need to be concerned of the neighboring towns that are just past the interstates.

Turning left onto Creek Highway immediately yields more untamed forest with access given by three small parking areas that are distanced by a half-mile or so. The region is not as popular as the Hidden Lake Forest Preserve, but is enjoyed by hunters and serious hikers alike. The very, first, graveled entryway leads to a narrow walking trail that soon opens up to a steep hill that only one fit for such a climb would ascend. It is here where most hikers turn around; not for the strenuous walk, but for the apprehensive thoughts that are often interpreted as danger.

The thoughts are overwhelming as one might ask, "What if I become seriously injured, bleed profusely and am unable to reach the bottom in time for help?"

Most believe it to be a premonition of some wild animal that is just around the corner and about to attack. But people familiar with the gruesome discovery of 10 years ago know that the apprehension along with sensation of inevitable danger are residual emotions of trauma that call out for help. And it was a place where a concerned husband would daydream of a bloody scene that involved his wife. The vision was so powerful, that he emailed her with a desperate warning. To understand the gruesome discovery, one must venture a decade into the past, to the turn of the century.

As the world anticipated the arrival of Y2K and the silly bug that would create havoc on the magical day of January 1st, Stephanie realized she was soon to reach thirty-years-old. Stephanie refused to be overtaken by those apparitions most women encounter in adult life. Shortly after the birth of her 1st child, she noticed herself changing into the very woman that she promised herself to never become. Stephanie despised the idea of identifying with one of those plain, frumpy, used-up and often overweight moms who knew nothing other than the confines of their homes and the activities of their children. Domesticated, aged and somewhat lacking an understanding of the outside world, these women often have a reputation of being undesirable by their husbands and most often abandoned for a younger, more energetic woman. Of course, in reality, there is nothing wrong with being a woman who stays at home to take care of her family. But as you will soon learn, Stephanie had all sorts of erroneous beliefs and distorted perceptions.

Only shy 4 months of 30, Stephanie realized she was quickly approaching the threshold of "getting old". 30 was still young, but it seemed like just a few months ago that she was in college and celebrating her 21st birthday. 40 could arrive in a time comparable to next week! It was then that Stephanie decided to gain control of her life.

Strict diet and extreme exercise are most often the initial remedies that most women in this mindset follow. These things were followed by trips to the hairstylist, new clothes and time spent at the tanning bed; all activities which produced a seemingly new Stephanie. In comparison to the fellow moms on her block, Stephanie was anything but plain, frumpy, used-up or overweight. But she still hadn't surpassed the apparitions that sought to overtake her. Although maintaining her youth and vitality, Stephanie remained domesticated and on her way to lacking an understanding of the outside world. It was then that she introduced the idea of venturing back into the world of work to her husband over dinner one night.

"Back to work? Steph, we don't need a second income! And what about Paul? Who's going to take care of him? And I thought you wanted another baby. We cannot have a second baby with you being a working mom."

She knew he wouldn't understand. And she realized that this dream of being a stay-at-home-mom only seemed like a good idea once-upon-a-time. As Stephanie felt, a woman should have the right to change her mind and enjoy a life with more purpose and direction. Stephanie could be both a mom and professional woman if given the chance.

Despite what the bitter wife assumed of her husband, and how much she now hated him, Joe was a very understanding and patient man. He was aware that people change throughout the years and that his wife wasn't quite ready for the fulltime mom status. Perhaps if his wife spent some time in the work force, she would find what she was looking for and once again be happy. Joe finally supported his wife's decision to go back to work. Within months of job hunting, Stephanie landed a position in the career she worked prior to being a mother.

Ask someone at the time to describe "the new Stephanie", words such as energetic, dynamic, intense or high-spirited would be supplied. "The new Stephanie" was so much better than the Stephanie of younger days. She had a drive to get the most out of life and prided herself in being super woman with an ability to do everything all the time. I mean this woman could do it all! Not only was she a rising star in her successful career, but remained a fulltime mother and wife; meeting and succeeding her responsibilities at home. She awoke at 3:45am each day for a grueling workout. Then fueled by a yogurt, banana and a half-pot of coffee, Stephanie spent time with her toddler son, Paul, giving him breakfast and shuttling him off to day care. Oatmeal bar and more coffee in the midmorning supplied just enough energy until lunch when Stephanie would devour a salad. While most might give in to temptation at night, Stephanie religiously ate grilled chicken stir-fry with vegetables for dinner. Of course she didn't expect her husband to eat this each night. Stephanie also prepared the steak and baked potato or some kind of down-home, cooked meal for Joe.

Those apparitions were left somewhere in Stephanie's dust, and for the first time since being married, Stephanie felt in control of her life. But could she have taken it a step further? She felt so young and alive. Could she have gone back to the days of 21 and embrace the playful, silly mood of once-upon-a-time? One element that Stephanie couldn't have back was the playful, teasing games that were once enjoyed with the opposite sex. Flaunting an irresistible sexiness in her younger years, Stephanie took great pleasure in having guys chase her, only to deny them and cause frustration. Oh, there might have been a couple who were fortunate enough to have a sample, but she couldn't be held down for too long. The playful game was too, much fun!

As a married woman at the turn of the century, Stephanie had a realm where she could safely embrace those sorely, missed days of play and teasing. It was a place where she could post a profile and photo while watching the hungry men jump in a frenzy for a chance to have some sort of piece of her.

The Internet today is different from the Internet we had at the turn of the century. Socializing, today, takes place on sites such as My Space, Facebook and Twitter. And if you are reading this 5 or 10 years after today, it's probably much different! Today, we network, maintain relationships and keep a vast collection of friends among people we know. But some people might recall a time when Internet socializing meant logging into an IRC or Internet chat room to make new friends and basically talk to complete strangers. Sometimes an actual cyber friendship could be formed, and eventually the communication merged from chat room to private emails. We don't hear too much about this phenomenon anymore. And I predict that in 10-15 years, if you discuss cyber sex or cyber romances, your mention will be received with wrinkled eyebrows and perplexed looks. Oh, the phenomenon isn't completely dead; but if you've experimented with this activity many years ago, trying logging into a chat room today. The users seem to lack any stimulating mentality.

Back in those fun days of chat room relationships, Stephanie created an exciting profile based on the person she imagined herself to be. She did this late one night while her husband was asleep, as creating the profile involved posting a risqué photo that would most certainly bring the wrong kind of attention. If the photo didn't attract the wrong people; her alias, sxyblonde, would.

From the moment Stephanie entered one of the rooms, there were so many men sending messages and requesting private chat sessions with the sexy woman in the photo. They just couldn't resist sxyblonde who stood naked, yet face-up against the wall while exposing her bare bottom. Stephanie felt so powerful turning down the instant messages. Some were compliments; some were downright, dirty, nasty comments. Still, others were requests to join in a private room where Stephanie suspected would lead to online sex. She was no tramp, of course, and wouldn't agree to such a rendezvous.

One night, Stephanie decided to accept an invitation into a private room with an individual who went by the name of 2Big4U. It felt like allowing a stranger to buy a drink while sitting down with him at a private booth. Requesting her ASL was confusing as Stephanie wasn't quite sure what that meant. But she soon learned it was protocol used by guys like 2Big4U to learn of a woman's age, sex and location.

In Stephanie's eyes, this guy was pretty stupid! It was apparent in her photo that she was a female and still young. But what business was it of him to ask where she was?

In his explanation, 2Big4U certainly could see that she was a woman; but he needed to make sure as he stated, "I don't do trannies… nor do I do grannies…"

Seconds away from Stephanie abruptly ending the disappointing chat session, 2Big4U added an interesting question. "Do you think you can handle this?"

"Handle what?"

"C'mon, don't you see my pic? Look at my profile!"

Stephanie looked at the list of names on the screen and clicked 2Big4U. His profile picture was simply a close-up image of that which makes men different from women. It was really quite large! Of course! His alias implied that he was much, too big for women to handle! But was it really his?

2Big4U answered, "Of course it's mine! I'll send some more pics if you want."

The stranger was most certainly eager to "get off" and send more photos, possibly a form of sex for him. But Stephanie wasn't going to reward him or lead 2Big4U into believing she was interested.

Seeing that his hope had failed, 2Big4U attempted a different angle. "How about you; is that really you in your profile?"

But Stephanie was on to the stranger. He was like all men, drooling in a desperate craze to have a piece of the gorgeous Stephanie. But as always, she took great pleasure in being impossible and appearing uninterested. "It's me, and I'm not going to send you any other pictures."

And then he asked of her social status, "Married/engaged/BF?"

"Married, but not happily…" Stephanie wasn't sure why she declared her marriage unhappy. There wasn't anything particularly bad about it, outside the typical challenges people experience. It's interesting to observe Stephanie's behavior online. Not even 5 minutes passed, and already she lied about her age and the state of her marriage. This was a virtual world where Stephanie could be whoever she desired. But she hadn't thought about the stranger on the other side of the screen. She hadn't considered that 2Big4U might be dishonest. Throughout the conversation, he claimed to be divorced and spent much time bashing his ex-wife in many obscene words.

Stephanie engaged in an online conversation for nearly an hour with this stranger. Once they got past the first few minutes of attempted sex talk that was initiated by the stranger, it appeared to Stephanie that 2Big4U was a really nice guy. But it was getting late, and Stephanie needed to retire for the night.

But before ending the chat session, 2Big4U hit her with another question. "Hey, can I have your email address? Keep in touch?"

Stephanie wasn't that easy and desired to test 2Big4U, gauge how serious the man was about her. She left him with, "You'll see me around. Maybe I'll be online tomorrow night at the same time."

* * *

The following afternoon, Stephanie sat at a PC in the Sillmac Public Library while creating an alias email account under a user named, Julie Gresky. She certainly couldn't allow prying eyes at her place of work to observe this new cyber life of hers. And she couldn't have evidence of her altered-identity on the family PC at home! It was probably best to do questionable email correspondences at the public library. The building was only 10 minutes from her office, and the secret mission would only require perhaps an additional 10 minutes of work. The untruthful excuse of a late-afternoon meeting at work would explain her reason for coming home late.

That evening would be Stephanie's last night in the chat rooms. She had her fun playing with the men, and wanted to devote energies in exploring this new adventure with 2Big4U.

As Stephanie hoped, the stranger who she chatted with for nearly an hour the previous evening was in the same room waiting for her. Stephanie threw out her bait, said some nice things and within 5 minutes let him know that it was necessary to retire early.

2Big4U asked again, "How about your email address? We could talk more during the day?"

It was the question Stephanie hoped for. "Sure, you seem like a safe person." She supplied an email address with JGresky for the ID. "That's my actual name, Julie Gresky."

"Well Julie, nice to meet you. My name is Brad."

* * *

Now it didn't take long for Stephanie's husband, Joe, to notice the downright, suspicious behavior coming from his wife. Mostly it would provoke a quick double take and a peculiar consideration that things were very wrong. But he pushed these thoughts away in a desire to maintain the much valued trust in their marriage. And as the man slowly emerged from the caverns of denial, Joe suddenly found himself sitting at the desk of his office one morning, typing the phrase in the search engine, "signs that your wife is having an affair".

If it was necessary for Joe to enter such an alarming phrase into a search engine, then it was certainly an indicator that there might be a problem. Many of the articles Joe read brought this fact to light. But there were other indicators. Increased time spent working out at the gym along with improvements to physical appearance could be an alarm. Staying up late on the Internet, long after the spouse has gone to bed could indicate communication over the internet. And a sudden increase or decrease of sex might point out a spouse's drive is being misdirected. These signs made perfect sense, but some of the articles discussed items that Joe hadn't considered.

It's the glow that a man remembers when his wife first fell in love with him. When a woman cheats on her husband, she's got that glow and cannot hide it. And a cheating wife will suddenly sleep with her purse next to her bed. She's almost fixated on the purse and won't leave it too far from reach.

Simple conversations turn into arguments. And it often appears that idle-like statement made by the husband is rejected, argued or disagreed upon. As Joe read these items throughout various articles, he realized that his wife was exhibiting many of these behaviors.

But why the purse? What did Stephanie have in her purse that she didn't want Joe to see? He crawled through more web pages, looking for possibilities. But he found nothing. His memory reminded him of the strange times that Stephanie came home and seemed to make a point of neatly placing the purse on the counter or tightly carrying it when leaving. And as the articles pointed out, Stephanie did take the purse to bed each night and set on the floor next to her side. Joe always had a respect for his wife's privacy; but under the circumstances, he felt obligated to invade. The question was, when?

Just as Joe slept with one eye open, waiting to see when his wife came to bed, Stephanie appeared to carefully watch her purse while she slept. The ideal time to invade was when she was sound asleep. But how connected to the purse might his wife have been? Would a subconsciously-watchful eye arouse her from sleep once the purse was removed from their bedroom?

It was almost as-if Joe set a subconscious alarm of his own! It was as-if some part of him scanned his wife's mind while she slept, and finally gave the okay that he could get out of bed and remove the purse from the room. Her breathing was slow and deep, indicating that the suspicious wife was someplace else and unable to see the violation of her privacy. In contrast, Joe's heart raced while his breathing increased as he took the purse into the kitchen where the oven range light was turned on. The moment had come to invade the secret life of Stephanie.

A woman can sense if something is out of place. There is no way a man can rummage through a purse and leave the invasion undetectable. Joe was aware of this and created a rule to leave things as untouched as possible. But the rule was quickly forgotten as he made the very shocking and quirky discovery of a long balloon filled with water! It was the type of balloon that a clown might use to make animal sculptures, but was small and no more than seven inches in length. Next to the discovery was a bag of such balloons, all red in color. Certainly lacking the density and rigidness to be used in "fallacious" adventures (at least for his wife's anatomy), the only conclusion for Joe was that Stephanie had some kind of balloon fetish.

Further probing, Joe discovered that tucked next to the wallet were some neatly folded sheets of paper. He further violated the "untouchable rule" and carefully removed the folded papers, believing them to be something incriminating. They were printed emails, a correspondence between a man named Brad and a woman named Julie. But why was Stephanie hiding these? It would require that Joe read a couple paragraphs of an email to understand that Julie was an alias name belonging to his wife. At least she was being careful.

Unlike you, Joe didn't understand that Stephanie refused to check her alias email account at home or work, much less send emails from those locations. She would type an email at home late at night, and save it to disk. (Yes; back in those days, floppy disks were still in use). Then she would go to the Sillmac library after work, and print up his emails to read at home. Whatever she typed and saved to disk would be copied and pasted, then sent off from the library.

There were so many personal details about her life, private elements of her marriage and exaggerated accounts of Stephanie's day. She was lying to herself; feeding a superhero ego and rationalizing the marriage had gone sour. And to add insult to injury, the emails revealed that a stranger had been permitted to see the most beautiful and valued treasure of Joe's, his wife's naked body! How could Stephanie allow that? The very beauty and splendor had been forever stained by the sharing of pictures. And the stranger's disrespectful and careless mention of what he called, "your *ass*... your gorgeous *ass*... slap that *ass* of yours." catapulted Joe into a fury.

What sort of man had control over the woman he cherished so dearly? She told him everything; but he remained in the background, only reinforcing her self driven beliefs of a life that needed change.

Brad would say, "You are realizing that you married the wrong guy. It's obvious that you are unhappy in your marriage. You are so beautiful and your husband doesn't appreciate what he has."

Then Brad would often follow with, "I think you are too good for your husband. We should meet sometime. Why don't we meet one night?"

Meet, meet, meet; it all came back to one, common motive. The stranger desired to meet Stephanie. She was so stupid and blind; caught up in a fantasy that was easily fueled by compliments and encouragements. It would only be a matter of time before Stephanie took the bait and met the stranger somewhere. He probably played this game numerous times, never thinking of how he destroyed marriages.

How would it end; a harmless date, coercion of sex, maybe murder?

Despite the infuriating details read, nothing could prepare Joe for the shock that was discovered, buried midway in the thread of responses. Stephanie had truly lost her mind as she went on to say, "I was looking up adoption online today. Need to know the facts in case I want to leave him and remarry. Nothing is more important to me than my son, and making sure that his new father is nurturing and caring would be the prime objective if I found someone else.

Maybe I'm living in a fantasy world, but it just amazes me that we hooked up in an Internet chat room where you can meet people all over the country. But through fate, I find out that we live only 20 minutes apart! Although I believe there was a guiding hand and that you and I could possibly be meant for each other, I still want to make sure that you are right for my son. Perhaps you are right. Maybe we should meet face-to-face."

Joe put the emails down on the counter and raised his hand to his forehead in dizziness. The very thought of his wife considering leaving him and allowing some unmet stranger to be the new father of his son just sickened him. He took notice of a small post-it note under the collection of printed emails. On the note was the name, Brad, along with a telephone number.

Suddenly, a voice could be heard at the kitchen's entrance. "What are you doing in my purse?" Apparently, Stephanie returned from the far-off places in her dream-world and regained focus on the purse. It wasn't there, and she needed to verify the terrible certainty that her husband had it.

Joe didn't care that he had violated Stephanie's privacy. Instead, he asked, "Who is Brad?"

She was so nonchalant, "He's a friend, and what business do you have going in my purse?" Stephanie snatched up the emails and proceeded to store them back where they belonged. She was not aware of the post-it note with Brad's phone number that remained in Joe's hand.

It was like a dream for Joe. He couldn't believe his wife's non-chalant attitude along with sudden dishonesty. "Stephanie, are you really going to tell me that's a friend? Are you aware that I read those emails?"

Her defensiveness grew, "He's a friend, Joe! Won't you just let me have a friend? I met him online one night, and he's a nice guy."

"Stephanie, he doesn't talk! The only thing he says is that you should leave me! You do the rest! You tell him everything; show him everything like pictures of you naked! And what's this you want him to adopt our son?"

Joe walked over to the phone while nearly shaking in outrage. That's when Stephanie saw the post-it note with Brad's number. She darted over to her husband, snatched the piece of paper from his hand, put it in her mouth and swallowed. "Good luck finding that! And you know what? This conversation is over!"

The last time Stephanie checked, she was the one in control of the world. It was her life, her marriage and her purse. If she desired a friend on the Internet, all-be-damned she would have one! The moment belonged to Stephanie; and just like all sadly mistaken spouses with such delusions, she believed that the pointless conversation no longer needed to be continued—conversation over.

Unfortunately, delusional people lack the understanding that the world doesn't work that way. Take for example the instance of a wife who has discovered her husband in bed with another woman. I suppose after the famous, "It's not what you think" phrase is given, it may also be followed with, "and this conversation is over." Was anything really solved?

A boss catches an employee stealing from the company. "I didn't steal; this conversation is over!"

The police have a suspect in custody with overwhelming evidence of murder. "I didn't kill anyone; this conversation is over."

I suppose in taking control of the world, he or she might have attempted to just walk away. But again, it doesn't work that way!

Ah, but Stephanie was fully prepared to just walk away. As she snatched her purse from the counter in full control of the world, she learned that although a gentleman, Joe was very strong. Joe was so strong in fact that he grabbed his wife's wrists in a force of uncontrollable fury and slammed her back against the wall. "No, we are not done, Stephanie! You can't do this! We will talk about this, and I will fight you every bit of the way if you walk off with our child and try to let that stranger be his new father."

If Stephanie believed herself to be strong and in the best shape of her life, she was soon realizing that Joe was much stronger with an ability to throw her flimsy body around like a ragdoll. She had never seen her husband that way, and was hit with the hard reality of being overpowered by an increasingly, rage-full husband who shook the living daylights out of her while surrounding the air with his late-night, stale breath.

Joe growled like a monster, "Tell you what, Steph! Let's go in the living room and login to your JGresky account. Let's see what else you are writing him!"

She was grabbed by the back of her neck and thrown into the living room with a force of disbelief. A quick retreat to the corner enabled the wife to impose her perception on the rage-full monster that violently approached.

Stephanie let out bloodcurdling screams, "Oh my God! Oh my God!"

The escalated violence had awoken their son, Paul, who began to cry. Joe was the true villain. This was exactly how women were murdered by their husbands. And yet Stephanie wanted this, the sick woman that she was! Joe acted in a manner that Stephanie had wished for as control had been given back to the cheating wife's world.

While she cried hysterically, the now calm husband studied in disbelief. What was happening to his wife? Why was she creating a twisted world of lies?

Transformed back into a miraculously-sane woman who finally had control in the house; Stephanie stood calmly, appearing to carefully weigh a decision before executing the unbelievable words. "I'm leaving you. I want a divorce."

"What? Are you crazy? Where are you going?"

"To live with my parents."

'"Steph, they live 4 hours out of state. What about your job?"

Stephanie only walked away. "I'm leaving. I can't take this anymore. And you better hope there's no bruising on my wrists and arms from your beating."

All Joe could do was sit in a chair and listen to the activities on the other end of the house. Stephanie rescued the crying child, 'It's okay; I'm sorry. We're going to Grandma and Grandpa's house, now, and everything will be alright. You want to help Mommy pack?"

Closet doors were opened; hangers rattled; suitcases unzipped. And then Joe's wife could be heard while speaking on the phone. "Mom, Joe and I got in a really bad fight... I don't know, he thinks I'm cheating on him... Yeah, tell me about it... Well, we're getting a divorce, and I don't want Paul being exposed to things here... Can I live with you for now...? Okay, I'll be there some time in the morning."

Moments later, Joe's wife and son walked towards the door. The child was too young to understand as he clung to Mommy who pulled suitcases behind her. Little Paul needed his father to fight and prevent his removal into a world of possible danger. But Joe could do nothing. Any further fighting would provide the irrational wife additional ammunition for the courts and police. As it stood, Stephanie would most likely run home to Mom and Dad in tears, "Joe thinks I'm cheating on him! See the bruises on my wrists?"

The sound of the trunk closing shut was heard outside. The engine started up and his wife quickly pulled away. Joe was now alone.

* * *

Joe had remained in that chair since 2:20 in the morning. Hours were spent in contemplative grief, sometimes attempting to imagine his wife was dead. But this was no help. When a loved one dies, the survivor continues to be loved from Heaven. A spouse who leaves for another lover, no longer loves the original. That being said, Joe would have gladly taken the death of Stephanie over reality. Perhaps this is why he was so willing to make peace in the afternoon hours as his wife suddenly stood in the entryway of the living room, offering to come back and make up.

"I don't want to fight anymore; I'm sorry. I can't take the stress and anxiety. You're right."

Joe couldn't believe what he was seeing and hearing. "Excuse me?"

"Honey, you're right. I thought about everything you said. He's just some stupid guy from the Internet and not worth destroying our marriage. I got carried away in the fantasy world. I called him and told him to never email or call me again. It's over."

It would require work and much healing; but for Joe, it would be worth every moment and a testament of true love for his wife. The remainder of the afternoon was spent cuddling on the couch and gently going over the details of Stephanie's mistake. Their son, Paul, slept on the loveseat as he hadn't rested since leaving in the predawn hours.

This event took place on Good Friday, a dark and challenging day indeed. But a dinner of forgiveness and reconciliation at the brand-new Hotlicks Sports Bar and Grill, offering the Lenten

Friday fish-fry value, would be an excellent step in healing the pain.

And after dinner, the married couple who had seen their first serious marital strife had made a left onto Creek Highway, just to cruise around and relax after a long, stressful day.

Stephanie suggested, "We should have a home built somewhere out here. It's so beautiful."

Not that much could be seen in the darkened hours, but a curious phobia was noted by Joe and kept to himself that night. He wasn't fond of heavily wooded areas and would hate to be alone out there where unspeakable things could take place. Perhaps it was best to stay in the main town of Mapleview, where the trees could be observed from a distance.

* * *

Easter came and went. But something tuned Joe to the possibility that his wife's infidelity was far from over. Easter dinner was to be held at Stephanie's, parents' house. And Easter dinner did happen on that lonely, Sunday afternoon; but Joe was not invited. As his wife explained, the in-laws could not understand why she and Joe were going to work out their marriage. Stephanie and Paul could come, but not Joe! How could Stephanie have abandoned her husband on Easter Sunday? She did, and it was a long and lonely Sunday for Joe.

Chapter 13

The knotted, rubber stem was wedged in the closed drawer of Stephanie's office desk as the long water balloon hung several inches below. Eventually it would burst and spray water on the floor. To remedy this certainty, a wastepaper basket was positioned below the balloon, ensuring the water would be collected.

Stephanie was very fortunate to have a brick-enclosed office with a door that locked shut. And just like many days at the office, she would often take her frustrations out on the balloon by biting it, sometimes in frenzy, attempting to make it burst. The teleconference call was most boring. Fortunately Stephanie she had a friend to torture.

"Stephanie, is the cord on your phone making a rubbing sound?" Her manager interrupted the teleconference call as a distracting noise could be heard from his employee's line.

Oops! Stephanie's frantic biting and chewing of the water-inflated rubber could be heard by coworkers and business associates. "I'll fix that! The cord is loose."

It was such a disappointment for Stephanie. She desired so strongly to break that balloon and see the water burst and spray out! Now the only means to nibble and chew was to do so, quietly, with it in her mouth.

Bursting long water balloons was a pleasure Stephanie learned at a girl's sleepover many years ago. Actually, the pleasure was further developed some nights after the sleepover. But on the night of the party, the pleasure was born as the creative and decorative person that her friend's mother was, used many balloons, some of which were the elongated type. Stephanie grabbed a collection of these and invented a game in which daring girls would take turns biting at the balloon, hoping to be the first to make it pop! Needless to say it was a silly game that caused much laughter and rowdiness among the group of teenage girls.

Stephanie took the game into her bedroom some nights later where it would be brought to a whole new level. An elongated balloon was filled with water and placed on a towel that sat on her bedside table. She bit in frenzy, each nibble a desperate wish for the water to gush out in an explosion of tragedy. It would no longer be a rigid balloon filled with liquid. It would be an empty shell of a disaster; a poor, sad balloon that lay dead from a violent assault. And when the short-lived burst of pleasure finally happened, the world was so much better for Stephanie. It all went away; her frustrations, disappointments or silly teenage anxieties.

The game developed into a nightly habit, lasting sometimes an hour past bed time. Realizing the ritual was cutting into her sleep, Stephanie would place a bath towel near the pillow where a long water balloon would lay. She would bite in frenzy, sometimes awakening in the morning to a balloon that had yet to be burst. The survivor was placed under the pillow to be tortured later in the evening.

* * *

"Ha! It sounds like someone lost a cup of coffee!" Stephanie finally burst her balloon and the water that gushed into the wastepaper basket could be heard by those in the teleconference call. What could she do now to pass the boredom?

Chapter 14

Obsessed with the vastness of deep wilderness and the dangerous seclusion it can bring; Joe laid awake on the night that followed Easter Sunday with his mind in those untamed woods that bordered Creek Highway, wandering and searching through a place of imagination that terrified him.

Out of that maddening obsession, he drove home from work on Wednesday and turned on the stretch of road commonly known as Creek Highway. He placed awareness somewhere deep in those woods. Things happen out there, terrible things, Joe just knew it! These abominable happenings remain unseen, buried way inside the woods.

Joe shouldn't have been thinking of these things for it was necessary to pull over at the intersection of Creek Highway and Route 4, overwhelmed with a daydream of blood, terror and desperation. It was like a vision that provided scenery in the seclusion of dense trees where useless screams were muffled. No one cared to venture that far into the forest where the repeated pain inflicted on a helpless woman was enjoyed by the deliverer. Just another story, one of many; this chapter was soon to close. And in the end she hung from a tree, life slowly draining from the wide open slice while growing ever cold, surroundings blackening. Final thoughts were those of loved ones. How she wished for one last sight of someone who cared.

The vision haunted Joe so deeply that he found it necessary to send his wife an email the following morning.

"Stephanie,

I am sending you this email to your JGresky account in case the affair is not over. Some part of me believes that you are still communicating with him, and I believe I sense something not right. I read those emails last Friday, and picked up on a very frightening vibe. What if this man was not who he says he is? What if he convinced you to meet him privately where he killed you?

Call me crazy, but I had a terrible daydream that seemed so real. It was nearly hallucinatory and almost like a vision. I became so overpowered by the daydream that I needed to pull over on the side of the road until it passed. In the daydream, you were brought deep into the woods where you were tortured and raped for hours. At the end, you were hung, midair, by your wrists with feet bound. He deeply sliced your body open from chest to groin. With the pressure of being hung by your wrists, your organs were exposed. He walked away and left you there to die. As the blood poured from your body, you thought about how you wished you hadn't met this man.

I hope you are not still communicating with him.

Love,
Joe"

On a Thursday morning, nearly a week after Stephanie's activities had been discovered during that late night purse invasion; Joe sent the email to his wife. And at the same moment the button was pressed, Stephanie pulled her SUV into one of the entryways of untamed forest that hugged along the asphalt of Creek Highway. She took a personal day from work and made plans to finally meet Brad. But she was careful! Although the two agreed on meeting at the first entrance adjacent to Route

4, Stephanie drove two entryways down and parked her SUV. Then she pulled a mountain bike from the back and rode to the entryway where originally planned to meet Brad.

And she did something else to protect her identity. She wore a baseball cap with sunglasses. Upon reaching the vehicle that Brad described in the email, Stephanie could see him sitting in the driver's seat.

Brad wasn't expecting the woman to be on a bike and was very surprised. "Julie?"

She affirmed, "Yes, Hi."

Brad emerged from his car and gently shook Stephanie's hand. "It's nice to meet you, finally. You rode your bike here?"

She nodded and half-heartedly giggled. "I figured it was a chance to get some extra exercise."

Brad was a bit disappointed. "What's with the sunglasses? You promised I would have a chance to finally see what you looked like."

Stephanie did not smile, but stared at him through her sunglasses. "Patience is a virtue. Let's go for a hike in the woods. I don't want people to see me here. Small world you know?"

Surely, the woman Brad had come to meet wasn't going to take her bike in the woods. He offered, "You want to put your bike in my trunk?"

But she remained on the bike while saying, "That little trunk? The bike is too big for your trunk. I'll take it with."

Although nearly May, it was still a bit chilly on that Thursday morning, April 27, 2000. Stephanie wondered if it was out of place for her to be riding a bike through the woods on such a day.

Brad broke the silence by continuing a conversation that was exchanged over email. "So I took your suggestion and got that new computer. I sent you one last email, opened my bedroom window and threw the computer and monitor on the lawn. Then I went outside, threw it in the fire pit and smashed it to pieces with my axe. After that, I doused it with lighter fluid and set it on fire. It was the coolest thing, ever! The cheap plastic melted, all the little components inside bubbled and the hard drive turned all black and warped."

Up until the mention of the hard drive, Stephanie remained mostly silent as Brad chatted away, giving the details of the ridiculous execution of his troublesome PC at home. She had to ask, "Did you damage the hard drive?" Being the office champion of proprietary information, Stephanie urged her cyber lover to destroy any possible means of someone rummaging his private life in an evening of dumpster diving.

"Oh yeah, it got wacked a few times by the axe and split in half. It's black and warped. No one's gonna be able to use it! No one!"

There was a note of perked interest in Stephanie's voice, almost a tone of concern. "How's the new computer? You send me an email from it yet?"

"No, the new one's still in the box. I suppose I should have opened the new one and tried it out first. Oh well…"

The two ventured into the woods on a narrow, gravel path that eventually turned into a steep hill. Much of the wooded regions of the Mapleview area are hilly as the location was carved by glaciers thousands of years ago.

Stephanie was in the best shape of her life. Although the hike up the steep hill was a moderate exercise for her, it was a grueling high-impact workout for Brad. Trying to hide his fatigue was useless. Stephanie could sense the urgency to pause. But she coaxed him onward while pointing out a flat area of the trail that was some 100 feet uphill. Brad pushed and pushed with all his might, sweat leaking from every forehead's pore while nearly gasping for air. He collapsed at the well-received flat area, and Stephanie found his lack of endurance amusing. Not only did she climb the hill with ease, but she did so while pushing a bike.

"You okay?"

"Yeah, just need to rest. Not in good shape like you."

Moments passed as Stephanie watched the stranger regain his breath while calming his body down. And when it looked as though he had stabilized, she wasted not a second in asking, "There's something I've been dying to find out."

"What's that?"

"Your profile pic. Is that thing real?"

What an unexpected surprise! Brad produced a facial expression of delight. "What, you want to see it?"

Stephanie nodded.

Brad pushed himself off the ground so that he now proudly stood atop of the hill as an almighty lord who issued a serious warning to the little lady that was curious of his anatomy. "I'm going to warn you. It might scare you. Let's just say that I'm well-endowed."

Only minutes ago of lying on the ground and half in death, he now unbuckled his belt. Mushy blubber hung over his waist as he pulled down the baggy jeans.

Brad announced in a voice of greatness, "A real man needs to wear boxers to make room for all that meat!"

And then the meat was fully exposed as Stephanie was welcome to explore in all her satisfaction. More like "dead meat", the proud display would not do as expected. Maybe he was nervous.

Stephanie led Brad over to a large, dead tree trunk that had fallen to the ground. She gently coaxed the excited man to lie down and urged him to rest with hands behind his head while enjoying that which was long overdue. Stephanie knelt beside him and amorously worshipped as if it were her own, wishing it belonged to her. Brad could only lay with eyes closed on the greatest day of his life!

The Ever Sharp Cutlery set boasted a collection of knives that could cut through anything. Stephanie watched one holiday season as a salesperson demonstrated the knives in the Mapleview department store. They were truly amazing as the salesperson sliced through wood, vegetable cans and bones. And no matter what was cut with these knives, they forever retained their sharpness.

As Brad laid in overwhelming pleasure with eyes closed, Stephanie saw the perfect opportunity to reach in her windbreaker and pull out the Ever Sharp butcher knife that was mounted to her side. She was so mean! In one slice, Brad was abruptly Bobbittized, robbing him of the very thing that made him proud. Blood shot gunned and gurgled in a search of something now missing. He stood up in shock, screamed with trepidation and took sight of the stranger he met online, jump on her bike and race downhill.

"Julie! Julie! Give it back! Please give it back!" Clearly less than a man, it wasn't unreasonable to cry out of panic. Was she really going to run off with it? Maybe this was a cruel joke in which she would leave it on the side of the trail for him to discover. But what if an animal found it and ran off?

The Bobbittization was soon the least of Brad's worries as a considerable amount of blood was lost. High up on a steep hill, it was urgent that he reach the bottom and somehow drive to the hospital. Keep in mind that not everyone owned a cell phone in those days to call for help.

Shock leads us into making strange decisions and following unexpected actions. Brad couldn't make up his mind of how to stop the loss of blood. Pulling up his jeans would only allow the blood to flow out as it was impossible to block the gap with his hand. Leaving them pulled down to his ankles made it difficult to hike down the hill. With no other choice, Brad removed his jeans and hiked down the hill, desperately covering the robbed manhood in an attempt to stop the blood. But he left the car keys and wallet in those jeans! Halfway down the hill, this was realized which left Brad no choice but to hike back to the top. It only increased his heart rate, weakened his body further and placed him into a deeper state of dangerous shock.

Somehow Brad managed to make it to the top where he grabbed the wallet along with keys. Not sure of how hospitals handled emergencies, Brad could just hear the words, "Sorry Sir; if you don't have an insurance card, we can't treat you here."

Shaking, confused, cold and extremely weak; Brad stopped to lie down on top of the hill in a last moment effort to regain some strength and energy. How could she do this to him? It was a lesson well learned; never trust the strangers met on the Internet!

* * *

In the dark of the late night hours while her husband slept, or possibly lay awake in stewing suspicion of his wife, Stephanie hid in the darkest, most, isolated corner of the house where she could be alone with her new possession. The closet in the basement, located under the stairs, was an area that she and Joe called the crawlspace. Although a filthy place of cobwebs, mold and dust; this was where Stephanie had the most satisfying balloon session of her life as she nibbled and chewed at the water-inflated rubber, covered by the flesh of a dead man. But she was careful not to be too rough! There could be no damage! The thing now belonged to Stephanie as she merely played in a delightful celebration. Brad's body had yet to be found. But at that very moment, Stephanie knew he was dead. He reached for her leg from around the corner in the crawlspace. It was a cold, angry presence that had come for something taken. But he couldn't have it, never! It was Stephanie's new, cherished treasure.

Mother took hers away when Stephanie was too young to remember. Oh, she was certainly a woman; but Stephanie knew Mother had taken it the first time she laid eyes on Father's, which proudly hung between his legs. But where was poor Stephanie's? She realized in sadness that Mother, the cold-hearted bitch, had taken it away. But anger and resentment would only lead to losing Mommy's love. Mother was forgiven and internalized while Stephanie accepted the fact that it was gone.

The new one was preserved in such a way that it would never rot. Slipped over an elongated water balloon, Stephanie attached it to herself and proudly let it swing between her legs. It was worn out in public, at work, in the stores and during outings with her husband (behind clothing, of course!). And it was better than any other man's as the technique of preservation made it ever stiff. Joe had no reason to worry. It was only a dead man, a man whom Stephanie murdered, that now made love to his wife.

But for Joe, there was something not right with his marriage. Initially he felt that Stephanie was being satisfied by another man, but he could not prove this. Thinking that perhaps irreversible damage had been done since discovering the emails, he decided it was best to divorce, leave his son with Stephanie and move out of state.

Chapter 15

"Frank, we need to get that furnace fixed."

Remarried some years later, Stephanie moved into the Maple Sap subdivision with an arrogant, dominating and sometimes abusive husband. One might say that he was just the man that Stephanie deserved, offering the type of relationship she needed. A man of jerky bullying, Stephanie initially admired his qualities as those belonging to an aggressive manly-man. Stephanie quit her job, had two more children and stayed at home as a wife and mother who devoted her days and nights to ensuring Frank's comfort and happiness. A sudden raised backhand with a threat to strike or even a shove to the wall often inspired Stephanie's devotion of love to Frank. Perhaps Joe should have done these things while married to Stephanie!

Stephanie now spent her nights in solitude while Frank worked the graveyard shift and the 3 children soundly slept. And certainly not worn all the time, the thing that was robbed from Brad often sat covered in a shoe box, buried in the back of Stephanie's bedroom closet.

On this particular morning, Stephanie voiced a concern to her husband about getting the furnace fixed. It made the most awful sound when starting up. It was a sound that echoed the ever-angry, tormented cry of Brad who howled for vengeance and the return of something that rightfully belonged to him.

The previous night was unbearable! Although April, the furnace continued to be used as the temperatures outdoors dropped below 50 degrees. In combination with another night of Brad howling through the furnace, something shocking had visited Stephanie during a heavy rain with, of all things, a rare occurrence of cold weather lighting.

The house purchased in the Maple Sap neighborhood was an older, sprawling ranch on a slab. Seated on an acre of land with mature trees, a farm field was located directly next door. Spring was in the air, but still cold for Mapleview. The gradual thaw of the distant breath of warm air restored life in trees while softening the ground. It's a rebirth that many of us feel. But for Stephanie, it was always a reliving of days similar to those with Brad. Morbid thoughts often experienced at the decay of autumn while one sits alone with a self conscience of wrongful deeds, are often forgotten by Thanksgiving or Christmas. But for Stephanie, they remained through the birth of spring; year after year, after year.

Sitting in the dimly lit family room with a cup of coffee was Stephanie's newly found sanctuary of peace and quiet. No TV, no computer; just alone with the sound of rain drops that randomly tapped against the sliding, glass, patio door. It was suddenly joined by the blasted sound of the dreadful furnace. It was another calling and reminder from the grave. As usual, it went away as the mechanical parts began to work. The world outside the glass door was studied in a hope to ignore and forget Brad's cry.

Rain drops; rain drops; increased rain… then Stephanie spoke out loud, "Ooo! Lightning!"

Lightning was such an unusual thing to see in cold April. But the spectacle was not intended for Stephanie to enjoy! The wind picked up and the raindrops began to thrash upon the glass. The frightful display only reminded Stephanie of the calling heard seconds ago.

Although nearly the opposite distance from Creek Highway where the murder took place years ago, Brad's body now resided in the farm field next door. The rain and thawing ground enabled the pale, lifeless, mud-caked corpse to emerge from the ground and walk slowly to the house in a quest of retribution.

Stephanie took a sobering sip of her coffee. It was such a silly thought, imaginary corpses rising from the ground. And Brad wasn't buried in the farm field next door. Family had a funeral and put his body to rest at the cemetery.

Suddenly, the rain came to an abrupt halt which was followed by a violent flash of lighting that streaked across the sliding, glass, patio door. The dance of falling water along with light and shadows produced the clearly, recognizable face of lifeless Brad peeking in. The cup was dropped on the floor as Stephanie ran out of the family room and into the hallway. Somehow she would have to return to close the curtains and clean up the stain on the floor. Obviously, Stephanie had too much caffeine for the day. Maybe it was best for her to switch to hot cocoa or decaf during her late night sanctuaries.

* * *

At the mention of getting the furnace fixed, Stephanie's new husband, Frank, only looked in annoyance at his wife. "What? We don't need to worry about the furnace, now. Spring's here! We can get it fixed in the fall. I'm not worried about little noises."

To silently suffer her own torment, Frank and everyone else would never understand what haunted Stephanie.

* * *

The imagined emergence of Brad's lifeless corpse along with his screams of torment through the furnace wouldn't be the only thing resurrected in the neighborhood of that year. Residents of the Maple Sap subdivision were unaware of a murder that had taken place during the 1970s.

Nearly three decades previous; a wealthy, illegal immigrant from West Germany had escaped into the United States after committing a series of murders along with the theft that helped him gain that wealth. Mapleview was the ideal town to hide. A renovated house for rent in the Maple Sap subdivision was easy to obtain. The fugitive named Adahelm simply met the landlord with a briefcase full of money that contained two years worth of rent, upfront. Adahelm consistently paid cash for whatever needed. No background checks or bank accounts were necessary.

Without friends or family; maintaining a low profile; and in possession of an exorbitant amount of money, Adahelm was soon in need of female companionship. He heard of the shameful boulevard located in the heavily populated, urban-like town that was a 45 minute drive from Mapleview. Adahelm hoped that a sizable stack of money would ensure that only the best of high class escort ladies who stood outside a nightclub and offered dates for the evening would be obtained.

When greeted by the perfect escort lady, Adahelm simply brought her into the nightclub for an evening of drinking and dancing. She actually took a liking towards the wealthy immigrant with his intriguing accent and the money that was often flashed. Mixing business with pleasure, the escort lady saw her client as one who would be ideal to offer ala carte services somewhere in private. But she didn't expect the party to resume in a small home in the Maple Sap subdivision.

Towards dawn, Adahelm was disappointed with the additional companionship provided. Intoxicated, he refused to pay for the services. That's when the escort lady made the mistake that would prove deadly by threatening to tell her manager of Adahelm's refusal to pay. She reminded him that the manager had an underground justice system. Of course this would only open the possibility of exposing the West German fugitive's hideout. So in Adahelm's massive strength, he seized the escort lady from behind and slit her throat.

There, the problem was solved! Adahelm simply left the dead woman in a pool of blood and went to bed for the night! Awakening 4 hours later in a more sobered state of mind, the fugitive was now hit with the reality that he had senselessly murdered an escort lady. Why didn't he just pay her? That would have saved him some serious headache. No time to ponder his stupidity, Adahelm temporarily hid the body, cleaned up the mess and began to plan a more permanent means of disposal.

By afternoon, there was a terrifying knock at the door. It couldn't have been the escort lady's manager; unless, of course, she was followed from a distance. No trace of a body and all fluids thoroughly cleaned with bleach, it wouldn't have been too difficult to play dumb. Adahelm could have simply replied, "No, she left early this morning."

But the horror that stood at that doorstep was far worse than an escort lady's manager. The FBI had successfully tracked down the fugitive and was now at the end of their manhunt. Adahelm was sent back to West Germany where authorities awaited the thief and murderer.

* * *

And then we have a little boy named Jeff, who for some years before moving to Mapleview with his mother and father had triggered a disturbing telephone call from his teacher to Mother. It was in the autumn months as small rodents such as mice and moles sought shelter from the cold. Many a home without a cat has been plagued by the sudden intrusion of unwanted small creatures at this time of year. Most homeowners resolve to lay out poison such as deacon in hopes to rid the presence of the unwelcome rodents. And because of this, Jeff discovered an unfortunate mouse, lying dead, near the outside corner of his garage. Never examining death so closely, the small boy concluded that it was a real mouse. The difference now: he could handle the small, furry creature; pet its head, even put it in the pocket of his jacket and keep it as a new toy.

Of course Mother and Father should not have been able to see this new plaything! At night it was brought to bed with Jeff and tucked under the pillow as he awaited the good night kiss from Mother. He always wanted a mouse of his very own. Now he could pet one on the head while falling asleep at night.

The following morning at school, Jeff slipped the dead mouse in his desk with the intention of bringing it out for company. Learning to add and subtract was the least event of excitement for Jeff. Perhaps a visit from Mousey would have entertained the boy while drowning out the discussion as to why four minus two, equals two.

The girl who sat next to Jeff suddenly called out, "Jeff is playing with a mouse on his lap!"

The teacher quickly approached the young boy and overshadowed his desk. Needless to say, she was deeply disturbed to see a dead mouse lying on her student's lap. She nearly panicked, bringing a garbage can over and demanding that Jeff pitch the dead mouse in.

But Jeff refused, "No! He's mine!"

"Jeff, honey; that mouse probably ate poison that could make you sick. Even worse, he has bacteria and germs on him."

The teary-eyed boy did as asked and then followed the teacher's escort to the restroom where she made sure he scrubbed his hands. Jeff's mother, Karen Greenstart, received a midmorning call from the school, advising her that a dead mouse had been handled and played with by her son.

But it wouldn't end Jeff's fascination with creatures under the spell of suspended animation. An unfortunate bird that hit the window; a squashed toad that had seen its end under the tire of a bicycle; these often ended up in Jeff's pockets. And poor Mother would discover them in one place or another. There was just no convincing the boy that collecting dead creatures was a sick and disturbing habit.

But nothing could have prepared the boy's mother, Karen, for what she observed through the kitchen window one autumn, Saturday morning. Little Jeff was making piles of leaves. It's nothing unusual for a child to play with leaves. But throughout the morning, Karen would glance out the kitchen window to notice that a neat, rectangular pile was placed next to another, next to another and next to another. By midmorning, she was horrified to see that nearly all the rectangular piles had wooden crosses at the heads.

She called out to her husband, "Bill? Bill!"

Karen scampered out into the living room where her husband read the newspaper and only looked up to reply, "What?"

"Look out the window and see what your son is doing!"

Both watched little Jeff driving his toy go-cart along the perimeter of a dozen-some rectangular piles of leaves with crosses at the heads. Father didn't understand Mother's concern, "What? He's playing with leaves. What's so wrong about that?"

"Bill, he's playing cemetery! That's so morbid! Did you ever do that as a kid?"

"Oh, I'm sure there are worse things he can be doing right now. Let the kid play."

By noon, little Jeff was called in for lunch. Father asked, "So whacha doin' out there, Sport?" He rubbed the little boy's head. The smell of autumn's sun and leaves spread through the air.

"I'm playing hearse driver. See all my graves out there?"

"I sure do! Maybe after lunch we can throw the football around, huh?"

Little Jeff looked at the ground in sadness. "I don't wanna. I wanna keep playing hearse driver."

But Father ensured him that the game would not be interrupted. "Sure you can, Son; as long as it makes you happy."

Later that night, Bill was startled awake upon the sound of the backdoor quietly opening. Was there an intruder? He quickly opened the sliding, closet door. The squeaking of the rollers and hardware woke Karen.

She asked, "What are you doing?"

"Shhh, someone was opening the backdoor." Bill reached to the top shelf of the closet and pulled out his magnum .357 handgun. Karen soon stood in the corner of the bedroom, listening for any indicator to phone police while Bill sneaked through the house and into the laundry room where the backdoor was located.

Then she heard her husband yell, "What are you doing outside, huh? You had me thinking someone was breaking in!"

The voice of little Jeff provided an explanation as Mother darted out of the bedroom through the living room and to the backdoor where her son stood, holding a life-sized Raggedy Ann doll. It was a toy of Karen's when she was a little girl. It was now soiled with leaves stuck in various places.

Mother had to ask, "Jeff, why do you have my Raggedy Ann doll, outside?"

The bewildered boy softly replied, "I buried her in one of the graves but forgot. She was cold and crying; so I went out side to dig her out and bring her to bed so she can be nice and warm."

Although purely innocent and certainly not to be taken as it may have appeared, Mother and Father looked at each other in disbelief. Then Mother finally declared that any further games of cemetery or hearse drive were thereby forbidden.

* * *

Years later, grown from playing make-believe to playing games of sport, Jeff moved into the nice neighborhood of Maple

Sap with his mother and father. Weary and very bored with the grueling task of carrying boxes and furniture into the new home, Jeff was later expected to assist his father in bringing items down into the crawlspace. Not terribly damp, the storage area had the smell of dirty, wet rocks that crunched when crawled through. The unflattering light of exposed bulbs that hung from the 4-foot ceiling revealed that the crawlspace reached through the entire area of the home. And in the orderly, meticulous habits of Father, Jeff was required to neatly store the items and boxes at the far wall.

Upon returning from storing the last box, Jeff crawled over a 6 foot region of rocks that felt softer and produced the sound as-if hollow. In Jeff's imagination he believed that a hole had been dug in the ground, something was buried and the rocks now covered whatever that mysterious object was. But why tell Father? What if it was something unique and valuable? Perhaps it was a treasure that Jeff could enjoy all to himself. He waited in a longing fantasy for a time when Mother and Father were gone so that he could return to the hollow region and uncover the mystery.

It would be nearly the entire summer before Jeff found himself alone. Although Father worked throughout the week, Mother was temporarily laid off from her job as the company was experiencing a lag in growth. This enabled her to settle in the new home and get acquainted with the neighborhood.

Finally, one Sunday afternoon, Mother and Father announced that they would go to the store and return in a couple of hours. They felt confident that Jeff could be left alone. Aside from that, he would need to become accustomed to spending time alone as Mother would soon return to work.

Every child knows in their stalking of parents that an occasional, quick return home for forgotten money or coupons is possible. Jeff sat motionless in the living room chair for several minutes until he could intuit that the embarking of Mother and Father was in solid motion. Then he excitedly ran into the garage for a shovel then brought it into the kitchen closet where the crawlspace entry was located.

Unflattering lights were flashed on. The boy crawled through the damp smell of crunchy rocks as he pulled the shovel along his journey until reaching the area of hollow ground. And after a few minutes of digging rocks, he uncovered something that was both intriguing and disappointing. It was an old, wooden trunk which definitely peaked his interest. But it was sealed with a padlock. What could he do now? Jeff pulled at the rusty lock and hit it with a shovel, but did not have the strength to break it open. What in the world could have been locked and buried beneath the floor of a crawlspace? Was there treasure? Was there a sack full of money hiding from a bank robbery?

Father once lost the key to the tool shed back at the old house. And as Jeff recalled, a large cutting tool that Father called "bolt cutters" had been used to snap the padlock open. Yes, of course; the very bolt cutters that now hung on the wall of the garage could be used. It was a decision paying no mind to consequence as only he knew of the buried trunk.

Jeff returned to the treasure chest with an ever-growing sense of excitement. The padlock was snapped open just as easily as Father had done back at the old tool shed. The lid of the old chest creaked when opened and revealed nothing more than salt! Why in the world would someone bury a locked up collection of salt? As Jeff pondered on his treasure hunt that seemed to be in vain, he suddenly heard the sound of the garage door opening outside! Mother and Father were home!

Quickly slamming the trunk shut and throwing the tools down the hole, Jeff barely had enough time to crawl out of the storage area, up into the kitchen where he would replace the panel on the closet floor.

"Jeff, the knees of your pants are dirty! And those are your good pants! I told you to wear old clothes when going outside to play."

Like all mothers, Jeff's was unhappy to see her son's clothing soiled and stained, possibly ruined from the careless play in dirty areas. But little did she know he was on all fours, in the crawlspace and on a treasure hunt while she was gone. She sighed, "Well wash up for dinner."

Dinner conversation between Mother and Father revealed that Mother fretted over a box of dishes that may have been accidentally brought into the crawlspace. She had always been this way, senselessly worrying over petty things. And Jeff silently agreed with Father that it was unnecessary to journey down into the crawlspace in search of a supposed missing box of dishes. The conversation soon evolved into a small argument until Father had no choice but to give in.

"Alright, I'll go down after dinner and give a look. I mean you would think we had enough plates as it is!"

Jeff panicked! His father would surely find the hole he uncovered in the crawlspace and the old, wooden chest. "I... I'll go down and look for you, Dad."

Mother and Father looked at each other in surprise of their remarkable child. Why would he offer to do something like that? Father only roared in pride, "Well, I believe our little Jeff is becoming a big man, now! He wants to help his old man out! Sure you can, Son!" And as always, Mother reminded him to change into his old pants before crawling around in that filthy crawlspace.

* * *

Mother was striking up a friendship with some woman named Stephanie who lived across the street. In the summer months of living in the new neighborhood, Jeff often observed the woman who had a way of displaying her legs in what appeared to be runner's shorts. Children are more observant than we know. Although not bad-looking, Jeff found the woman to be peculiar in her appearing to worship her own legs. The neighbors across the way had a boy Jeff's own age named Paul. But despite Mother and Father's persuasion, Jeff was the least bit interested in deliberate introductions. Parents just don't understand the code that kids follow. Only a dork would have gone out of his way to introduce himself as the new kid on the block.

With Mother entering Stephanie's house and Father at work, Jeff saw it the perfect opportunity to, once again, sneak into the crawlspace for a closer examination of the treasure chest. There just had to be something buried beneath that salt! There was no point in locking it up and throwing it down into a hole to be covered by rocks.

Carefully pulling back a mound of salt with the blade of the shovel, he soon learned that there was something, in fact, hiding underneath. More and more salt pulled back, his heart accelerated in joyful pleasure which produced the most frightening smile one could ever see a child wear. He always wanted one of his own, something dead to play with. The corpse of a woman who had been perfectly preserved under the salt for nearly 3 decades now lay before Jeff. But there had to be rules to follow! The first and most obvious was to only enjoy his treasure during moments when Mother and Father would not discover him. Second, the wooden chest must be closed shut with the rocks pulled over, each and every time he was finished with his play.

Finding something dead to play with should be every boy's dream; at least Jeff believed this. A preserved woman who remained under the spell of suspended animation could have her clothes removed without resistance. And beyond this disturbing initial fact, I care not to even think of the adventures Jeff had during his remaining two weeks of summer vacation.

The first day of school would be, as Jeff felt, a more natural introduction to the boy who lived across the street. They made the casual greetings at the bus stop, sat in seats nearby on the bus and even discovered that they would share the same teacher for the year. But by midmorning recess, Paul and his friends seemed to have mutually concluded that there was something not right about Jeff. Whisperings from behind Jeff's back offered immature suggestions that the new kid was gay or queer. Many can remember the unpleasant days of middle school social disasters. Defeated, the only thing Jeff could do was mention to his neighbor of the treasure buried in the crawlspace.

Paul only called out, "Yeah right! I don't believe you!"

This only outraged Jeff. "Wanna bet? You think I'm a liar? Come over after school and I'll show it to you. Both my parents will be at work."

Later in the afternoon, both boys placed their book bags on the kitchen countertop of Jeff's house. Paul stood at the closet while the new kid in the neighborhood opened the entry to the crawlspace.

Maybe the new kid was serious about this. If he was joking, how far would it go? Paul thought it was best to remind him, "You better not be lying!"

Illuminated by the unflattering, exposed light bulbs, Paul crawled behind Jeff through the crunchy rocks with the smell of dampness in the air. In a need to display toughness, Paul could not admit an unexplained phobia of a crudely, unfinished area below the house. And he couldn't help but begin to suspect that there was, in fact, the naked body of a dead woman down there.

But Paul wouldn't lose control! He was the one in charge. The new kid was the one who had to put his money where his mouth was. "Okay, so where is it? Are you lying?"

Jeff remained calm, "It's buried under these rocks, Dummy! You think I have that out in the open for everyone to see?"

The anxiety was masked with a growing display of a badass who continued to threaten behind a prepubescent voice. "You better not be lying! I'll tell everyone at school and we'll kick your ass!"

Jeff only remained silent, picked up the shovel and pulled back the layers of rocks which soon revealed the old, wooden chest. He looked up at the now pale-faced Paul who was on his way to becoming Jeff's best friend. The old chest creaked when opened which produced a horrified, agape look on Paul's face. Boys that age feel comfortable using profanity when not in the presence of adults. Paul certainly exercised every right of profanity at that moment.

"I dare you to touch her. See, I touch her." Jeff stroked his hand over the corpse's right breast.

"You're sick! You're freaking crazy! I'm not touching that!"

"Come on, don't be such a wimp. Touch her! Girls at our school don't have these! Go ahead; haven't you ever wondered what a titty felt like?"

Paul laid his hand on the corpse's left breast; but quickly pulled it away upon feeling that the woman would suddenly come back to life.

Jeff was understanding and offered the usefulness in the treasure that was now shared with Paul. "Do you have any idea the power we have with this thing? We can charge all the kids in this neighborhood to come down and look at it."

Chapter 16

The only thing that had changed in Bill and Karen Greenstart's life was their address. Moving wasn't much of a life-change event for the couple as it may have been for people in different situations. Moving to Mapleview, for some, might require landing a new job or leaving a career to be a stay-at-home parent. Even more stressful might be the requirement to distance oneself from close family and friends. But Bill and Karen simply lived in the next town over and merely wanted to enjoy a new setting in the nice town of Mapleview.

With her son now finished with summer break, and on the second day of returning back to her job, Karen was suddenly plagued with an unexplained amount of anxiety. Nothing was out-of-the-ordinary at work and things were fine at home. But the anxiety would mysteriously surface during a quiet moment, as-if a warning of some calamity in the not-so-distant future. Suffering from acute anxiety only a few years ago, Karen was armed with the mechanisms to battle the irrational feelings.

Has the reader ever been on vacation or in the middle of a long holiday and discovered the sudden wish for Monday to return? Sure, the time away from work is nice as much as the time spent with loved ones. But sometimes it feels as though that vacation or that holiday is a fast-paced track of nonstop events, along with constant smothering of loved ones. Monday restores everyone's return to their old routine along with a sense of peace and quiet. For Karen, her summer months of moving into the new home; doing cosmetic improvements along with becoming acclimated to the new neighborhood was a nonstop vacation of work, work, work. How she longed in those summer months to return to her quiet cubicle where she might answer a phone call or work on some project; then finally have a more healthy and balanced dose of Bill and Jeff in the evenings. In all the months at home, Karen had yet to relax and unwind! This was a seemingly rational explanation for the mysterious invasion of anxiety.

When shopping for the new home, the advertisement boasted a nice house in the quiet town of Mapleview, in the much sought after neighborhood of Maple Sap. A good selling point for Karen was the recently installed hot tub of her private, master bathroom. But despite living in her new home for months, Karen had yet to enjoy it! Tonight, a nice cup of chamomile tea while soaking in the hot tub and surrounded by a few flickers of candle flame would finally be enjoyed.

She lay there, melting in the tub with her eyes closed while enjoying the sensation of warm water relaxing her muscles. But never mind those noisy jet streams that produce nothing more than agitation and uneasiness. Karen only wished for the sound of peace and quiet in the still water.

There must be countless people who have been murdered and their bodies dumped in unmarked, shallow graves. The owners of those bodies wait patiently for someone to discover them and finally bring closure to loved ones. And it must be a lonely feeling to know that your body has been abandoned, left to rot in the ground beneath some log or a bush that has now grown over you. This is the thought that intruded Karen's mind as she imagined herself laying outside in nature while soaking in the rays of the sun. They were merely unwelcomed manifestations of anxiety, and somehow the unpleasant thoughts should have been pushed from Karen's mind. She was quite alive and the same could be said of her husband and son. Outside of Karen's father, all other close family members were still alive. And she didn't have a friend or family member who had been murdered. Reminding herself of how fortunate she was, Karen placed her mind back in that same spot, lying outdoors in the warm sun.

In an imagined moment of astral projection, the very place where Karen lay out in the sun was one such grave of an unfortunate, murdered soul. The astral realm proved dangerous as it allowed the intimate infusion between the rotting corpse a few feet below, and the woman who was alive and appreciating a place of serenity and nature. Karen's skin absorbed the vile carrion and the residual terror of that corpse's final moments alive.

She quickly sat up, now back in the hot tub with heart rate increased from a surge of anxiety. Examining the surroundings didn't help much. The hot tub suggested lying in a coffin.

"Bill?" Something needed to break the powerful daydream. "Bill! Bill!"

He finally entered the bathroom to see his wife holding her chest and having trouble breathing. "What? What's wrong?"

"It's happening again! I'm, I'm having…" It was nearly impossible to breathe which made it difficult for Karen to speak.

Bill filled in his wife's words. "What? Are you having another attack?

Karen nodded.

Bill was now alarmed with the knowledge that his wife was suffering another acute anxiety attack which was the same sort of attack that she experienced some years ago. Placed on medication, his wife learned to gain control and was weaned from the drugs so that she could once again live a normal life. But the move and the return back to work must have triggered another spell of anxiety. Bill could only do his best to calm his wife, "Okay, sit tight. I'll call the doctor and have him fill a prescription for you!"

* * *

Now the best-of-buddies, Jeff and Paul stood in the corner of the school hallway with a group of kids, challenging those who might be interested to view the naked and preserved body of a woman. "It must have been buried in that crawlspace for a hundred years!"

As Jeff explained, bodies that are buried in the desert never rot because of the dryness. The salt would have had the same effect on his mummy—such a strange piece of knowledge for a child to have. But just as Paul doubted Jeff before actually seeing the corpse, the kids that now surrounded the pair of newfound friends cried out in their badass, prepubescent voices that Paul and Jeff were lying. They speculated that at most, a life-sized Halloween decoration of a corpse was probably buried in the crawlspace.

$2.00: that was the cost to view the mummy. Any turndowns would be proof of being a wimp. Jeff and Paul certainly weren't afraid of their dead plaything. But could the other kids stroke the breast of a dead woman, maybe more? Talk was cheap; the other kids needed to prove their boldness!

A list of 19 kids had been accumulated throughout the day, but only 7 had come home with Jeff and Paul. These were kids from the neighborhood, each with $2.00 and a promise to "kick some ass" if the show was disappointing.

9 kids crawled through the crunchy floor, towards an area that was seemingly void of that which had been promised.

"Alright, where is it?"

"Yeah! I want my money back!"

"We're gonna kick your ass!"

The crawlspace echoed with a wild party of rowdy, middle-school-aged kids. Jeff only smiled and took hold of his shovel, "Don't worry, you'll see it."

Layers of rock had been pulled back which exposed the familiar, wooden chest. "And now that you have paid your dues to join our club..."

The chest creaked open, and all was silent. The kids had seen many life-like Halloween decorations, but this one looked real! It looked so real, that perhaps it was real!

And as each boy had finally come to the conclusion that there was, in fact, an actual dead body lying in the new kid's crawlspace, they each took turns in whispers of, "Whoa... wow... holy..." These things were only read about in books or seen in movies. But there one lay in a hole of a crawlspace, pale and lifeless; a suggestion of suspended decay; mummified as Jeff had said.

"Go ahead, touch her!" Paul delighted in challenging the now disturbed boys who sensed a barely detectable iota of awareness from the woman, a vibration of death that no decoration could duplicate.

"I'm not touching that!"

"What are you afraid of? See?" Paul laid his hand on the corpse's breast and squeezed. "It's a real titty! Go ahead!"

And one-by-one, in a demonstration of conquering fears, the corpse's breasts, thighs and many other areas were fondled in a morbid fascination that would disturb the boys for many years to come. And of all things, the area that no one would touch was the woman's hand. The one touch that could be considered an act of love and affection was strictly off limits for the boys, as they feared that the woman would resurrect and seize the hand of life.

The group of 9 boys who lived in the neighborhood had suddenly been closely bonded by a new "club" that collectively owned a treasure of power. But they didn't go into the crawlspace every day to admire it. In fact, the corpse was left to rest in peace for weeks as the kids performed normal activities such as playing basketball or video games. On occasion, the boys would journey on all fours to the place of burial and raise the dead in admiration and play. And of course, Jeff's rule was always followed to cover the wooden chest with rocks while leaving the ground appearing undisturbed before climbing out of the crawlspace.

* * *

Pulling into the driveway on a late afternoon, Karen spotted her son playing basketball with the kids on the block at Frank and Stephanie's house. Initially wondering if the boy had homework, she soon found herself in a sense of relief that Jeff had successfully made friends at the new school and neighborhood.

Jeff apparently had friends over, earlier. Walking into the kitchen, her footsteps were met with stickiness over by the pantry. Perhaps it was soda. She didn't mind, terribly, that Jeff had friends over. But she was going to have to mention that groceries were not purchased for the neighborhood kids to enjoy. Why else would they be in the closet? And Karen was going to have to mention that if someone spilled soda or juice on floor, it would be nice if he mopped up the stickiness.

It was a bit chilly from the kitchen windows left open; but Karen opted to leave them alone as the oven would soon heat up the kitchen. Today was Wednesday, and as planned on the week's list of meals, meatloaf would be prepared and probably done by the time Bill came home from work. If you've ever made a meatloaf yourself, then you're quite familiar with the task of mixing raw meat, seasoned breadcrumbs and a couple of eggs in a bowl. Then the slop is mixed with the hands, squeezed and flipped over until a workable substance can be dumped in a loaf pan.

But Karen was different in her preparation. With a sizable Mixmaster on the counter, she dropped the meat in the bowl then cracked open the eggs and dumped the breadcrumbs. Why experience the unpleasant sensation of slimy, ice-cold meat numbing the hands? Simply flip the switch of the automatic mixer and let the machine do all the work.

The Wienerdorfs, located behind and on the next block, had begun their project of constructing a new deck in the backyard. They mentioned this to Bill and Karen over the weekend. Apparently, the Mister was getting a jump start by making cuts with the electric saw. The wood screamed as it met the toothed, circular blade which was a sound never a favorite of Karen's. While Mr. Wienerdorf made his cuts, the meat which mixed in the blender almost called out in a plea to stop the bloody mess.

Karen ignored the terrible thoughts of imagination. But the dreaded, circular saw continued to produce more horrific screams by the wood. They were nearly the sounds of a terrified woman who begged for it all to end. Why such senseless torture? Why so many little cuts?—a snip here, a snip there and then aggravation of those terrible injuries with further torture.

The blender was turned off and the bowl nervously lifted over to the loaf pan. And then the tortured woman let out one, final, bloodcurdling scream of unbearable agony. It was a cry for it all to end, a plea to break the realm of solitude of her captors. Karen could see in her mind the defenseless woman, lying in the crawlspace with tearful longing for a final departure from Hell.

It was too much for Karen; the meat mixture never made it into the loaf pan. She ran out of the house, truly feeling that someone was screaming down in the crawlspace. But how irrational; she knew it was only the sound waves from Mr. Wienerdorf's saw that bounced off the walls and to the pantry closet.

Now standing in the garage while desperately clinging to sanity, Karen called out to her son across the street, "Jeff, do you have homework?"

"Only a little, Mom!"

"Well I suggest you say goodnight to your friends!" Yelling at the boy was the much needed outlet that restored her sanity. And as he walked into the garage, Jeff was met by an unfriendly face of anger, "What were you doing in the kitchen this afternoon?"

"What? Nothing!"

"Yeah, you spilled something all over the floor! Why didn't you clean it up?"

"I did!"

"Jeff, it was all sticky!" Karen lowered her voice so neighbors would not hear the rest. "And I don't buy food for all your friends to eat. We don't have money for that, understand?"

Jeff only walked away, believing that mother was merely crazy and looking for something to yell at.

Karen wondered if perhaps the boy would hear the same thing that she heard. But after waiting several minutes, she concluded that the screaming stopped.

20 minutes later later, as Bill pulled into the garage, he took sight of his distraught wife sitting up against the bumper of her car. Bill immediately suspected that Jeff had done something wrong. "Where's Jeff?"

"In the house, doing homework."

"Did he get into a fight at school?"

Karen's face remained to the floor, saying not a word.

Needless to say, Bill was concerned. "Honey, what's wrong? You have to tell me!"

"I was making dinner, and I heard screaming coming from the crawlspace."

"Screaming?"

"Yes; it was a woman, screaming. It sounded like she was being severely tormented and it was the most awful thing I ever heard."

"Well did Jeff hear it?"

Karen shook her head, no.

Being the sensible man that Bill was, he stepped back in a moment of assessment. Why would someone be screaming from the crawlspace? Perhaps his wife was having an adverse reaction to the anxiety medication. But the possibility of someone actually injured in the crawlspace needed to be disproved. He entered the house, alone, walked into the pantry and opened the panel door. Descending the stepladder, he called out, "Is anyone down here?"

There was nothing but silence.

"Hello?" He flicked on the crude lighting and could see nothing but an empty storage area with boxes and junk stacked at the opposite wall. Satisfied that all was well, he turned off the lights and ascended back up the ladder.

Maybe Jeff could have provided insight. Bill entered the boy's bedroom and took sight of his son working math problems on the roll top desk that was illuminated by an overhead light. "Jeff, were you doing something down in the crawlspace?"

The boy turned flush, "No! I wasn't down there!"

Noticing the peculiar reaction, Father had to further probe. "Jeff, I'm going to ask you again and I want an honest answer. Were you down in that crawlspace when your mother came home from work?"

Realizing he was not guilty at the moment, Jeff reaffirmed the original answer. "No, I wasn't down there." In truth, Jeff and his friends hadn't gone down to admire their treasure that afternoon. They played basketball until Mother called him home.

Bill's final evaluation would be a confirmation of Jeff's answer from his wife. He met Karen back in the garage and asked, "Was Jeff downstairs in the crawlspace when you got home? I asked him if he was down there and it looked like he was getting nervous."

"No, Jeff was across the street with his friends at Frank and Stephanie's house."

Bill sighed, "Honey, I don't know what to say. I went down in the crawlspace and saw nothing. And even though Jeff was acting suspicious, I saw no evidence of him fooling around down there. You must have heard the screaming coming from outside or on someone else's TV."

His explanation only provoked tears in Karen's eyes. The screaming was so real for her and she wanted to help that person.

Bill was comforting to his wife. "It's okay; you're under stress, getting used to the new house and working that stressful job. The mind plays tricks on you when you feel anxiety." Bill was getting very hungry and wanted his wife to cheer up. "Come on, I'm starving. Let's go out for pizza."

And so the Greenstarts went out for their family dinner that evening, and the horrible screaming heard in the crawlspace was forgotten. Of course Jeff was clueless of Mother's incident and unaware as to why Wednesday night was a pizza night, instead of the usual meatloaf.

Going to bed at her usual time, Karen woke up around 2:15 in the morning under a terrible spell of thirst. Although she enjoyed pizza as much as you and me, Karen found that sometimes the sausage was very salty, which required she shoot down a couple tall glasses of water in the middle of the night to get back to sleep.

In between gulps, she paused and listened to a faint noise. Did the Zickmans get into another fight? The newlyweds next door were so young and appeared to be so much in love. But quarreling was often heard through their windows. Tonight the very, young Mrs. must have stepped out for a bit of weeping from maybe another fight of "you-don't-love-me-as-much-as-I-love-you." Karen gently pulled the curtains back but could see no one standing in the Zickman's driveway. But the weeping continued, very disturbing and agitating.

Now Karen slowly opened the backdoor and stepped out into the chilled, autumn, night air. The smell of burning logs, probably from someone's fireplace, hung in the distant air. But no weeping was heard outside. Surely this wouldn't suggest that the sound came from within her own home! She stepped back into the warm house where the soft cries continued to be heard. Pretending to be clueless of the origination, Karen walked through various rooms of the house. But the sound was loudest in the kitchen... in the pantry... from the floor where the crawlspace panel was located!

Rather than fall spell to another attack of anxiety, Karen laid there on the floor with her ear to the weeping, listening to a poor woman who questioned how and why such a terrible misfortune could have happened to her. Karen really wanted to help, but wouldn't dare go down into the crawlspace. No one would probably be down there, anyway.

The experience in the hot tub; the screams heard earlier in the day; and now the cries of sadness from below the floor: perhaps it was time to be strong and consider that someone was reaching out and offering a premonition. Bill mentioned that Jeff appeared suspicious when asked of the crawlspace. It was so obvious now; Karen's son was doing something down there in the afternoons, something awful! The weeping was met with a promise to get to the bottom of whatever terrible thing Jeff hid from his parents.

* * *

A child who approaches the teenage years should draw new concerns for any loving parent. Being that Jeff was in a new school and neighborhood, perhaps he was exposed to drugs or promiscuous girls. And maybe these things were done in the crawlspace after school. There was only one way to learn the truth. Karen left work early, mentioning a family emergency and headed home where she parked some distance down the street. Carefully approaching the house, her intention was to avoid any detection from Jeff. But the rapidly, beating heart and heavy breathing suggested another attack of anxiety. Not now! Karen needed to be strong! The truth can sometimes be painful and disturbing. But it's needed in those challenging moments of motherhood.

Karen slowly opened the backdoor and softly walked across the ceramic, tile floor. Sure enough the pantry was open, and the panel to the crawlspace had been removed! A group of noisy kids could be heard crunching along the crude flooring. And then they emerged before Karen had a chance to peek down into their realm of taboo activities. It was their conversations of filth that were most disturbing; her own son declaring that he would never stick his "manhood" in that "crevice", citing that he was saving it for something real.

One of the boys challenged "Oh yeah; well what if we threw Kristy down in that..."

"Oh; Hi, Mom! You're home early!" Jeff immediately recognized his mother.

So did one of the other boys, "Hi Mrs. Greenstart!

Mother only glared at the rowdy, obnoxious boys who wore faces of guilt and that of up to no good. "What are you doing down there, huh?"

Jeff resembled a startled deer. "Nothing! We were just down there. That's our fort."

"Yeah Mrs. Greenstart; that's our fort. We have a club, Grave Robbers Anonymous. Call 911!" Paul laughed

Karen didn't find Paul's explanation the least bit funny and met the attempted joking with firm rules. "You do not play down there! That's not a place to hang around and do whatever while I'm gone!"

Her son exhibited signs of defensiveness and smart mouth. "Okay Mom, we won't. Jeez, we get the point."

But Mother wasn't done with her investigation. With dread, the boys watched as she descended the stepladder while dictating that Jeff send his friends home and begin homework.

Now the #1 of rule of Jeff and his club was to always close the trunk and cover the hole up with rocks before going back upstairs. And it's a good thing for Jeff that he continued to follow this rule. Mother looked around the crawlspace and journeyed over to an area where a collection of crushed soda cans, a shovel, bolt cutters, some screwdrivers and a wooden handle for a paint roller laid. She wasn't sure what they were up to with all the tools. Maybe they were just being boys and playing. The rest of her time was spent looking at the boxes of items along the far wall, planning a day to go through them all.

That night, during dinner, Father broke the silence. "Your mother says you were down there in the crawlspace with your friends. Do you have anything to say about that?"

Jeff once again became nervous. "It's our fort down there."

Father spoke with a tone of disappointment and that of suggesting dishonesty. "Now yesterday I asked if you were down there and you told me, no. And today I find out you and your friends *are* down there. Now I want some answers. What are you doing down there?"

Mother added more, "Jeff, I found a shovel, some tools and lots of soda cans. You guys play with tools? And what's this grave robber game you're playing?"

Father dropped his fork on the plate as a psychological effect that would suggest sudden outrage. "You better not be digging holes down there! Are you digging holes?"

"No sir."

"Alright, I'm going to tell you this once, and only once. You get those tools out of there and clean up your mess. And if I find that you've been going down there any more, there will be hell to pay; you hear?"

"Yes sir."

Chapter 17

Working the nightshift is a challenge for anyone. The mind and body must be tricked into living during the dark hours and sleeping while the rest of the world goes by without you. Remove merely one hour of a day's rest, a nightshift worker is catapulted into a walking coma as he or she struggles to remain conscious. And the old saying of "you can't get something for nothing" applies while maintaining consciousness in such a walking coma. Irritability, lack of concentration, fits of rage or anxiety and an occasional sensation of passing out could be experienced. With these facts in mind, why in the world would Stephanie's husband, Frank, stay up during the morning and afternoon to drink? I suppose it's similar to the functional alcoholic who stays up until midnight, passes out and rises at dawn for work the next day. But as you read Frank's story, you might wonder if the 3rd shift hours in combination of alcohol abuse turned Frank into the monster that he was.

A couple years before Jeff moved in the neighborhood, Paul learned of his stepfather's potential of violence on an afternoon upon returning home from school with friends. Being the inconsiderate beasts that children can be, Paul became rowdy in his bedroom while Frank tried with all his might to sleep in the next room that was darkened with shades and exterior noise drowned by the sound of FM radio static. Usually Frank slept like a rock. 12 beers in the course of the morning and early afternoon would ensure of this. Not to use outdated phrases, but a bomb could go off in the next room while Frank continued to soundly sleep. But on that day, Frank had difficulty.

The young boys giggled and laughed. And then there was a slam that rattled the floor.

"Those damn kids!" Frank jumped out of bed, grabbed a bowling ball from the closet and hurled it through bedroom wall towards the direction of the rowdy kids. The ball punched through both layers of drywall so that Frank could see the startled faces of boys who had aroused the Incredible Hulk into becoming angry. He used colorful adjectives while ordering them to "shut up". Fortunately, the destructive bowling ball did not hit one of the children. And Stephanie learned that night of what would happen if she ever scolded her husband again!

Then there was the year that Frank's favorite professional baseball team appeared in the World Series playoffs. Just as many fans felt that a title was long overdue, Frank truly believed that his team would make it that year. He sat in the chair one early evening, having already guzzled 10 beers. But it was anything but a party. His team wasn't doing so well.

A recent litter of golden retriever puppies lay near their momma in the kitchen. Stephanie and Frank felt that mating the pure bread golden retriever might prove to be a small business to earn additional Christmas money, vacation money or whatever. But the puppies were getting bigger, bolder, louder and anxious to play. They now interpreted Frank's shouting at the TV to be calls for play as they answered his shouts with excited barking.

He growled with colorful adjectives, "Shut up!" Then Frank crushed an empty, aluminum beer can and whipped it at the dogs. The golden retriever puppies saw it as play and a toy to entertain them.

Then Frank rose from his seat and staggered into the kitchen for another beer. Popping the tab, he stopped dead to watch another poor play on the diamond. "You could have stolen base!"

An excited puppy rose on its hind legs and put its paws on Frank's legs. Outraged at what he interpreted as another stupid move by his team, Frank vented the frustration by cocking his right leg back and kicking the dog, like a football, into midair and on the other side of the family room.

Serious, internal damage had been done as the lifeless puppy lay on the ground. Its mother nervously approached and sniffed the tragic end. But Frank didn't care. The puppy deserved it. He left it to lie on the ground, a message to the mother that her puppies needed to be controlled. And at the end of the game, Stephanie had entered the family room. Frank belched, smashed his final, empty beer can on the end table and told his wife, "I think there's something wrong with the dog! Why don't you check it out?"

* * *

It was an unusually warm, Saturday afternoon in November with the thermometer at 65 degrees. Paul's mother put on her jogging shorts to enjoy a run on a day that was totally unheard of in Mapleview (for November). Playing with his friends and secret "Grave Robber club" outside, Paul was briefly called in the house by his stepfather to help move a large, awkward recliner chair from the family room and into the den.

But the chair would not fit, no matter how angled or flipped up-side-down it would be. Frank was becoming increasingly irate, producing the odor of metabolized beer that wafted through the air.

"Turn it this way, Pauly. Pauly, turn it this way. Hey, you payin' attention?" The chair was shoved in brut force but only smashed the boy's fingers.

Paul cried out, "Ah! Ouch! You crushed my fingers. It won't fit! I'm trying to tell you that the other end is too big!"

Frank dropped the chair on the floor, "You know Pauly, we're all alone and no one is here to see anything. I'm gettin' a little fed up with your crap and your smart mouth attitude." He dragged the recliner chair out of the way so he could get to the boy who ran into the corner, in cover, from his stepfather. "I think it's about time someone knocks the crap out of you!"

Paul's entire body was lifted over Frank's head and then thrown to the ground. Although the wind had been knocked out of the child who now gasped for air, Frank repeatedly picked him up and body slammed him to the floor; again, and again and again. Not satisfied with the beating, the large man knelt on the ground and proceeded to punch Paul's feet and twist his ankles. As Frank always said, "If you want to beat your wife or kids, you beat their feet. No one can see the bruising underneath shoes and socks."

Finally catching his breath, Paul screamed in agony from the twisting of his ankles. He managed to kick his stepfather over, get up and limp over to the corner of the room. But the monster quickly approached and repeatedly clobbered Paul's head with the bottoms of his muscular, tattooed forearms. Although the forearms didn't bruise Paul's head, it really hurt and caused a strained neck that was accompanied by a headache for a couple of days.

"When I tell you somethin', you listen!" Then Frank stormed over to the door in his testosterone and beer-fueled rage to yell out to Paul's friend, "Pauly's grounded for the day! You can go home now!"

Stephanie returned some time later to take sight of the recliner chair on its side near the entrance of the den. "Oh, were you moving that?"

Frank sat on the sofa, finishing his beer. "Yeah, I want you to help me move it in there. Your smart mouth kid is grounded. He wouldn't help me."

Stephanie was ordered in the den and told to take the other end of the recliner chair. But just as Paul had discovered, the entryway was not wide enough to accommodate the chair.

"Frank, it's too wide! Maybe if we take the door off the hinge?"

Snapping a reply of BS with colorful adjectives, Frank insisted that the chair could make it through. He used brut force to push the chair through. But Stephanie watched as the paint from the woodwork chipped which soon turned into torn wood with splinters sticking out.

"Frank, you're damaging the wall!"

It was a mistake that cost Stephanie dearly. She knew not to raise her voice to the man. The chair was dropped and then dragged out of Frank's way. Stephanie nervously apologized and ran over to the corner of the room. And just like Paul, she was picked up and slammed to the floor. Then he punched her feet in all his strength and twisted her ankles. From his bedroom, Paul could hear his mother screaming in torment. How he hated his drunken stepfather!

* * *

A surprise, early arrival home by Mrs. Greenstart, combined with her mysterious need to investigate the crawlspace, was taken as a warning by the boys. It was time to dispose of the mess that lay in the wooden chest. But disposing of their treasure took on a meaning that was different from simply disposing of a body just to avoid getting caught. The boys wanted one last party, the grand celebration of them all! Just about every possible abuse and mutilation had been done to the corpse and the boys had grown tired of it. But what could be done that would both dump the body to a new location, while at the same time serve as major entertainment?

The afternoon following Paul's severe beating, an outrageous suggestion had been provided. Although funny, the boys decided to take a serious risk with an end result that had the potential to permanently change the neighborhood, forever.

Now I don't think the reader can fully appreciate the near impossibility of the ghoulish plot. To begin with, there was no way that the wooden chest could be transported out of the crawlspace and to its final destination in one sweep. The project would require that it be done in steps. And if the boys could actually find the perfect moment to move the chest in these successive steps, the question remained if they actually had the strength to move it. There were two things that worked in their favor. Each of the boys was comfortable with handling the corpse. And it was mid-November which meant that darkness fell on the neighborhood by late afternoon.

Wasting not a moment, all 9 boys of the club gathered around the burial after school on Monday, and positioned ropes behind the woman's body. The woman alone probably weighed 130, or more, pounds. The old, wooden trunk probably added an additional 50 pounds. First lifting the corpse from her burial and then pulling the "coffin" from the ground eased the total weight required to lift.

The body was gradually carried to the stepladder and then all 9 boys stood around the entry, above, barely pulling the lifeless corpse up onto the kitchen floor. Little did the boys know that she lay very near the spot where Adahelm murdered her 30 years ago. The wooden chest was much easier to transport and lift up onto the kitchen floor. And while the 2nd step of transport went under way, Jeff remained in the crawlspace, filling the robbed grave with stones, only to discover that more needed to be taken from other areas of the storage space. He had to act quick! Mother would be home soon!

"Are you guys getting that thing out of here?" Jeff was frantic!

"Yeah, they're rolling it out behind the garage, now!" The "coffin" had been placed on a sheet of plywood which rested on a large, Radio Flyer wagon. Waiting just outside the backdoor, the corpse was successfully placed back in the wooden chest; the lid shut and then rolled out underneath a bush behind the garage. Not quite dark and soon time for the neighborhood kids to go home for dinner, the transporting project needed to be interrupted where it would wait for the next step.

With the crawlspace restored to normal, Jeff climbed back up to the kitchen, replaced the panel and noticed a collection of dirt, salt and yucky fluids spread along the floor. This would be an afternoon when Jeff thoroughly swept and mopped the floor before Mother arrived home. She warned him about sticky soda and juice. But this sort of mess might be the last straw. He often observed Mother use the disposable wet-mop cloths that were located under the kitchen sink.

In the middle of mopping, the sound of the garage door opening could be heard. Jeff scrubbed the area in such frenzy! It all had to be cleaned! But so what if she caught him mopping? He was expected to clean up after himself.

"Jeff are you okay?" Karen took sight of her son busily mopping an area near the pantry. She had never seen him take hold of a mop before.

"Sorry Mom; I spilled some soda on the floor."

* * *

Just like Jeff, Paul was unable to go out after dinner. But Paul's reason was different from Jeff's in that tonight was Monday which meant that his mother, Stephanie, would go to the gym for evening aerobics. His stepfather, Frank, slept in the late afternoon / evening hours which meant that it was necessary for Paul to remain at home and watch his younger siblings. He would, however, be part of the sinister plot as he needed to keep his younger brothers in another area of the house.

Just about all of the houses in Maple Sap are sprawling ranches. Some are on a slab; some have a crawlspace underneath. In the darkness of a November, early evening; seven members of the Grave Robbers club rolled a Radio Flyer wagon with a wooden chest across the street to their friend, Paul's, house. It was wheeled to the backdoor where pallbearers lifted the "coffin" from the wagon, and quietly moved the wagon and plywood into the house. The naked corpse was removed from the wooden chest and rested directly on the plywood in the house.

Some of the boys experienced Frank's flaring temper on the day he was disturbed from sleep and hurled a bowling ball through the wall. Needless to say, they were concerned that the man would wake up. But Paul insisted that his stepfather was usually passed out cold. 14 beers were counted in the trash can that afternoon, and his continuous snores verified deep sleep. With Paul and his siblings in the opposite wing of the house, seven pallbearers quietly rolled the wagon down the hall, and opened the door of Frank's bedroom. The smell of metabolized beer hung in the air.

Seven pallbearers summoned the strength to not only lift the naked, dead woman; but gently place her on the bed, next to Frank, while exercising caution not to wake him.

Keep in mind that the corpse had remained in that wooden chest for 30 years. The head and feet were elevated at the top, while the hips had sagged at the bottom. Setting the stiff corpse on the bed had caused her locked legs to pull the weight over so that she suddenly turned, causing the bed to shake. All the boys stopped breathing!

Frank awoke slightly and mumbled, "Whuh? You want some, Baby?"

Then he rolled over and spooned the naked corpse from behind with his hand over the mutilated breast. And just when the boys thought the end was near, Frank's snoring resumed!

The boys did everything in their power to hold back the laughter. They wheeled the wagon out the backdoor and burst out spasms of uncontrollable laughter. They ran down the street like a pack of wild hyenas with the Radio Flyer literally flying behind them! The wooden chest was brought to the neighborhood park where it was dumped in the drainage pond. In celebration of a mission accomplished, the seven boys cheered out, "Grave Robbers Anonymous!"

* * *

9:00 in the evening, Stephanie opened the door of her bedroom to awaken drunken Frank for work. Paul was getting ready for bed, but listened attentively to the activities of the room next door.

"Frank?"

"Hmm…"

"Frank, you need to wake up for work."

"Frank, who do you have in bed with you?"

The click of the light switch could be heard followed by a gasp and scream from Mother. A thud sound indicated that Frank had jumped out of bed. It was followed by a series of profanity as the confused man tried to process what he was seeing. "What is *that? Is that thing real? Is that **real? It's real! Pauly, get in here!**"

Mother argued back, "Frank, are you out of your mind? You think he did this? You think he found a corpse and put it in bed with you while you were sleeping?"

There was no other explanation as Frank argued back, "**Well how did it get there?**"

All Frank and Stephanie could do was stare in numbing shock at the naked, mummified, female corpse that lay in their bed. Its fingers had been cut off and stuck in the mouth. Screwdrivers had been jammed into the eye sockets. And paint roller sticks had been inserted throughout various orifices. How would such a thing end up in their bed? Even worse, who would have abused a corpse in such a disturbing manner?

Bill and Karen Greenstart watched from their living room window as swarms of police cars and other emergency vehicles parked up and down the street. Karen wasn't sure why, but she suspected that, somehow, Jeff was involved.

* * *

And so was nearly a decade in Stephanie's life. It was a decade that started as a wife and young mother; married to a kind and patient gentleman. It would draw to a close; married to a drunken, abusive monster that slept with a mutilated corpse! The relationship between her son, Paul, and second husband, Frank, had grown increasingly worse so that Paul moved out of state to be with his own father and his new family. But Stephanie's story was far from over! A couple years later, she would contribute to another disappearance in the town of Mapleview.

Chapter 18

Certainly a mysterious character who lived in one of the apartment complexes of downtown Mapleview, those who took sight of Steve Coldsworth might have wanted to know more about him. Outside of a uniquely-creative, starving and frustrated artist, what did he do? Surely he must have worked.

Traveling through Mapleview each day; past the Trivelli house, past Hotlicks where Route 4 begins; Steve further ventured to a rural, farm-like community just outside of Sillmac that was home to a major sawmill and lumber distribution warehouse. This was Steve's place of employment.

Work was not too important for Steve. He couldn't be bothered with the small, miscellaneous tasks as a warehouse associate. His manager noticed that Steve appeared unmotivated and easily distracted while exhibiting occasional, poor workmanship. Such an employee couldn't be trusted with high-tech machinery that could damage precious, raw materials or cause fatalities. The easily distracted, frustrated artist was given duties such as stacking lumber, transporting bundles to the warehouse floor and sweeping when needed.

It was a fine, September morning with October a day-or-so away; and a couple weeks since the disappearance of the Hotlicks girl, Kelly. Steve turned onto the main road of Mapleview on his way to work. Some distance down the road a pair of gorgeous, muscular legs jogged. They belonged to middle-aged wife and mother, Stephanie. (It was at least over a year since the corpse had been discovered sleeping with her husband) If there was ever a woman who maintained her youthful exuberance while finding a means to freeze time, Stephanie would fit that description. But outside of a pair of legs that would look perfect on the Tree Goddess painting, Steve knew nothing of the woman.

Steve couldn't help but wonder, "Who is she? Where does she live? Where could I see her again, preferably close enough for study and examination?"

Time was running out for another possibility of studying the subject's legs, for the days were getting cooler, and autumn was pretty much in the air. Soon, the woman might not be able to wear shorts to expose her beautiful legs and thighs.

Steve spent that morning of inspiration at work, stacking small 4' x 4' cuts of plywood and then binding them for delivery. Through the monotonous, mindless task, the frustrated artist was able to remain obsessed with the woman who jogged as he realized that finding legs for the Tree Goddess wouldn't be as easy as finding the arms. Legs had to be strong enough to support the weight of a tree. A pair of muscular thighs and legs was ideal; but they couldn't be too thick as the limbs needed to suggest graceful femininity. Stephanie's legs had both qualities of muscle and that of being a woman. How he wished to see this woman again!

This day of discovering Stephanie's legs was a Thursday. With one final weekend of somewhat warm conditions forecasted for Mapleview, Steve had to find the mystery woman within the next couple of days. But how? It would require diligent search and stalking. It might involve calling in sick the following day in hopes to see the woman running. Then he could carefully follow behind and learn of where she lived. But it was still only chance as success depended on the mere possibility that the mystery woman was a stay-at-home mom, never leaving for work. Considering the importance of his new master-piece, Steve left work at his usual quitting time with the decision in mind to call off sick the following day.

6:00 am Friday morning, the obsessed artist drove up and down the main road of Mapleview in search of the beautiful, gorgeous legs that jogged only yesterday. Maybe she took a different route that day. She had to live nearby! Maybe her residence was in the tree-lined, single-family-home subdivision of Maple Sap. But a drive through the winding roads and cul-de-sacs would produce no encounter of the jogging woman who possessed the legs of a goddess.

Discouragement needed defeat! Steve took the day off in a sacrifice for his art and he couldn't give up now. The possibility that Friday mornings wouldn't involve the ritual of jogging could not spell the end for his search. He was determined to find the woman, even if it meant seeing her in a car driving to work. If needed, Steve would follow the woman to her place of work, wait for the day to end and then follow her home for further stalking.

For Steve, that Friday morning would be the Mapleview 500! His search followed a repeated route that went up and down the main road, through the apartment complex, through the winding subdivision of Maple Sap, through the business streets in town and around back to the main road. The sun continued to rise in the sky; morning commuters cluttered the roadways; and children stood at the bus stops. There was still no sign of the jogging woman.

9:00 am, the streets had cleared of commuters and school buses. By now, Steve was devastated with despair upon the realization that he would not find his study. The persistence of cruising the Mapleview 500 was soon a devotion that enslaved the obsessed artist. Although he may have lost the chance to study the woman's legs, he still had the undying determination of an artist. Vincent Van Goah cut off his ear to show love for a woman. Steve would die of starvation in a relentless search for his jogger woman.

Then, in an unbelievable reward for purely, mad obsession; Steve found his study (Stephanie) at the local park in the sub-division of Maple Sap. It was 10:15 in the morning and she appeared to have taken a small child, perhaps her son, to the park. Whatever her reason for being there, Steve needed to act quick and come close to those beautiful legs.

Parking his car down the street, he inconspicuously walked over to the playground and to the monkey bar area where the jogger's apparent child played. His plan was to blend in as another parent who might have been visiting the park with his own kids. In an effort to be convincing, his right hand saluted over both eyes to block the sun as he gazed in the distance for his imaginary children. Appearing satisfied, Steve was now at ease and then turned to the small child who played on the monkey bars. "Are you big enough to go across that yourself?"

The little boy gave the strange man a blank stare and watched as he turned to Mommy to give a friendly, "Hi."

Mommy cautiously returned the greeting with a short, "Hi" of her own. To the little boy, the situation looked ordinary and went back to his play on the monkey bars.

Although Steve may have felt avoided, he persisted in his small talk with the woman in shorts. "Man, it's a beautiful day out here. I love having Fridays off, and my kids like when I have it off, too. This is supposed to be the final weekend of nice weather."

Stephanie only nodded with an uninterested smile and walked a few feet to a wide-open area. She didn't know who Steve was and didn't care. She wasn't at the park to socialize with some strange guy, only there to let her kid play while she did leg exercises. But little did Stephanie know that the mini-workout was the perfect opportunity for the gawking artist to fully study every line and curve of her lower limbs. Each step the woman took while dropping her knee to the ground showed the well, defined tone and highly developed muscle.

Stephanie returned to the monkey bars with colored face of circulation while masking her discomfort of being watched by halfheartedly smiling at Steve.

It was misinterpreted as friendliness and provided the quirky artist the confidence to draw near the woman and provide a compliment. "If you don't mind me saying, you have some really, nice legs. I can tell you exercise them and keep them muscular."

"Why thank you!" Certainly open to receiving compliments on her legs, Stephanie warmed up to Steve, even smiled with a hint of a blush. But it was soon replaced with angst as the strange man quickly knelt down to fully caress her things and legs.

"I mean they are just gorgeous!"

Stephanie was livid, "Whoa, whoa! You don't need to touch my legs! Do you want me to call my husband?" She grabbed her son who cried out in defiance that he wasn't done playing. Then she set him down in another area of the park where the boy continued to whine while mommy pulled out her cell phone.

While studying the woman's legs from a distance, Steve became acutely aware of the chirping of birds surrounding the park. A single engine plane passed overhead which mesmerized the artist to the point of viewing the activities of his surroundings through a panoramic, high-definition screen. Very much confused and perturbed of the sensation, Steve was only pulled closer into the vision until he stood before the woman's bed as she slept. Being ever-so-careful not to wake the oblivious dreamer, he slowly pulled her hands onto the pillow and secured them to the bedposts with a chain of nylon tie wraps—one of the strongest ties known to man. The woman could struggle with all her might, but the nylon would be impossible to break!

Next, a blindfold was carefully applied to her head so that it covered her eyes. With the sleeping woman now fully secured and blinded, Steve pulled back the blankets which revealed her sleepwear to be nothing more than a t-shirt and panties. It provided full access to her warm, silky thighs and legs as Steve caressed, rubbed and squeezed in all his delight. Of course this provoked startled screams as the helpless woman, unable to see, fought desperately with the only limbs she had free. But Steve had a firm lock on each thigh, kneeling in between, and maintaining them at his sides. He continued squeezing and caressing while she screamed in horror, obviously unnerved with the inability to see her attacker.

* * *

"Yes! He was holding my thighs! He's still here!"

The angry voice of Stephanie pulled Steve out of his panoramic vision. What was he playing with? Ever since accepting the challenge to create the Tree Goddess painting, many unexplained sensations and visions overpowered Steve. This was the most frightening of them all, placing him in the driver's seat of some twisted crime. As his logic and bearings slowly restored, Steve was soon hit with the realization that an outside party was being contacted to handle the curious assault in the park. It was time to leave!

And quickly he did! Steve ran at top flight to his car. But Frank's voice could be heard from some distance away, "Hey! Hey you! Where are you going? You like touchin' my wife?"

Stephanie shouted to Steve from the park, "There he is! There's my husband!" Intuitively, Steve turned his head towards a group of houses where a shirtless, muscular man ran towards the park. Steve barely made it to his car! As the ignition turned over and the engine made the familiar, "vroom", the furious man banged at the closed window. But he was too late; the car peeled off and the strange, quirky artist was able to assault Frank's wife without consequence.

Chapter 19

Poor Mary; stricken with guilt for allowing her younger, misguided and misunderstood cousin to suddenly leave on a short note. Although family didn't seem to cast blame on her, Mary couldn't help but feel responsible for the disappearance and a possible worse reality. It was Mary, after all, who invited Kelly to come stay at the Trivelli house while becoming established in the rural town of Mapleview. And really Mary didn't mind the additional company. Kelly could have stayed as long as desired, indefinitely for that matter. Her presence provided a comfort on those many nights when Daren was out of state. And although not close in earlier years, Kelly was gradually becoming a friend to Mary. Why did she have to go away so quickly?

On a late, brisk, September evening with October a day-or-so away; Mary stood outside while overlooking her deck with the moon rising over the Hidden Lake Forest Preserve. In the distance was the familiar call of wolves—old friends of Mary. It wasn't until after discovering Grandma Trivelli's skeletal hand in the vase, that Mary realized not one shred of hostility was ever projected onto those wolves. She should have been fearful of them and hated them. But maybe some part of Mary knew that the large beasts had never taken Grandma. Perhaps the call always served as a reminder of a truth yet to be known.

The distant call was most likely foreign to Kelly, being that she originated from the city. Perhaps Kelly witnessed the beautiful call when leaving Hotlicks for the night. But as far as Mary was concerned, the sound was most appreciated while standing over the Hidden Lake Forest Preserve, restoring a sense of peace and renewal. She listened for a while and then retired for the evening, another night alone with Daren out of state.

It was such a peculiar environment to dream of in the late night hours during October's approach. Mary knelt on the ground on a warm, spring day while planting flowers along a garden that perimetered her backyard. Just then, Kelly emerged from around Daren's mausoleum.

"Mary?" The call was urgent with a face of distress.

Not aware that she was dreaming, Mary stood up and quickly approached her lost cousin. "Kelly, where have you been?"

The face produced by Kelly had not been seen in many years. Only when Kelly was a young girl would such an expression of horrific distress be made after scraping her knee or some injury that terrifies a child. "Mary? I'm so sorry!" Her face contorted as it shifted to a sob.

Being the nurturing woman that Mary is, she quickly embraced her cousin and offered a shoulder to cry on. "What is it? What happened?"

"I'm just so sorry!"

"Oh, it's okay. Whatever you did, it couldn't be that bad."

Obviously concerned, Mary secretly wondered what her cousin could have possibly done. And in the peculiar, mechanical laws of dream-world, Kelly suddenly escaped the comforting embrace so that she now stood before Mary and spoke in a clear warning, *"Daren!"*

The announcement startled Mary awake in a tremor that could only be broken with the click of her nightstand lamp. Now sitting upright and trying to shake the dream's eerie sensation, she began to ponder the meaning. Such a cruel suggestion of her subconscious; a late night visit from Kelly could only mean one thing. And how much denial covered Mary? Perhaps the dream was only a revelation of something she already knew of Daren.

Only 4:21 am, Mary had nearly 2 hours of sleep remaining before awakening for work. And she wasn't about to telephone Daren over a silly dream. He'd kill her over a late night call, especially when rest was needed to make sales at whatever biomedical convention he attended that week. Aside from that, asking her husband a question or two in person would serve a better gauge of his honesty. Mary could only turn off the light, close her eyes and hope for another dream or two (not of Kelly) before awakening for work.

* * *

Silent suspicion only stews within. Fortunately for Mary, she was a well-grounded person and kept further suspicions from flaring while speaking on the phone throughout the week with Daren. Oh, she'd ask a bothersome question such as, "So how was your night?" or "Did you go anywhere in the evening for entertainment?" But his answers were mostly boring, suggesting that he ate dinner alone and watched TV in the hotel room. Is that all his life was, selling some CAT scan machine during the day while eating at the hotel restaurant, alone, in the evening? How long can one endure tiresome hours of watching whatever paid programming a hotel room had to offer? Daren was the sort of man who could not stay in one place for too long. Extended hours being confined to indoors would certainly cause the man to grow irritable. So what did Mary's husband do for entertainment?

Daren came home the Friday afternoon of that week while Mary was still at the flower shop. To surprise his sorely, missed wife with a Friday night celebration of his return, Daren stopped at Lee's Chinese Tacos and Pizza.

Lee's Chinese Tacos and Pizza is an interesting twist on our favorite, American fast foods. The dishes offered are somewhat similar to Mexican tacos and Italian pizzas, except they are better! It's literally chop suey on a taco or pizza! And don't forget the egg-foo-young burritos! The TV commercial that advertises the restaurant to Mapleview and surrounding areas features the proud, elderly, Chinese owner who speaks before the camera, "Lee's Chinese Tacos and Pizza is a healthy alternative to eating because you never see fat Chinese people!"

Upon Mary's arrival home, she was surprised with two pizzas: a large chop suey and a large chow mein. Greeted by a loving kiss, Mary sat down at the candlelit table and pulled away at pizza that was infested with bean sprouts, water chestnuts and pea pods. She would have been happy with a regular cheese and sausage, but perhaps Daren was trying to eat healthy.

Daren was in such a good mood, speaking of the successful week in Santa Fe, but also of how great it was to be home with his lovely wife. And they made love, beautiful as ever! It reminded Mary of how "made for each other" they truly were.

In the hours past midnight while Daren lay beside her sleeping, Mary pulled out of the evening's first REM and watched her husband while thinking of their Friday night together. She recalled a strange vibration, almost deliberate of Daren that suggested any questions of suspicion would be inappropriate. It was almost a mental control, sort of a subliminal brainwashing. Most likely, this skill would have been acquired in the years of gaining trust from potential purchasers of biomedical equipment.

So what was Daren thinking? What was he hiding? They were questions that nagged at Mary throughout the night while drifting in and out of dreams. By early morning, she awoke and head downstairs to brew coffee. Daren's little Friday night celebration of his return was over, and it was time for a long, overdue, heart-to-heart talk. In the additional two hours that her husband slept, Mary rehearsed all the scenarios thought of in response to one simple question of truth.

Eventually his footsteps could be heard descending the stairs. Daren greeted his wife with a cheerful "good morning" followed by, "Saturday morning coffee! And I bet it's the ole Trivelli recipe, huh?" He was referring to Mary's ability to make what many have described as the best coffee ever tasted. It was some secret, family technique of brewing that Mary had sworn to secrecy. But on this Saturday morning the compliment was unnecessary.

Mary quickly responded, "Yeah I brewed it so we can have a little talk this morning. You want to sit down?"

Daren was surprised, "Sure, okay. It's Saturday morning and I though we'd go for a bike ride before you left work." He pulled the chair close to the table, "So what's up? What do you want to talk about?"

Mary took a sip of her coffee, "Did you do something with Kelly while she was living here?"

Daren followed with a nervous sip from his cup, but it wasn't the coffee that opened his eyes wider! "Excuse me? Like what? Go through her panties drawer? Say something rude to make her leave?"

Just as anticipated, Mary's husband was going to dance around in riddles, but she had a backup plan. "Daren, did you have sex with Kelly while she lived here?"

Now he set the cup down while exhaling, "What brought that on? This is what you wanted to talk about? I mean I can't believe you would ask me something like that."

This was one of the things that Mary disliked of her husband. How she wished the man could have had a heart-to-heart talk without appearing to be some dishonest politician who indirectly answers questions with roundabout statements and questions of his own. Mary projected a fierce glare while sternly asking, "Daren, I would appreciate a simple yes or no answer!"

He violently shook his head in outrage while gently reaching his hand forward to pull the answer out, "*No!* I can't believe you! I surprise you with a little celebration last night along with some great sex, and I wake up to this! You know, I work hard out there! You think it's a party once I leave out of state? I don't have time to fool around with your cousin and I don't have time to waste on something petty like this!" Daren paused while watching the tears stream down Mary's eyes. He made his impact and it was now time to close. I assume you're working today?"

Mary shook her head, yes.

"Good; well, you better get ready! *I'm* going for a Saturday bike ride. *My* time home is too precious to be bothered with silly accusations from you!" Then he stepped away leaving his half-finished cup of coffee, and Mary to sort through the aftermath while feeling ashamed of herself.

There was no need to call out goodbye to his wife as she showered; Mary was being punished for the day. Before jumping on his bicycle, a quick breakfast of Pop Tarts (plate, wrapper and crumbs left on the table) was eaten along with a glass of orange juice (glass left on the table as well). Skip the coffee! Daren was in no mood for Mary's special, Trivelli recipe; not today. Maybe he could stop in town for a cup at the Mapleview Coffeehouse.

Oh, but how could he forget? A quick dash was made upstairs. The sound of Mary's blow dryer behind the closed, bathroom door indicated it was safe to enter the bedroom. One certainly can't go for a bike ride without some cash! Maybe Daren could go on an extended bike ride and enjoy lunch afterwards.

Sorting through the collection of bills, a stack of 100s was grabbed. Nah, that won't have the right effect. A stack of 20s would be more impressive; maybe $500 worth would make an impressive roll. And to add to the genuine appearance, a handful of 10s, some 5s and some singles from his wallet were added. There, now Daren could go for a bike ride!

Coasting down the long, Trivelli driveway and peddling along the main road of Mapleview; Daren approached downtown where he often enjoyed the scenery along with residents and tourists alike. Leaves were already falling from trees; browns and golds highlighted the edges of roads. Since being married, Daren was developing a slight gut which he attributed to his wife's down-home cooking. Of course it wouldn't be all that beer that he drank! Fortunately for today, he wore a light jacket to cover the slight protrusion.

One scenic part of his usual route was the winding streets of Maple Sap. Daren coasted along the midmorning neighborhood where he took sight of a nice-looking blond (Stephanie), playing with her son at the park. Certainly worth checking out, he made a momentary stop near the area where she stood, just to take a hearty guzzle from his bottle of natural spring water.

Refreshed, he called out to the small boy and mother, "Let's see you go across those bars! Come on!"

Stephanie took sight of the tall, dark and handsome stranger who stood so athletic near his bike. *Where did he come from?* Interested, she laughed.

The small boy watched as the stranger approached who continued to encourage his swinging across the bars.

Stephanie spoke to the stranger, "He loves doing this!"

Then she encouraged her son, "Go ahead; show him how you can go across!"

With mommy's reassurance that the stranger was safe, the little boy took hold of the monkey bars and swung from one to the next, each bar leaving his hands increasingly tired. 3/4 of the way, he could no longer endure the exhaustion and let go. But Daren applauded and congratulated for a job well done.

Then Daren stuck out his hand in a gesture of greeting towards Mommy, "I'm Daren!"

"Stephanie!" She did the same.

"So your son's a gymnast?"

Stephanie laughed, "No, he'd like to sign up. He loves watching the high beam on TV."

And then Daren spoke of his imaginary children. "Yeah, my two daughters are in gymnastics. You know the generic building in town that says,"Gymnastics"? That's where they go."

Stephanie was impressed, "Really? That's great! My son would love to go, but I keep telling him someday."

"Well what are you waiting for, Mom?" Daren knew Stephanie like a book in those few seconds of exchanged words as he quickly glanced at her left hand to make sure she wore a wedding ring. And just like clockwork, Stephanie would mention that finances were tight and gymnastics lessons were not in the budget.

And while she spoke, Daren reached into his front pocket and flipped out his massive wad of cash while counting it, making sure it was in Stephanie's face. He put the bills back in his front pocket and looked up at Stephanie, just to make sure she wore a face of disbelief. But her sunglasses made it difficult to interpret. Still, he continued to lay on the enticement. "Forgive me for saying, but I always found it a shame when a man cannot afford the simple necessities of raising a child. I mean your kid wants to take gymnastics lessons, and your husband can't even afford that? That's so sad."

Flipping out money to entice women was 2nd nature for Daren. Early in his career, he formed an unusual, paradoxical belief that exposed the secrets behind what motivated men and women. Men, Daren believed, were driven by one thing and one thing only: sex! That man-part often referred to as a "compass needle" was most appropriate in Daren's philosophy. The very chase of women led to the purpose, direction, careers and family life of a man. Women, on the other hand, were motivated by something else. The very sight of Benjamin Franklin on a green promissory note that says $100 would put the silk on a lady's panties in Daren's world.

Visiting countless, late night hotel bars where traveling business women sat alone; Daren learned through experience that it wasn't good looks and muscles that tickled a woman's fancy. They sat there, so innocent, sitting pretty while sipping a cocktail. Many of these women were married and showed no desire for sex as they got plenty of that at home. Mr. Husband was already good-looking with charming personality. Daren needed something that Mr. Husband didn't have, something to give him that edge.

On many occasions, Daren would walk past a 30-something blonde who was dressed in her business attire. Immediately he pulled out a thick wad of cash, "What are you drinking?"

Her pheromones would suddenly spike as the scent of fresh bills flipped in the tall, dark stranger's hand. She would sit up and tightly close her legs together, "A strawberry daiquiri!"

Then Daren would yell out to the bar tender, "Get this lady another drink; and I'll have a martini!" Now with his foot definitely in the door, it was easy to lay on the charm and intrigue while offering tales of traveling the globe, people met and activities experienced. Daren often considered learning Spanish so he could mimic a Columbian accent. A tall, dark stranger with money and an accent; a woman would literally drag such a man to her own hotel room! Still, Daren was satisfied with the results.

Once-upon-a-time, the money-love-struck blond in business attire would have never thought of accompanying a stranger to his hotel room. She loved Mr. Husband and declared before family, church and God to remain faithful to him through the years, for richer or for poorer. But time unfolded and she grew wiser while learning the true meaning of financial strain. Her "compass needle" would become the scent of crisp, fresh cash. And it wouldn't be necessary for a man such as Daren to share any with her. Simply possessing the smell of money was powerful enough to cause the woman to remove her own clothes.

And Daren's compass needle certainly took delight in knowing that another precious marriage had been corrupted.

Now on this fine, Saturday morning; he stood before Stephanie, taking pity on her because Mr. Husband didn't have the money. "Tell you what; I'll do you a favor. Your kid wants to take gymnastics lessons? I'll pay for it!" Daren would financially support Stephanie in many ways including mortgage, utilities, groceries and clothes for her kids; even the clothes on her own husband's back! Daren was a man with money who was looking to buy an alternate wife in town for those moments when Mary was not so pleasant.

But Stephanie wasn't one of those late night tramps in a hotel bar, looking for sex on the road. She said what any decent woman would say, "No, that's okay; I don't think so."

"Awe, come on; it's nothing! Your kid wants to take gymnastics!"

She was growing impatient, "No! I'm fine!"

Just then, Stephanie's cell phone rang. "Hello…? What…? No…! He just came over here…! Nothing…! Fine; goodbye!" Putting the phone back in her pocket, she looked up at Daren. "You know; I just want to thank you! That was my husband, and we live in those houses over there. He saw you talking to me, and now I have to go home!" She grabbed her son and walked away.

But the chase wasn't over for Daren. "You want me to talk to him for you?"

But the chase was over for Stephanie as a slight beating awaited her at home. She knew better than to talk to strangers, especially after being assaulted not more than a week ago. She angrily replied, "You don't want to meet him!"

* * *

About a week passed and Daren was out of town.

October officially begins the season of Halloween for Mary. Maintaining the family tradition of elaborate, seasonal decorations; a weekend with Daren on the road was the perfect opportunity to bring a sense of autumn festiveness to the home. Starting with pumpkin-spiced candles, autumn-harvest centerpieces and outdoor, decorative corn displays; a touch of Halloween was soon added with colorful bat lights, ghostly decorations and an assortment of carved pumpkins with candles. You've got to love Mary! She went all out with seasonal and holiday decorating, and the Trivelli house probably hadn't seen the likes of it for many years.

Ah, but the stigmatism of the Trivelli house! With the ghostly, creepy displays that invite the mood of Halloween, some might say that Mary was doing poorly to erase the bad reputation of the house. But in Mary's opinion, that was just nonsense! Halloween is a fun holiday that brings warmth to the season and a reason to celebrate.

And so she carved her final pumpkin in the late, Sunday afternoon hours. Halloween was under a month away. How could she carve pumpkins so early in the season when they would only rot? Her secret to prevent this? For a modest price, realistic-looking, foam pumpkins were purchased at the Mapleview Arts and Crafts store. Already hollow, they only needed to be carved with a Dremel tool and candle placed inside. This particular pumpkin was to go out in the backyard, near Daren's mausoleum, exactly where Kelly had emerged with her look of distress.

Of course Mary forgave her! Whatever Daren had done, he should have been the bigger person. In the spring, Mary planned on planting some white tulips in the area as a symbol of her forgiveness.

Chapter 20

"Mommy, can I sleep with you tonight?"

"No I'm sorry, Honey. You're a big boy now, and old enough to sleep by yourself." Stephanie tucked her youngest child, Sean, into bed on a crisp night in October. Although he posed many arguments and negotiations to stay up longer or sleep in Mommy's bed, Stephanie was firm with the child. His older brother wasn't staying up late or sleeping with Mommy. The same treatment should have been given to Sean. Besides that; once the children were tucked into bed for the night, Stephanie enjoyed her quiet time with a nice cup of hot cocoa.

Thankfully, the furnace had been repaired which meant the unmentionable calling from the grave was no longer heard. And for the thing hidden in the closet, perhaps it was time for Stephanie to finally get rid of it. She thought of visiting Brad's grave and somehow burying it nearby. But then his eyes would most likely be felt along with a silent persuasion to confess to her horrific crime. Burying it under the dead tree trunk where he had lost it would be the next best thing. But again, Brad's presence would most likely be felt in the whisper of trees or the sounds of animals that stirred in the forest. Probably the best thing to do would be to whip it out her car window on Creek Highway, and let nature bury it. But what if a hiker discovered it? Stephanie's DNA was all over the thing and... Well, it was certainly no easy task to get rid of body part!

Some time passed as Stephanie took a relaxing shower, slipped into a comfy nightgown and replaced the lights with the glow of an autumn-scented candle. Halloween was less than 30 days away, and the time was near to drag out the decorations and prepare for trick-or-treaters. Soon the orange, purple and green glows of Halloween decorations would illuminate quiet evening moments alone.

Stephanie sat down with her cherished cup of hot cocoa, listening to the sounds of treasured silence. At the other end of the house, Sean was halfway in slumber as he experienced an interruption of his peaceful rest with one of those unpleasant nightmares that are incomprehensible to a logical mind.

A ticking noise could be heard in the dream, similar to that of a pocket watch. Along with this, a large boulder drew closer to Sean's face with every tick until he shook out of his sleep in a desperate attempt to avoid getting hit. Now awake and distressed from the bad dream, Sean quickly rolled out of bed in a simultaneous hop to the floor with a full intention to run towards Mommy for comfort.

But Mommy could be heard from the family room, making bloodcurdling screams. The terror of the nightmare and the now reality that Mommy was in danger overwhelmed the little boy in a pendulum that swung from one fear to the next. Her screams grew softer as Sean approached the family room. And upon finally reaching the place where Mommy was supposed to be, he only discovered the glass, patio door open which allowed the cold, night air in.

Mommy was out there! Under normal circumstances, a terrified boy who was under the influence of hypnagogia would never enter the night world alone. But the light of his world had escaped outside, and the need to find her increased with every second of desperation.

The small boy ran out into the night crying in a panic, "Mommy? Mommy? Mommy?" The cold, autumn air ripped through his pajamas. Instinctively, he followed the concrete patio onto the small sidewalk that led to the driveway. Down the driveway he ran where he turned left and followed the neighborhood sidewalk, all the while calling out for Mommy.

4 doors down, Mrs. Stanhill pulled into her own driveway where she took sight of the small boy. The poor child was in need of comfort and possibly in danger. Mrs. Stanhill called out, "Sean?"

Being a familiar face in the neighborhood with the ability to be nurturing, Sean collided and embraced the woman. Tears and mucus were wiped against her coat.

"Sean, Honey, what are you doing out here?" Needless to say, Mrs. Stanhill concluded something tragic had happened and was affected by the child's anxiety.

"My Mommy is gone!"

"She's gone?"

* * *

Pulling into the neighborhood on a Monday morning after a long night from his job, it was necessary for Frank to park his car some houses away as numerous police cars and other emergency vehicles crowded the street near his home. He ran up to the house as any startled spouse would and yelled out to the police officer who greeted him, "What's going on? I live here! This is my house!"

The children were okay, but the house was now a crime scene that was taped off by police line barricades. Stephanie was missing. And the evidence inside that remained suggested foul play. This was one morning that Frank would be unable to drown the sorrows of his night job over half-dozen or more beers.

Inside, Detectives Tom and Larry evaluated the only evidence available: muddy shoe prints that led from the corn field to the inside of the house; a scented candle that now burned near the bottom; and a cup of cocoa that had been spilled on the carpeting, cup laying on its side.

These sights along with the information supplied by the little boy, Sean, led Detective Tom to state the obvious. "Well, there's no denying it; the patio door was left unlocked and the intruder surprised her by coming in. She didn't get far."

This conclusion was made from the story told by the muddy foot prints. They showed exactly where in the family room Stephanie had been taken and showed the struggle as she was removed from her home. And the cup that lay on its side had been further knocked into and rolled to another area of the floor as it didn't lie near the stain of cocoa. Stephanie had been dragged out the patio door, back into the cornfield (or should be called "soybean field" as the farmer alternated soy and corn each year) and then dragged about a half-block to where the field met road.

In avoiding barefoot contact with cold, wet grass; Sean followed the patio sidewalk to the driveway. Had he turned the opposite direction, he might have seen his mother being dragged off! No blood found in her path of dragging, the question remained if Stephanie was still alive. Police were already questioning neighbors of any unusual activity in the previous evening hours.

Suddenly, a voice emerged at the entrance of the room. "Detective Tom, Larry; gentlemen, I think you need to see this." An investigative force had been searching Frank and Stephanie's home for any clues. The most startling and bizarre discovery had been found in the bedroom closet, on the shelf, behind a collection of boxes. Detectives Tom and Larry followed the lead into the bedroom where an open shoe box sat on the dresser. Inside the box was the preserved part that had been taken from Brad nearly a decade ago.

And let that be a lesson to the reader: Most of us will never murder or have gruesome secrets hiding in our closets. But do dispose of unwanted items wished not to be found when you are gone. Imagine the faces and reactions of your loved ones!

Part Three: Hello?

Chapter 21

Mapleview Road is the main road that travels through town. It runs north and south, beginning from the southerly border, but eventually curves east just beyond the Hidden Lake Forest Preserve where it travels past Hotlicks Sports Bar and Grill and crosses Creek Highway. From there it changes its name to Route 4 where the road stretches towards Sillmac.

Homes located north of downtown Mapleview are often historical (such as the Trivelli house). Although there are two newer subdivisions in the mostly historic area of Mapleview, the older homes of this section do not belong to any particular subdivision. These are embedded along the heavily wooded region as if they were part of the forest preserves.

Maple Sap was one of the first official subdivisions of the area which is located in downtown Mapleview. But just as any city or town, new neighborhoods are created which offer bigger and better homes. Circle Point would have been the 2nd official subdivision that was part of Mapleview. Known for its main drive that circles along the neighborhood, there are 4 streets that dissect the area encompassed by Circle Drive. And what makes this particular neighborhood interesting is the fact that single-family homes are located on the west side of the dissecting streets while duplexes run on the east side. All residences that sit on Circle Drive are exclusively single-family homes.

This is the neighborhood where Sara lived, a young woman who rightfully earned the recognition as a contributor to the mass development and improvement to Mapleview's economy. For decades the area was one of those independent, small towns with nothing more than some basic stores, a couple of churches, schools, necessary places of business and other municipal offices. Aside from that, nothing was in Mapleview! There was no reason to even travel through the town on vacation, outside of stopping for fuel and a quick bite to eat. But then a great transformation took place which suddenly gave Mapleview the appearance of being the ideal vacation spot. Surrounded by deep wilderness, it now serves as an oasis of every shop, restaurant and luxury. Why wouldn't people want to visit?

Aside from a 4 year stay at an out-of-state university, Sara lived in Mapleview her entire life. And once-upon-a-time, she lived in the area north of downtown where, as a little girl, she could safely peddle her bike to the Hidden Lake Forest Preserve. And she remembered with clarity the tunnel that had once been blocked by chain link on both sides.

A roaring stream, likened to a small river, rolls through the center of Hidden Lake Forest Preserve as it joins with the small lake. Some decades ago, improvements had been done to route the water and prevent flooding to the walking trails. A large hole, 8 feet in diameter, was carved through a large ravine and filled with a concrete tunnel so that the water could be channeled from the natural stream and guided under the ravine. To prevent possible transfer of debris from one area of the forest to another, chain link was cemented to both sides of the tunnel. This unnecessary blockade had been removed some years later, as it only accumulated forest debris at the incoming down flow side of the tunnel; sometimes clogging the flow of water where it would rise to undesired levels. In fact, the decision to remove the chain link was driven by a very, frightening event that had residents of Mapleview outraged.

For Sara, it was her first moment of terror experienced in life. Peddling her bike down the entrance of Hidden Lake Forest Preserve, the little girl traveled to the bank of the rolling stream with the purpose of collecting small stones and pebbles. While filling a cloth sack of her precious gems, the sensation of a rain drop could be felt on her nose. It was soon followed by a tiny rain drop that fell on her arm. Hearing thunder way off in the distance, it was easy for little Sara to conclude that rain was on the way. The darkened sky which rolled the colors of alarming danger in the horizon suggested urgency for Sara to return home. Thunder was terrifying, and it was best to seek shelter indoors and behind curtains where she could run to Mother for comfort if frightened.

Just then, the cries of a boy nearby could be heard, "Hey! Help! Help me! I can't get out of here!"

Pausing momentarily to look in the direction of the cries, Sara found that a boy had been trapped inside the tunnel, imprisoned behind the chain link that was cemented on the outsides. Hoping to find turtles, snakes or other reptiles, the boy managed to stand on top of the tunnel and wedge himself through a damaged part of the chain link located on top. Unfortunately, he lacked the strength to pull himself out and had been trapped for nearly 6 hours.

Sara remained petrified for a brief moment. At such a young age, she was easily overpowered by fear and quickly raced off on her bike with raindrops spiking her face and neck throughout the short ride home. Sara left the bike in the corner of the garage and ran to the safety of her bedroom where the jewels of the pebble hunt could be inspected.

All afternoon it rained and rained. Puddles accumulated on the sidewalks while gutters routed lakes of water into the sewers. Occasionally, the boy trapped in the tunnel appeared in Sara's imagination. But she quickly removed the thoughts with the self reminder that it wasn't her that was trapped. "Stupid boy; what was he doing in that tunnel, anyway?"

A child's imagination forms many strange beliefs and ideas. As Mother poured glasses of water from the tap and set them on the table for dinner, the young child imagined that the stream in the woods was somehow connected to the kitchen faucet. In Sara's belief, the very water that sat in her glass had been in contact with the boy who was trapped. With all the rain, perhaps the tunnel was flooded and he had drowned.

Drinking the water was difficult to do as the mouthfuls taken had surely been choked on by the drowning boy.

"Drink your water Sara; it's good for you!" As always, Father expected his daughter to finish her food and drink.

"I don't like it."

"You don't like it? What's wrong with it? Drink it!"

Reluctantly, Sara finished the boy's choked-up tunnel water. The quicker she pee-ed, the better!

At night, Sara lay in bed while hearing the rainwater trickle along the downspouts. She considered that the boy might still be alive, keeping his head up above the water which may have been near the top of the tunnel. It was only a matter of time before he finally died; then she wouldn't feel so guilty. His body would be found, but no one would be aware that Sara had seen him in the final hours, alive.

On and on the rain water trickled; but Sara couldn't get the boy out of her head. The evening hours intensified the disturbing thoughts to the point of finally breaking down. She scampered into Mother and Father's bedroom in tears. The mumbling and crying made it impossible to understand. But through a couple minutes of listening, Mother and Father quickly interpreted that a boy may have been trapped in the drainage tunnel.

Across town, a frantic mother who had reported her son missing received a phone call from the Mapleview police, informing her that the boy was found alive. But as a precaution, he was taken to the hospital for observation as he had been wet and cold for many hours. It was a very, close call and an outrage for the residents of Mapleview. That boy could have died, thanks to the unnecessary fence. Within 1 week, both sides of the tunnel had been removed of the chain link.

* * *

Spending an average of 4 years for a quality education at the university of one's choice, many people work diligently to obtain degrees ranging from business, to accounting, to engineering, to art. And in those 4 years, the plans of a highly, successful career with a large corporation are often dreamed of. Summers are spent showcasing one's talents during internships with the hopes to land a job shortly after graduating. And for many, this course of action proves successful. Oh, there are many other avenues to success; such as military, entrepreneurship, even skilled trades. But the most popular throughout America is a 4 year degree, followed by a successful career with a large company.

Sara was different in that she did earn her 4 year degree in business management. But upon completion, she returned home to the quiet, peaceful town of Mapleview where she felt that the area was lacking one important thing.

Being a lover and connoisseur of coffee, she spent a few months after graduation, doing research on the various coffee beans along with proper methods of brewing and the equipment required. Not long after, Sara obtained financing and leased a storefront to be called, The Mapleview Coffeehouse.

Of course starting a small business is no easy task. For two years, Sara was the only person who manned the operation and barely earned enough sales to cover operating expenses. Mother and Father were proud of their daughter's entrepreneurial endeavor. But a 20-something, living at home for free was a bit uncomfortable to say the least.

As luck would have it, Sara was part of a growing trend in Mapleview; a surge in businesses that bloomed along the main road of downtown Mapleview to include small shops, restaurants and outlet stores. Suddenly, Mapleview was the town to be! And upon waking early for work in the morning, or requiring a 10:30 java-jolt (or even one in the afternoon), the Mapleview Coffeehouse was known to serve the finest brew in town. Some years after its conception, Sara's business became so successful that she expanded the shop to include a small bakery, offering morning pastries to commuters or tourists who needed a quick breakfast.

A regular customer at the Mapleview Coffeehouse, Brian appeared to visit each morning with the purpose of another greeting and possible conversation with the delightfully pleasant and very, attractive blonde who worked behind the counter. A real man likes a woman such as Sara: a rubenesque frame and well endowed. And through time he learned that Sara was the owner of the Mapleview Coffeehouse. They shared something in common. The two were business owners in downtown Mapleview as Brian operated his small insurance company just down the street.

Was it necessary for Brian to be perfect? Is that what people ask of in a significant other, to be perfect? Some minor flaws and a bit quirky, he was a good-looking man and well mannered. Along with the right chemistry and that sparkle in his eyes, Brian gave quite an impression of being seriously interested in Sara.

Dates soon followed and Sara learned of their ability to talk for long hours. She enjoyed Brian's humor and how he made her laugh. And he was so affectionate with warm embraces and passionate, yet gentle kisses. Sara was falling in love with possibly the man of her dreams. But it was too early to even talk about marriage; you know the "safety threshold of time" that many young couples imagine.

Things were certainly on the up for Sara with her business that had flourished along with those wonderful moments of falling in love. And it was finally time to move out of Mom and Dad's house and enjoy her own place. Brian accompanied Sara to check out a duplex condo, shortly before she made an offer to purchase. He gave her reassurance that it would be a great buy. And although both remained silent while walking through bedrooms, thoughts of "the baby nursery in here" and "our marital bed in there" seemed to be dreamed simultaneously. Brian knew that Sara was the one and vice-versa.

Chapter 22

In adulthood, outside of acquired experiences, 5 or 6 years apart in age has little-or-no difference. In childhood, 5 or 6 years can make a world's difference. As a girl, little Sara had rarely been exposed to the older boy named Kevin who she had left for dead, trapped in the tunnel. Occasionally, she might have seen him in a car or noticed the familiar face who stocked shelves in the grocery store. Kevin was considerably older and probably didn't recognize Sara. But needless to say, Sara felt a bit uncomfortable whenever locking eyes with the person she had let down earlier in life.

Now older in age, Sara certainly knew better and would help anyone in need. In fact, the incident so early in life had traumatized Sara to the point of obsessively answering anyone's cry for help. Some might have said that a woman like Sara was easily taken advantage of. Junkies that parked at the gas station often walked up to her, asking for a few dollars. "I'm trapped here and I can't get home."

How could Sara say, "No"?

It was a week before closing on the duplex condo that Sara had purchased in Circle Point. Sara was working her coffee shop in the early, AM hours when suddenly, eyes were locked with a stranger who had entered the establishment. Immediately, Sara felt the familiar, uncomfortable feeling. It was Kevin, the once boy who was left to drown in the tunnel. She hoped he wouldn't recognize her.

"Good morning, can I help you?"

He placed 3 dollars on the counter, an unusual act in comparison to other customers. "Give me your house blend; large, black."

"Sure, right away!" Sara grabbed a large, specialty cup with wraparound heat pad and poured the daily blend made just an hour ago. As the coffee filled the cup, the nagging guilt combined with a longing to "clear the air" with the stranger who had haunted Sara for many years was suddenly overpowering.

The lid was snapped on and brought over to the counter. Then she looked up and stuttered some before speaking. "Are you... did you get trapped in that tunnel over at Hidden Lake when you were a boy?"

Kevin was surprised; eyes soon revealed his sudden awareness of who Sara was. "Yeah!"

Heat flushed on Sara's cheeks and ears, obviously blushing. "I'm sorry; I was the girl that you called out to. I was so young."

"Oh, so that was *you*?"

Sara nodded.

Kevin didn't seem to care. "Bah, don't worry about it; water under the bridge; no pun intended! If anything, I learned a valuable lesson that day. Don't get myself in places I can't get out of. How much do I owe you?"

And just like that, the apology was quickly accepted. But Sara continued to feel the guilt. "It's on the house; no charge today."

"No, come on! I'm not going to take a free coffee. Here, keep the change!" Kevin slid the 3 dollars across the counter; wedding band was seen on his left, ring finger. And then he walked out, bell chimed as the door opened while holding it for a woman who now entered.

One week later; the day after closing on her new, duplex condo; Sara had arrived in Circle Point and parked in the street in front of her new home. The rented trailer was soon to arrive with furniture. But Sara stopped dead in her tracks once exiting the car. Directly across the street, Kevin wore a military uniform and was loading luggage in the back of his vehicle.

The neighborhood was silent, not a bird chirped in the trees much less a gentle breeze. The two had quickly taken notice of each other.

"Hey, good morning! You're my new neighbor?" Kevin spoke out across the street—handsome in a uniform with shiny boots.

"Good morning; yes! I closed yesterday and I'm moving in."

"Well welcome to the neighborhood; you're going to like it here! Listen, I'd hate to cut you short, but I've got a plane to catch!" And with that statement, Sara's brother and her boyfriend roared down the street in the moving truck. Furniture had arrived.

She spoke over the approaching noise, "Well, I'll catch you around! Good luck to you." Suddenly, heat could be felt over her cheeks and ears. Was "Good luck" the right thing to say to soldier who was going away on duty?

The moving trailer backed into the driveway with high pitched beep. Out of the corner of her eye, Sara observed the activities across the street and noticed that Kevin's wife had sat in the driver's seat of the vehicle, apparently taking her husband to the airport.

* * *

Perhaps it was the near three days of moving, placing furniture and becoming situated in the new home that made her oblivious to the activities across the street. In Sara's perception, not more than three days after Kevin's return to duty, his wife had a regular visitor. It was a man who parked his Dodge Charger in the driveway and would spend much time in the house. Initially suspecting that he was a brother, Sara eventually questioned just how close a brother and sister can be. Sara loved her own brother, and she visited him once or twice a week. But the man who visited Kevin's wife did so on a daily basis.

And they often went out together, sometimes in the evening. The man would drive off with a soldier's wife in his passenger seat with the strong scent of perfume blowing out the window.

Then came a Friday morning when the two had entered the Mapleview Coffeehouse. Finally seeing the pair up close, Sara quickly surmised that the relationship was strongly taboo.

"You let us sample coffee, here?" The man spoke as if Sara owed a reason to be a customer. He looked like a typical, lowlife scumbag that would see the opportunity of a soldier away on duty to fool around with a wife.

"Sure, what would you like? We've got the house blend of the finest South American beans. There's also smooth-vanilla nut, and a fresh brew of mountain berry."

"Mountain berry?" The histrionics coming from the scumbag were most unappreciated. "What else do you got?"

Sara remained patient, "Well, I can brew anything up for you."

"To sample?"

Sara was dumbfounded. Surely the man wasn't that stupid and inconsiderate. She wasn't going to brew an entire chamber of coffee just so he could sample.

But the scumbag persisted, "Come on! Brew 'em all up! We want to try each one!"

Kevin's wife added a flavor she was interested in, "I want to try Irish coffee."

The scumbag slapped his hand on the counter. "Irish coffee; that one first! The lovely lady wants Irish coffee!"

It was followed by a giggle from the unfaithful wife as she backed up against the scumbag's chest while his hands caressed her shoulders. Sara could handle Irish coffee as many customers enjoyed that flavor. But she wasn't about to brew every blend in the store. From the looks of it, the sickening love birds had sampled plenty in life.

Grabbing two cups, the fresh blend was poured and handed to the samplers.

The scumbag was quite demanding, "Come on; what's this? Fill it up!"

Apparently a half-filled cup (about 4 ounces worth of Irish coffee) was not enough. Sara entertained his demands and returned with 8 ounces each. They drank and giggled while Sara went about her morning duties.

"So what are you going to make us next?"

"I'm sorry?" Sara was very close to losing her patience as she approached the counter from behind.

"You said you would brew up all your blends for us to try."

She paused, "Sir, we don't do that here. I only have so many chambers."

But the inconsiderate man continued, "No, I want your minty, chocolate surprise!" Kevin's wife whispered something in the scumbag's ear that was followed by another order. "And another sample of your Irish coffee! He slapped his hand on the counter as if cracking a whip, "Let's go! More samples!"

Now at the end of her rope, Sara did something she had never done at the Mapleview Coffeehouse. "Sir, I'm going to have to ask you to leave!"

"What? Why?"

"Unless you're going to make a purchase, you're going to have to leave."

"Are you serious? Can I see your manager?"

"I'm the owner, and I'm asking you to leave. I will call the police if necessary."

Including colorful adjectives, poor Sara was given derogatory names as the scumbag took hold of Kevin's wife and walked towards the door. "My brother's a lawyer, you know. I'll have him take care of you! And you know what else? I'm going to tell everyone in this town about the rotten service I received here." Another derogatory name was given and the sickening couple left the store.

Sara wondered if the unfaithful wife knew that she was a neighbor.

Chapter 23

Bizarre things happen in the charming town of Mapleview—in case you haven't already noticed. But if you merely visit while traveling on vacation; the sentience that blankets the town is most likely unnoticed. It might require moving in the area; and even then, Mapleview would appear seemingly normal.

Craig was one such individual who moved in from out of state. He would have done this around the time that the Mapleview Coffeehouse had finally seen success, and the owner had moved in to her duplex condo in Circle Point. And although his first couple years were very eventful, nothing supernatural or incredibly bizarre had taken place.

But there was one, small event that Craig experienced that served as a precursor to a terrifying discovery, which sent him to the Mapleview Police where he would babble like an incomprehensible fool. The event would have been terrifying for anyone, as equally irrational and impossible.

Even still, the third disappearance of Mapleview was two years into the future from that terrifying discovery. Pay close attention; one of the characters in the upcoming series of events will contribute to another mysterious disappearance. See if you can determine who it is.

* * *

Craig was born to a family of small business entrepreneurs. His father saw an unfortunate layoff from his company as an opportunity to work, full time, in the residential real estate sales business. Of course this is a difficult career for anyone to start. And while Father waited patiently for steady commission checks to roll in, Craig's mother began a short-lived career as an Avon sales representative.

Craig received his first taste in sales, as a boy, when Mother expected him to assist her as the Avon lady. Walking the neighborhood streets with Mother's car behind, the task of delivering Avon catalogs at various customers' doors was nothing to be proud of. And since this activity was done in the afternoon hours, after school or on weekends, there were often kids outside his age.

Poor Craig can recall with sharp clarity the Saturday morning that Mother dropped him off in front of a house where some boys were playing basketball. They observed the unfamiliar kid who walked up to the house and left something behind. And of course, the crowd of boys quickly ran to the door, eager to see what was left.

"Hey! Check out this new shampoo!" One of the boys commented on a shampoo advertised on the front page of the catalog. "Hey kid! Are you the Avon lady? He's the Avon lady!"

Walking to the next house with Mother's car following behind, Craig did his best to ignore the surroundings and hoped the moment of shame would soon pass. He hated this torture, and often argued that delivering Avon catalogs was a thoroughly, embarrassing afterschool or weekend activity. But Father declared that it was unacceptable not to help the family earn additional money. As Father put it, "You eat here and have a roof over your head! It's not too much to ask that you help your mother!"

The crowd of kids on that Saturday morning surrounded poor Craig at the next house. One of them asked, "Hey kid! Can I ask you something? Why are you so gay? You're such a gay rod!"

Craig could only hang his head low while answering, "I don't know."

By the time he met Mother at the end of the block and entered her car, she asked, "Were those some friends of yours?"

If there was one thing Mother had plenty in surplus, it was the paper, Avon, cosmetic bags; the ones that the Avon lady delivers to the door for a customer who purchased makeup or perfume. With hundreds of these bags at home, there was no reason to purchase brown, paper lunch bags at the store. Poor Craig was expected to bring his lunch to school each day in an Avon bag! Kids are so cruel! Although Craig desperately attempted to cover up the bold icon on the paper bag, he was nicknamed "The Avon Lady" during lunch.

By the time Craig was in high school, Father's career as a residential real estate salesman had flourished which meant that it was no longer necessary for Mother to hustle the streets as the Avon lady. But the family was expected to assist Father in one, small aspect of marketing. Canvassing is an activity that involves hand-delivering advertisements to neighborhood doors. This activity proved successful for Father as an afternoon of canvassing would generate several inquiry calls, which often led to a sale or two.

In those days, Mother owned a powdered-blue Subaru station wagon. And it was in the winter months when Mother and Craig's two brothers would bundle up in bulky snow suits, moon boots and stocking hats for an afternoon of canvassing. But not Craig! He wouldn't dare dress up in such ridiculous attire! Mother and Father simply declared that Craig was a "big boy", and if he was "too cool" and stupid to wear his bulky snow suit and moon boots, then he would join the family activity wearing only his jacket and hiking boots. There was no way Craig could get out of assisting in the family business.

It was very fortunate that Craig did not dress in such heavy clothing. For whatever reason, Mother found it necessary to crank the heat on full blast, which would make anyone want to run out of the car and into the cold before vomiting or passing out from the heat. Perhaps that was her secret means of motivation!

Mother discovered the 1980s tragic release of "Hooked on Classics" that sped up classical works of Beethoven, Bach and Tchaikovsky while blending a poor attempt of snappy beats. The music would have been more suitable for a 1980s aerobic class for senior citizens.

Craig would sit in the back seat of the powdered-blue Subaru station wagon with a family of astronaut-looking family members, hoping no one his age would recognize him or hear the corny "Hooked on Classics", blasting in the car. How thankful Craig was to escape the roasting heat and maddening nursing home music. He secretly referred to this activity as Torture in a Subaru.

Years later, Craig was turned on to the idea of starting a career in residential real estate sales. Doing research into the various areas throughout America that experienced a market growth; Mapleview, Craig thought, was America's little known secret. It was during a time when the economy for Mapleview had surged with an increase of new businesses. The town seemed attractive to people of surrounding areas, and much new construction was planned for the extending region beyond downtown.

Ask anyone who has worked a career as a Realtor, he or she will tell you that it's a highly challenging industry to break into. One might think that an agent only sits in the office of Century 21 or Re/Max while waiting for the telephone to ring. After all, many individuals with the intention of purchasing a new home call the local real estate office, right? But the fact is the phone will never ring unless inventory is built up. Because of this, a brand new agent is faced with the challenge of accumulating a personal inventory to advertise. He or she must convince a homeowner to allow the exclusive marketing of a property. And while this is attempted, countless other real estate agents are competing for inventory!

This is the point when most aspiring, young Realtors give up. After months of prospecting without so much as one sale, the need for food on the table drives what was once a motivated agent to seek a new career. And after months of unsuccessful prospecting at Mapleview Realty, Craig had already decided that a change of career was best.

Hope suddenly appeared on the day that he went through his office mailbox and discovered a flyer from the competing office of Jack Swieley Realty. The broker/owner was in search of an assistant and promised not only training from one of Mapleview's finest agents, but a weekly salary as well! Desperate for income as Craig's savings were near depletion, and not wanting to go back home to family and friends defeated, he walked into the office of Jack Swieley Realty for an interview. Within 5 minutes, Craig found himself to be hired! Of course the original broker would have to release his license and conduct the daunting exit interview. But those things could wait. Jack Swieley Realty offered fast-paced training that was to start that day!

Jack Swieley Realty: It wasn't exactly what Craig had expected. For the successful track record and reputation of being one of the top producing offices in Mapleview, the brokerage establishment was nothing more than a small, rundown office with a retired-age secretary up front. The only agent working was the broker/owner, Jack Swieley. He was an old man in his 60's, very large, perhaps 400 pounds and wore the most obnoxious, checkered suit with loose necktie. From the looks of him, Jack Swieley could have passed for a cheesy car salesman.

Craig sat in the chair before his new broker's desk, hearing the tales of glory and how Jack Swieley defeated all obstacles. Despite the fact that Mr. Swieley had been humped by dogs while trying to go over a marketing program with clients; threatened by people with shot guns to get out of their homes; and at times, received the reputation of being the most ill-reputable salesman in town, Jack Swieley managed to turn tragedy into triumph.

Suddenly an alarm sounded from a digital 1980s watch that Mr. Swieley wore with pride on his left wrist. "It's almost 9:30. You've got your first appointment with a seller, today."

Expecting a boring lesson from "Telemarketing 101", Craig was very surprised that his first day of training would begin with some field work. It was, as Mr. Swieley described, a homeowner wishing to sell. They drove to the residence in an old Cadillac convertible with the roof down while Mr. Swieley puffed away at a fat cigar.

The broker/owner reaffirmed that Craig was now working at the "country club" of real estate. "Ah, feel that sun? That's what you call the Realtor's tan! It's what you get from driving around in a nice, Cadillac convertible. I bet you didn't get that at Mapleview Realty!"

It was an average, single-family home on a quiet, residential street. A For-Sale-By-Owner sign announced to the world of its availability. The old Cadillac pulled into the driveway. The transmission was shifted into park and the ignition turned off.

Mr. Swieley ordered, "Here; take my keys, go in the back trunk and pull out one of my signs. Take out the For-Sale-By-Owner sign in their lawn and replace it with mine. I'll catch up to you in a minute."

His first day on the job, Craig quickly went to work and did as the boss asked. And while pulling out the For-Sale-By-Owner sign, he could see the sellers standing up through the living room window. Worried that the sellers noticed someone other than Jack Swieley tampering with their sign, he gave a friendly wave that, he hoped, would indicate an operative from Jack Swieley Realty.

The front door flew open, "Excuse me! What are you doing? Uh; no! We didn't ask for any Realtors to sell our home."

Confused, Craig looked behind for some help from the boss.

Mr. Swieley was already behind him, giving official introductions. "Jack Swieley; how are you this morning? My office said you set up an appointment to list your house for sale with us?"

"No we didn't! Get your sign out of here. We don't need any agents!" By now, the homeowner was irate.

Mr. Swieley bent over and put his cigar out on the front lawn. "Now there must be some kind of mistake. I have an order here from my office to list your house for sale."

The homeowner's irate demeanor escalated to near outrage, "Look, I don't know what this is all about, but we are not looking to hire agents right now!"

It was Mr. Swieley's cue to take over and reassure the homeowner he meant no harm. He gently put his hand on the seller's shoulder in some kind of calming effort that appeared to work. "Now, now; I realize this is a big mistake and I didn't mean to pull a fast one on you. You certainly didn't call us out here, today. We'll get to the bottom of this. Let's go inside; I'll contact my office and find out what the mix-up is."

At this point, it might be worth commenting on a strange effect that Mr. Swieley had on people. Perhaps it had something to do with his size and age. A tall man and easily 400 pounds, one might wonder if this is what contributed to his ease of manipulating people. If you or I motioned someone to let us in the house, we would be ordered to leave and possibly threatened. But for some reason, people (such as the homeowners of that morning) allowed Mr. Swieley into their homes, even though they were outraged that he had a bogus order to market their property.

They all stood in the kitchen; Mr. & Mrs. perturbed Sellers, top-producing Jack Swieley and his new assistant who worked his first day on the job. Mr. Swieley proceeded to speak to his office while everyone else listened in silence. "Dora, we have some kind of mix-up here today. I'm at the house on 422 Crescent Drive and they say they never called us out... Well I don't know; I can only go according to what they say... Alright, let me know."

Mr. Swieley put the phone down for a moment and whispered, "They're going to get to the bottom of this." Then he attempted some small talk. "So how long have you folks been for sale?"

The seller loosened up some. "About 2 months, now. Does your office have any buyers?"

Mr. Swieley's eyes opened up as if surprised they would ask. "Well sure we have buyers!" Then he looked at his new assistant and motioned with hands while whispering, "Go preview the home with the seller and take some notes."

Touring the home with Mr. Seller, the voice of Mr. Swieley could be heard in the background, arguing with the office on the phone. And at the most adjacent corner of the house with Mr. Swieley furthest away, Craig was asked in confidence, "Is that his ploy to get in the door and offer sales pitches?"

Craig hadn't thought about this. But it suddenly became a nagging suspicion. Was this the top producer's technique? But being the loyal employee he was, Craig simply answered, "No, Mr. Swieley doesn't do business that way. He's actually a very, professional agent and has been in the business for over 30 years!"

By the end of the tour, Mr. Swieley was ending his telephone call with the office. He removed the extinguished cigar from his mouth, "Folks, my office wants to apologize for this mix-up today. You have a lovely home and I know my assistant has done a preview in case we get a buyer." And then he went right for the kill! "In a motion of apology for the terrible mix-up, the office is extending a full marketing package to include advertising, open houses and network Realtor marketing for an unbelievably, low commission rate."

For such a great deal, made possible by an inconvenience, how could the sellers have gone wrong? After a couple minutes of guided decision making (led by Jack Swieley) the sellers entered an exclusive agreement for his office to market their home.

On the ride back to the office, Mr. Swieley puffed his cigar with a big smile on his face. "You see that? See how I turned tragedy into triumph in there. Now that's what I'm talking about."

Chapter 24

It was soon learned that erroneously placing Jack Swieley Realty signs in the front lawns of homes that were For-Sale-By-Owner was no accident. It was part of Mr. Swieley's technique. In fact, it was no longer necessary to instruct Craig of the sign's replacement. He simply exited the old Cadillac (Mr. Swieley driving), obtained a company sign and went to work. And Craig was sure to bring a notebook for purposes of jotting down home details inside the residence while the boss straightened out the mess.

But not every attempt to win exclusive rights of marketing a For-Sale-By-Owner was successful. After some time, Jack Swieley's "comedy of errors technique" was experiencing a losing streak. Mr. Swieley was exhibiting signs of worry while Craig grew increasingly concerned.

"We better start building up some inventory or I'm not going to be able to keep you as my assistant." Although spoken as joke, it was a serious consideration. Mr. Swieley mentioned this around 11:00am, his next appointment not until 12:30 in the afternoon. With an hour and a half to kill, perhaps the broker could have drowned his anxieties at the all-you-can-eat luncheon buffet, held daily at Mapleview's Country Diner. "It'll be my treat. But you better start gettin' us some inventory or we won't be in business long." Again the boss was joking; but in a way, kind of serious.

The huge beastly-of-a-man exited the old Cadillac as the shocks raised the car off the ground from a relief of overbearing weight. Onlookers immediately took notice of the enormous stomach with blood-pumped face that huffed towards the building, eyes intently focused on the door. The Mapleview Country Diner should have locked its doors! Jack Swieley was in the mood for some serious feeding!

How was it possible for one man to load such a phenomenal amount of food in his body? Being that it was the all-you-can-eat luncheon buffet, he continuously stacked up 2 plates... 3 plates... 4 plates... even 5 plates of food; each one being a mixtures of heavy meats, pastas with rich sauce and vegetables such as sweetened yams or sauerkraut soaked in bacon grease.

By 12:15, the Mapleview Country Diner had experienced a disaster of unimaginable totality. Mr. Swieley simply pushed the table away, nearly crushing the bewildered assistant and announced that it was time for the appointment.

Craig was accustomed to standing in kitchens with a pairs of irate homeowners while his boss spoke to the company on the phone. But that day was different from the others. Suddenly, Mr. Swieley produced the most urgent look while whispering to the sellers. "Hey, can I use your bathroom? I just had the all-you-can-eat buffet over at the Mapleview Country Diner"

The seller was not so hospitable. "I don't think so, buddy! You better wrap up the call and head out of here!"

He whispered, "Okay, sorry for asking. I'll be out of here in a minute... Yeah Dora (grunt) they say (grunt)..." Mr. Swieley breathed heavily with an ill and pale face, beads of sweat dripped down. Then he flatulated which appeared most painful and shouted to the seller, "In the name of all that is holy, you gotta let me use your bathroom!"

Slapping his forehead in annoyance and disbelief, Mr. Seller was reluctant. "Alright, hurry up! I can't believe this!"

A sound mightier than a sudden, broken dam that could have never held back the Niagara Falls was released. It was a gush followed by belts of firecrackers that only announced another breaking dam. How one man could hold that much matter in his bowels was equally amazing as the damage done back at the Mapleview Country Diner.

Then he shouted at his secretary, Dora, that he was using the bathroom and would call back momentarily. 10 minutes passed as more firecrackers ripped and built-up dams collapsed. The toilet was flushed numerous times; moans and whimpers could be heard from under the door crack.

In such an uncomfortable situation, Craig finally spoke up. "So, how long have you folks been for sale? Would you let me preview your home in case I have a buyer?" He toured the residence with Mr. & Mrs. Seller for about 15 minutes, all the while discussing the company's success and the proven marketing strategy. Cries and flatulence from the far corner of the house cheered the assistant on as he laid the final touches on a presentation well done.

Craig returned to the bathroom door and knocked. "Mr. Swieley; you almost done in there?"

"I'll be out in a minute. I'm done. So sorry!" And then he flushed which sounded to go terribly wrong. "In the name of all that is holy: Have pity on me!"

Mr. Seller gasped as about a minute's worth of violent plunging was likened to emergency room doctors that pounded on the chest of a trauma victim. The blockage finally broke and the water went down.

Mr. Swieley emerged from the bathroom with a cold, wet towel around his neck. "Folks, I'm really sorry about all of that and I want to thank you for letting me use your bathroom. Because of today's inconvenience, my office is prepared to offer an amazing deal". The closing statement of the offer promised advertising, open houses and network Realtor marketing for an unbelievably, low commission. Would you believe the home-owners entered an exclusive right to market with Jack Swieley Realty?

It was necessary to drive Mr. Swieley back to the office as he lay in the reclined passenger seat with a cold, wet rag on his forehead. "My God, the things I have to do just to get some business!"

Craig had to wonder: How many times did Mr. Swieley visit the Mapleview Country Diner, just to get some business?

Chapter 25

It was a typical Friday morning as Sara sat in the small, closet-sized office of the Mapleview Coffeehouse, paying bills to vendors and preparing weekly paychecks to part-time employees. Although still considered a modest operation, she had come a long way in success. The morning and afternoon hours were staffed by her and sometimes the morning employee, Dianne. They worked together until the "mature" high school students who rotated manning the coffeehouse in the evening hours throughout the week arrived. Not totally free for weekends, and yet to have enjoyed a week or two of vacation since opening business doors, Sara merely arrived in the early-morning, week-end hours to let employees in and bring the coffeehouse into operation. Then she stayed in tune with the business from a re-mote location while enjoying the weekend, occasionally making a cameo appearance just to check on things.

Logging the expenses into the spreadsheet, she proudly wore a sparkly, diamond rock on the left hand. It was a gift from Brian on the night he proposed, knelt on the ground with tears in his eyes. The wedding was 6 months away; so much had happened in a little over a year since Sara moved in her duplex condo.

Just then the bell sounded from the door, announcing a customer. Much to Sara's surprise it was Kevin, her neighbor on another temporary leave of duty as a soldier.

"Good morning! Nice to see you!" Kevin was greeted so warmly and made to feel welcome. Should that not be for all men and women who fight for freedom?

He returned the greeting, "Good morning!" Then he placed 3 dollars on the counter. "I'll have your house blend; large, black."

"Sure, right away!"

Being that Sara was Kevin's neighbor along with the fact that the two went way back, it was certainly appropriate for Kevin to make small talk. "So how's the neighborhood treating you? Everything okay?"

"Oh ya! I love Circle Point!"

"Have you had the opportunity to meet my wife, Debbie?"

Being that Brian and Sara referred to her as "The Woman across the Street", this was the first time Sara had become aware of her actual name. Aside from that, Debbie, as Sara now knew her, maintained a distance and for probably good reason!

"Yeah, I've met her briefly…"

Sara filled the large cup, all the while "patting herself on the back", knowing that she would never be like Debbie. Thanks to Debbie, her husband earned the disgraceful reputation as the soldier whose wife cheats on him. He probably knew about it, too! The poor guy most likely felt trapped in his devotion to placing life on the line, while receiving bitter welcomes home from a deceitful wife who couldn't wait for her husband to leave. Sara and Brian would have no such shackles to confine them in life. And being the center of love in a marriage, Sara would always maintain that happiness for the decades, onward to evermore.

And just like a child who zipped off on a bike to escape the rain while leaving a boy trapped in a tunnel, Sara was suddenly burdened with overwhelming guilt. She placed the large cup of coffee on the counter, "You know, I'm sorry; this is probably none of my business, but your wife spends a lot of time with another man while you're gone. He spends the night and stuff."

Kevin's face turned grave, "Are you sure?"

She nodded slowly, "Yes; they came into the coffeehouse one morning and she was leaning up against him, cuddling. He's a creepy, jerky kind of guy. I actually had to throw them out because he was disruptive."

With that, Kevin slid the 3 dollars across the counter, "Keep the change!" Then he stormed out, holding the door for a female patron, never losing his sense of chivalry, even when confronted with a possible crisis."

* * *

Owning a business on Mapleview Road and very much a part of downtown Mapleview's culture, one might desire an escape and enjoy an evening out, elsewhere. Sillmac provided such an environment for Brian and Sara as they traveled Mapleview Road in the late afternoon hours, past Creek Highway and due east where it changed to Route 4. Similar to Mapleview, Sillmac has its share of restaurants, shops and even small museums for the town's yearly tourists. But Sillmac is considered a prestigious area in comparison to Mapleview. Taxes are higher, housing with no set price. If you want to ask $350,000, $450,000, or $600,000 for your home; it will sell as no one could set a price on Sillmac.

The historical residences and places of business had been renovated to eliminate any appearance of decay and maintain that 1800s charm. And just like Mapleview, the town is surrounded by thick, forested wilderness. But many of the preserves are improved to the point of qualifying as botanical gardens with paved, nature trails outlined in beautiful flowers; countless ponds with lily pads and meditational gardens at the center of flowing creeks.

Brian and Sara had their own nature path that they regularly walked or biked during their escapes from Mapleview. Since the dinner reservation at the elegant Perry's Seafood wasn't for another couple of hours that Friday night, a casual stroll along their nature path for about an hour was enjoyed

Holding hands with her beloved Brian in the quiet, late afternoon hours, Sara spoke of the incident at the Mapleview Coffeehouse earlier that day. "Oh, the Lady across the Street: her husband is home and he came in this morning."

"Oh yeah?"

"Yeah; and I found out her real name is Debbie. And I probably shouldn't have done this, but I told him about was going on across the street."

"Sara, you didn't! You actually told the guy that his wife cheats on him? We have to live with her, you know?"

"I know, I know. But Brian, I felt so obligated to tell him. I just never stopped feeling guilty after what happened when we were kids. He just doesn't deserve it."

There was a long pause as the engaged couple followed the bend around the lily pond until Brian finally spoke. "I suppose you're right. I see what you mean. Anyway, maybe not the first year after our wedding, but eventually we should probably move out this way."

"To Sillmac?" Sara was excited.

"Yes! I'm building up clientele and Sillmac isn't that far from downtown Mapleview. We should get some old, historic house in the woods."

Sara interrupted, "Not like the Trivelli house!" (Remember, this was a couple years before Mary moved in and made the discovery in the vase).

Brian reassured her, "We'll make sure of it."

And so the engaged couple in just one of many happiest moments in love finished their walk before heading over to Perry's Seafood for dinner.

By evening they drove Route 4, westbound, until reaching the border of Mapleview while holding hands as Sara's thumb stroked Brian's back of his hand. And in those moments, plenty of reminders were given of "I love you" followed by similar loving responses.

Family and friends who sometimes rode with Brian and Sara took notice of how Sara could not be a silent passenger as she would often call out, "Why are you turning here?" "Why don't you get in the other lane?" "Watch out..."

If you've ever been victim to a backseat driver, you might have noticed how such a person can cause near accidents! But on this night, Sara remained silent as she was trying to repair her reputation of "backseat driver". Just as Brian had followed the bend where Mapleview Road turned, he slowed down on the dark road for no apparent reason. But Sara remained silent; maybe only sighed.

And just as Brian resumed speed, he quickly swerved to avoid a collision with a deer that crossed the highway. He must have noticed something up the road which caused his unexplained slowing down seconds ago. Although avoiding the deer, the swerve caused the vehicle to run off the road, and down a ditch some 50 feet below. Of course an insurance salesman would have worn a seatbelt and so did Sara! But a large tree had been cracked in half during a recent storm so that the broken top was bent 90 degrees. The windshield rapidly approached towards it. The velocity of descending the slope was enough force for the 90-degree, bent tree trunk to penetrate the glass and make contact with Brian's face. It was completely unrecognizable, no longer part of Brian's body.

Once the vehicle had come to a complete stop, Sara used a second or two to evaluate the new surroundings and then quickly looked over to check on her beloved Brian.

"Brian? Brian? No! No!"

She quickly exited the vehicle with her voice echoing throughout the forest while calling out, "No!" They were cries that anyone would understand to question life's cruelty and the grand scheme of things.

And to add insult to injury, her fiancé's closed-casket funeral would include the most hurtful words from Brian's mother, who did everything in her power to keep from falling apart. But she finally broke down in front of Sara with a seriously damaging accusation, "Maybe if you weren't such a backseat driver, my son would still be alive!" Unfortunately, Sara was the only living witness with no one to defend her.

Chapter 26

Seasons passed since Kevin's last visit home, which was the time when Sara advised him of the strange man who often stayed at his wife's house. The death and burial of Sara's beloved Brian had come and gone. And once again, Kevin was on another leave of duty for more sadness at home.

At one time or another, you might take notice of a female neighbor or coworker who mysteriously develops plumpness along with a certain "glow". The beauty of being with child cannot be masked, even in the earliest weeks. But are you bold enough to approach your neighbor or coworker and ask if she's pregnant? Consider the embarrassment if you were wrong!

While home on another leave from duty, Kevin noticed this plumpness and certain "glow" from his wife. Unfortunately the "glow" lacked the appeal of something beautiful as Debbie remained disconnected and somewhat bitter towards her husband. Had it not been for Sara's mention during Kevin's last visit, along with many months of stewing suspicions overseas, he would have never suspected that his wife was pregnant with another man's child. He certainly had this suspicion, now. But there was just not enough evidence. And quite frankly, Kevin didn't want to deal with combat and stress at home. I suppose denial was easier to tolerate.

For Debbie, she had reached the point in her affair of coming to terms with no longer loving Kevin. But strangely, she was unable to voice this realization to her husband. Only a halfhearted attempt of bitterness and despise would be manifested when she really should have confessed a love that had grown cold. Pregnant with another man's child and very much in love with this other man, Debbie held back the words she had rehearsed over and over again of, "I no longer love you."

But why did she hold back? She wanted the end of her marriage so badly! And sometimes the words nearly rolled out of her mouth during moments with Kevin.

Her announcement was never made during Kevin's brief time home. Seeing her husband off at the airport, she hated him for his strong will and persistence. He gave his Debbie a kiss and reminded her of his love. Most men would divorce a wife who rejected any and all attempts for sex along with continuous animosity. But Kevin was a soldier who played the role very well. There was a war to be fought, and in such times the battle can be felt at home in a marriage. Kevin could go the extra mile; two, three; lengths that the average man could not.

The scumbag remained supportive for many months of Debbie's pregnancy, citing that he understood the difficult challenge she was faced. It wasn't so easy to simply announce to a husband that a love had ended. For this reason, Debbie's boyfriend had promised that the next time Kevin came home from duty, he would stand beside the woman he loved along with the child they created together. As he worded it, Debbie needed a man in her life to take charge.

And then one cold, early, winter morning—towards the end of the third trimester—the scumbag's salty Dodge Charger zipped into the driveway. Debbie watched as he approached the door in his leather jacket with sunglasses on. There was something in his walk that Debbie did not like.

She opened the door to let "Freebird" in, "What's up? Aren't you on your way to work?"

A "Freebird" has no reason to give explanations. He simply stated a need to move on. He did provide a cowardly excuse that he had ruined a marriage long enough. And although Debbie begged and pleaded while promising to break the news once Kevin returned, the scumbag's mind was made up. He was a real man who maintained his decision. The time had come for him to move on as he relied on partial lyrics from 1970s guitar rock to drive his point in.

Then he left her, the wife of another man, pregnant and sobbing with an entire world crumbled to pieces.

So vulnerable and standing in the middle of crisis, the only solution was to realize that she had been wrong. Perhaps this day had been foreseen the last time Kevin was home. Maybe the ignored precognition explained her inability to announce marriage over. Debbie could see it with such ever clarity as her lesson had truly been learned.

She decided to give birth when the time had come and place the baby up for adoption. By the time Kevin would come home, the affair would be long over and the soldier would be welcomed with open arms.

But much to her surprise, it was only hours after Debbie gave birth that Kevin made an unannounced visit! Not sure what to expect in his element of surprise, Kevin discovered Debbie in a very frazzled and worn appearance. And although receiving a most welcome hug and a seemingly change-of-heart since his last visit, Debbie cried much and claimed to be sick with the flu throughout his entire visit.

It was bothersome for Kevin; some mystery was shrouded in his own home. He lay awake at night with the sensation of something being very wrong. How much more could he take? Was his life at home healthy for him?

On the morning of his departure back to duty, Kevin rose early, woke his wife and announced his desire to end the marriage. And although she confessed to an affair and promised it had been long over, Kevin could see right through his wife. She was covering something, masking feelings and being untruthful.

6 months of waiting for some sort of message or indication that he forgave her, Debbie had grown impatient, decided to file for divorce and place the home up for sale. Could those things really be done with the spouse overseas? Whatever the limitations, she felt it was best to initiate the ending of their life together. She hurt Kevin enough and the man would never heal.

* * *

Craig sat in his broker's office one afternoon, receiving a good talking to about casually flirting with an attractive, young, female buyer that was met at an open house. The severely, obese broker/owner sat behind his desk, wearing a checkered car salesman suit from the early 80s while puffing a fat cigar. Although corny, cheesy and the type of salesperson one wouldn't immediately trust, Jack Swieley had lived it all in the real estate business and was someone any young agent would want to know.

He spoke to Craig, "Now, I ain't God's gift to women. I mean just look at me! But there came a time early in my career when a lady seller of mine seemed to take a liking to me. And she wasn't bad-looking either. I thought she liked me because I was a growing star in the business and was starting to make money and drive a nice car and all that.

Well, one thing led to another and you can imagine what eventually happened. I figured this was just one of the many perks of my job and was going to enjoy it like everything else. Wanna know what happened?"

Craig was expecting to hear that the woman's husband discovered the infidelity and nearly removed Mr. Swieley's unmentionables with a shotgun blast. So he voiced this.

"No! Worse! When the time came to accept an offer on her property, she let me know that she wasn't going to report me to the police for rape. Since she was being so kind, she expected me to sell her house for free!"

Craig didn't find his broker's tale of terror so realistic. "Come on! She could have just gone to the police and said that anyway. I could go to the police and say you threatened my life. My word against yours; who are they going to believe? There's no proof."

"Suit yourself if you don't think there's a problem with flirting, getting personal and sleeping with your clients. I'm just telling you that you never, never, never get close and personal with a client. Keep it business and professional. Address them as Mr. and Mrs. Seller. You're not there to be a friend, boyfriend, or anything else; just a Realtor to make a sale. Remember that!

Oh... evidence? There was plenty on her sheets. Plus if any rumor surfaced out there of me attacking clients, it would hurt my business."

Although appearing not to believe the possibility of tragic results for sleeping with clients, Craig made an effort to conduct himself professionally. But then he met Mrs. Debbie Cordsmullen, soon to be divorced. She was several years older than him, very attractive and irresistibly sexy. And mindful of his resolution to maintain professionalism, Craig did his best to keep it strictly business, despite how challenging it was.

"Do you have a baby Mrs. Cordsmullen?" Craig sat at the kitchen table with Debbie (Kevin's soon-to-be ex-wife), filling out the paperwork to put her house on the market. He could hear the sound of a baby crying in the background.

"No! No baby!" She was unusually worried at Craig's mention.

But Craig insisted, "I hear a baby crying."

Debbie gazed up as if listening. "Oh that? That you mean? That's the neighbor's baby crying next door. It sleeps next to the window and when the window is open, you can hear it crying."

Mr. Swieley always stressed the importance of making small talk with clients, just to maintain a casual environment. In addition, Craig wasn't comfortable calling a baby an "it". He asked, "Boy or girl?"

Debbie quickly replied, "Boy!"

Craig checked off the paragraphs to the contract while explaining the terms and conditions; all cancellations must be done in writing, 6% commission for a successful sale, be out in an agreed time with the buyer on the day of closing. As the contract was filled out, the baby screamed louder and louder. Craig took pity on the crying, little one. "Wow! That guy sounds hungry!"

Debbie nodded her head in agreement. Not open to small talk, it seemed as if she wanted to hurry things up and get Craig out of the house. Craig didn't mind as it was early evening and he just wanted to get home and relax.

Once all was signed and explained, Craig was immediately shuffled out the door where the sound of the baby was no longer heard. He didn't care. Craig figured that if his client did, in fact, have a baby and was attempting to hide it, the situation was none of his business.

Chapter 27

Although Debbie's house was now listed and able to show to potential buyers, there was one, slight problem; a dark horror that remained in the house which needed to be removed. This is why she sat at the kitchen table, drinking an extra, strong glass of vodka and cranberry juice. The familiar buzz followed by mental numbing indicated that all things would soon be possible. When finished, a second glass of straight vodka was poured. It was brought down in the basement along with a garbage bag and small suit case. In the event that Debbie's emotions take over, a few gulps of vodka might put them on ice.

It had been months since Debbie opened the 4ft x 4ft dry walled enclosure in the corner of the basement. It contained a panel door on the side that was secured by a simple latch with hinges. Opening the door, the sump pump could be accessed. But on this afternoon, there was something else for Debbie to access.

The latch was disengaged and the panel door opened. Behind the sump pump was the naked and unfinished wall that was constructed by large, industrial-sized bricks. The mortar of one had been chiseled through some months before, so that one of the large bricks could be removed.

Debbie pulled out the large brick; the rotting stench gave alarm to a crypt which had been disturbed. But the smell was ignored as Debbie's heart ached and her soul was jolted by the saddening realization of her mistake. In a drunken sincerity, she cried and apologized while her mind traveled back to that fateful day in winter when Kevin made a surprise visit home.

It was in the coldest death of winter when Debbie's water broke which soon followed serious labor pains. No one knew of the pregnancy as she had covered it up quite well with winter coats. And she wasn't about to check into the hospital so that bills would be incurred along with evidence of her mistake claimed to insurance. Debbie planned to privately deliver at home, anonymously drop the baby off at a safe haven and then clean her life up for good.

Life is filled with irony! Not many hours after delivering, Debbie rested some, cleaned up and was about to leave for the safe haven. But Kevin had surprised her with an unannounced visit and took a taxi cab home! Obviously, the man was suspicious of his wife and saw the perfect opportunity of an inconsistently-timed leave-of-absence to check on Debbie's activities.

In such an inconvenient irony, Debbie had to wonder why Kevin was given so much ample leave-of-absence. Most families sorely miss a loved one while he or she fights overseas for two or three years while waiting for a much needed leave-of-absence. But Kevin was given time away from war, it seemed, nearly twice a year! What was he doing home?

What could Debbie do? The baby cried in her arms as the soldier home from duty could be seen through the window, removing luggage from the trunk of the cab!

The child's life was quickly extinguished, body thrown in the 4ft x 4ft dry walled enclosure in the corner of the basement. By the time the front door had opened, Debbie ran upstairs to greet her husband. But somehow he knew; somehow Kevin was aware of things not right.

* * *

Months later, numbed by excessive vodka and cranberry, Debbie knelt within the sump pump enclosure, crying before the disturbed crypt at the sight of her exhumed baby. "I'm so sorry; I'm so sorry!"

Rubber gloves were stretched over Debbie's hands and the decayed baby was pulled out from the wall. The slimy stench was enough to make one gag. The child was now a lifeless skeleton with perhaps a few shreds of remaining organic matter, carrion at most.

And then the stiffness of tiny bones suddenly creaked as it gave the appearance of self movement. The skull partially covered in wasted tissue turned on its own so that the shriveled, rotting eyes looked directly at Mommy. The skeleton's jaw opened to produce the shrilling sound of an angry baby, crying!

Louder and louder with a fury that would tell the tale of months abandoned, the skeletal remains continued to cry. It was a hellish fright for Debbie, as she dropped it on the floor and backed out of the sump pump enclosure while screaming in a way that only drunkenness could produce.

Instinctively, Debbie ran up to the main level; the psychological distance of stairs and a closed door provided safety. It was such an unreal phenomenon that called for desperate measures. And it's amazing how one is prepared for such an experience! Debbie flashed open the coat closet where she removed an unused, wire coat hanger. Unwinding it from factory form, she descended into the basement where the reality of something so unreal continued to be heard.

Imagine bringing oneself to pick up that sort of anomaly! Made possible by a few gulps of vodka, the mysterious life was choked from the screaming, infant skeleton. The wire coat hanger was left around the neck bone as a tourniquet. Debbie placed her baby in the suitcase along with the rubber gloves and zipped it up. By the time it was temporarily placed back in the sump pump enclosure, the possibility of a very, bizarre hallucination was considered. For months she supposed the occasional, heard crying to be guilt-induced hallucinations. But they were so bad that even the Realtor heard them. It would soon be over. Debbie simply needed rest after the experience, along with some hours before driving as drunkenness would certainly result in a pullover by police.

Awakening some hours later, Debbie laid on the family room sofa upstairs. It was now dark and time to execute the 2nd phase of the plan. A shovel was placed in the trunk of her vehicle. Then she entered the basement in fright and opened the sump pump enclosure to remove the sealed suit case to be carried up into the garage.

A drive up Mapleview Road, through town, past the Trivelli House; Debbie pulled into the wayside entrance of the Hidden Lake Forest Preserve. Tonight would be a very, dark and lengthy hike through a nightmarish world. Never a fan of walking through the woods, she did recall a time earlier in life of following a path with friends that hugged around a lake and headed west into deep forest.

Debbie speculated that walking further into the woods would reduce the possibility of the unmarked grave's discovery by hikers and nature lovers. It was a good hour of exhaustive travel, alone in the darkness with the corpse of her child she had murdered, twice. Only in the realm of Hell were such symbolic journeys taken. Creatures of the night stirred in darkness while the skeletal remains in the suitcase sometimes felt to have moved.

Feeling that further travel was no longer possible, Debbie ventured a few feet off the path and began the process of digging the hole. Once large enough, the suitcase was dropped in, dirt covered and then the shovel carried some distance to be discarded elsewhere in the forest. Then she hiked back to the car.

It was some hours past midnight by the time Debbie returned home. Two bottles of water were guzzled along with some Aspirin for a headache. And while drifting off into slumber, dreams would bring her back to the darkened forest where the skeletal baby's screams echoed throughout the trees. By dawn, she had terrifying nightmares of the skeletal baby, screaming, outside her bedroom window.

Chapter 28

Clients receive one or two open houses during their time listed with Jack Swieley Realty. With such a large collection of inventory, it isn't possible for two agents to conduct open houses for every home, every weekend! And today just so happened to be Debbie's Sunday for an open house, hosted by Jack Swieley Realty and conducted by the young agent, Craig.

Mr. Swieley had taught Craig well. Following the recommended guidelines, the seller was asked to leave for the afternoon; all lights were turned on; all closets opened; and person's touring the home were required to register upon entering. In addition, small talk was made with people and highlights of the home were pointed out.

But Craig had an additional rule created that was based on observation. Some people enter a home and walk around with eyes focused on windows, room size and usually make comments such as, "We can put the table here...The sofa would look good over there." These people in Craig's mind were to be approached and treated as interested buyers.

Then there are people who come in the house and study the furniture, the decorating, family portraits and then make comments such as, "The lay out is opposite of ours...I can't believe they made this room the master bedroom." In Craig's conclusion, these were nosey neighbors that had no interest in purchasing a home in the neighborhood as they already had one. A simple, "Thanks for stopping by." was the only thing needed.

By 4:30 in the afternoon, the tours dwindled down until Craig made the decision to do one, final inspection of the seller's home and ensure all was in order for the homeowner to return. It was a productive day and Craig had spoken to a few seemingly interested buyers. With their names and phone numbers listed on the guest registry, he would surely call tomorrow and follow up.

But just before closing his brief case and heading for the door, Debbie Cordsmullen arrived home.

Rats! Now Sunday afternoon, Craig wished to drive off, loosen the neck tie, head home for a couple of beers and possibly see the end of the game. And how he hated updating a seller just moments after an open house or showing! Time was needed to digest the events and rehearse a briefing to be spoken over the phone.

Still, every seller has the right to know and every seller deserves friendliness and small talk. "Welcome home Mrs. Cordsmullen. I was just packing up to leave."

"Oh, please don't rush! How was it today?"

Craig spoke of the countless, potential buyers who had toured her home; showed the list of names on the guest registry and promised to call each one in the morning as a follow up.

Reaching into the refrigerator and pulling out a couple of cold ones, the irresistibly-sexy Mrs. Cordsmullen seemed very pleased. "Well that's great! I'm in the mood for a little celebration!"

"Now Mrs. Cordsmullen, I don't want you to think I sold your house, today. I'm just saying it showed well and I have some people who might be interested."

His attempt to downplay success was ignored as both bottles of beer had been opened, and one handed to Craig. "You worked hard today. It's Sunday afternoon, nearly 5:00, and it's gorgeous outside. Let's just have a couple beers together and I'll put something on the grill later for dinner."

Too focused on developing his career in residential home sales, Craig hadn't so much as a young lady that he courted for marriage. And although drinking beer with a married woman felt wrong, Craig rationalized after a couple guzzles that Mrs. Cordsmullen was in the process of getting the home sold and finalizing the divorce. And what is so wrong with allowing a client to make dinner on a Sunday night?

There's absolutely nothing wrong with accepting a seemingly, harmless invitation. A couple hours passed as beers turned into mixed drinks and Mrs. Cordsmullen (who now asked to be called Debbie) set two filet mignons on the grill and invited Craig inside to escape the mosquitoes.

After dinner a cozy, side-by-side seat was shared on the sofa with additional drinks. It was in these moments when Debbie opened up and shared her deepest feelings of a marriage gone sour, citing that perhaps she wasn't ready for matrimony so early in life; and then theorizing that perhaps Kevin's duty at war was to blame for such loneliness.

Debbie confessed to the affair and how she truly believed that the other man was supposed to be the one. Craig would hear of her pregnancy and the desire to announce the need of divorce. And then the sad story of "Freebird" who declared it was time to move on had the near drunken Debbie teary-eyed and overly emotional.

"I put the baby up for adoption before my husband came home on leave. But he still found out about the affair. I think he learned it from talking to one of the neighbors across the street. And that's how I got where I am."

Not the least bit interested in hearing of Debbie's personal problems, Craig hung onto his mixed drink buzz as best as he could, all the while appearing interested while the irresistibly-sexy face of Debbie remained only a foot from his. Inhibitions numbed while noticing her need for someone to care. Craig drew his face close to hers and kissed softly as if "testing the waters". An eager return was all that he needed; both had waited for this moment but held back for so long. The kissing grew into intense and frantic making out. If only Mr. Swieley could have seen his agent, then!

Suddenly, the sound of the sump pump could be heard from the basement which caused Debbie to jump up. "Oh no; it's the sump pump!"

Confused and nearly frustrated, Craig joined her. "What? What? Is there a problem? Want me to check it out?"

That was the last thing Debbie wanted! She shouted, "No!"

How odd; what in the world could be wrong with the sump pump? But Craig wasn't about to let this strange incident ruin his moment of "hitting the jackpot". Aside from another turnover of the dreaded sump pump downstairs, he ignored the incident and resumed his conquest. In a final gesture of willingness, Debbie seductively led the young man into the bedroom, closed the door and brought him over to the sinful bed where both Kevin and Freebird once laid.

* * *

Just as with every business, there are slow times of little or no revenue. The real estate industry is no exception. Many independent brokers suffer weeks and months of stacked up inventory while waiting for a sale which would hopefully lead to a closing and commission check. Although the now dynamic duo of Jack Swieley Realty possessed one of the largest inventories of homes in Mapleview, they waited patiently for a wave of buyers to finally purchase their collection of real estate.

For Craig, the slow time was bearable with the existence of his new girlfriend who regularly made dinner, offered plenty of drinks and continued to provide fantastic sex. Needless to say, she was anything but a serious relationship. Debbie was more of a distraction from his career, as Craig would often daydream of another steamy session of romance with the sizzling, hot Mrs. Cordsmullen.

Still, Debbie had her own life, her job and whatever other responsibilities. So did Craig. One responsibility Craig had was to report to the offices of Jack Swieley Realty, daily. But with a surplus of inventory and homebuyers who appeared to be doing anything but shopping for homes, Craig was experiencing "downtime". And it was in these times when Craig noticed that Mr. Swieley could be a real bear!

"Boy, what are you doing?" Glancing out his small office, Mr. Swieley noticed Craig at his corner desk, reading a novel from his Kindle. His desk sat in the dark corner of the main office and was nothing more than a card table with a PC, telephone and desk calendar. Mr. Swieley insisted that Craig use the old-fashioned desk calendar instead of the electronic calendars on computers or hand held devices.

Needless to say, Craig found the question a little uncomfortable. "I... I was..." Under the circumstances, what did the broker/owner expect?

Mr. Swieley stepped out into the main office and approached Craig's desk. "You're reading that Kindle thing, again? Boy, don't you know reading ain't gonna make us money? Your job is to make me money! Now get to work!"

"Well, what do you want me to do, Sir? You want me to handle some appointments for you?" Craig speculated that perhaps their current inventory was "dead" which meant time to build up fresh, new homes for sale.

The broker/owner found his assistant's suggestion insulting. "Excuse me? I do the appointments around here! You haven't been trained to do that, yet. Instead of wasting my time and money by reading from your Kindle, why don't you do some telemarketing? You can find some buyers for our homes. The phonebook is over there on the file cabinet."

Keep in mind that while receiving his training at Mapleview Realty, Craig was instructed that telemarketing during certain times of the day was more successful than others. Midmorning to mid-afternoon often resulted in nobody home. But with the bear-of-a-man that Mr. Swieley had become, it was necessary to follow orders and aimlessly dial various telephone numbers throughout Mapleview with no answers. Aside from that, Mr. Swieley had a phonebook from 1999! Many of the numbers were disconnected or wrong numbers.

An hour passed, and Mr. Swieley looked out his office door. "Boy, haven't you gotten one lead, yet?"

"Sir, nobody's answering!"

"Well you're calling at 10:30 in the morning; nobody's home!" Realizing he was losing control, Mr. Swieley rested his fingers to his forehead and exhaled. "Look, I'm sorry. I got a lot going on. The wife is fighting with me, nagging whenever I'm home. And you can see we're at a low, now. Tell you what, let's go out and do an appointment. I'll show you how it's done."

Apparently, Mr. Swieley decided that it was time to find inventory that would replace the stale, old homes for sale. Was that really the way to work the business?

They went through the usual routine at another Mr. & Mrs. Seller's house. Craig stood in the kitchen with Mr. Swieley who reassured the homeowners that all would be well. And just as he pulled the cell phone from the inner pocket of his checkered suit jacket, a phone call came through.

Mr. Swieley answered, "Hello...? Yeah, I'm workin' right now. I don't have time for... WHAT...? Baby, no! You can't do that! It's been over 30 years!"

Call apparently ended, Mr. Swieley lowered his arm while still clutching the phone. He sighed, "Folks, I'm sorry; that was my wife. I just found out that she is filing for a divorce. It's all over."

He raised the phone back to chest level and proceeded to dial with a hint of a tear in his eye. "Hang on, let me call my office and find out why they sent me here even though you didn't call us out."

For sure, Craig wondered if this was another one of Mr. Swieley's tactics, perhaps a "feel-sorry-for-me" pitch. And by the looks of the homeowners, they most certainly thought the same. But then Jack Swieley lowered the phone from his ear with a troubled look and then dropped the plastic device on the floor. He soon grabbed his chest while gasping for air.

Mr. Seller was in bitter disbelief. "You've got to be kidding me! You're going to have a heart attack in my house, now?"

But a closer look at the pale face with beads of sweat and an overall air of something terribly wrong, all gave testament that Mapleview's top producer was not pulling an act.

"You gotta... you gotta... you gotta call an ambulance!" Mr. Swieley breathed as if running a marathon.

It's amazing how people can change their attitude while witnessing a struggle for one's life. But the world never realized that poor Jack Swieley had struggled his entire life. He struggled to hold together a business; put food on the table; maintain a rocky marriage; send his kids to college—the list goes on. And while struggling all those years, people kicked him to the ground with hurtful words and bitter reputations. This moment was different as the homeowners took pity on the man. "Hold on buddy! I'm calling an ambulance! They're only two minutes away."

And even in that moment, the broker/owner continued to think of selling homes while stating, "That's a good selling point."

Then, while gasping for air in a cold sweat, Mr. Swieley mulled over his recent, disturbing news. "Uh, how much more can I take? She's leaving me for my competitor. He's a snake and a con artist! And she loves him, instead of me!"

Mrs. Seller placed her hand on Mr. Swieley's shoulder. "Try not to worry. Try to relax. Everything is going to be okay. The important thing is that you stay alive." It was such an encouraging piece of advice!

Mr. Swieley called out, "Oh Lord, either help me or take me! I can't handle much more!"

Not much time after his cry out, it appeared that the good Lord was going to help Jack Swieley as the ambulance siren was heard not so far off in the distance. Listening as it drew nearer provided a mesmerizing calmness that was followed by relief at the presence of paramedics.

Craig and the homeowners watched as Jack Swieley was stabilized and hauled off on a stretcher. The siren screamed away into the distance, leaving the kitchen quiet and motionless.

It was the perfect opportunity for Craig to speak up while pulling out an exclusive-right-to-market contract. "Well, Mr. Swieley usually charges 6%; but because of our mishap here, today, I'll give you a discount."

No presentation or sales pitches were needed. Mr. & Mrs. Seller were most eager to list their home with Jack Swieley Realty.

* * *

"Please tell me you got them to sign." Visiting his boss in intensive care, Craig brought the medicine that would provide a temporary relief to Mr. Swieley's broken heart. Just how far will the top producer of Mapleview have to go to keep his business afloat? Hopefully this would trigger a winning streak for a while!

Chapter 29

One Saturday afternoon, while showing Debbie Cordsmullen's house to potential buyers, Craig learned, with certainty, that Debbie had a peculiar phobia of the sump pump in the basement.

"What's in that box?" The husband and wife pair took notice of the 4ft x 4ft dry walled enclosure that was located in the corner of the basement with a 3 ft panel door on the side. It apparently granted access to whatever it covered.

Craig answered, "I believe that's the sump pump. Debbie is that what this is; a sump pump?" Debbie's presence was with them as she remained home that afternoon, and followed Craig and the buyers downstairs during the showing.

"Yes, that's the sump pump."

The wife-buyer grew increasingly curious. "The panel with a lock on it: Is that the door to get in?"

Craig could see that Debbie was struggling to maintain patience as she calmly answered, "Yes."

But another inquiry was soon followed by the husband-buyer. "Could you unlock and open the door so I can see the pump? I'm sorry, but I hear a lot of horror stories about those pumps."

Knowing his client much deeper than a sales professional should, Craig could clearly see that his seller was thrown way out of her comfort zone as she stuttered and stammered, "Ummm; oh jeez, this is embarrassing. I don't have the key for the lock. But I will have it open if you come back for a second showing to take a look."

If you were a potential buyer in a situation like this, wouldn't you grow suspicious? The husband-buyer hinted his suspicion, "I never heard of someone locking up a panel to access the sump pump. That is strange."

But the Realtor quickly came to the rescue, "Rest assured folks, if you get an offer accepted on this home, you will be entitled to a full home inspection." The tour resumed, but Craig's confidence in selling a home of structural and utility soundness grew weak. Was he hiding known, latent defects from potential buyers? And to further add to his discomfort, Debbie had lipped the words, "Thank you" as he left the house.

Just about every (if not all) states mandate that a Realtor use care when representing a buyer. This means that a Realtor must make known any defects of a home to buyer, even if the Realtor is on the seller's side. Considering this and the realization that his client may have been hiding something wrong with her sump pump, Craig visited his wise and seasoned broker, Jack Swieley, who was recovering well from his mild heart attack and soon to come home from the hospital.

He stood before his boss's hospital bed. And amazingly, Mrs. Swieley now stood at her husband's side while lovingly tending to his needs. Craig hated to disturb the man from recovery, but he was in need of some important advice.

Mr. Swieley was back to his usual self with powerful words of sales experience. "Now you listen here and you listen good! Did you see anything wrong with that sump pump?"

Craig responded, "No."

"Did the seller tell you there was something wrong with the sump pump?"

Again, Craig responded, "No."

Gazing out the hospital window, the broker/owner was in a moment of contemplation before returning with advice made possible through decades of experience. "Whatever that seller has in that box of hers is none of your business! If she's hiding something from you and the buyers, then it's her problem. Let her try to figure out how to cover up some defect. You stay out of there and let the seller show the sump pump when she's good and ready. You did nothing wrong, you hear?"

Craig could hear the important piece of wisdom loud and clear. "Yes sir!"

Being confined to the hospital bed had caused Mr. Swieley to grow impatient. "I got to hurry up and get better and get out of here before my business falls apart!"

Mrs. Swieley patted her husband's shoulder and reminded, "Now, now; you relax like the doctor said. I think your partner can handle things while you recover. He's good and young enough."

Mr. Swieley continued, "Do me a favor. My secretary, Dora, had some people call on Mrs. Rudi's house. Are you up to showing it if these people are interested?"

"Yes, of course!"

Although Craig had shown numerous houses in the time worked at Jack Swieley Realty, the broker/owner found it necessary to continue coaching his apprentice. "Just be friendly. Let the house show itself and answer any questions, only the ones you know answers to! Don't say anything stupid! And make sure you give them my card. Can you do all that?"

Again, Craig reassured him, "Yes, of course! I'll take care of them for you! Maybe I'll sell it!"

Mr. Swieley only snorted a halfhearted laugh through his nose. "Well I hope you do."

* * *

With her house on the market for nearly four months, the day elderly Mrs. Rudi met the dynamic duo from Jack Swieley

Realty is an interesting story in itself. The poor Mrs. Rudi lost the love of her life some months ago. After living in the Mapleview bungalow with Mr. Rudi for over 30 years, she thought it was best to sell and leave the memories of a life that had passed. Only two days after placing an ad in the paper and a sign on the front lawn, Mrs. Rudi looked out her front room window and took notice of a good-looking, young man replacing her For-Sale-By-Owner sign with one that contained the name of a local real estate company

She drew close to the window while sipping her cup of tea. The young man simply smiled and waved. How cute! The good-looking, young man made such a bold gesture in suggesting that she should allow him to sell the house.

Mrs. Rudi stepped outside and approached the Realtor who now wore a sheepish grin. "Oh ya? You think so, huh?" It was best to play "hard-to-get" with such a fine, young fellow. He was probably accustomed to beating women off with a stick. But Mrs. Rudi was experienced and knew how to handle a chase so that she could win.

Suddenly, a voice could be heard from behind the good-looking, young man. "Good morning! Jack Swieley! I have an order to list your house for sale?"

What was this? A large, old man appeared with stinky cigar smoke! Taken back, Mrs. Rudi wasn't about to let the obese, sloppy man interrupt the game of the good-looking, younger man. Mrs. Rudi wasn't interested in Jack Swieley as she informed the broker-owner, "Look, all I know is that this young fellow put his real estate sign in my lawn, first! You're going to have to get in line. I'm talking to him, first!"

It took a few minutes of explaining before Mrs. Rudi's fantasy deflated back to reality. And by now, you are full aware of Jack Swieley's "comedy of errors technique" of obtaining exclusive rights to market. But the interesting thing about Mrs. Rudi: She never quite understood that placing the sign on her front lawn was only an accident. To this day, she believes it was the real estate broker's charming way of suggesting that she should use their services. It kind of makes you wonder if elderly people have difficulty understanding, or if they simply know the truth.

* * *

Sure enough, the buyers who saw Mrs. Rudi's house in an advertisement wanted to see it. And so Craig drove to Mrs. Rudi's house and took notice that her front door was shut and locked. It was 30 minutes before the potential buyers were to arrive. He knocked first and then used the key to enter. Mrs. Rudi was out doing busy Mrs. Rudi things. And just as Mr. Swieley had always done, Craig prepared the house for showing by opening curtains and windows, turning on closet lights and making mental notes of the outstanding features to mention. Then he sat down in the front room and waited.

A small, marble box that sat on the side table caught Craig's attention. Little, decorative knick-knacks often intrigued him. This one looked to be an interesting souvenir purchased at a gift shop while on vacation, perhaps during a cave tour. Craig lifted the box for an examination, but unfortunately did so at the lid which soon pulled out of the box in midair, causing the other 5 sides to fall back down.

Ashes and small chips of bones scattered on the table. It was then that Craig took notice of the candles surrounding the box along with photographs of the late Mr. Rudi. Apparently the intriguing, marble box was used as an urn, and Craig had violated a sacred altar of memory.

He frantically swept up the ashes while his skin crawled at the texture of a dead man's ashes and bones. While doing this, Craig took sight of the potential buyers who had exited the car and were now walking up to the house. In all the frantic sweeping, the ashes had somehow gotten in the air and found their way into Craig's nostrils. While gagging and choking, doing his best to restore the altar, the doorbell sounded. With the taste of Mr. Rudi at the back of his throat, it was necessary to force a pleasant greeting and engage in a moment of conversation.

Grittiness remained on Craig's teeth along with a maddening desire to down a bottle of water. If the buyers finished up, a trip to the gas station would have been near in the future. But they took their time, inspecting every room and closet while planning this room or that room to be one child's or another's.

"We'd like to make an offer!"

An offer? No, no; anything but an offer!

Mr. Rudi was truly with Craig in more than spirit. He called out, "You'll sell this house, today, for my wife!"

And the offer needed to be written up on the kitchen table as there was no room for clients back at the small, rundown office.

Chapter 30

Although curiosity has been known to kill a cat, some might claim that satisfaction brings it back! As far as Craig could determine, there was something in Debbie's sump pump access box, something other than a latent defect. And despite the strong words of advice, Mr. Swieley was unaware of that Sunday evening of mixed drinks and fantastic sex between his assistant, Craig, and seller, Mrs. Cordsmullen. Mr. Swieley was unaware of the panic-stricken Mrs. Cordsmullen who nearly had a nervous breakdown at the sound of the sump pump.

Now a Sunday afternoon and Debbie's 2nd open house, she had left for a few hours so her Realtor could handle business. It was an unusually hot day as Craig remained isolated in the air conditioned house. Considered the dog days of summer, the real estate market slowed down which resulted in an uneventful open house.

45 minutes passed, an hour, an additional 15 minutes; Craig sat in the chair as he fought the temptation to sneak into the basement and defeat the locked panel door. It used one of those cheap, hinged locks that mounted to the door with the use of screws. Craig simply needed to find a screw driver, remove the 6 Phillip screws and separate the hinge from the panel door.

Another 10 minutes passed and the bored Realtor finally rose from his seat, entered the garage for a screwdriver and descended the stairs into the basement. Carefully...Carefully...Each screw needed to be removed in such a way that his seller would never find out. At this point it would be worth mentioning that the makeshift panel door had the hinges on the outside. Under most circumstances, hinges are attached on the inside so that a person such as Craig cannot unscrew them and access what is protected inside. But the 4' x 4' enclosure with hinged panel was constructed by an amateur. And besides that, the initial construction never considered that one day a lock would be installed. As the potential buyer had mentioned only a couple weeks ago, "Who locks up a sump pump?" Yes; in recent events, Debbie found it necessary to install a lock!

The 3 foot door now dangled from the locking mechanism as Craig popped his head inside the enclosure. Nothing out of the ordinary was noticed. Simply a hole with sump pump and large PVC mounted to the wall, the discovery was just as anyone would expect. Then he observed the mortar that had been chiseled around one of the bricks and appeared removable, as if something was shrouded behind. With the use of his fingernails he wedged and pulled until enough of the brick could be grasped by his fingertips. The sound of grinding stone against the exterior wall produced the peculiar feeling of guilt that one might experience when accidentally walking over another's grave. The stench suggested something deathly. The moment was very similar to discovering ashes that lay on a side table and figuring out that they belonged to an urn which had been carelessly disturbed. It wasn't until the tiny bones of an infant surrounded in remaining carrion were noticed that the morbid reality struck Craig in the face.

It held a rusty, dismantled coat hanger in its skeletal hand. And then it moved, attempted to sit up in the crypt with restricted space while screaming a most terrifying cry; the same cry heard the afternoon Craig had signed the right-to-market agreement with Debbie.

Impossible! How could such a phenomenon exist? Words cannot describe the fear-driven speed in which the Realtor exited the enclosure. And his crouched body which bounced and flew out collided with the unexpected presence of the seller who now joined the screaming baby in a duet tears.

Debbie ran upstairs in the duet's refrain of "No" and "Oh my gosh!"

Craig followed, truly sorry for what he had done, wishing to have taken Mr. Swieley's advice. His broker was right. Pandora's Box should not have been opened!

Once upstairs, the basement door was closed which softened the shrilling cry of the skeletal infant. Craig did the only thing he could do at the moment and apologized for his ill-mannered snooping. "I'm so sorry Debbie! I'm so sorry!"

Debbie sat at the kitchen table with an emotionally distraught face, appearing to worry of the consequences.

"Debbie, I don't know where to begin. How in the world...Why in the world is this happening?"

It was in this moment that Craig finally learned the full truth from Debbie. She spoke of the child birth at home and the surprise visit of her suspicious husband. The infant-child had been murdered in a matter of seconds and temporarily thrown in the sump pump enclosure. But it came back to life many months later as Debbie carried out its removal. And as further punishment for her wicked deeds, the thing would only crawl back home, miles from its forest burial to scream for Mommy near the bedroom window.

"*And somehow it figures out how to take that damn coat hanger off from around its neck!*" It was necessary for Craig to step aside as Debbie had nearly run into him while darting for the door. Once reaching the bottom of the stairs, it wasn't long before the cries of the decomposed phenomenon silenced.

Slowly ascending the stairs, Debbie sat at the top step in complete, emotional drain. She gazed up at her Realtor for pity, "This has been going on for many months. You have to help me get rid of it."

Apparently, opening Pandora's Box meant that Craig now shared the torment of a woman who was not only unfaithful to her soldier overseas, but had committed a savage crime which resulted in terrible consequence. But Craig would not have it! He sharply replied, "That's not in the contract! I don't have to help you get rid of anything!"

He was sadly mistaken! The now ugly Mrs. Cordsmullen cracked the most devious and unsettling smile. "And neither was having sex with me. Maybe I should call your broker and report how you inappropriately touched me."

Funny thing: The impossible sight of a skeletal baby, which had come back to life, could not compare to the anxiety that Craig felt, now! He stormed out of the house an hour before the scheduled Sunday open was to end, and drove right to the Mapleview Police Station.

The very confused Officer Ralph took the delirious report and concluded that a possible murder of a child had taken place in the Circle Point subdivision. As luck would have it, the lead detective of the Mapleview Police was in his office, wrapping up the paperwork of a Sunday afternoon car crash which appeared to be a homicide.

How should Officer Ralph have relayed the information? "Detective Tom, I think you should check this guy out. He says some decomposed baby was coming back to life in his seller's sump pump."

"Well is he hopped up on goofballs? Come on Ralph! I've been going all day long and don't want to deal with stuff like that. Send him to the local bad trip center."

But Officer Ralph persisted, "No, he just looks like he's shook up from what he saw. You think there might be a dead baby in someone's sump pump?"

Just as-if on cue, Detective Larry walked in on his partner's sigh that was immediately interpreted as a longing to go home for the day. "What's going on?"

Officer Ralph briefed Detective Larry of the strange report.

Then the tired and weary pair of detectives entered the report room to meet the very disturbed Craig who sipped a cup of water as-if it was a good, stiff drink. As usual, Detective Tom began with his dry and annoyed humor. "Alright Sir, what's this all about? I hear a dead baby is in your sump pump and trying to get you?"

"No! I am an agent from Jack Swieley Realty. My seller has a dead, decomposing baby in her sump pump enclosure and it keeps coming back to life. She wants me to help her get rid of it and I just can't!"

Realizing the impossibility of what the hysterical man was claiming; Detective Larry attempted to draw some shred of reality. "Now wait a minute. Do you mean to say that your seller is neglecting her child and keeping it in a sump pump closet?"

Why was the delirious man growing impatient? "*No!* It's dead, but it's moving around and crying. I can see its bones and stuff."

"Okay, so she's starving her baby and keeping it in her sump pump closet?"

Accepting the detective's suggestion was the only way to get the police to Mrs. Cordsmullen's house. "Yes, it looks starved and severely abused. It's just horrible, simply horrible."

* * *

The following morning, Craig nervously reported to the office where, as usual, the broker/owner sat at his desk as-if eagerly waiting for Craig. Mr. Swieley was now out of the hospital and back in the saddle, eager to hear of yesterday's open house.

"So how did the open house go yesterday?"

Craig simply replied, "It was dead."

Mr. Swieley made a snorting laugh through his nose. "That's what I hear. It was dead! Last night I had my old buddy, Detective Tom Morehausen, stop at my house. We go back some and we went to high school together.

Anyway, he wanted to know if I knew anything about our seller, Mrs. Cordsmullen, who might have a dead baby in her sump pump. I told him I didn't know anything. But apparently you ran into the station having a freak out session, insisting that she had a dead baby coming back to life in her sump pump. But when he and his partner arrived at her house, they found nothing in the sump pump. Imagine that!

The only thing Detective Tom Morehausen has to go on is a delirious witness who swears a dead baby was coming back to life. Oh, he has his theories, but that's all."

Craig was at a loss of words and only looked at the floor, realizing he had disappointed the great Jack Swieley. In the broker/owner's decades of wisdom and intuitive insights, surely he must have been aware of Craig's inappropriate client relations.

But it appeared to Mr. Swieley that his assistant had been through enough. "Well, I think you learned your lesson. If the seller is trying to hide something, let it be the seller's problem, not yours." Then he stood up from the chair and walked towards the door. "Come-on, we got an appointment with a new seller."

Halfway to the door, Mr. Swieley stopped and looked at Craig. "I bet you want to know what Mrs. Cordsmullen did with that dead baby, don't you?"

Of course Craig did! How did Mrs. Cordsmullen cover the evidence from the police? What about the chiseled mortar around the brick? Did she use toothpaste to cover the cracks?

But Mr. Swieley had no information, only another piece of wisdom. "Well that's none of your business, right? Oh, and one other thing…" Mr. Swieley gave the young agent a good, hard kick to the seat of his pants. "That's what you get for getting close to a client!"

Chapter 31

On a brisk, Saturday morning in October, Sara walked a lonely nature path in the heavily wooded area of Sillmac. It just so happened to be the same path that she and Brian once shared. Just over two years since the tragic ending of a beautiful love, poor Sara experienced more than heartache. In those two years following the tragedy, Sara lived her life and operated the business both on automatic copilot as she struggled to cope with the loss of her fiancé. She had gotten much better. Through counseling, gradual healing and a will to live on, the Mapleview Coffeehouse continued to thrive. And once unimaginable, Sara began dating; more of a casual relationship.

She certainly hadn't forgotten Brian, she never would! And Sara would always love him. Many who have been touched by a special person remain altered for years and decades beyond a departing; whether it is a sad breakup, or in Sara's case, a tragic death.

Just then, Sara's cell phone rang. It was an unrecognizable number. "Hello?"

No one replied, but there was a static in the background accompanied by buzzing and a few pulses. Concluding it to be a misdial or crossed connection, the "End" button was pressed and the nature walk resumed.

Just as every year, autumn typically arrives around September 21st. But for all practical purposes, it still feels like the edge of summer in many places. The region that Mapleview and Sillmac belong to, however, feel autumn air somewhere around early September. Fall had already placed its grip in these woods as brilliant, October, colored leaves scattered throughout the nature path and forest. And the contrast of temperatures was most peculiar; cold, crisp air mixed with the hot sun that beat down in the clear, morning sky. The weather forecast predicted temperatures to reach nearly 60 degrees on the day of that Saturday morning walk. But the overnight temperatures were cold.

Halloween was soon to arrive. Considering herself to be an adult, the holiday, in Sara's mind, was meant for kids. But to be festive, her coffeehouse brewed the pumpkin spice blend throughout October and November. Mark, her new boyfriend, often stopped by and nearly expected a fresh chamber to be made for him.

The path made a curve as it hugged the small pond. The walk was, once again, interrupted with another unrecognized caller on her cell.

She answered, "Hello?"

Just as before, all Sara could hear was static in the background. But the pulsed buzzes gave hint to possible speech, maybe someone saying her name, perhaps someone asking, "Can you hear me?"

Unsure as to why, the second call was a bit eerie for Sara which resulted in a phone call to her mother. It was difficult for Sara not to obsess over a possible attempt to reach her. Was it important? Was there an emergency?

"Hi Mom, were you just trying to call me...? I got a couple calls from a number I didn't recognize and all I could hear was static... I don't know; whoever it was tried calling twice, but I couldn't hear... Just wanted to make sure you weren't trying to reach me... Yeah, I was going to try that next. I'm going to let you go and give him a call... Okay, bye."

Everyone has received a call on a cell phone from an unrecognizable number. Sometimes that person hangs up upon realizing the wrong number was reached. And sometimes all that can be heard in the background is dead silence or maybe some choppy words buried in noise before losing the call. It's a combination of a wrong number and bad reception. Often this phenomenon takes place at 2:00 in the morning as we explain that someone was looking for drugs or other illegal activity and dialed the wrong number. Only 7:30 on a Saturday morning, these explanations could certainly hold true. But Sara wasn't going to give in to those explanations. There was a near urgency in solving the mystery caller, and it was necessary to ensure that none of her loved ones were attempting contact.

Sara called her boyfriend, "Mark? Hey, were you trying to call me...? I don't know; someone tried calling a couple of times and there was just static... No, I didn't recognize the number... What? No!"

Mark playfully accused Sara of handing out her number to other men at the bars. He played this game many times and although annoying, Sara speculated it was his way of showing he cared. He often asked, "Who are you texting, your other boyfriend?" Or sometimes he would comment, "Going on Facebook to find some old boyfriends from high school?" Although cute and funny, once or twice, Sara was growing rather tired of it.

Unfortunately, Sara now found it necessary to explain herself to Mark as to what she was doing alone on the nature path. "I'm going for a walk over at the bike path... It's not bad outside..."

Oh, but it was bad outside! Mark would see that she understood this. No one in his or her right mind would ever consider hiking in frigid temperatures. And to make matters worse, Sara was woman, alone in the woods at 7:30 in the morning. Reminded that it wasn't quite 50 degrees, she was next asked if mace or a taser was carried.

"Mark, I'm fine! I've been doing this for years... Well, I'm going to let you go so you can get back to sleep... Okay, bye."

Brian wouldn't have thought that it was too cold outside. The woods were beautiful, especially in autumn. This was the same path that they shared together; walking, jogging or biking at least twice a month. And although Sara was alone, Brian's voice spoke as-if walking next to her. It was a welcome fantasy that often filled the gap of his sorely, missed presence.

His imagined voice declared, "Yep, fall is here. Pretty soon we won't be able to walk. We'll have to get the snowmobiles out." And of course he would throw in some silly joke, a jab that made fun of insurance agent stereotypes. "Do you have insurance, Sara?"

Uh-oh! Not again! Smiling at the joke of someone who was not there, Sara deliberately replaced it with the gentle reminder that Brian was truly gone. Then she reminded herself of the need not to relapse into those overpowering fantasies.

People mourn in different ways, and Sara had an unusual way of coping with the loss of the man she loved with all her heart shortly after the tragedy. She heard of people who maintained relationships in the "astral world" with the use of directed dreams and fantasies. Strangers sometimes connect this way; why not people who were close in life with a desire to maintain a loving bond? Sara may have lost Brian's love in this world, but she knew he was someplace else, continuing to love her. She simply needed to focus on that realm and continue the bond with the man she felt was her soul mate. Hugging her pillow at night while hoping to have another vivid dream of Brian, or having strong daydreams of him at day; his sorely missed presence was still with Sara to the point that it was very real. It was almost too real.

For months, Sara lived in this fantasy realm while talking to her deceased soul mate. He was with her while she drove; he was with her at work; and he was with her during breakfast, having detailed conversations. Eventually, Sara realized this to be unhealthy and had considered that perhaps she was having temporal lobe hallucinations. Counseling was soon followed.

There are healthier ways to mourn the loss of a loved one. And it's true; we can resume a relationship with someone who has passed into the next world through prayer, feeling that person watching over us and maintaining certain traditions followed when he or she was alive. But we must accept the fact that a loved one is gone. Having strong, overpowering fantasies that a deceased love one is still with us, in person, can be detrimental. During her therapy, Sara followed the suggested homework, visited Brian's grave and spoke out to him that she needed to move on. And after weeks of taking it one day at a time, she pulled out of the overpowering fantasies and moved on.

Still, on that Saturday morning in October, Sara felt that a much-deserved, fleeting fantasy wasn't a bad thing. Besides that, Brian probably was with her on that nature path.

She softly replied to Brian's suggestion of riding snowmobiles, "Well Brian, I don't think snowmobiles are allowed out here, not in this town; you know Sillmac."

After the morning walk, she stopped at the bakery where she and Brian often visited. Since the bakery offered a dining area, she sat down and enjoyed her fresh bagel and orange juice. "So how are things up there, Brian? Sorry I couldn't order your cinnamon bun and coffee; you understand."

Being that Sara offered a mini-bakery at her own coffeehouse, Brian often playfully reminded her of supporting the competition. He did so at that moment as well. "How do you like that? The owner of the Mapleview Coffeehouse is sitting down at another bakery, drinking their coffee. It's not as good as yours, right?"

She had to be careful not to smile too much. Only crazy people smile and laugh to themselves. And then she thanked him for the time spent on that Saturday morning while throwing away the wrapper and empty orange juice bottle. He was gone and it was time to come back to reality.

A short drive back to Mapleview, Sara quick showered and then paid her Saturday, morning visit to the coffeehouse where employees had greeted their boss. All was in working order and her small bakery was nearly depleted. That's okay; having too much waste at the end of the day was not a good thing. The coffeehouse closed at 5:00 on weekends. Since midmorning was nearly over, people wouldn't be looking to eat donuts and pastries in the afternoon.

Sara offered, "Do you girls want to go on break while I'm here?"

Jessica and Lynn had been working since 6am and handled the Saturday morning rush. Now slow, Sara could man the counter with maybe only one or two customers; customers like Daren who now entered and greeted Sara.

He was a regular customer, most friendly and a very, good looking man. He spoke while approaching the counter, "Hey there; how's things?"

The need for Daren to make deliberate small talk was so obvious. Sara often wondered if he came in just to see her.

She exchanged the greeting, "Good morning!"

Ah, but despite his good looks, wonderful charm and money; the man had one turnoff that prevented Sara from having any interest. Daren was married, as evidenced by the wedding band that held the massive wad of cash—20s and 10s rolled up and counted with his right.

Daren made his request, "I'll have a medium pumpkin spice coffee."

Did he really need to count the ridiculous amount of money to verify there was enough for the beverage? Sara responded, "Sure, coming right up."

Sara was an incredible woman to drool at, and Daren painfully yearned for her. Mary was well endowed, herself; but

Sara probably had the biggest pair of breasts in all of Mapleview. Mary had a robust body frame, but certainly not rubenesque like the woman who owned the Mapleview Coffeehouse. Daren liked women of all sizes, shapes and colors. There were so many that he was literally in love with. And there was something so intriguing, so sexy about a chunky lady. As far as Daren was concerned, a little "muffin top" gave the appearance of being healthy, cute and very cuddly on a cold, winter night.

Sara filled the medium sized cup with the popular blend for the season. Suddenly, her cell phone rang. Not a big fan of answering calls in front of customers, she merely checked the number with the intention of calling back. But it was the unrecognizable number that had called twice while on the walking path earlier that morning.

She looked up at Daren in apology, "Excuse me." And then she answered her phone, "Hello?"

This time there was definitely a voice as it called out, "Sara?" The voice rang through the static and produced a flood of memories, bringing Sara nearly to tears. It was the voice of Brian—impossible! And he continued to call out, "Sara, can you hear me?"

The memories and near tears were quickly replaced by distress and confusion as she quickly snapped the phone shut and focused on the customer. The lid was placed on the cup and brought over to the counter.

Even Daren in his selfish quests took notice of the disturbed look on Sara's face. "Is everything okay? You look like you've seen a ghost."

"No, I'm fine, just a wrong number. That'll be $1.89".

He flipped through the ridiculously, oversized roll of money and pulled out a ten. It's funny; only moments ago, Sara resisted any possible hints of flirtations from the good-looking, married customer who often entered. Now she savored every moment in giving him the change back. Being that Daren was the only customer in the store, Sara would soon be alone in the case of another baffling and frightening call.

How do you tell a stranger to stay for company, much less explain an impossible phenomenon? There is no way to ask a stranger of this. Daren took the change and brought the cup of java to the cream and sugar table where a quick pour and stir happened all too quickly. The bell sounded as the door opened. Sara was now alone. Hopefully the girls would soon return from their cigarette break or whatever they were doing outside. Maybe they were having a quick and sensible breakfast at one of the fast food restaurants nearby.

Steve Coldsworth was up late the previous evening, touching up parts of his masterpiece painting, the Tree Goddess. He could have slept in later, but Steve accepted an offer for some Saturday, afternoon overtime at the sawmill and lumber distribution warehouse. Much in need of a serious java jolt before work, he stopped at the Mapleview Coffeehouse for his regular cup of Joe with a shot of espresso.

Sara nearly appeared relieved to have seen him enter. Steve recognized her from the numerous times previous of visiting the coffeehouse. But this was the first time Steve had taken notice of Sara's enormous breasts with cleavage that she proudly displayed in her low, cut blouse. If that weren't enough, nipples protruded through her bra and blouse, and it wasn't easy for Steve to keep his eyes off them. They were the perfect breasts for the Tree Goddess!

"Hi, can I help you?"

Steve peeled his eyes away from Sara's breasts and gazed up at her face. "Yeah, give me a medium coffee and throw in a shot of espresso."

Sara wasn't unfamiliar with requests like this. Many people came in asking for two or three shots of espresso in a cup with ice. There's been an age-old argument of whether or not espresso contains more caffeine than regular coffee. Some experts claim there is less while others claim there is more. Still, the Mapleview Coffeehouse seemed to be gaining a reputation as a legal pharmacy for liquid crack. Sara didn't mind. Shots of espresso added to the charge so that an ordinary cup of coffee could be double, even triple in price.

She gladly announced, "One hammerhead coming right up!" A coffee expert certainly boasts her knowledge of the various beverages made.

While preparing the customer's beverage, Sara's cell phone rang. Why would she do the unthinkable? Why would she answer to the unrecognizable number that had spooked her moments ago? Maybe it was curiosity. Maybe it was a need to prove to herself that Brian's voice was only imagined through the harsh static. She looked up at the customer and apologized before answering.

"Hello?"

The voice spoke through loud and clear, "Sara, it's Brian!"

Such cruelty! Such a mean joke! Sara darted into the backroom, barely withholding her tears. The phone was no longer at her ear, but she could see the call was still active. And Brian's deceased voice yelled through the receiver, "Sara!"

The phone was snapped shut and the battery removed. Who was doing this? The voice was so perfect. It couldn't have been her imagination that time. Was Brian's family so cruel as to play a wicked joke?

Nervously pressed for time, Steve watched as Sara emerged from the back room with eyes that had been crying. She sniffed while speaking nasal, "That'll be $3.78"

* * *

Saturday afternoon overtime at the sawmill and lumber distribution warehouse required the simple task of transporting grosses of plywood from the sawmill to the showroom floor. Licensed to operate a forklift, the uniquely-creative, starving and frustrated artist spent a few hours slowly and carefully driving the lift with hundreds of pounds while observing safety.

Such a job required strict attention to detail. But after a few hours of monotonous driving, backing, raising and then lowering, Steve began to think of his Tree Goddess painting. The woman at the Mapleview Coffeehouse had remarkable breasts, indeed. But would breasts that large disturb the essence of the painting while distracting the onlooker from the art?

And then there was the reality that outside her protruding nipples and smooth cleavage that displayed through the low, cut blouse, Steve had yet to see much of anything. Too bad there wasn't a small device that would enable Steve to freeze time. He could enter the Mapleview Coffeehouse where the small device would be activated.

Steve created a daydream in which everything in the Mapleview Coffeehouse had stopped! One second, the well endowed woman behind the counter was preparing his beverage. The next, she was in suspended animation—thanks to the small device that enabled Steve to freeze time! As if walking throughout a stationary image, Steve freely entered behind the counter and lifted up her blouse which exposed a bra about to burst from enormous mass and weight. Undoing her bra let it all hang out! Smooth and milky white, the breasts were ginormous in size, almost frightening. Steve caressed, squeezed and explored every inch of her bare breasts, taking mental photographs while admiring how the breasts, themselves, nearly bulged as if to burst.

Satisfied, he struggled with the ginormous mass and barely refastened her bra. The blouse was pulled back down and Steve walked in to the position behind the counter where the time-freezing device was deactivated. Clueless of what had just happened, the woman behind the counter merely had the sensation that things didn't fit right, underneath.

Customers at the sawmill and lumber distribution warehouse observed as the crazed, forklift driver sped down the main isle of the showroom floor and past the cash registers. He looked as though having some sort of mental seizure, completely oblivious and just staring off into space. It was necessary for parents to yank their small children off the deadly path of the runaway forklift. Hundreds of pounds of plywood approached the brick wall that had an employee break room on the other side.

CRASH!

The explosive crash snapped Steve out of the daze. "Damn it!" The uniquely-creative, starving and frustrated artist had another unfortunate vision from the Tree Goddess while driving the forklift. The mess that lay before him was a pile of bricks and drywall dust that lay over the pushed break room table. Fortunately, the only person on the other side of the wall was his supervisor who sat on the adjacent side of the table as the forklift battered through the wall.

Poor Steve, he was in big trouble now as the supervisor called out, "That's it, Coldsworth! You've just lost your forklift privileges!"

Chapter 32

Years ago, when originally conceiving of owning a coffeehouse in Mapleview, Sara planned to remain closed on Sundays. I'm sure many of the business owners in downtown Mapleview thought the same. And perhaps some of these small shops and outlets do observe the old fashioned rule. But when it comes to coffee, do lovers of this drink refrain from their daily java jolt on Sunday? The fact is Sunday brings in many weekend shoppers, tourists and simple residents who can't get enough of the Mapleview Coffeehouse blend. Guess what! Sundays became regular days of operation for the Mapleview Coffeehouse!

People could wait until 8am, of course. Throughout the workweek and Saturday, Sara's business opened the door at 6am. But when first starting years ago, Sara was the sole operator and needed at least one day to sleep in. And the same can be said of the girls who now open the shop on Sundays. They should be able to get some rest after a Saturday night, out, perhaps even join the family for church.

And it's a good thing that her business had grown to the point that there were shift supervisors who handled the business opening on weekends. On the Sunday morning that followed the Saturday of terrifying phone calls, Sara needed to make a trip to the cemetery where Brian was buried. It was about an hour drive from Mapleview. Maybe that fleeting fantasy during Saturday morning's hike made it necessary for a gentle reminder that Brian was gone.

Sara hadn't been to Brian's grave in over a year-and-a-half, much less seen his family members since the funeral. It wasn't that she felt awkward visiting her deceased fiancé's grave as much as she feared encountering his family. Recall that at the funeral, Brian's mother had spoken the damaging words, "Maybe if you weren't such a backseat driver, my son would still be alive!" But no one rushed in to hold back the woman from speaking further. No one did so much as to apologize for the mother's frazzled emotions. It was as-if Brian's family truly did believe that Sara's backseat driving resulted in the tragic death.

Sara pulled into the mortuary and memorial gardens that Sunday morning and drove her car to the area closest to Brian's grave. It was a large, old cemetery. Her fiancé was buried some distance from the road which required a small hike through fresh, cut grass mixed with small and barely noticeable remains of autumn leaves mulched from the tractor.

This lonely walk through headstones was a symbolic confrontation of that which tormented her the previous day. Perhaps this is why she willingly answered the ring of the cell phone that displayed the dreaded, unrecognized number.

"Hello?"

"Sara, it's Brian; don't hang up! This is really important!"

The sound of his deceased voice returned Sara to distress. Whoever it was could emulate Brian's voice so perfectly. Outraged, Sara shouted, "Damn you! It's not funny! Leave me alone and stop calling me!"

Tears ran down Sara's face as she ended the call and threw the phone in her purse. What was wrong with that person? Maybe it was someone in Brian's family finally getting revenge. It was a cruel, sick joke indeed!

Sara reached Brian's grave while close to sobbing. "It's been a while. I haven't been to see you lately. I bet you wonder what brings me here. Well someone keeps calling me and pretending to be you!"

She stopped her words short upon noticing something smashed into the ground near the headstone. Apparently a supposed tractor tire had rolled over the mysterious object and wedged it into the ground. It was a sight that would lead one to ask, "Do cemetery groundskeepers roll tractors over the graves?"

Whatever the thing was, it didn't belong there. Graves do not include these unusual items. Sara bent down and used her fingers to dislodge a sun-faded, water-damaged cell phone from the ground. The LED display was cracked and the buttons were caked with dirt. It surely belonged to a member of the living at one time, but it was now part of Brian's grave.

Although damaged and certainly beyond repair, Sara lived in a world where anything was possible. The coincidence of receiving calls from an unfamiliar number with Brian's voice, only to discover a cell phone near his grave, yielded quite an ironic overtone. She laid the old cell next to his grave and then pulled out her own while selecting the call option for the unfamiliar number.

This time, Brian answered. "Hello?"

"Brian, it's me! I'm sorry; I didn't know."

Waves of static overshadowed his distant, choppy voice until the message of "Lost Call" displayed on her own screen.

Realizing how nearly impossible it was to reach the dead, Sara persisted by calling the number again. But the callout tone would only ring and ring. For some reason, Brian did not answer.

How long could she stand over his grave while calling and calling? What if someone recognized her? What if she encountered a member of Brian's family? There had to be a way to hide the phone near his grave so she could continue until he finally answered. But digging a small hole near his grave would damage the sod and alert family members or groundskeepers to something buried. There had to be an alternative.

Brian often commented on the strength of Sara's legs. Although nearly impossible to do, Sara pushed and grunted with all her might, ignoring her lack of knowledge of monumental masonry. Could a headstone break? Was the base heavy enough to damage the marker that displayed Brian's name? Cemetery desecration is a serious crime and toppling over a headstone, possibly damaging it, could be met with harsh penalties.

Soon her deceased fiancé's headstone lay on its side as the bare ground that was underneath the marker only seconds ago lay exposed to the sun. With her fingers, Sara dug a hole into the dirt. The soil of her lover's grave caked under her fingernails. The phone equally as dead as Brian and found near his grave was dropped in the hole and then covered up with soil.

But poor Sara learned that lifting the headstone back upright was twice as challenging as the near impossible task of toppling it over. She lifted and lifted with all her might, but efforts were in vain.

And then Brian spoke out as he had always done since leaving this world, suggestions to help his struggling Sara. "Come on! Use those powerful legs of yours! You can't lift that thing yourself! Push it upright; don't lift it!"

Sara called out, "I'm trying! Come on, Brian! You have to help me! This is not easy, this whole thing! Look at me; I'm a crazy woman who is playing with a grave!"

Brian could only offer suggestions as he was dead. But he was correct to suggest that she used her legs. A few grunting-pushes landed the base and headstone back into place. Any possible evidence of molesting, Sara hoped, would be washed away in the next rain.

As for Brian, he wasn't going anywhere. Brian was in that ground forever and would answer the phone eventually.

Chapter 33

Sound asleep on a crisp, October, Sunday night; Mary dreamed of her backyard where she stood overlooking the Hidden Lake. Suddenly, thoughts of that eye-sore-of-a-mausoleum invaded her mind. Fighting the urge not to look was impossible in dream world. Just thinking of the building caused its sudden view in front of her face.

And who would appear from around Daren's mausoleum? It was Kelly who approached with a look of seriousness. "She's sorry, Mary. She wants you to know that she's sorry."

Poor Kelly; Mary never held anything against her. Daren should have been the bigger person, and Kelly most likely learned her lesson. Mary reminded the young girl of this, "I forgive you, Kelly. Don't worry about it."

Is the reader a dreamer, like me? Has the reader ever taken notice of the transition of motions and actions in a dream? If so, then you are quite aware of how the unusual communication took place. Kelly was already aware of Mary's forgiveness and let this fact known without even speaking. And then she continued, "It's the other woman who lives here. She's sorry and wanted me ask your forgiveness. I want you to know that she never did anything with Daren. But she did a lot of bad things in her life and she hopes someone could forgive her."

Mary awoke, lying alone in her darkened room. It was nights like these that she wished Daren lay beside her. Away in Omaha at another product demonstration, he wasn't in bed to draw close to and provide body heat and safety from another bad dream.

Although forcing herself to pull from the residual fear, Mary remained trapped in her desperate need to understand the dream's meaning. What did Kelly mean by "the other woman living here"? And why was Mary suddenly an authority to give the Sacrament of Reconciliation?

Piercing darkness penetrated Mary's nightshirt as her feet touched the floor and she drew close to the entry of the bedroom door. Slowly and reluctantly walking along the hallway where invisible fingers laid their undetectable touch to her skin, Mary approached the stairs. Just a breath away from screaming, she descended while fighting in vain with whatever forces possessed her to do the unthinkable.

At the landing, her resistance to opening the main, entry door to the outside world was numbed by the seizing presence. The chilled, night air was most unrecognizable in comparison to the heavy, looming presence that blanketed the house and grounds. The deepest fear one could ever feel; the weight of the unfathomable ocean; it illuminated every pore on Mary's body. Still, Mary continued towards Daren's mausoleum.

Around the tall bushes that perimetered the yard; Mary soon faced the back of the building. Crying, it came from behind the stone, brick walls. Was it the actual building crying, or was it someone inside? The faint light of early dawn revealed the mausoleum's texture and crevices along with a sickly color that appeared vile and repulsive. Still, Mary placed her ear against the wall, listening to the saddened cries. Maybe if she walked around to the front and listened through the door, the crying might be recognizable.

She was greeted by the pale and deathly body of Kelly who stood before her with black, sunken eyes and lifeless expression. Is the reader a dreamer? Those haunted words of "I'm sorry" were never heard from Kelly's open mouth as Mary was quickly startled awake and sat up in bed.

Daren lay beside her, snoring.

Mary gave a quick pinch to her arm just to verify that she truly was awake.

* * *

Monday morning means that Mary must report to the flower shop for another 5 or 6 days of her job. And although a boring first-day-of-the-week sort of morning, Mary followed the practice of having a nice breakfast with her dear husband while he was home. Every bit of time together was precious as Daren often traveled out of state, demonstrating medical products. And precious time can mean, at times, to sneak a gentle mention of a concern that is hoped to be met with reassurance that all is well.

Daren sat at the kitchen table, eating Mary's homemade French toast with bacon.

Mary soon joined him with her plate and poured some blueberry maple syrup over her French toast. "So, I had a bad nightmare last night."

"A bad nightmare? What happened?"

Nearly regretting her mention of the silly dream, deep down inside Mary needed her concern to be heard. "Well, I've been having these weird dreams since Kelly disappeared. It started one night when I dreamed that I was outside working in the backyard and Kelly came out from around the mausoleum, apologizing to me."

Daren looked up, "Apologizing?"

"Yes. Well the dream was scary and I woke up. But then last night, I dreamed that Kelly came out from the mausoleum, again, and told me that the woman who lives there is sorry, too."

Daren wiped a dribble of blueberry maple syrup from his chin, "Huh? Wow!"

She waited for any further comments from Daren and then continued. "Anyway, I thought I woke up, but was in another dream. You were out of town and I started to wonder about the mausoleum. And even though I was terrified, I went downstairs and out into the backyard. There was crying coming from the mausoleum! And suddenly Kelly stood before me like some walking corpse. She looked dead! Daren, it was scary!"

Daren set his fork down and looked up at his wife in compassion. "Mary, I know this thing is really hard on you with Kelly suddenly disappearing. But I don't want you to blame yourself. You know how she was always the black sheep of the family, right?"

"I know, Daren. I just… I'm looking for some kind of closure, that's all. I really think that if I went into the mausoleum, it would make me feel better."

Daren's face froze for a second, "Why would you want to do that? It's the family mausoleum, sacred."

Mary sat there in a silent expression of persuasion and a hope that her husband understood. And then she continued, "I know, Daren. But no one's in there and it would just make me feel better. It would help me stop having the nightmares."

Sitting back in his chair with a couple taps of his fingers, Daren agreed. "Okay; sure. Come on, let's go outside and you can see the mausoleum."

But Mary was cautious. "I'm sorry Daren. You're not mad, are you?"

"No, I'm not mad. What's there to be mad about? Come on, put your jacket on and let's go outside. I'll get the keys."

Although no one would see Mary in her bathrobe, covered by a jacket, she still had a desire to step into a pair of pants. And then she followed Daren to the far corner of the yard where they walked around to the front of the mausoleum. Daren unlocked the door that smoothly glided open.

It was the first time that Mary had ever seen the inside of the building. All that greeted her was a wooden bench at the center and two sidewalls of closed crypts. Daren walked in the building and over to the far wall where two sconces illuminated the area. Mary was invited to join him.

While approaching her husband, Mary could see that Daren masked his rattled feelings. The building truly was sacred for him and allowing her to see the inside for the sake of Mary's piece of mind was quite a sacrifice.

Daren commented, "See, this is where you and I are going to rest together. Isn't it nice?"

And then his rattled emotions manifested. His voice rose, "What, you want me to open the crypts so you can look inside? You don't believe me? Here, I'll open one for you!" Daren walked towards the entrance of the building and undid one of the crypt locks.

"There, see? No one in there! You believe me now?"

"Daren, stop it!" How Mary wished she hadn't disclosed her silly suspicion! She was supposed to trust her husband but failed. No wonder he was so upset.

But Daren continued, "No, why should we pretend? We both know why we're in here! You think that I killed your cousin and put her in here with someone else!" He pounded the hammer of his fist against the wall while shaking his head in disbelief.

Mary laid her hand on his shoulder. "Daren, I'm sorry. If I knew it would have made you mad..."

But he only shouted louder, "I just can't believe this!"

The monster of years ago who was nearly abusive, suddenly appeared before Mary's eyes. She was about to experience words and behavior that hadn't been witnessed since before Daren cut back on his drinking.

Daren now spoke like a ferocious demon with hands that could smash anything nearby. He was always frightening while doing this; and Mary often stepped back as she did this time, allowing Daren to yell. "I'm always gone, busting my ass, doing what it takes to make money! Then I come home and you ask, 'Gee Daren, did you murder Kelly and lock her in the mausoleum?'

I'm sick of the suspicion and hostility coming from you! And let me tell you, there is truth to the statement of, 'wedding cake is the food that kills a woman's sex drive!' Ask if you want to have sex and it's like I'm the most disgusting thing, ever! And when I'm home, you feed me that down home cooking crap! Look at my stomach!"

Such verbal damage seriously wounded Mary's feelings. The attacks were completely uncalled for. Mary understood the sacredness of the mausoleum, but did Daren have any sacred feelings towards his loving wife. All poor Mary could do was run off, crying. Why didn't she listen to Aunt Loraine?

Before locking up the mausoleum, Daren opened his favorite crypt for a quick beer inventory. Running low, it would be necessary to visit the store while Mary was at work. And Daren didn't drink the low-carb/low-cal stuff, either!

Chapter 34

Weekdays were very much different than weekends for Sara in that she certainly couldn't sleep in late and then report to the nature path for a relaxing hike. There were things to get done throughout the workweek such as inventory, deliveries and other necessary tasks of running a business. And although there were no early, morning deliveries scheduled on a Tuesday morning, it was best that Sara maintained her weekday schedule and arise at 3:30am.

The Sunday phenomenon at the cemetery had certainly changed circumstances for Sara. For you see, Sara had convinced herself that those fantasies of Brian's presence (shortly after his death) were nothing more than the harmful effects of imagination. And in the case of Saturday morning's "breakfast with Brian" at the bakery in Sillmac; again, it was fantasy that combined some prayers to Heaven as-if Brian could receive them and shine his light back down.

But there was a new reality. Sara realized this as she picked up her cell phone in the darkened living room and dialed the once unrecognizable number which now belonged to her late fiancé. Fantasies used to be sweet while offering a brief escape from reality. But as the callout tone could be heard while waiting for an answer, the seriousness of what Sara was attempting ate away at her conscience. It was almost frightening and eerie. Who calls the dead from a cell phone?

Sadly and equally relieving, Brian did not answer. Was he angry with her? Surely he had to understand what a confusing moment it was for his Earthly fiancée to receive a call from another world. And from what Sara remembered of him; Brian was a very, easygoing sort of guy who rarely became angered, much less hold extended bitterness for a silly misunderstanding.

During weekdays, The Mapleview Coffeehouse opened its doors at 6:00am. Just like every Monday through Friday, Sara entered the backdoor of her business a couple minutes before 4:30am, and disengaged the alarm.

Coffee was well overdue! Maybe the first chamber to be brewed would be the dark French roast followed by the regular blend. And of course the third chamber would be Mark's favorite, pumpkin spice. The sacred java could not brew fast enough as Sara waited while mentally planning the morning. She was just like her customers, depending on the fine blends of the Mapleview Coffeehouse to start the morning off right.

Just then, the main business line rang. It was an unexpected sound that sent a jolt through Sara's body. But it was best for her to answer professionally, considering the possibility of a customer or vendor. "Good morning; Mapleview Coffeehouse."

It was a man's voice on the other end. "Yeah, I've got some paper supplies, boxes and bags."

Sara was confused, "Is this a delivery?" Boxes, bags and cup holders were not scheduled to be delivered until Thursday. This unexpected arrival would throw the morning off.

The voice replied, "Yeah, I'm parked in back. I'm covering for the usual driver while he's on vacation."

That would certainly explain his strange way of delivery. The regular driver walked through the front door and usually came around midmornings. Although not even quarter-to-five in the morning, the untimely delivery was still needed as paper products were running low.

Poor Sara hadn't a chance to drink her morning coffee as she answered, "Okay, I'll walk to the back and open the door. Be there in a second."

Walking past the small ovens, Sara turned the dials to preheat. A couple batches of pastries and other baked goods were needed for when the doors opened for the day.

The unexpected, predawn delivery was certainly a bother. She deliberately scheduled visits from vendors during the later morning hours for when her employee, Dianne, could assist.

Just seconds away from the backdoor, Sara's cell phone rang. It was Brian—unbelievable! Of course she would answer it! While pushing open the backdoor which automatically unlocked it, the speaker of the cell phone went right to her ear as she spoke the word, "Hello?"

* * *

50 year old Dianne reported to the Mapleview Coffeehouse at her usual Tuesday morning start. Often is the case when she raps on the front door for her boss to open. But Sara did not appear on that Tuesday morning as Dianne continued to knock harder and harder.

Sara had to have made it to work that morning; the lights were on.

Pulling out her cell phone, Dianne called the Mapleview Coffeehouse and then Sara's personal number. Still, there was no answer.

Being older with a trustworthy reputation, Dianne had been given a copy of the shop's key along with the code to disengage the alarm. These things were provided in the event of an emergency or for a possible morning when Sara would be unable to come in. Dianne walked around the establishment to the backdoor where the alarm could be disengaged if needed. As further proof to Sara's presence, her car was parked in the back. Where in the world could Sara have been?

Walking in the backdoor, Dianne noticed that the alarm had already been disengaged and the aroma of coffee hung in the air. But something wasn't right. The morning smell of baked goods was absent.

"Sara?" Dianne called out to her boss, but no answer. She walked past the ovens to take notice that they were preheated but no pastries. Did something happen? Did they run out?

"Sara?" The cash register had yet to be opened! There was only one chamber of coffee brewed. Where was the pumpkin spice? Where was the regular brew? And why in the world hadn't Sara started baking?

Dianne had seen nearly 30 years of marriage and the raising of three children. She wasn't about to face the morning completely helpless. Apparently there was a problem and the store was about to open. Hurriedly, she dashed into the freezer where an assortment of pastries and other baked goods were removed. And then she flung the frozen goods onto baking trays as if dealing a deck of cards.

In the years of being a housewife, Dianne could rotate a load of laundry, flip the omelet, wake her children for school and have her husband's coffee and vitamin at the table in less than two minutes—yes, all of those activities in less than two minutes! And at the very moment that her husband spoke, "Where's breakfast?" his perfect omelet would be placed on the table. Dianne was proud at that.

With the greatest of ease, she grinded the beans, filled the baskets of the chamber and pressed the automatic brew button. And by the time that had all been done in less that 4 minutes the first customer of the day stood outside the door that was locked.

Dianne was about to pour a cup of coffee for herself. But the customer comes first! She dashed over to the door and unlocked it.

"Good morning!" Customers were always pleased with the service and friendly greeting as they entered. But on this morning, a small inconvenience would be brought to the customers' attention. Dianne apologized, "Sorry, we had a little problem with our ovens this morning. The first batch of pastries won't be done for another 45 minutes or so."

Throughout those early morning visits, Dianne apologized to the regular customers who were used to their jalapeño and cheddar bagels, cinnamon rolls or muffins. But she remained graceful and held down the fort—a one man (excuse me!) *one woman* band that could proudly do it all!

By midmorning, the rush of java addicts had ended. Where was Sara? Dianne peeked her head out the door and could see Sara's car. This wasn't right! Surely Sara wouldn't leave the shop unattended.

At exactly 10:30, Sara's boyfriend, Mark, entered the coffeehouse with his usual, energetic greeting. Asking for a tall pumpkin spice blend with two shots of espresso, he next asked Dianne, "Where's Sara?"

But Dianne didn't know. "I don't know. I was hoping you could shed some light. Her car is outside."

Chapter 35

With two recent disappearances in town, there was no delay in adding Sara's mysterious absence to the string of investigations led by the Mapleview police. All it took was a phone call from the concerned Dianne who grew increasingly worried as the day progressed. Sara's car was in the back parking lot and she evidently entered the coffeehouse in the predawn hours. But it wasn't like her to suddenly vanish. Something was wrong, and Dianne felt it was her responsibility to convey the phenomenon to police.

It might be easy to conclude that cameras would have recorded the business owner's final moments that morning, but it was an expense that Sara hadn't invested in. From what detectives Tom and Larry could see, there was no sign of struggle much less a hint of anything which suggested foul play. And the only item that might have provided evidence was the establishment's records of transactions of the week (and month) that contained times of the days and hopefully names of customers who used debit or credit cards for purchases. At the time, this request was considered merely procedure by the pair of detectives. But when they returned to the station, the guiding hand of events would encourage a diligent examination of the Mapleview Coffeehouse's sales records that would lead to the first suspect in the Mapleview disappearances.

Officer Ralph had been a clerk of the Mapleview Police Department for many years. Despite his lifelong ambition to fight crime, the poor man worked the beat of traffic patrol early in his career until it was decided that the pudgy and good natured member of the police force was better suited for office duties. But he never lost sight of his ambitions and refused to accept the fact that a lifelong career of desk duty was his destiny.

Such was the case on the day when Detective Tom and Larry returned from the Mapleview Coffeehouse with nothing more than records of transactions. Officer Ralph had some information that he hoped would blow the case of the Mapleview disappearances wide open. "Gentlemen, we had a visit from one of the bouncers over at Hotlicks earlier."

"Oh yeah; what'd he say, Ralph?" Detective Tom's skin often crawled when approached by the office clerk who sought every chance to, one day, become a detective like him

"It's not what he said, it's what he provided. This is the name of a customer who harassed that Hotlicks girl who disappeared. According to the bouncer, he used a debit card that night to pay for his beer. And he was parked outside, waiting for her, a few nights before her disappearance."

Detective Tom's expression of disinterest suddenly changed as he looked at the report. "Steve Coldsworth, huh? Well why wasn't the bouncer so forthcoming with this information before?"

Only moments ago, the veteran detective entered the station with a heavy gait and the burden of another disappearance. Now he was supercharged, spewing out orders and creating a plan of action. "Larry, why don't you and Ralph go through the coffeehouse sales records and see if the name Coldsworth pops up. I want to look up the address of this guy and see if he has any records."

Coffee which had sat on the burner for over 8 hours was poured into a Styrofoam cup with a packet of Sweet and Low. Most would cringe at drinking such a nasty beverage, but Detective Tom needed the elixir which provided a boost of his noteworthy intuition.

Not more than five minutes had passed as Detective Tom looked up the name of Steve Coldsworth who lived in downtown Mapleview at one of the old apartments. Soon, Detective Larry entered his partner's office with the excited Officer Ralph trailing behind.

"Hey Tom, Steve Coldsworth visited the coffeehouse on Saturday and purchased a medium coffee with a shot of espresso."

Officer Ralph quickly gloated, "That's right Detective Tom! He used his debit card! *I* found it while searching the receipts!"

The seasoned veteran of the Mapleview Police briefly glanced at the computer screen, "Coldsworth, huh? Well Larry, should we pay this guy a friendly visit? It's late in the afternoon and he's probably home."

Detective Larry agreed, "I think we should."

The pudgy, good natured office clerk who aspired to join the detective force could hardly contain his excitement, "You want me to come with, too?"

Detective Tom was so mean, "No Ralph; it's dangerous out there. You better stay in the office and monitor any possible updates to the case."

"Okay; but Detective Tom, can I go home now? It's past my shift."

"Sure you can, Ralph."

* * *

It was near 6:00pm on a Tuesday twilight in October. Steve stood alone in his one bedroom apartment, before his masterpiece mural in the living room with a frozen pizza cooking in the oven. The sounds of neighbors could be heard from the outside hallways along with the muffled babbles of TV news anchors in other apartments. Steve preferred silence and loathed the disturbances from those who lived around him.

The Tree Goddess paining was nearly complete; only the head was needed. Still, the effect was all wrong. Something was disproportionate with the painting; and the more Steve examined it, the more frustrated he became.

And then to further disturb his much, needed silence a loud rap was made at the door.

Steve would have ignored the knocking, assuming it to be a door-to-door salesperson or some kid selling candy for a school function. But the announcement of, "Mapleview Police" inspired him to quickly answer.

"Steve Coldsworth?"

"Yes"

"I'm Detective Tom Morehausen with the Mapleview Police Department, and this is my partner Detective Larry Copperwright. I was wondering if we could have a word with you."

Steve opened the door all the way. "Yes, of course. Please come in!"

Immediately the pair of detectives was drawn to the mural-sized painting of what appeared to be a half-tree, half-human that stood in the middle of a clearing in the woods. Very careful detail had been given to the painting and every aspect and tone of human limb representation had been created. Steve Coldsworth was a very gifted artist, indeed.

Although impressed with the work of art, Detective Tom had a case to solve. He flashed a picture of Kelly in front of Steve's face. "You ever seen this girl?"

Uh-oh! Steve certainly did recognize Kelly as evidenced by his expression of anxiety. He could only tell the truth at that moment, "Yeah, she's a waitress down at Hotlicks."

Detective Larry corrected him. "No; *was* a waitress down at Hotlicks. She's missing. You can't tell me you don't know that. It was all over the news!"

Steve appeared so surprised and even apologized. To make matters worse, he provided an excuse for his lack of knowledge. "I don't pay attention to the news. It's the same crap every night: corrupt politicians and CEOs, global warming along with the Middle East about to blow itself up. I'm a painter who gets involved in his work. I wasn't aware that she had disappeared."

Detective Larry took the conversation in a different direction." Tell me something, Mr. Coldsworth; where do you find inspiration for a painting like that? Why does the tree have women's body parts painted on it?"

Steve was quick to answer, "I do nature hiking. I found the tree in the woods and the way it was shaped reminded me of a half-human, half-tree goddess. That's why I am calling it the Tree Goddess."

And then Detective Tom attempted to hex his suspect with the ole' Jedi Mind Trick. "Mr. Coldsworth, there is no need to get defensive, here. We're just asking a few questions. You have a guilty conscience or something?"

It was Steve's first indication that he was a suspect in the waitress' disappearance. But he wouldn't fall for the detectives' tricks as he answered a firm, "No!"

Without asking, Detective Tom walked over to the mural painting and carefully examined it while appearing to admire the work. Then he turned around while reaching in his coat pocket, "Well, Mr. Coldsworth, if you have anything you might want to tell us about this missing waitress down at Hotlicks, you give me a call. I'll be all ears."

Detective Tom handed his business card to Steve. Accepting it was the most insulting thing Steve had ever experienced.

Once the pair of detectives made it back to the car, the seasoned veteran of the Mapleview Police Department made mention of his key impression which labeled Steve Coldsworth as the prime suspect. "Larry, did I ever tell you that I spent two years of college, pursuing an art degree before deciding on law enforcement?"

"Why no, Tom; I don't believe you ever did."

Detective Tom pulled onto Mapleview Road while continuing. "Yeah, and I found art to be fascinating. Let me tell you something about that mural in Coldsworth's living room. There's a problem with it and he knows it. The entire tree and body parts are exquisitely detailed; so much, in fact, that the various body parts don't match. It's sort of a twisted Mona Lisa, a collection of various women. And I bet the body parts painted on that tree belong to the missing women.

He has them, Larry. He's got the women buried somewhere or maybe even hiding in his closet."

* * *

The following morning, Detectives Tom and Larry stood over a fresh pot of coffee at the Mapleview Police Station.

Detective Tom was not happy with the brew, "Ralph, this coffee is weak! Can't you make coffee right?"

Detective Larry came to the clerk's defense, "Well you need to let it sit for about 10 hours, Tom. I thought you like the stale, burned stuff."

"Very funny!" Detective Tom took a sip from the Styrofoam cup, hoping the morning elixir would bestow the secret powers of intuition. "I just wish I can get a warrant based on the tree painting. I'd love to go through Coldsworth's apartment."

"You really think he's got the women in there?"

"I know he does, Larry."

Just then, Larry suggested a brilliant idea. "Well supposedly it's a real tree out in the woods. Maybe he goes there and talks to it. Maybe we should find the tree and ask what it knows about Coldsworth."

Detective Tom didn't find the suggestion helpful. "You're a real comedian this morning, aren't you, Larry?"

Just then, Officer Ralph appeared. "Gentlemen, did I hear you mention something about a tree in the woods?"

Detective Tom rolled his eyes, "Oh boy…"

Detective Larry encouraged the office clerk to continue.

"There's some kind of urban legend about an old tree in the woods, something about an Indian massacre which had taken place because of this tree. I guess there's some sort of ancient well that's next to it where victims were sacrificed by being cast into it. I say that if you find this tree and ancient well, you'll find those missing women."

"Well where is it Ralph?" Partly humored, Detective Tom was willing to explore the possibility.

"Look, I'm not trying to say that the tree and ancient well is really out there. But if your suspect believes he found the tree, then maybe he's burying the bodies nearby. Maybe you should pay him another visit and ask him to bring you to it.

Chapter 36

As do many regions of the United States, Mapleview has a history spanning hundreds of years as it was occupied by civilizations long before the New World was explored by the white man. And most of these civilizations remained scattered about the country long after it was given the name of America. You've taken history classes, I'm sure of it. Our country is thousands of years rich in Native American history.

Like most tribes of Native Americans, the ones that existed along the regions of Mapleview, Sillmac and beyond were peaceful people. This is why the supposed legend which, at some point, was passed down to the modern day residents of Mapleview is so unusual. It would suggest that a disturbed individual had led a small cult into a killing spree. Believed to have taken place some 300 years ago, modern day historians in Mapleview immediately discredit the tale because of its inconsistencies and lack of evidence.

The name Nukpana would have been most unlikely for the supposed Native American serial killer who terrorized the region of Mapleview before the arrival of the white man. Nukpana is a Hopi name, and Hopi is a tribe that is primarily located in Arizona and quite some distance away from Mapleview. Further more, why would someone be given the name of Evil (English translation of Nukpana)?

But according to the persistent urban legend, Nukpana was a Native American tribesman who lived some 300 years ago and had become obsessed with an unexplained hole which, as far as inhabitants of the region knew, had always existed. People had a fear and aversion of the deep, dark hole in which a stone could be dropped into without the splashing sound of water. Its purpose and origination was a complete mystery.

Often dreaming of the fearful place, a need to face the hole alone in a moment of conquering was an appealing prospect. And so Nukpana ventured from his people and village for an afternoon in solitude with the mysterious entrance into the Earth.

Sitting at the very edge and gazing deep into the blackness, Nukpana thought about his own life. He examined events, memories and the current state of his people's village. Every face of his own family and neighbors had appeared as daydreams. Each person had been labeled by Nukpana's own likes and dislikes. The hole, he concluded, possessed a spirit which he had befriended. There was nothing evil or to fear of the anomaly. It granted the power of omnipresence or that of all knowing.

Nukpana returned to the village, seemingly altered and changed, almost as-if a wise man who was many years beyond his age and so aware of everything around him. To the actual elders and wise men of the tribe, the altered and changed Nukpana was nothing more than a wiseass who needed to be cut back down to size.

Within a day, the previously enlightened and omnipresent tribesman was the laughing stock of the village. As the elders saw it, any gift of nature should have been accepted with humbleness and humility, not boasted while arrogantly insulting members of family and neighbors. If he had gained some insight in his private moment with nature, he was not wise enough to understand its purpose. The elders saw to it that arrogance was knocked back down.

Returning to the anomalous hole in the Earth, Nukpana pleaded with whatever perceived spirit that existed. There had to be a way to restore the power of omnipresence. Was there a cost?

He imagined of a payment that would ensure a more perpetual state of greatness. Surely, he speculated, there were people in his village who residents could have done without. Perhaps the purpose of the hole was to discard these individuals. In return for eliminating those who, Nukpana believed, were a waste of life, the spirit, he imagined, would grant a more constant state of omnipresence.

It was a young boy who unfortunately was born deaf and mute. And although nothing particularly troublesome with the boy, Nukpana always maintained a strong dislike towards the child. Why should he be allowed to live while burdening family and tribe people with his handicap? Nukpana carefully led the boy some distance from the village, where he was murdered and then dropped into the deep hole.

Returning to the village with an imagined restoration of being all-knowing and wise, the man who sacrificed the deaf and mute child felt respect and regard which came from the tribe people. In reality, many people associated him with the disappearance of the handicapped boy. And as time went by the man who imagined himself to be, once again, omnipresent concluded there to be an additional cost that he hadn't considered for his greatness.

Due to his arrogance, Nukpana interpreted everyone's negative feelings as a certain jealousy and animosity for the power which he possessed. In reality, they were the wiser ones who had sneaking suspicion of Nukpana's evil deed. For Nukpana, the solution was so clear. Younger members of the tribe needed to be inducted into this strange cult that involved a perceived spirit in the deep hole.

A handful of boys who were at the threshold of becoming men were one-by-one persuaded to join Nukpana out into the wilderness. The task of persuasion was nothing easy as it needed to remain secret. And it took quite of few days to convince each boy that a mystical event out in wilderness would guarantee reaching manhood with ease.

But once away from the tribe, Nukpana led the boys to the anomalous hole and introduced them to the perceived spirit. Those who would join would gain an unparallel power along with the life of freedom to do whatever desired. To demonstrate freedom of desire, Nukpana had abducted a young woman from a neighboring tribe where she was bound, awaiting her final moments alive, when one of the young men would forcefully enjoy his desires. When her purpose was fulfilled, the young woman was killed and dropped into the hole. Nukpana congratulated the boy on becoming a man.

Within a few days, additional youth of Nukpana's following had been secretly inducted into this new cult that was now boasted by its first followers and soon to branch off from the village. In the predawn hours the small population left their families and friends to live as nomadic killers and rapists who enjoyed (which was more imagined) an unparallel power brought on by sacrifices to the hole. Women, children and the elderly; victims were abducted from various villages to be murdered and casted into the Earth.

Now terrorized with the new evil that prowled out there, warriors had joined from neighboring tribes to hunt for this cult and do away with its leader. A small scrimmage with boys on the threshold of manhood was no match for the skilled and hardened warriors. The cult was rounded up. Nukpana was executed and dropped into the anomalous hole which would forever be his realm of Hades. His followers stood trial before the chiefs and elders of the several tribes that had been tormented by their evil. As punishment, the boys would be banished for some years to continue wandering as nomads in hopes that they would learn to value and respect what they had before turning against the tribe.

It was a harsh winter for the boys who had to learn to fend for themselves and hunt for small animals which barely kept them alive. Feeling defeated and low in spirits, it was a sight in mid-spring which restored a sense of awe and that of hope. Perhaps they were looking for some sign that Nukpana was still with them. Maybe this is why they ventured to the mysterious hole in the Earth where it was noticed that a baby tree grew next to it. It was a sign that Nukpana had become a god. Nukpana would be their protector, an invincible leader who most likely encouraged the boys to continue their lives of human sacrifice.

But there was an addition made by the nearly starved cult of adolescent boys. The tender flesh of young women who were abducted for pleasure and sacrifice would be roasted in the fire. Nukpana's followers had become a cult of savage cannibals that resumed its terror along the region of Mapleview and surrounding areas.

Once again, finding and capturing the adolescent boys, who had yet to be named men, was no difficult task for the assembly of warriors. The boys stood a serious trial, received many hateful words and insults; and were finally executed to be discarded in Nukpana's realm of Hades.

Historians and archaeologists have difficulty accepting the urban legend and see it as just another creepy, ghost story to be told around the campfire. Lack of evidence along with the unlikely name of Nukpana is not even half the problem. Anyone educated in archaeology knows that Kivas (holes in the ground that lead to chambers) are constructions of Pueblo Indians; who would have been a far, far distance for tribes that existed in Mapleview some centuries ago. An ancient well would be an unlikely theory for the supposed hole because there are plenty of lakes, rivers and fresh water streams throughout the Mapleview and Sillmac area. Digging a well would have been unnecessary, even thousands of years ago.

And then certain details of the legend sound exaggerated and unreal. Why would so many boys choose to leave their families behind for a disliked man to live as nomads? And just how did this renegade tribe abduct its victims without being discovered?

How about you? Do you believe the Legend of Nukpana's Cult?

Chapter 37

Detective Tom wasn't a historian or archaeologist. He didn't care if the Legend of Nukpana's Cult was accurate history. And if the legend really was just another creepy tale, the possibility remained that Steve Coldsworth was performing human sacrifices to what he believed to be Nukpana's hole. The legend did make mention of a nearby tree that would now be old and very large. All it would require was to have the prime suspect lead Detective Tom and Larry to the very tree that had been seen out in the woods. If Steve Coldsworth balked at the suggestion, it would provide further suspicion that something was hiding out there in the woods.

But it was necessary for Detective Tom to go about the casual investigation carefully. He certainly couldn't surprise the suspect at work and appear harassing to someone who was innocent. Despite Detective Tom's intuition, there was yet to be a reason for an arrest or obtain a search warrant.

Detective Tom couldn't show up at Steve's apartment on a Wednesday or Thursday night, asking to be brought to the tree. It was now autumn which meant that darkness fell upon Mapleview early.

A Saturday morning visit would surely have taken the suspect by surprise. The pair of detectives approached Steve Coldsworth's apartment at 8:01am. The knock produced the half-asleep Steve who peeked through the cracked open door that was secured by a chain lock.

Everyone enjoys a loud and cheerful greeting just seconds after being awoken, especially when it's designed to agitate. Detective Tom was the master of this. He warmly greeted, "*Rise and shine, sleepy head!*"

Steve had finally retired only three hours ago after another Friday night with the Tree Goddess painting. Groggily he replied, "Can I help you?"

"Mr. Coldsworth, why so unfriendly? It's only us, here to visit."

The chain was undone and door opened further. Steve stood motionless, waiting to hear more.

Detective Tom read the suspect's body language and then continued, "We just want you to show us where that tree is that gave you inspiration for your painting."

"The tree? You want me to show you the tree?"

"Yes! That's all we want: to see your tree out in the woods."

Needless to say, Steve was mistrusting. "Am I under arrest or a suspect?"

"Well that all depends if you've done something wrong. Now how about that tree? Show us your tree."

* * *

It was a gray, Saturday morning as Steve volunteered himself to ride in the back of the unmarked patrol car with Detectives Tom and Larry to the Hidden Lake Forest Preserve. Although seemingly cooperative with nothing to hide, Detective Tom treated the artist as though he was hours from being arraigned.

The trio exited the vehicle at the Hidden Lake oasis, the place where Steve often parked for his adventures in the woods. And then Steve led the Detectives some feet away where a small, dirt trail provided a pathway for hiking.

Detective Tom was never fond of the woods. "You come out here often, Mr. Coldsworth?"

"Oh yeah; I've hiked here on many occasions."

"Alone, in the deep forest like this?" Detective Tom asked.

"Yeah."

"Well that's kind of strange, don't you think, Larry?"

Detective Larry agreed, "It's a bit odd."

Detective Tom continued, "Aren't you afraid to come out here, alone? There are bears and wolves; and crazy, dangerous people often come out here to be alone." He clarified the subtle accusation with exaggerated emphasis, "Oh, *excuse me*, Mr. Coldsworth. I wasn't trying to say anything about you. I'm just making mention that strange people come out to the forest to be alone."

Steve softly came to his own defense, "I'm not afraid."

"What's that?" Detective Tom sharply asked.

"The woods, they don't frighten me."

"Of course they don't, but you should be." Then Detective Tom asked his partner, "Larry, remember that body we found up the road? It was some guy who had been left in the woods, castrated."

"Yup, I remember that one."

"He shouldn't have been out there alone. It's just proof that bad people do bad things in the woods. See, I like to go fishing and sometimes I find a lake off the highway. But it's out in the open, not hidden in the forest. If you ask me, I hate this wooded environment. Some day when I retire, I'm moving to a tropical climate with lots of sunshine and warm weather. Let me tell you, I love the sun and hot weather. It gives me energy. But you like cool, dark places; right Mr. Coldsworth? You probably like going into caves."

Steve confirmed, "Caves are cool; I've toured a few in my life."

Detective Tom quickly shot down the suggestion of caves being a nice place to visit. "Not me! I have no desire to go into the Earth and tour some dark and musty place. Caves are for creepy people who do creepy things. Are we almost there yet, Coldsworth?"

"Yeah, it should be coming up here any second." Then Steve paused for a brief moment and proceeded to pace in circles while looking at the ground."

Detective Tom was annoyed at the sudden, strange behavior of the prime suspect. "Larry, he reminds me of a school boy that didn't do his homework and is pretending to look for it in front of the teacher." The pair of detectives watched their prime suspect wander aimlessly in confusion.

It was frustrating for Detective Tom, "What happened? Did you forget where the tree is?"

Steve stuttered and stammered, "It... it was right here. This is where I saw it."

Studying the ground, Detective Tom could see no evidence of a tree ever being there. He was growing increasingly disgusted to the point of wanting to smack his prime suspect. Rather than hit him, he grabbed Steve by the back of the jacket and held a firm grip on his left shoulder while walking the man forward. "No, this must not be the place where your tree is! Come on, Mr. Coldsworth, let's find that tree!"

Steve resisted and pushed back. "But this is where the tree was! I'm telling you the truth. I don't know what happened to it."

Detective Tom sighed in disgust and realized it was impossible to force Steve to lead them to the tree. And he knew Steve wasn't at the point of confessing to any murders. But an unofficial, off-the-records interrogation out in the woods just might have had the possibility to produce a jolt that would cause a breakdown when evidence was finally collected against him.

Detective Tom lit up a cigarette and glared at Steve. "You think I was born yesterday? You think I'm a freakin' idiot? I suppose the tree ran away once it knew we were coming. In fact, I bet the tree is the one responsible for the disappearances.

Actually, I've got a better idea. I think that tree of yours is that Indian legend tree, and I think you are sacrificing women to it. I bet the reason you can't find that tree is because it might lead us to the bodies of those three women. Isn't that right, Mr. Coldsworth?"

Steve appeared shocked and horrified while shaking his head, no. "Detective I had nothing to do with the disappearances of those women. And I'm sorry I can't find the tree. I just don't understand why it's not here."

Detective Tom took a deep drag and exhaled. "Well if you ever find it, you give me a call. In the meantime, I'm watching you. I know you're just full of it right now and don't want to come clean.

Come on Larry; let's take Mr. Coldsworth back to his apartment; waste of my time today!"

Part Four:
The Ring

Chapter 38

Understanding the fourth and final disappearance of Mapleview requires that we venture back into the spring of that year. It was about a week after Mary had closed on her new home that was purchased from Aunt Loraine. This meant that Daren had yet to step foot in the Trivelli House. And Steve had yet to receive his vision of the Tree Goddess on that dark night in the Hidden Lake Forest Preserve.

The fourth disappearance had nothing to do with supernatural forces or any of the previously mentioned residents of Mapleview. It all had to do with a man named Wayne, who on a boring Friday night in spring sat before his desktop PC.

Actually, it is best to venture some 15 years before that night in spring, to the early 90s when a summer evening turned out tragic for Wayne. It did, after all, change his life forever and was most likely the reason for sitting before a PC on a lonely night some years later.

It was all Curt's fault; that's what Wayne believed for many years after the event. If it weren't for Curt's interference, Wayne wouldn't have lost the woman that he loved. Curt was always somewhere in the background. Considered in childhood to be a playground friend, and among one of his close peers at the start of 7th grade, Curt soon shared a fascination with Wayne towards the young and beautiful Eileen.

Children that age claim to "go out" with one another. For a week or two, Wayne would enjoy this status as Eileen would sit beside him at the Saturday matinee. And then word would spread that Curt was talking to her. Soon, she would be "going out" with Curt instead of Wayne. A couple weeks would pass, and rumor would spread that Wayne was talking to Eileen. And then the beautiful Eileen would, once again, belong to Wayne. It was a never-ending cycle.

By high school, neither young man had let up on the fascination with Eileen. Wayne was lonely during his freshman year as the girl he loved wasn't his. Of course they remained friends which turned to romance by summer. We could go on and on with the never-ending cycle of who would possess Eileen. But by senior year, Eileen belonged exclusively to Wayne. Curt had his own girl which meant that Wayne could finally relax and fully enjoy the girl that he loved.

A time shortly before high school graduation and throughout the summer months, Wayne believed this to be the happiest days of his life. Eileen spoke things such as, "Some day when we're married" along with many other hints that she believed to have found her destiny.

Adding to the high in life, Father cosigned and made the down payment for a "like new" 1984, midnight-blue Camaro. It was a handsome graduation present intended to launch his son into the adult world. Wayne would be expected to land a job to afford the payments and insurance. And as a little bonus to the graduation gift, Father already had a job lined up. A colleague of Father's who owned a construction company was happy to accept Wayne as an apprentice.

And I know what you're thinking, "Why in the world wouldn't Father have supported his son with college, instead?"

To answer your question, Wayne wasn't quite ready for college. Not all kids his age are. But Father hoped that a responsibility, along with the realization that life would be nothing more than banging away on wood, might have inspired his son to aim higher.

Who was father kidding? Wayne loved the construction job as it paid well. And Wayne was enjoying the best days of his life as the summer nights were spent cruising downtown Mapleview in his midnight-blue Camaro with Eileen beside him. He had plenty of money to spend on his girl. He had plenty of money for beer during those summertime kegger parties. And amazingly, Wayne and Curt appeared to be buddies while drinking beer side-by-side. Curt had his own girlfriend and Wayne had his beloved Eileen.

Then one Monday morning in August, Father passed his son's bedroom while leaving for work. He could hear Wayne snoring away. It was already 7:30!

Father swung his son's bedroom door open. "Wayne?"

"Huh..." Wayne sat up in bed with eyes partially closed.

"Don't you have to go to work, today? It's 7:30! You're supposed to be on the site at 6!"

"Nah, I quit. I gave 'em my notice last week."

Needless to say, Father was outraged. "Quit? Why?"

"I registered for school. It starts next week."

"School? What school? Where?"

"Over at the Sillmac Community College."

Father's feelings were mixed at the moment. He was certainly happy that Wayne considered continuing his education. And it was much sooner than expected. But there was one small problem. "Well that's fine, Son, but what about the car? How are you going to make the payments and afford insurance?"

"I'll get something part time, I guess."

"You guess? You damn well better get something or that car is history! So when did you register for school?"

"I took a day off last week. Eileen and I went down there."

It all became clear to Father, "Oh, so *Eileen's* going there?"

"Yup."

Such disappointment, Wayne didn't decide on bettering himself and continuing his education. Wayne quit his job so that he could keep an eye on the girlfriend while she attended classes at the community college.

And right Father was! Wayne did everything in his power to ensure that he would have the exact, same classes as his girlfriend. Although cute at first, Eileen soon perceived this to be a nuisance. Most bothersome was the need to seek Wayne's approval for taking one class or another. Her reason for attending the Sillmac Community College was to complete general education requirements and then transfer over to a 4 year university where a nursing degree could be earned. Certainly Wayne wouldn't follow her all the way through nursing school!—would he?

College writing was the very, first class of Wayne's very, first day. He sat next to Eileen with his textbooks, notebook and pen. Eileen didn't mind the company. Wayne was her boyfriend and it was nice to start a new chapter in life with a close friend beside her. Then much to their surprise, Curt entered the room and greeted them both with a friendly smile. He sat down at the other side of Eileen which didn't bother Wayne in the least— that is until he remembered that Curt's girlfriend left for college, out of state. But he controlled the jealousy while remembering the summer parties in which him and Curt stood side-by-side, drinking beer. They had buried the hatchet and left the years of archenemy rivalry behind. Still, Eileen noticed the peculiar feeling of being supervised while talking to Curt.

A writing class is all about writing. The professor didn't waste time in having the students do this. Maybe a 20 or 30 minute talk of how to go about writing, the first assignment was to be done in class. It was a simple introduction of who one is and why one is attending college. When completed, the work was to be read out loud.

Wayne used this as an opportunity to declare his relationship with Eileen and how he was very happy with her. And as expected, Eileen mentioned him while reading her assignment out loud.

The professor next encouraged that the students find a partner in class to exchange future works for feedback. No problem for Wayne! He and Eileen should have exchanged each other's work as they were boyfriend and girlfriend. And with Eileen being his new feedback partner, Wayne was most delighted when learning of the next assignment that was to be a small essay titled, "Who I Admire most in Life".

It would have been more appropriate for Wayne to title the essay, "How do I Love Thee? Let me Count the Ways!" After a short, Tuesday night out with Eileen, Wayne retired to his bedroom and wrote several paragraphs of flattery on his girlfriend. Knowing that Eileen would be reading it, the work was poetry in disguise, designed to melt her heart in class.

* * *

"I can't wait for you to read my essay!" Wayne took hold of his girlfriend's hand while driving to school.

She smiled back while disguising her dread, "Uh-oh; what did he write? Would it be necessary to read Wayne's essay out loud, in class?" His firm declaration of possessing Eileen was somewhat embarrassing on the first day of class.

That day caused heartbreak for Wayne. As he found out, Eileen did not write several paragraphs of flattery to him. Instead, Eileen wrote a nice paper that was dedicated to her mother who had triumphantly survived breast cancer. Never losing her grace while maintaining strength and faith, she pushed on as a full time mother of three children, loving wife and continued working her career. Needless to say, Eileen was most admiring of her mother.

But Wayne was crushed that his Eileen was not on the same page. He poured his heart out on paper, declaring eternal love for his soul mate. Eileen, however, wrote about her mother.

Another writing assignment involved describing a place that students would like to one day visit. Wayne wrote of his future honeymoon with Eileen on some tropical island where two weeks would be spent snorkeling, boating and laying out on the beach. At night they would make love and create their first child together.

Eileen, however, wrote of her longing to visit Paris, maybe even live there for a moment in her life. She continued to describe that Paris was often believed to be a romantic place where one can fall in love.

This writing seriously disturbed Wayne as it showed that he and Eileen were not in synch. And what did she mean about "falling in love"? She was already in love with him! And Wayne had no desire to live in Paris. The only way she could live in Paris was to break up with her boyfriend and maybe meet the love of her life, half a world away! Wayne offered much criticism on this work, citing that it was too dreamy and not realistic. Eileen's sentences were full and somewhat lengthier than Wayne's. Of course Wayne declared these to be run-ons and a serious fracture of the rules of writing.

All these events occurred under the stress of Curt's presence who sat very near Wayne's precious Eileen. College writing was every Tuesday and Thursday. College writing became emotionally traumatic times of the week for Wayne. Curt's girlfriend was far away and possibly broken up with. Wayne feared the potential of losing his girlfriend to Curt.

And then Wayne's worst nightmare happened in class. The professor announced that it wasn't good to receive feedback from the same partner. On the fourth writing assignment, Eileen and Wayne were required to turn to the neighbor of the opposite direction. The end result, Eileen and Curt exchanged papers!

Although a harmless, persuasive essay in which Eileen chose to state her reasons against capital punishment, Wayne imagined with slippery slope anxiety all the sensitive things that Curt would learn of the girl he loved. Wayne's presence could be felt as he listened from two seats away.

And it killed him to hear Curt compliment Eileen's writing style. "You are truly a brilliant writer. Have you ever thought of doing this professionally?"

Driving home in the early afternoon hours, Wayne's dependent girlfriend, who had yet to own a car, sat in the passenger seat. As far as Wayne was concerned, it was every bit his right to ask, "What was your paper about?"

"Capital punishment; why?"

"I don't know; I just want to see what Curt thought was so spectacular about your assignment."

This was the moment when Eileen finally lost patience, "You know Wayne, ever since we started college, you've turned into a big jerk. It's like your jealous or something. What if I don't show you my writing assignment? Would it kill you?"

Wayne's blood boiled, "I would almost expect you to show me your paper. I don't like seeing secrets between you and Curt. Show it to me, now!"

He quickly pulled over to the shoulder of Mapleview Road, just past the bend where the road transitioned south. Seeing that she had no choice in the matter, Eileen removed the paper from her folder which was quickly snatched by trembling Wayne.

Wayne's parents were fundamentalist, ultraconservative republicans who often spoke of how the country would soon collapse with Bill Clinton in office. And it wasn't uncommon for his father to preach that it was cheaper to put a bullet in criminal's head than to keep him alive in prison. Reading Eileen's humanitarian essay that defended the lives of those who should rightfully serve their debts in prison went against just about everything that Wayne believed. "Eileen, this stuff is wrong! You're obviously not educated enough! Don't you get it? A killer will serve his time in prison and come out to do it again! Why waste money? Execute him!"

And then he insulted her writing style; the length of sentences along with a couple spelling errors. "I don't know what Curt is talking about. You suck as a writer and your ideas are stupid!" He flung the paper back at the glassy-eyed Eileen and tore off, spinning stones from the shoulder until gripping the asphalt.

How Eileen missed Curt at that moment.

* * *

A year-and-a-half passed and seasons transitioned. Despite how the young Eileen desired to end her relationship with her mentally abusive and possessive boyfriend, she remained with him. There was just no way to break up with him. Any suggestion or hint that it was best to spend some time apart would be met with rage and fists pounding the seats, hood of his car, or whatever inanimate objects were nearby.

It was necessary to request in advance nights out with her friends. And somehow, Wayne would end up at the same club or whatever function was planned.

And then came a warm, summer night when Wayne would learn the truth of Eileen's Friday night outings. As usual, it was necessary for Eileen to call her boyfriend in the afternoon and ask if it was okay to go out with her friends.

Wayne wasn't the least bit receptive to the idea. "You know, it would be nice if I could spend a Friday with my girlfriend. You went out last week, too."

"Well Wayne, you could spend some time with your friends instead of stalking me. They probably forgot about you."

And right Eileen was. Wayne had no friends as every moment of his life was devoted to Eileen.

He continued to probe, "Where are you going?"

"I don't know; Lynn and Julie want to go out for pizza and maybe see a movie. Is that so terrible?"

"What movie?"

"Wayne, I don't know! We just want to go out and have some fun."

There was a slight pause before the lord and master spoke. "Well I don't see how you can go out without making plans. If you ask me, a bunch of girls wandering without plans is a bunch of girls asking for trouble. I don't think so, Eileen. You're not going out tonight. I'll be over right after work."

It would appear that attempting to go out unsupervised by Wayne would entail another nasty fight along with one of those pseudo breakups. She spoke sharply in reply, "Wayne, don't bother coming because I won't let you in. And if you don't like it, then we can end this!"

Now I won't go into the pathetic afternoon of harassing phone calls that threatened to breakup along with plenty of crying, rude hang-ups and accusations of, "I know you don't love me". Such things needed to be endured by Eileen. But strangely, Wayne didn't show up after work. In fact, she heard nothing from him in the early evening hours. Perhaps he decided to visit some old friends like a normal guy should.

But unknown to Eileen, her possessive boyfriend hid at the park down the street! It was 7:00 in the evening as he sat inside the top of a tornado slide. The entrance area provided a porthole view of his girlfriend's house. She wouldn't see him, nor would anyone else. A pair of binoculars remained on Wayne's lap. He would find out, once and for all, if his suspicions were correct. For some reason, Wayne did not trust the girl he loved.

By 7:03 a Pontiac Grand Prix pulled into Eileen's driveway. Wayne quickly raised the binoculars to his eyes which yielded the most shocking and unwelcome sight. *Curt* exited the vehicle and walked up to Eileen's door!

10 minutes passed before the couple came out. Along with no flowers brought into the house, there was no opening of the passenger door so Eileen could get in. And before pulling away, the two kissed. These were all suggestions that they had been dating for some time.

Oh how Wayne's hands trembled! How his breathing became erratic as the tips of his fingers tingled from an abrupt change in circulation. Wayne's suspicions were confirmed. Eileen was lying and cheating. Wayne sat at the top of the tornado slide for some time as twilight faded into evening. What could he do? How could he handle this situation? Perhaps it was best to use that evening as an opportunity to learn of where Curt lived. Although buddies before starting college, they weren't on a "go-to-each-other's-house" basis. If Wayne could hide out at the park and wait some hours for Eileen to return, he could follow Curt. Keep in mind that this was the early 90's, a time when computers were not exactly a common house appliance and sites such as Zaba Search were nonexistent. Back in those days, it was necessary to physically follow one in hopes to discover his or her residence.

Wayne's midnight-blue Camaro remained in the darkened lot of the neighborhood park. He waited at the top of the tornado slide with binoculars until 1:17 am when a car pulled into Eileen's driveway. In the dark, Wayne jumped off the slide and ran to his vehicle. Driving up to the edge of the road, he waited with headlights off while carefully observing their activities through binoculars. He imagined that his cheating girlfriend and Curt were oblivious to the distant presence as the couple made out for some 5 minutes.

And then Eileen exited the vehicle and ran up to the front door. As a gentleman, Curt waited until she made it into the house, safely.

Curt remained oblivious to the midnight-blue Camaro that followed some distance behind. The pursuit took Wayne northbound through Mapleview Road, into the old section of Mapleview, past the Hidden Lake Forest Preserve and then a right turn onto Vine Road. It was so easy! Curt actually turned into his small, heavily-wooded subdivision where he finally pulled in front of his house. And he remained oblivious as the midnight-blue Camaro passed, drove half a block and turned around. Wayne watched the man he hated most enter the home. For now, his residence was found.

* * *

"Hello?" Eileen answered the phone the following morning, sounding as-if disturbed from slumber.

"Hey…" It was Wayne of course.

"Hey…" was given in return. With the previous afternoon of immature fighting, Wayne was not her favorite person at the moment. Besides that, she had a wonderful date with Curt the previous evening.

Wayne quickly asked, "So where'd you go last night?"

"What do you care? You broke up with me, right?"

"Come on Babe, I was just upset. I didn't mean that. And I thought about everything and you are right. Why shouldn't you be able to go out with your friends?"

There was a long pause that was broken by Wayne. "So where'd you go last night?"

Eileen sighed, "We went out for pizza and then went back to Lynn's house for a few hours. Not much of a night, just girl stuff."

"Oh yeah? That was nice. You wanna go out tonight, make up?"

Again, there was another pause followed by a sigh, "Sure, you can come over around 6:00."

"I can't get there that early. I've got to work for a few hours and cover for Rick who called off." Wayne was the fry boy at Big Boy's Beef and Ribs. "Maybe I can be there around 9:00?"

"Sure; I'm going back to bed."

But before she hung up, Wayne's voice could be heard through the receiver. "Hey Eileen?

"What?"

"I love you."

She threw the phone back down on the receiver. Next to it laid Wayne's promissory ring, a piece of cosmetic junk to be worn in the place of a real engagement ring. It spoke to the world and pretty much said, "She's mine, but my modest salary as fry boy makes it impossible to have a fiancé." Eileen whipped the ring across the room, something often done when frustrated with Wayne.

Only a split second after the ring bounced on the floor, Eileen's phone rang. No problem, she pulled the cord from the outlet. Wayne would be calling all morning, and Eileen needed her sleep.

* * *

And so the very, much, disliked, midnight-blue Camaro zipped into Eileen's driveway at just a dot past 9:00 that night. How she wished she could break up with Wayne. How she hated the sensation of sitting in his passenger seat.

"Where's your ring?"

Uh-oh; Eileen forgot to put her ring back on. Most likely it remained in the corner on the floor. "Oops! I put some lotion on and left it on the dresser. Do you want me to get it?"

Wayne remained motionless with a blank stare.

It was Eileen's cue to dash out the passenger door and back into her house. She returned with his ring on her finger, expecting another fight for trying to leave the house without it.

But surprisingly, Wayne was nice as they pulled away. "Ah; nice night tonight, huh?"

It was best to agree with him, "Yeah…"

"Again, I'm really sorry about yesterday. I've got to learn how to control myself. Let me make it up to you." Wayne drove through downtown Mapleview with some song by Nirvana playing on the local radio station. Eileen had grown sick of that song along with many others that were heard on Wayne's radio station of choice. They were so off-tune and harsh. At least Curt didn't play that crap.

Eileen asked, "Where are you going?"

"A little surprise for you, tonight." He edged the downtown section of Mapleview and headed into the old, forested section. Was Wayne taking her to a restaurant in Sillmac?

The peculiar sense of adrenaline could be felt as Wayne turned right onto Vine Road. She was familiar with this route. It was the way she often took to Curt's house. Wayne looked over and smiled while continuing to drive. He turned onto the street that entered the small, heavily-wooded subdivision; all the while Eileen's face grew increasingly flush. Did Wayne know something?

There was no denying his knowledge once the car stopped in front of Curt's house. "So do you know this place? Have you ever been here before?"

Eileen considered flashing open the passenger door and running up to the house. Even if he wasn't home, Curt's parents would gladly let her in once hearing of trouble. She was fearful of Wayne's anger and how the night would turn out. But Curt's parents were unaware of Eileen's dilemma. Although Curt was patient, his parents might have been misunderstanding of her difficulty in breaking up with the original boyfriend. Wayne's violent and possessive behavior would surely bring him to the door where he would pound his fists and scream to open up. It would be an embarrassment, to say the least.

Instead of running up to Curt's door for safety, Eileen remained seated in the passenger seat. "Yeah, I've been here before."

Wayne tore off, "So you're not going to lie? You're not going to tell me that you've never seen the place?" He quickly u-turned at the end of the block.

Eileen answered a soft, "No."

Wayne revealed his knowledge of the previous evening. "You didn't go out with your friends last night. Curt picked you up at 7:00. I saw you both from the park."

His voice increased in volume and began to tremor. "*I saw you* **kissing him** *through binoculars! And I waited all night for you to come home and watched you make out in front of your house!*"

Wayne was now out of Curt's subdivision and halfway down Vine Road, rapidly approaching Mapleview Road. "You lied to me and you cheated!"

Eileen could only remain motionless and speechless. He was right. But she hated Wayne so much and couldn't get rid of him, no matter how she tried.

Now Wayne peeled right onto Mapleview Road and traveled north. "There's just one thing I want to know, Eileen. If you wanted to go out with him, couldn't you have given me the decency of breaking up?"

Eileen finally spoke up in defense, "Wayne, I've been trying to break up with you for some time, now! You just don't get it! We're not like we used to be! You've changed since graduating high school! It's time for us to move on!"

The suggestion threw Wayne into a fitful rage! "**Don't ever say that!** You have no idea what we have! The midnight-blue, 1984 Camaro roared down the wooded highway while approaching the bend that transitioned the road east."Don't you understand? You just can't stop loving someone! No one ever does! You will always love me; I will always be in your heart! Why don't you just accept that?"

There was a long pause as the strained couple traveled the dark road. Eileen was tired of his drama and inability to let go. And she grew increasingly fearful of wherever he was taking her. "Where are you going?"

"Eileen, there are too many obstacles, variables and changes of events that I think distract you from me. Can't you just find it in you to forget about Curt? I'm the one who is meant for you! And the quicker you accept that the quicker our problems will go away. And you'll be happy again, I promise! Don't do this; don't end this wonderful love that we've had since 7th grade."

They now approached Creek Highway, near the spot where Hotlicks Sports Bar and Grill would stand if it were several years later. Eileen softly replied, "I love him, Wayne. There's nothing you can do about it and it's time for us to breakup."

Wayne didn't bother to stop at the intersection. He merely slowed down and then violently peeled left onto Creek Highway, "Fine! Fine and dandy! I try to be nice and reason with you; but, no!"

"Where are you going? What are you doing?"

Wayne remained an adrenaline-fueled maniac who continued to speed along the pitch, black road. He had no business doing this and no right to hold Eileen against her will. The anger inside Eileen suddenly rose above all other emotions. "***What the hell?***"

But Wayne remained silent.

As the seconds passed, his breathing accelerated as Wayne grunted and pounded the steering wheel. It was like watching someone turn into a horrible creature, like the 1970's Incredible Hulk or some sort of werewolf. Then he finally spoke, "I just don't know how I'm supposed to reach you!" The vehicle came to a screeching halt until the tires met the gravel entry of a closed forest preserve. "I don't know what else to do!" He quickly exited and slammed the driver door shut.

"Wayne, what are you doing?"

The sound of the trunk opening could be heard. Nervously, Eileen exited the passenger door. "What the hell are you doing?" She backed at an angle towards the forest in hopes to see what the crazed monster was doing in his trunk.

The dulled ring of iron was heard, and then Wayne quickly approached with a tire iron! "I'll teach you who to love! I'm sorry Sweetie, but you leave me no choice."

Instinctively, Eileen ran towards the forest. But which was the lesser of two evils? Should she have run into the dark woods and get lost, possibly attacked by an animal. Or should she have allowed herself to be beaten with a tire iron? Holding her hands out in defense was the best Eileen could do at the moment.

The assault was more like slaps to the shoulders and upper arms, enough to cause pain. It was certainly frightening to be beat with a metal object while having the man she hated demand love. And when Eileen turned to avoid further strikes to the arm, the tire iron's assault landed on the back of her upper thigh.

"End it with him! End it!" Wayne paused his beating while Eileen cowered against a tree. Then he delivered another harsh blow to her thigh, just to reinforce that he could hit harder. It was the worst strike of them all and probably caused damage. "I can't hear you! You gonna end it?"

Eileen finally cried out, "Yes!"

"Yes what?"

"Yes, I'm sorry. I'm so sorry!"

"And what else? Do you love me?"

"Yes, I love you. Please don't hit me anymore!"

With that, Wayne stormed back to his car, threw the tire iron in and slammed the trunk shut. He opened the driver side door and sat down. Then Wayne yelled out the passenger window, "Get the hell in here! I'm hungry and we're going to Taco Mile!"

Poor Eileen didn't want to be left alone in the dark. She did as her boyfriend demanded, but it was necessary to limp to the car. The last strike must have bruised her muscle which made it painful to walk.

"What the hell are you limping for? I didn't hit you that hard! You're lucky tonight because I could've killed you!"

She sat down; but before having a chance to close the passenger door, Wayne tore off and u-turned on Creek Highway, heading back towards Mapleview Road.

* * *

Customers inside the Mexican fast food establishment watched as the young girl limped through the door with her apparent boyfriend who demanded that she walk normal. Since it was summertime, Eileen wore a pair of shorts and sleeveless shirt. Most disturbing were the many bruises that now covered both her arms and shoulders. Mascara ran down her eyes, a suggestion that she had been crying.

I'm pretty sure Wayne expected people to mind their own business. And we do live in a world where we are told not to jump to conclusions, judge a book by its cover—all that. But are people really that stupid? Fortunately, there remain individuals who have learned to follow gut instincts and use some common sense. Such was the case when a middle-aged husband and wife stood in the line next to Wayne and Eileen. They immediately noticed the beaten appearance of the young girl.

Wayne announced his need to use the restroom followed by, "If I don't get back in time, get me a macho burrito with extra jalapenos and a jumbo soda."

The older man standing next to Eileen waited for Wayne to disappear. Then he laid his hand on her shoulder which jerked at the touch. "Honey, is everything okay? Are you alright tonight?"

The mascara-smudged eyes looked up with tears that were about to run.

The older man's wife asked, "Did he beat you?"

Eileen nodded yes, followed by a flood of tears.

"I'm going out to my car phone to call the police." The older man walked away while his wife remained.

The wife gave the young girl some important advice. "Honey, I hope you don't stay with him. You're way too beautiful to tolerate that. And if he does this now, imagine what he'll do when you're married. Leave him."

Moments later, Wayne returned from the bathroom. "What are you cryin' for? You still mad?"

She felt like a child who had been beat and scolded by a parent. It was all Eileen's fault for the punishment. Eileen had no one to blame but herself. At least that's what Wayne told her as they sat down with the tray of food.

"You can stop putting on the little act and making people feel sorry for you. You're the one who lied and cheated. I suppose you should tell people that, instead."

They sat at a small table in the middle of the dining area. Although Wayne would have preferred a booth at one of the perimeters, the crowded restaurant made it necessary to sit at the center. The establishment had entry doors at both sides of the building. Wayne felt as though he had the greater vantage point as he could see the same entry that he and Eileen passed through. Eileen sat opposite where she could see the entry that the older man had used, announcing he would call the police.

"Is that all you're eating, a taco and a diet soda?" asked Wayne as he unwrapped his ridiculously large burrito while grinning at his defeated girlfriend.

"I'm not hungry. I had dinner, earlier."

Of course this was the stupidest thing Wayne ever heard. It was his world and he proved to be lord and master. He just shook his head in disbelief while taking a hearty bite of the burrito.

For Eileen, this moment was the most pleasurable in which she savored every second. As two officers of the Sillmac police passed the entry of Eileen's vantage, she waited until Wayne looked up and then gazed deeply into his eyes. She held the ring finger before his face, pulled the stupid promissory ring off, and then laid it down on the tray.

Before Wayne could voice anything or show disapproval, a stern greeting was made from above. "Is everything okay, tonight?"

Much to Wayne's surprise it was the police. And Eileen was sure to put on quite an act that night! Outside of court, it was the last time Wayne ever saw the girl he loved.

Chapter 39

A sorely missed love haunts the one who misses. A sorely missed love can often be seen on a stranger's face in the crowd. Throughout the years, Wayne would take sight of a woman who had much of the same appearance of the one he lost. That new coworker, that face in the grocery store, the woman in the car next to him; they all looked like his beloved Eileen. But they weren't, and even if he fancied the idea of substituting one of these women for Eileen's absence, they were all taken.

It was probably not best for Wayne to sit before a desk in front of a PC where he explored a downloaded web program that utilized detailed satellite imagery from around the world. Type in the town of Mapleview, Wayne could zoom in on the high-resolution imagery of houses, stores and forests. And the web program included a nifty flight simulator that emulated the appearance of flying a small plane. Wayne soared about 5000 feet, following Mapleview Road and through the forests. Such technology was not available 15 years ago when Eileen was his. In fact, Wayne hadn't heard of the Internet back in the early 90's. It certainly would have been a useful tool, then.

An old buddy recently mentioned to Wayne of Eileen's whereabouts. Surprisingly, she still lived in Mapleview in a new subdivision that was located off the wooded section of Mapleview Road. According to Wayne's friend, Eileen lived on the main road of the subdivision and had the sprawling ranch with in-ground pool in the back.

In his virtual plane, Wayne located the wooded subdivision that sprung up 5 years ago. He circled the main road and found the sprawling ranch that boasted the in-ground pool. "Hmm, looks like she didn't do so bad for herself." Eileen's home certainly was impressive in comparison to Wayne's condo which he barely afforded on a modest salary. Eileen was so smart and beautiful; no wonder she flaunted success later in life. In less than a minute, Wayne's old feelings of envy resurfaced.

"I wonder what she looks like, now." Then he snorted a deliberate laugh through his nose, "Probably fat and plumpy."

Still, curiosity took the best of Wayne. He continued circling Eileen's supposed house while decreasing elevation. Perhaps he could see her in the backyard or out in the street, getting mail. There was a chance that Eileen may have been outside on the day the satellite imagery was taken.

With no sight of Eileen or the likes of any people, Wayne fancied the idea that it was possible to circle close enough to the house and glance through the windows. And then he saw something through, what looked to be, the front room window. Being necessary to circle the house a few times, Wayne determined that his beloved Eileen could be seen through the window. Most disturbing, she appeared to be naked!

This possibility infuriated Wayne. Eileen was somewhat promiscuous in high school and wore clothing that he felt was too revealing in college. Obviously this need to show herself continued later in life. Eileen was probably aware that the satellite would photograph her neighborhood that day, so she stood in the front room window while posing nude. All day long she probably waved at neighbors, the mailman or utility workers while dressed in nothing more than her birthday suit. How Wayne's rage grew by the second.

The small plane continued to circle and descend. To avoid crashing, he pulled the rudder (controlled by the mouse) so the plane would gain altitude and the flight simulation could resume. Now a thousand feet in the air, Wayne realized just where his ex-girlfriend's house was.

Only a walk to the end of the block would bring Eileen to a patch of trees that appeared to provide a small path for accessing the other side. Beyond that patch of trees was a large park that offered a playground, a couple baseball diamonds and a soccer field. And if Eileen ventured beyond the park, she would find herself on Curt's street, just a few doors down from his house!

It was all in front of his face. The satellite imagery showed exactly why Eileen had chosen that house. For years Wayne speculated that perhaps Eileen had forgiven him, maybe even missed him. He imagined there was a special room in Eileen's heart that waited for Wayne's return. He wrote several letters of apology in those years that also confessed his longing for her. But a restraining order was plain and simple; keep away from the victim and attempt no contact. He wasn't sure if the order had expired, and if so, had Eileen renewed it? Wayne was lucky enough to have avoided prison. Testing the waters with an attempt to contact would have been most unwise on Wayne's part.

All those years of wondering, and all those years of feeling her presence that longed for his return through some imagined, psychic connection: Instead, Eileen moved not more than a block away from Curt's house. It was more than Wayne could handle. He smashed his fist on the desk and quickly stood up while mumbling, "How could she do that to me?" And then violently punched his fist in the air, "I can't believe her!" Wayne lived alone and never married. No one would see or hear his tantrum.

It's interesting to observe Wayne's perceptions and actions. One might conclude that there was something seriously wrong with the man. The very fact that he assumed Curt was living with his mother and father some 15 years later was testament to his mentality. Wayne was a man who never grew up. None of us really do; but Wayne was seriously stuck in that summer after high school graduation, somewhere in the early 90s. Ever since his bad experience in college, he tried desperately to return to what he believed to be the happiest days of his life with Eileen.

Wayne was unable to move forward, accept that life progressed and that people change along with the times. Self-perceived as a man of nostalgia, in reality his life was a music CD that continuously skipped and reverted back to the beginning. Hopes and dreams were nothing more than a haunting and the impossible desire to return to the past.

That midnight-blue Camaro was replaced by a midnight-blue, used Mustang GT. And the same songs of the 90s grunge that were played with Eileen continued to be played as he left his job at Big Boy's Beef and Ribs each day. Being promoted from fry boy to franchise manager in 15 years of dedicated employment, he laughed at the kids who cruised in the parking lot with thudding bass that vibrated the paint off their vehicles. These kids weren't even babies when Wayne was the king of the streets. Unfortunately, Wayne didn't understand that they were the kings who had replaced him.

* * *

"Nobody has fun, anymore! Nobody parties like the old days!" This is how Wayne felt about life. On a late, Friday afternoon in April, Wayne cruised over to the Mapleview liquor store where a 40 ounce bottle of beer was purchased. Then he drove to the secret party spot in the woods with his imagined Eileen seated beside him. What if this could be real? What if he and Eileen finally reconciled?

Standing in the middle of the woods with a half-finished 40-ounce bottle of beer, Wayne had a good time with all his friends, people who only existed in his imagination. Eileen stood beside him with her head on his shoulder. Even Curt laughed with him while drinking his beer. This was a great Friday night!

"So what's the plan? The night is still young!" Wayne was in the mood to party. He guzzled the final bit of beer in his bottle and finally accepted the fact that he was alone. "I guess the only plan for me is get to the bottom of a 40."

Wayne hiked back to his Mustang GT and roared down the road with a mild beer-buzz. The only words he could ever recognize from that Green Day tune, which now played on CD, was the refrain, "Welcome to Paradise!" It almost made fun of Wayne who was beginning to suspect that life would be nothing more than loneliness and heartbreak.

Perhaps a quick drive past Eileen's house would have restored some sense of connection. He put on the sunglasses while entering her subdivision and slowly drove by, hoping to catch a glimpse of the girl (now woman) who he loved. It was only the month April, and the air was rapidly dropping to a chill as the sun fell low in the horizon. No one was outside in front of Eileen's supposed house. But Wayne noticed something that immediately caught his attention.

Apparently, Saturday was garbage day, at least for Eileen's neighborhood. Cans and bags were lined up at the edge of her driveway on that Friday night. Wayne would come back later in the evening and play garbage man while collecting the bags and placing them in his trunk. Garbage can tell much of a person who is stalked.

* * *

Late in the evening, Wayne lugged four kitchen garbage bags up the flight of stairs to his condo. He excitedly carried them in and hauled the bags into the bathroom where they would be placed in the bathtub. Scissors cut the ties loose so the bags could ultimately be opened.

This was the greatest thing, ever! Eileen's garbage laid before him to be inspected to heart's content! Wayne stripped down to his boxers and entered the bathtub. Then he embraced the garbage bags against his bare chest while breathing in the scent of rotting meat, rotting vegetables and used coffee grounds. "Ah-hhh… Eileen!"

He rocked back and forth while resting his face against the side of one of the bags. Then he burst out in tears, sobbing. "I'm so sorry; I'm so sorry!" Wayne loved Eileen so much. Her garbage was precious and the next, best thing to Eileen herself.

After the moment of sweet reconciliation and re-unitedness, Wayne carefully opened one of the bags as far as it would go. "So what do you have here? There is much catching up to do."

A copy of the Mapleview Daily Herald had been discarded. The front page story announced, "Skeletal Hand in Vase Settles 1830s Legend of Trivelli House!"

It was nearly a week since the discovery was made in the vase, but Wayne wasn't interested. Pulling out the newspaper, he discovered mail underneath that looked to be unopened credit card solicitations, junk mail and…

"Oh no! *No!*" Wayne beat his fist on the edge of the bathtub. "Why, why, why, why, why?"

Poor Wayne couldn't even have a sacred moment, alone, with Eileen's garbage. The presence of Curt remained in that moment as Wayne discovered an envelope addressed to Eileen Saulmon, the same last name as Curt. This was evidence enough that proclaimed the terrible reality to Wayne that Eileen had married Curt!

Chapter 40

Awakening the following morning, Wayne now had someone's garbage in his bathtub. The stench of rotting trash filled the bathroom which caused Wayne to gag. Those bags needed to be disposed of. They were of no use to Wayne now. During the excitement of the previous evening, it was no work at all to bring Eileen's trash upstairs and into the bathroom. But now it was a grueling task to reseal the bags, carry them down the two flights of stairs and haul them over to the dumpster.

It was Saturday morning around 7:00am. Big Boy's Beef and Ribs wouldn't open until 11:30am, and Wayne could have enjoyed sleeping in. Employees wouldn't arrive to work until around 10:00am. But Wayne had difficulty sleeping being that his world was crumbling around him. He groomed and shaved, leaving the trimmed mustache and goatee. And he plucked another gray hair from the side of his head and inspected the hairline for any signs of receding. Those hair growth products appeared to be doing the job.

But it was all in vain. For years Wayne maintained his appearance for the day when Eileen would finally take him back. He did his best to remain youthful which was not difficult for Wayne as he had the unusual phenomenon of appearing much younger than he truly was.

Consider the progression of a man's aging. Throughout a man's teens and early twenties, a thin and often toned body is most noticeable. But as a man ages, the whole fattening-of-the-cow phenomenon takes place. He builds more muscle from either labor or exercise. And despite any strenuous activity throughout the days, he gains weight as metabolism slows down, giving the appearance of being somewhat larger from a younger man.

Wayne had yet to cross this threshold of aging. His thin appearance was most likely brought on by years of anger, nervousness, neurosis and a mind that never grew up. That in combination with his young man's choice of clothing; his use of hair growth products; and the trimmed facial hair, such as a goatee and sometimes sideburns, made Wayne appear very much as he did 15 years ago.

But what good was this gift of youthfulness, now? Eileen would have nothing to do with him. All the years of fantasies, dreams and hopes were now gone. It was almost as if a loved one was now dead.

And this is probably why Wayne spent his Saturday morning sitting at the park near Curt's old house; looking to be a disheveled, heartbroken mess. Wayne was visiting the lifeless corpse of hope in a moment when he struggled to bring closure to the dreams that were now dead. It was a moment of mourning for the, once again, lost love. And whether Wayne though of it or not, the moment was more symbolic than he could have realized, a subconscious revelation of the many years of stalking in the background of his ex-girlfriend's life.

Two girls emerged from the wooded patch that separated the park from Eileen's subdivision. It momentarily brought Wayne back to his early youth when he would visit the parks with his friends. The memories were so cruel. They reminded him of 7th grade when he and Eileen would walk hand-in-hand down neighborhood streets. Somehow, Wayne needed to forget. That was his problem in life. Wayne realized this during an epiphany of the moment that revealed 15 years had been lost in some neurotic depression, unable to let go of Eileen.

But it was no easy task for Wayne. For years he hoped of a possible chance to go back in time and do it all over again. Wayne wished that opportunity would grace him. He knew the things he had done wrong, but it took some years to admit his foolishness. He was so jealous and possessive at a young age; no wonder Eileen disliked him more and more. If he could go back to those days with the knowledge of the present, perhaps conditions would turn out differently.

Sitting back in the bench and looking in the direction of the playground, Wayne could not believe his eyes. Eileen was there! After 15 years of her absence, Eileen was no more that 20 feet before him. And it wasn't just Eileen; it was the Eileen that Wayne remembered from 7th grade! He blinked, rubbed his eyes, shook his head and continued watching. It was the same voice, the same laughter and the same gestures. Her hair was much lighter as it was in her early teens. Did opportunity grace itself for Wayne to have a second chance?

The young Eileen looked in the direction of Wayne and then turned to say something in private to her friend. For Wayne, it was the exact same moment when he and Eileen first met. As he remembered, Eileen once showed interest by whispering to her friend.

But times were different now. Wayne was much older and had to approach gentler, as if not to frighten the young girl. He stood up and walked over to the pair and spoke directly to Eileen, "Hi there! You girls just hanging out at the park on a Saturday morning?"

She was cautious, "Yeah..." The child looked a bit unsure, but in the same not wanting to blow a possible chance with the older, cute guy who approached.

Wayne quickly thought of a way to appear harmless. "Yeah, I'm thinking of buying a house in this neighborhood and just checking out the park. So there's some nice people living here, huh?"

"Yeah, we live over there." The young Eileen pointed to the newer subdivision where the older Eileen and her husband lived. "But I guess there's some nice people here, too."

"My name's Wayne." He extended his hand towards the girl.

She did the same and they shook, "Alexi; and this is my friend, Angela."

"Nice to meet you, Angela." And then Wayne looked back at his young Eileen (Alexi) who only gazed in return with her bright, blue eyes.

She was so beautiful, just as Wayne remembered. Then his senses yelled out from within as he realized what was truly happening. "And you're much, too young for me, aren't you?"

The young girl only smiled and shrugged her shoulders.

But Wayne was curious, "How old are you?"

"12…"

"12? Wow! I thought you were a bit older, like 17."

The young Eileen was flattered as she blushed and smiled, "Get out of here! Seriously?"

"Seriously!"

It was apparent that Wayne was interested, but the young girl was equally curious of his age. He looked to be out of high school, maybe college-age. She asked, "How about you? How old are you?"

"Well, let's just say I'm much older and not 12. See, I drive; got a Mustang." He pointed to his car parked in the street.

Girls that age aren't thinking of driving, and they certainly don't get excited over cars. But she supposed it would look "mature" if she showed interest while replying, "That's cool!"

"Yeah, maybe I'll give you a ride sometime."

Big Boy's Beef and Ribs was scheduled to open in about an hour-and-a-half. Soon, the Saturday employees would report to work for opening. It was Wayne's job to oversee the opening and operations throughout the day as he was the franchise manager.

Wayne announced, "Well girls, it was nice meeting you, but I've got to get to work." He looked directly at the young Eileen, "See you around sometime?"

Although Mother may have been horrified, the young Eileen (Alexi) answered, "Sure…"

* * *

Out of sight; out of mind. In a 12 year-old girl's world, this way of life certainly applies. Not more than 10 minutes after the encounter with the stranger, she forgot about Wayne and most likely spent her Saturday texting her peeps, hanging out with friends her own age and gossiping about who's going out with whom. By dinnertime, the encounter that morning was ancient history, completely forgotten.

But Wayne hadn't forgotten. Wayne developed an obsession with the young girl. Every day after work he would return to the park, but the young Eileen was nowhere to be found. It caused him to wonder if kids these days played outside after school.

It was exactly one week since the encounter with the young girl. Another Saturday morning with a couple hours to kill, Wayne drove through Eileen and Curt's neighborhood in search of the girl who seemed to be his answer for a second chance. Still, she was yet to be found.

Patience is a virtue. Wayne continued to remind himself of this as the frustration continued. He exited Eileen and Curt's subdivision by pulling onto Mapleview Road, and then traveled a half block to Vine Street where the route was followed to the park. He exited the midnight-blue Mustang and strolled over to the bench. Sooner or later, whether it was today or next week, the young Eileen would be found.

No sooner had this been thought, the young girl suddenly emerged from the patch of forest that separated her subdivision from the park. She was alone that Saturday and appeared to be passing through while walking to a friend's house.

Apparently, the young girl recognized Wayne as evidenced by a quick smile and wave. But she didn't stop for any further greeting, much less show interest.

Wayne called out, "Eileen!"

She stopped in her tracks and continued smiling to cover her sudden alarm. It was the first time the young girl had sensed something eerie of Wayne. She knew him, somehow, or more like he knew of her in a strange way. Was Wayne a relative or an old friend of the family? What was it about this guy?

She carefully approached while maintaining her cautious smile. He was a cute guy and somewhat older, but his interest was a bit alarming. And was a moment like this considered talking to strangers?

The stranger spoke, "I haven't seen you in a while. How've you been?"

She answered, "Fine; did you buy a house yet?"

"Nah, I don't know what I'm going to do. I mean it seems like a nice neighborhood. Hey, I came by earlier this week, but you weren't around."

"My Mom grounded me." The young girl wondered if this information should have been provided. It sounded nerdy, and perhaps she was giving a stranger too much information.

But the stranger seemed harmless as he understood her grief. "Grounded? That sucks! Yeah, I remember those days. Wait 'till you move out; it'll be better."

The young Eileen agreed, "Yeah…"

And then Wayne thought of a subtle way to exchange contact information. "So did your parents ground you from the computer?"

"Yeah; computer, phone, Facebook—everything."

"What'd you do to get grounded?"

"I talked back to my Mom; that's what she says. I was just defending myself."

Wayne was so understanding, "I know all about it. I've been there." For a stranger, Wayne seemed like a cool guy. He wasn't creepy (in the young girl's eyes). He was good-looking and drove a Mustang. In the child's perception, dangerous strangers were the opposite.

Then Wayne threw caution to the wind, "I was going to say that you could have emailed me about it, let off some steam."

But kids that age don't email each other. The young Eileen suddenly asked, "What's your phone number?"

Seeing the girl pull out her cell, Wayne assumed she asked for his mobile number. Since he was the franchise manager of Big Boy's Beef and Ribs, Wayne was given a Blackberry for purposes of being reached. He gave her this number. Then he watched from a distance as the girl typed into her phone, assuming she was entering his contact number. As she put the device back in her pocket, Wayne's Blackberry made a beep.

"Is that you?" Wayne asked.

"Yeah, I sent you a text."

"A text?"

The young Eileen laughed, "Yeah, a text! You ever hear of that?"

Despite the fact that Wayne's generation made text messaging, IMs and social sites the reality in our culture; he had yet to send or receive a text. In fact, if Big Boy's Beef and Ribs hadn't provided one, Wayne would have never owned a Blackberry. And if you suspect that it's only tweens and teens who text, look at the adults who type away in their own vehicles at the red light. Sorry kids, it was Generation X (and the generation previous) that invented the LOLs, BRBs, BTWs and the notable :-)

Wayne pulled out his Blackberry which showed a message. "Hi dis is Alexi's nmbr." It was all intuitive for Wayne. He could clearly see the reply option and used the QWERTY pad to reply back, "Cool thanks".

* * *

It didn't take long for Wayne to master the art of sending and receiving text. At first he used full words and sentences, quickly learning that his young Eileen used acronyms and abbreviations. Sitting at his PC with a page that defined acronyms, he spent his evenings communicating with the young girl and getting to know her.

It was only necessary to quickly type in the names of artists or songs along with movies, videogames and other elements of preteen pop culture that were mentioned by the young Eileen. Through this diligence, it was very possible to hold a conversation with a girl young enough to be Wayne's daughter. It's frightening to think how easily a child's world can be learned with nothing more than a series of 150 character messages.

And then came a night in May when the young Eileen spoke of her aggravation with Mother.

Wayne suggested, "Maybe u need 2 get out of da house 4 a while."

She replied, "Ya rite…"

"Seriously, sneak out when ur parents r asleep. Meet me @ prk."

"Then what?"

"Go for a ride in my Mustang."

Father often went to bed early. And although Mother stayed up in front of the TV, in reality, she fell asleep around 10:00 until awakening at midnight to stagger into bed. Only a quick glance into the family room to verify that Mother slept, the young girl next fluffed her pillows under the blanket to give the appearance of lying in bed. Then she carefully climbed out the bedroom window and ran off into the night.

Wayne was full aware that his young Eileen was a nothing more than a girl. He wouldn't dare complicate her youth with adult affection; and in no way is this going to become another tale of, "What to Do with Little Lolita"! Wayne had more class than that and loved his young Eileen. But this doesn't mean to say that embraces, strokes to her beautiful hair, cuddling and occasional kisses were avoided.

The young Eileen received her first kiss from an older man on that May's night-ride in a Mustang. She was in love from that moment and equally obsessed with Wayne as he was with her. She couldn't wait to see more of him. The young Eileen texted him more and more while using words such as luv. As for Wayne, he returned to the happiest days of his life.

These secret dates continued through the late spring and early summer as Wayne would pick up his girl at the park. Her sleepwear was changed to "date wear" while walking through the small patch of forest that separated her subdivision from the park. She was a woman who would ride with her older boyfriend for a late night dinner at Taco Mile. Mother hated the place and avoided it like the plague. Thanks to Wayne, finally, the young girl would learn of what her friends bragged about.

But it was a little odd sitting in the Mexican, fast-food establishment as other late night patrons and servers appeared to look suspiciously at the couple who had quite an age gap. Was that his younger sister or niece? Little did they know that Wayne was old enough to be her father. And how eerie the young girl looked so lovingly in his eyes. Wayne would have to address this reality to his young Eileen.

This danger was communicated on July late night while cuddling near a small bonfire in the woods. Wayne purchased some beer for himself and Smirnoff ice for the young girl. Not only would tonight be a discussion of how to conduct one's self if the love were to last, but it would also be a special night for Eileen.

Wayne kissed his girlfriend on the forehead, "So, I've been thinking that you and I are really involved, lately. And obviously, others might look at us and notice the age gap. I've never said this before, but I'm sure you know I could go to jail for doing this."

"Yeah, I know."

Wayne continued, "I know you know, but I just want to make sure that you keep this thing as secret as possible. I hope you don't tell anyone, not even your friends. People talk and if someone's parents find out about us, they might call the police."

His young Eileen reassured him, "Don't worry, this is secret. It's no one else's business. You make me so happy and I don't want anyone to take this away."

Wayne was relieved to hear this, but who was the young girl fooling? She was so elated in love and could hardly contain the excitement for herself. She told her best friend, Angela, who in turn told some of her friends. This supposed secret was the gossip among the preteen-aged kids in town! But it wasn't necessary for Wayne to be aware of this! You know how children that age are.

Wayne pulled out a small box and held it before his young Eileen. "Eileen, I got this for you and want you to wear it." He opened the box and produced the same ring that was the older Eileen's promissory ring of some 15 years ago.

It was beautiful for the young girl. It made her tingle all over and shake from excitement. This was the moment that took the relationship to a serious level as she allowed him to put the gift of love on her finger. It was a bit larger and would need adjustments to get it to fit. Along with her excitement, the girl remained confused with Wayne's silly insistence of calling her by Mother's name. Yes, in case you haven't already figured out, Wayne was having an affair with Eileen's 12-year-old daughter. But his deliberate ignorance of her true name, Alexi, was merely ignored. She was completely blinded by her young and obsessive love; kissed him, and then wiped away her own tears of happiness.

Chapter 41

"Wayne, when you have a chance, I need to talk with you."

A Monday afternoon in August, just after the lunchtime rush, the regional manager of Big Boy's Beef and Ribs visited Wayne's franchise. Although a visit from one of the higher-ups can often be considered stressful, the regional manager, Jerry, was a laidback sort of guy who often wore a pair of jeans and a t-shirt (polo shirt if there was some big business). Jerry was a gloves-off man who talked straight with his franchise managers. Aside from that, Jerry was Wayne's boss for many years while he worked the position that Wayne now filled. After his own promotion, Jerry felt that Wayne had proved himself to be a dedicated employee all those years, and most qualified to run the operations of the very, successful beef and ribs grill.

Wayne sat in the backroom office with the now regional manager who appeared to have something serious to discuss.

Jerry broke the air, "So, as you may or may not know, along with everything else, I am also responsible for handling the bills for cell phones, internet service, electricity, water and stuff like that at each of our restaurants. And...Well... I'm looking at the July bill for your Blackberry and can see that you sent and received 2,781 text messages."

The regional manager paused and looked up with a puzzled look and then continued. "That's a little problem, actually a big one. You see, your account doesn't include unlimited texting and sending pics & videos. We have a corporate deal that includes each account to have 10 free text messages for the month. The remaining 2,771 gives us an additional charge of $415.65."

There was another moment of silence as Jerry gazed at Wayne without blinking an eye. Then his animation returned, "Here's the thing, Wayne. I hired you when you were just a kid in college, and I would expect something like this from someone that age. That's why we wouldn't supply our regular employees with a Blackberry. I mean that's a lot of money to expect me to pay for your own personal use. And might I interject that the Blackberry was not intended for personal use, maybe a few calls here and there, or one or two texts to your girlfriend that you're running late."

Although Wayne possessed a mind that had yet to grow up, he was adult enough to understand what Jerry was implying. "I'll pay for it, Jerry. I'm sorry; I had no idea the messages cost money."

Jerry was relieved, "Good man! And get your own phone if you want to text all day. They're pretty cheap, and a lot of packages include unlimited texting. I just can't justify to my boss that our franchise managers are running up hundreds of dollars in text messages."

Although Wayne was a franchise manager, don't think for one second that his offer to pay for the text messages was a drop in the bucket. Franchise managers at Big Boy's Beef and Ribs earn a modest salary in exchange for the fancy title and responsibility of running the operation. For sure, August would require some borrowing from the credit cards. In addition, Wayne visited Mapleview Wireless Solutions for an inexpensive cell along with unlimited texting and data.

For Wayne, financial strain was small in comparison to the new stress experienced in his relationship with the young Eileen. Knowledgeable that the young girl roamed the streets freely with her friends, Wayne often drove the neighborhood to check on his young Eileen's activities. And it wasn't uncommon to leave Big Boy's Beef and Ribs while claiming to staff that a quick errand needed to be run. These micro-errands lasted no more than 5 to 7 minutes as he drove to the wooded section of Mapleview and entered the old and new subdivisions near Vine Road.

One hot August afternoon, the young Eileen was walking with a group of kids her age that recognized the sound of Wayne's Mustang driving from behind.

"Uh oh; Alexi's boyfriend is checking up on her!" The kids enjoyed teasing Alexi. But Alexi ignored her boyfriend's car and was growing annoyed with his constant, surprise visits.

While passing, Wayne observed something that he didn't like. A boy was walking a little too close to his young Eileen. Although furious, he waited until exiting the subdivision and sent an inquiring text, "Who's da guy walking w/ u?"

Wayne drove back to Big Boy's Beef and Ribs, all the while waiting for the young Eileen's reply.

Again, he asked, "Who's da guy u were w/?"

Still, no reply.

10 minutes passed, "Hello? R u out there? I know u can get my msgs. Who's the guy?"

Alexi did, in fact, receive all the messages. And friends continued to tease that the boyfriend was angry. But Alexi announced in not so nice words, "Forget about him! I'm sick of him!"

In a 12-year-old girl's world, harassment is easy to handle. She simply selected the option to block Wayne's number. Imagine the shock that Wayne experienced when receiving the text, "Message undeliverable: user has opted to ignore all texts from this number."

Oh how Wayne's hands trembled! How his breathing became erratic as the tips of his fingers tingled from an abrupt change in circulation. What was his young Eileen doing and why?

Desperate situations call for desperate attempts. The midnight-blue Mustang became an alarming sight for the young girl which made it necessary to cut across people's yards onto other blocks, just to avoid Wayne's attempt of intercepting her at the end of streets.

But the cat and mouse game was getting out of hand. One evening, Alexi fought desperately on her way home while Wayne nearly cornered her in a confusing maze of dead-end streets. Almost trapped, she climbed over someone's backyard fence, only to be chased by a Doberman while jumping over to the other. Four yards of crossing brought her to the park. And as she ran across to the patch of forest that separated the old subdivision from the new, Alexi could hear the frantic Mustang roaring down Vine Road to meet her at the other side. The child merely hopped over several backyards until reaching her own. She was safe from his capture, at least for that night.

There was only way that Wayne could finally make contact with his young Eileen. He called off work on a Wednesday morning and headed over to the park near her neighborhood. Then he ventured into the patch of forest and hid near some trees off the small trail. Within a couple hours, Wayne could hear rustling and footsteps that approached. Sure enough, they belonged to his young Eileen who traveled alone. He jumped out as she passed and seized the young girl with his hand across her mouth, "I got you!"

The terrified child squirmed and squealed with all her might. But Wayne wouldn't let go until she calmed down, "Take it easy; sweetie, take it easy. I'll let go if you calm down."

The squirming ceased and Wayne's grip lessened. "Now, I'm going to let go; but if you scream or try to run, I won't trust you and will continuing holding, okay?"

The young girl nodded her understanding. Wayne carefully released his grip. She was a split second from running off, but remained in place by some sort of adult-to-child overpowering. Beside that, Alexi knew why Wayne was there.

He finally asked, "Why do you keep running from me? And why did you block my number?"

The young girl shrugged her shoulders.

Wayne continued, "Here I'm thinking that everything is going good between you and me, and then one day I get a message that you blocked me. Why?"

She was in near tears while confessing, "It's too much for me! Sometimes I feel like you want me to be all grown up. But I'm just a kid. I feel guilty hanging out with my friends, like you don't want me to be around them."

Wayne only returned a stare with a look of confusion. "Where did you ever get that idea?"

"'Cause you keep following me. You keep checking up on me throughout the day and it's embarrassing. I'm walking down the street with friends and we hear your car driving up. Don't you think I hate it when people tease me and make fun of me?"

Obviously, the poor girl was confused. She misinterpreted her boyfriend's actions and made a few wrong decisions. At least that's how Wayne perceived it! And since he was the bigger person, it was up to Wayne to take control of the relationship and correct the child's erroneous beliefs. "Eileen, you are sadly mistaken! I am not driving around to check up on you. Don't you think I have more important things to do with my time? And to be fair, yes I do like to occasionally drive by and see you. I miss you throughout the day and want to be with you. But I had no idea that other kids noticed this and made fun of you. I'll make you a deal. If I promise to no longer drive by, will you promise to unblock me so we can continue our relationship?"

Alexi nodded in agreement while wondering why Wayne insisted on calling her by Mother's name.

Wayne was relieved with her agreement. "Good! Go ahead and unblock me so I can send you a text."

About a minute passed as his young Eileen tapped away at the keypad, accessing her profile and settings page. "Okay, I have to reboot the phone for the changes to take effect."

"That's fine; I'll send you a text while it's rebooting." While messages and settings were being transferred through the air, Wayne made an offer for another late night rendezvous. "Tell you what; you want to go out this Friday night? I'll wait by the park and pick you up for another dinner at Taco Mile?"

"Sure..."

A message alert sounded on the young girl's phone. When checked, it was a message from Wayne, "I luv u!"

* * *

It just so happened that the upcoming Friday night was Alexi's last Friday before school resumed—the end of summer break. And on Thursday night her best friend, Angela, announced that there would an end-of-summer-vacation pajama party in which everyone would be sleeping in the backyard in tents. The party was planned for Friday night. Needless to say, Alexi was excited. All the girls in the neighborhood would be attending and Mom and Dad agreed to allow their 12-year-old daughter to join in the fun.

Of course this would mean her date with Wayne would have to be cancelled. No problem, she simply texted her boyfriend on Friday morning with the news, and promised another date the following Friday night.

His reply was short, "But we're going out 2nite."

Obviously, Wayne was disappointed. She responded, "Sorry pleze try 2 undrstnd. Its the last fri nite b4 skool."

Apparently, Wayne's young Eileen didn't understand the gravity of the situation. It's highly rude to cancel an evening with him, not to mention socially unacceptable. Although she was young, it was time to educate the girl of her priorities. He texted back, "U can't just cancel a date w/ me. That's not rite. I'll b @ the park waiting @ 10."

You remember sleepovers as a child, the excitement and anticipation of fun? As the day progressed and the other girls raved of the wild evening, Alexi leaned more and more towards "blowing off" Wayne for the night. Who was he to dictate her priorities? And she shrugged off any remaining guilt once Angela announced, "My parents are going to have a late night barbeque during the sleepover, and we can roast marshmallows!"

The girls did their usual, Friday night activities and then reported to Angela's house at 9:00. Angela's mother and father attended a dinner with some of Father's business clients, and were due to be home around 10:00. That's when the late night barbeque would begin.

Forgotten by his young Eileen, Wayne sat, parked, by the edge of the road in the other subdivision which was the usual pickup spot. Although trying to remain calm, tonight was somewhat nerve racking as Wayne was curious if his girlfriend would make the right choice. 90's grunge rock softly played on CD while the minutes of the clock moved further past 10:00. By 10:37, he nearly shook with adrenaline. Eileen had ditched him for the night!

Back at Angela's house, Mother and Father returned from dinner. The coals were near perfectly glowed on the barbeque as the silly, playful girls watched Mother go back inside for a tray of meat. That's when they heard the identifiable roar of Wayne's Mustang speeding along Vine Road.

The giggling and chatter paused for a moment. One of the girls looked up to ask, "Uh-oh! Is that…?"

Poor Alexi could only sigh with a dreadful look, "Yeah, I think so." She was a playful child only seconds ago, but had been brought back down to Earth with the frightening monster that roared and screeched closer as the seconds passed. Her stomach knotted and heart pounded faster. Wayne was mad—really mad!

Unsure of where Angela lived, much less his young Eileen's residence, Wayne slowly drove the streets until noticing what appeared to be a small party in a backyard. He parked his Mustang in front of the house that was next door to Angela's. And ironically, Wayne was now next door to Curt and Eileen's house as Alexi's friend, Angela, lived two doors down. If only Wayne's ex-girlfriend of 15 years ago was aware of his presence! But she was oblivious as the grown man crept up to the house where her 12-year-old Alexi stayed for the night.

Angela's house was without a backyard fence. Large bushes and trees perimetered the home. They were useful for the jealous and possessive stalker to hide. He watched from the corner of the house as the pimply-faced Angela stood before the barbeque with Mother and asked, "Are those bratwurst sausages? I love bratwurst sausages!"

Needless to say, entering the backyard was a bad idea at the moment. Someone his own age was supervising the young girls. The only option was to continue watching from behind the bush, using the moment to take note of his girlfriend's behavior.

10 minutes passed as Wayne observed some of the girls eat their dinner while nosily chatting. His young Eileen had yet to eat. More bratwurst sausages cooked on the grill. Suddenly, she rose from her seat and walked towards the side of the house. Maybe she was on her way to the front where she would check for Wayne's suspected presence. While doing this, Wayne emerged from the bushes and startled the young girl who was now alone.

"Oh jeez! You scared me!" exclaimed Alexi.

Wayne had no pity for her. "Come with me! I want to talk to you!"

"But I'm…"

Alexi's wrist was tightly grabbed as she was pulled in the direction towards the front yard. The young girl's reaction was similar to a child who is disgusted with the scolding of a nagging parent. While Wayne walked faster and faster towards his car, one of the girls from the party ran around towards the front of the house, curious of where her friend had gone. Alexi's boyfriend had her now, and it appeared as though the two were arguing. She wondered, "Why doesn't Alexi just break up with him?"

The Mustang peeled off while the curious girl returned to the backyard. Then she announced, "Alexi's fighting with her boyfriend, again."

Angela's mother was somewhat concerned, "Was that her boyfriend who pulled off like that?"

Several of the girls affirmed.

"He drives? Does Alexi's mother know about this?"

"I guess…" was an answer that came from the group of girls.

Mother shook her head in disbelief and then went back into the house where Father sat on the couch, watching the news. She announced to her husband, "You know Curt and Eileen's daughter, Alexi?"

"Yeah…"

"She's got a boyfriend who drives! And he just peeled off with her. I guess they're fighting."

Father remained slouched on the sofa while shaking his head in disbelief, just like Mother. Then he commented, "I don't get these kids now days. They're way too grown up. I mean, would you have been able to get into some guy's car at… What is she 12 or 13?"

"She'll be 13 next week." said Angela's Mother.

"Still, that's way too young to be getting into cars."

In the meantime, furious Wayne tore down the darkened Mapleview Road at open throttle with the very, frightened Alexi in the passenger seat. All she could do was listen to his spew of anger.

"*Who are you to blow me off, tonight? I told you that I would be at the park to pick you up! And then I find out that you go to your friend's sleepover, instead!*"

The young girl had never seen such a display of fearsome rage and could only cry, "I'm sorry. I'm so sorry. I forgot and really wanted to go to Angela's sleepover."

But this would only trigger a convulsion of punches to the dashboard as the midnight-blue Mustang raced the darkened road at over 100MPH. "*That's unacceptable! No, no, no, no, no! You don't do that!* You don't cancel plans with people and say that you forgot!"

Poor Alexi was fearful for her life. Although the young girl didn't drive, she realized that the dangerous speed had the power to take life. Sobbing while desperately apologizing was the only means to, hopefully, encourage her boyfriend to slow down. Fortunately for her, Wayne saw the parking lot of Hotlicks Sports Bar and Grill as the ideal place to turn around. Spinning a 180 and nearly colliding with a large, red pickup truck; Wayne now traveled east and hugged the bend that transitioned south.

Wayne appeared calmer but continued yelling. "So what are you girls doing tonight? Are there any guys?"

"No."

"What about when Angela's mother and father go to bed? Will any guys come over, then?"

"No."

He sighed, "You really got me ticked off right now! How dare you throw me in the corner and blow me off, tonight? You agreed to meet me for a date and then chose to go to your friend's party, instead?"

There was a long period of silence before Wayne turned left onto the street where Alexi and Angela lived. "So are you all sleeping in tents, tonight?"

"Yeah…"

He was facetious in his reply, "Awe, isn't that freaking nice? Sounds like you girls are going to have a good time!"

The car stopped on a dime in front of Angela's house. "Well, might as well go back to your little party! Thanks for blowing me off!"

The young girl exited the midnight-blue Mustang which soon tore off, made a 180 and headed back to Mapleview Road.

Warm tears flooded Alexi's eyes as guilt and sadness overcame her. She entered the backyard with an emotionally distraught face and swollen, red eyes. And the giggly girls cheered her name, "Alexi!"

Angela noticed her best friend's condition. "Did you and Wayne get into a fight?"

The curious girl, who looked for Alexi earlier, finally spoke up. "Why don't you just break up with him? He makes you upset all the time."

Another girl announced, "Oh, we saved your brat and potato salad, but the dog came out and ate it." Poor Alexi hadn't eaten since 2:00 in the afternoon. But that was okay, she was too upset to eat. And what a long, depressing night it was at her best friend's pajama party.

Chapter 42

There's a small, common item in this mother and daughter saga which I'm sure the reader is most curious of. At some point I'm sure you've asked, "What about the ring? How does Eileen feel about her daughter, Alexi, wearing the same ring that she wore 15 years ago?"

Well of course Alexi didn't wear the ring around Mother or Father! She knew that both would disapprove of her relationship with Wayne. If only Mother knew the truth!

It had yet to be discussed of the appropriate age to get into cars for Friday night dates. And this is why Eileen was much surprised on a midmorning in September when encountering Angela's mother, Janet. Eileen was doing work out in the front yard as her neighbor, Janet, walked by, cooling down after her daily run.

"Hi Eileen!"

"Hey Janet!"

"So this is the other side of summer, after the kids go back to school?"

Eileen smiled, "Yes, another summer has gone by with the kids. How was the party with the girls last week?"

"Oh, they had a nice time. They weren't noisy at all, just slept in tents outside. Doug fired up the grill in the evening and made them a late dinner." Then Angela's mother broke in with her burning question, "So Alexi's got a boyfriend, now?"

Eileen was surprised but took the news lightly, thinking it to be a puppy love with a boy her own age. "Does she? This is the first I've heard of it."

Seeing the unconcerned response, Angela's mother provided more information. "Yeah, he drives."

The mention of driving suggested a boy that was older, at least 16 and in high school. No parent would be happy to hear of this. All Eileen could say in the shock was, "Well this is *really* the first time I've heard of this."

Janet laid on more shock. "I guess he came over on the night of the party, and Alexi went up front to meet him. It sounds like he was mad that she went to the sleepover and they were fighting. She got in his car and he sped off, actually tore off like a maniac."

Eileen was livid, "You let her get into a car with some guy?"

"Well I thought you were aware of this. All the girls in the neighborhood knew. From what I understand, it's the big talk of the town."

Eileen could only cover her mouth in shock while shaking her head in denial. "This is the first I've heard of it." Shock soon turned to controlled anger, "And I'll definitely be talking to her about this. Janet, if you see her or even hear of her getting into this boy's car, I want to know about it. I'll end this relationship when she gets home this afternoon. And tell Angela that her best friend might be grounded for about a week, maybe a long time. I just don't know how I'm going to handle this, yet."

* * *

Alexi entered the house that afternoon. She was at the start of 8th grade and already a young lady. Years ago, Eileen would watch in delight as her excited girl ran home from the bus stop to greet Mommy. If memory went back far enough, Alexi was Eileen's baby who boarded the school bus one sad, sad day. But on this day, as a young lady who believed herself to be old enough to get into cars, Alexi strolled in the house and briefly gazed up at Mother while passing by.

Her only word of greeting, "Hey…"

Mother returned the greeting, "Hi, how was school?"

"Fine…" So non-verbose, Alexi continued walking to her room with Mother trailing behind.

"Where are you going? Why in such a hurry?"

Alexi continued walking which left Mother no choice but to call out, "Alexi, stop!"

Her daughter turned around with a confounded look, "What?"

"I want to talk to you. Come back in the living room and sit down."

She did as Mother asked but was curious, "About what? What do you want to talk about?"

"Well, I want to talk about boys. I want to talk about getting into some boy's car and driving off on the night of Angela's sleepover party."

Alexi looked surprised and forcefully annoyed, "What? What are you talking about?"

"You can stop pretending with me. I spoke with Angela's mother this morning and she told me about the older boy who came over that night. I hear he drove off with you?"

"Mom, that's not true!"

"So is Angela's mother lying? Should we have her come over? And why does everyone else know about this but me?"

"Mom, Angela's mother must have me mixed up with someone else! I did not get into some guy's car and drive off."

Eileen was a child once. That fact along with her motherly instincts gave Eileen the full awareness of her daughter's attempted deception. Alexi's behavior had been somewhat moody in recent weeks. And there was an increase of talking in her sleep, actually shouting as-if fighting. Mothers know all, despite what children may believe. There was a boy in Alexi's life that had a negative effect. And for whatever reason, this boy was being kept a secret from Mother.

There was only one way for Mother to gain control, "You're grounded!"

"What? Why? This is not fair!"

"For one week you are grounded. I want your phone, there is no computer and you will not be going out with your friends, understand?"

"Mom, this is not fair!"

"Your phone, give me your phone!"

Alexi's social world was about to crumble. She voiced her concern, "What about people calling or texting me? How are they going to know I'm grounded?"

But Mother didn't care. "That's your problem. I already told Angela's mother that you would probably be grounded after what I heard. At least your best friend knows." Mother held out her hand, "Your phone, please."

But Alexi remained rebellious and argumentative. "Oh, so you decided that you were going to ground me before talking to me?"

Mother's patience was growing thin. "Do you want an additional week tagged on to that?"

Keep in mind that Alexi's phone contained nearly 3 weeks of text message history with her boy friend, Wayne. Recall that she blocked him on a hot summer day in August. In the frustration, she also deleted all chat sessions with the man who annoyed her. And it wasn't until nearly a week before school resumed that Wayne had cornered the young girl and convinced her to unblock his messages. From that moment on, a history of text messages began with a phrase that said, "I luv u."

Alexi could have run past Mother who was still young and perfectly capable of catching her daughter, forcing the phone's release. And even if she escaped Mother for a chance to delete the chat sessions with Wayne, it would admit guilt and lead to greater punishment once returning home. Defeated, the teenage girl grunted in disgust and jammed her hand in her jeans pocket. But she had to be careful. Wayne's ring was in the same pocket and had the possibility of slipping out.

Now if Eileen were older, such as in her late 50s, she might have been clueless of how to search her daughter's archive of text messages. But Curt and Eileen had Alexi at a young enough age so that their way of life was not much different from hers. Eileen was Generation X and highly experienced with text messaging, social websites and any other technology wonder of the 21st century. She had her IPhone and downloaded Itunes. She had her Kindle reader with a vast collection of modern-day, 21st century literature. Along with heavily used Wi-Fi in the house; the modern-day family possessed 3 notebook computers, one for Father, one for Mother and one for Alexi. The Ipad Touch had yet to be released; but if it was, Mother and Father would surely have one. If you haven't figured it out already, the picture of clueless parents who are lost in a teenager's world of technology is a thing of the past.

Eileen took hold of her daughter's cell phone and noticed that it was password protected. "Oh, I need a code to get in? Cute!" Eileen simply unsnapped the battery from the phone and reconnected it as a hard reboot which, due to a manufacturer flaw, restored the phone to the homepage—password unnecessary. Such is the reality with inexpensive, poorly, designed phones (made in China) that are given to teens.

Horrified, Alexi watched Mother now browsing her personal data and history of messages. "You're invading my privacy! That's not fair! You can't do that!"

Mother looked up at her sadly mistaken daughter. "I'll do whatever I damn-well please. You're my kid, living under my roof; and this is my phone that I let you use. And don't you have homework to do?"

Alexi stormed out of the room as panic increased. What could she do now? Mother would learn of everything!

As Eileen discovered, it was a guy named Wayne who began the history of text messages with the phrase of, "I luv u". This was an indicator of additional history that had somehow been deleted. It would lead any parent to question, "How long was my child seeing this person?"

But that's not what vexed Eileen. As seen in the archived messages, this Wayne burdened her daughter with guilt while making demands to see her. Mother could see that hours before Angela's sleepover, Alexi cancelled some date with the older guy who felt he had every right to deny her the ability to be with friends. Was every man named Wayne some jealous and possessive monster?

Apparently, Alexi had sneaked out on the Sunday night before school. Wayne had asked, "Is 2morow ur 1st day of school?"

Alexi replied, "Ya"

"Then u can meet me 2nite. Its only a 1/2 day. Don't make me mad like fri-nite."

"Ok I'll b there."

Then there were the daily messages that were received around the time Alexi came home from school, "U home from school?"

"Ya"

"U going out w/ friends?"

"Maybe."

"With who?"

"Angela and a few others."

"Ne guys?"

"NO!"

Initially infuriated with the fact that her daughter had sneaked out on a Sunday night, Eileen grew numb with an eerie sensation which brought her back to those days with Wayne.

Did her ex-boyfriend have a son who was equally possessive and controlling?"

And as luck would have it, a live text message came through Alexi's phone from (whom else?) Wayne.

"U home?"

Eileen had so much power in that moment. The chat session could lead her to the very monster that controlled Alexi. She typed in the word, "Yes."

"How was school?"

"Good."

"U have homework?"

"Only a little. I think I'll go out today, if that's ok with you."

"No guys rite?"

Eileen imagined the Wayne on the other side of the text messages to be the same controlling Wayne who she dated years ago. In a moment of fantasizing revenge, she texted back, "Yeah, there'll be some guys. Do you have a problem with that?"

The monster responded back, "DONT GET SMART W/ ME! U know not 2 make me mad!"

Caught up in the fantasy, Eileen's blood boiled as she was fully prepared to destroy this Wayne. There had to be laws against a high school kid picking up a 13-year-old for unauthorized dates. She spoke out loud, "Oh, really?" Then she texted in reply, "I was just joking. When are we going out next?"

"Don't joke w/ me. And I'll b checking on u 2day. We can go out whenever u like."

The fish was now on the hook and moments from being pulled onto shore. Eileen would set a date with the pedophile and have police show up at the scheduled time. "How about Friday? Pick me up?"

Wayne texted back, "Sure usual spot."

This threw Eileen off guard. Where was this usual spot? Maybe if she asked which one, he would tell her.

But this didn't work. Wayne only responded, "The usual spot where I pick you up."

There was no other choice for Eileen. "Where's that?"

She waited several minutes and sent a second reply, "Hello, are you there?"

Several minutes passed before sending a third, "Are you mad at me?"

Eileen blew it! Whoever this Wayne was, he picked up on the bait and quickly ran. He was aware that Eileen wasn't Alexi.

* * *

Coming home from work to his fumed wife, Curt's reaction to the string of text messages was that of comparable anger. Friends and family often joked with the man by swearing that one day he would polish the rifle in the living room while some boy came in for a date with his precious Alexi. He knew the day of boys was coming soon as his daughter's lower torso boasted wide hips with curvy thighs. And then there was her well-budded chest. Alexi was turning into a woman and a spitting image of his beautiful wife, the same girl that Curt recalled back in 7th and 8th grade. Now some mysterious punk was demanding that his precious daughter sneak out past curfew, and past the eyes of Mom and Dad.

The hunting rifles remained locked in the gun cabinet. And Curt enjoyed his hobby of hunting. That's why he chose to live in the heavily wooded Mapleview area. He was a sensible man who knew that using a scope rifle to take out some punk was most unacceptable. However, Curt remained a very, angry man.

Demanding answers from the uncooperative, 13-year-old girl proved unsuccessful. Seeing that control had been lost, another week of grounding seemed the only option.

"Daddy, that's not fair!"

Her cuteness had no effect on Father. "Alexi, you lied to your mother, as proven by the text messages on your phone. I've got some creep out there, demanding that you sneak out of the house at night. And when I simply ask who he is, you refuse to tell us. This is a little too out of control for the moment. You're grounded for two weeks. I just don't like what I see."

The girl stormed off, sobbing in disgust. How she hated her parents and the way they controlled her life. But Mother softly knocked at her door before entering where Alexi lay on the bed, face down.

Mother sat down beside the child who wanted nothing to do with parents. "Alexi, I know I'm the last person you want to hear from. Your father grounded you to protect you. But I don't think you understand how serious this is. First of all, a boy who drives should be interested in other girls his own age. But there's more. I think you are too young to understand this, but there is a dangerous quality called possessiveness. Before I married your father, I dated a guy for two years who was very possessive of me. He wouldn't let me go out with my friends, and he was always checking up on me. And do you want to know he did to me one night? He brought me to a dark road and beat me with a tire iron. He was so mad, Alexi. And I was so scared that night. It's like he turned into a monster, all because he was jealous and possessive.

Anyway, the reason I say this is because I read all those text messages on your phone. And those were pretty much the same things he used to tell me. In fact, I thought I was talking to the same guy I dated many years ago. This Wayne is very possessive and controlling of you. You're too young to go through something like that and I think he's taking advantage of the fact that you're so young. I don't think he can get a girl his own age to control. That's why he has you.

I know you're mad and hate me right now. But I hope you use these two weeks to think things over and come to your senses.

* * *

Ask any parent with a teenage daughter, and he or she will say that the best way to keep a girl in love is to prevent her from seeing her boyfriend. Unfortunately for Curt and Eileen, the grounding only fueled Alexi's desire for Wayne. Only weeks ago, she wanted nothing to do with him. Now she would give anything to see him.

There was a double whammy which intensified this desire. It smacked Alexi in the face on the day she used a payphone at school to call Big Boy's Beef and Ribs. She hadn't spoken to Wayne in 5 days and realized the convenience of phones that required quarters to operate. They just so happened to be mounted in the hallway, just outside the lunchtime cafeteria.

She placed the quarters in and made the call; it wasn't so hard to figure out. But she once heard that these payphones had limited time. Hopefully it was enough to time to speak what was needed.

"Big Boys Beef and Ribs!" It was the voice of Wayne.

"Hi, Wayne? This is Alexi."

There was a short pause before Wayne spoke, "Where are you calling from?"

"A payphone. I'm grounded, Wayne."

"I kind of figured. Do your parents have your cell?"

"Yeah, they took it from me."

Wayne sighed, "Okay, we need to cool it for a while. I guess one of your parents was pretending to be you and tried setting a date with me. I could have gone to jail; do you realize that?"

Alexi apologized, "I'm so sorry. What do you mean by cool it?"

"It means not see each other for a while, or text, or call—nothing! I'm serious; I could lose everything and go to jail!"

It was the most disturbing news for Alexi, "But Wayne, I want to see you. I can't be without you."

He was so cleaver in keeping the young girl calm. "It's only for a while. Let me ask, are your parents getting in your business?"

"Yeah!"

"See, they won't leave you alone, even after you're grounded. So if I vanish for a while, they will back off and things can get back to normal. Can you do that, for us?"

The young girl sounded so disappointed, "Yeah, I guess."

And then Wayne was quick to hang up, "Okay, I've got to go. There's a customer coming! Please, don't call here!" There was a click and the eerie sound of a loud buzz which brought Alexi to a cold reality. She and Wayne were broken up.

Chapter 43

Alexi sat at the breakfast table, two weeks from the day that Mother and Father grounded her. Freedom was soon to be had as she ate her microwaved egg and sausage biscuit while longing for the announcement that she was finally ungrounded. Asking for this freedom and reminding Mother that the two weeks had ended might have brought bad news of additional punishment. It was only Wednesday. Perhaps she was to wait until Sunday to fulfill Father's idea of two weeks.

Mother walked in the kitchen and gently placed Alexi's cell on the table. "I'm giving this back to you. Your two weeks have ended. But your father wants you to understand a few rules."

Alexi remained motionless, listening attentively to mother.

"You cannot get into any boys' cars, understand? There is to be no sneaking out the windows late at night. And you cannot text, call or email whoever this Wayne character is. Do you understand this?"

Alexi nodded.

"We're serious about this, Alexi! If we so much as suspect that you have anything to do with that Wayne, you'll be grounded, maybe longer than two weeks."

Alexi reassured her mother, "Don't worry, I won't."

But there were two other items that Mother chose not to share with her daughter. As Alexi would find out, upon coming home from school, there would be surprise spot-checks of her cell phone. Mother would examine the archived messages once, twice, even three times each day. And Alexi was unaware that her mother conducted nightly bed-checks to ensure her daughter was in bed, sleeping.

Alexi's parents had high expectations of their daughter, demanding that she exceed in classes. As was always the understanding, if Alexi wanted keep her cell phone, maintain her social networks and enjoy the computer along with other sources of entertainment, it was necessary to maintain an A average. B's were okay, but frowned upon as Alexi was a bright and gifted child.

Because of this, weekdays were different from summer vacation. Mother and Father granted her the privilege of hanging out with friends before dinner. But after dinner, school work was to be done in the evening, nothing else. Seated at a desk in her room with an overhead light; don't think, entirely, that she was isolated from the outside world. School in the 21st century depends on the use of computers and sometimes web research. For this matter, the notebook computer was beside her. And Mother and Father were quite aware that Alexi often took breaks by visiting her Facebook page or texting a friend on the cell. She did well in school, so the distractions were fine with Mom and Dad.

Saturdays were more laidback for Alexi, and they should be that way for children. On a beautiful, October morning, homework completed for the weekend, Alexi woke up around 8:30 and immediately headed for the shower. The early, morning grooming was unusual for Mother to hear as Alexi often strolled into the kitchen for breakfast and then sat on the sofa while watching Sponge Bob Squarepants with the notebook computer on her lap.

Alexi must have really had plans for the day. She blow dried her hair and gave it some slight curl. Then she made up her baby face with cosmetics and glossy lipstick. It was all completed with a thorough spraying of perfume, which would remind someone more of cotton candy and bubblegum, instead of the desired effect of a sexy girl.

Was she doing the right thing? Alexi didn't care. She had the power! With her cute figure, the tight fitting clothes showed off all those things that Father would have preferred to be covered in an old-fashioned, Amish dress.

Alexi entered the kitchen close to 10:00 where Mother was making the preparations for dinner later that night. She took sight of her irresistibly cute daughter and finally asked, "So, what's up? What's the plan for today?"

"Oh, nothing; Angela and I are going to the park and stuff."

"Yeah? Well that ought to be fun." Mother knew it had to involve boys, but she wasn't going to say anything.

There was, however, a crucial warning that needed to be given to her daughter. "Alexi, you have to promise me that you will be very careful out there. There have been a couple disappearances in Mapleview and the police think they're related." Mother was referring not only to the disappearance of the waitress at Hotlicks Sports Bar and Grill, but the woman who had been abducted from her home, earlier that week. "Please be careful, okay?"

"I will…"

Whatever the plan was for the day, it wasn't to take place until around lunch. Alexi remained at home, doing her typical Saturday morning activities. Then around noon, a knock at the door produced Alexi's best friend, Angela.

Five minutes later, Alexi entered the house. "Mom, do you know where the bicycle pump is?" It was an unusual request because Eileen's daughter usually walked to the park. Why was a bicycle necessary that day? Obviously, there was something that Alexi was hiding. A bicycle was only needed if long distance was to be traveled.

Mother hid her suspicions while waiting for more evidence. But she wasn't sure where the pump was. "Honey, I don't know where your father keeps that. Did you check the garage?"

"Yeah..."

"Well, that's the only place I can think of."

More rummaging could be heard from within the garage. Alexi returned with the announcement that she would fill her tires at Angela's house. Several minutes later, Eileen took sight of both Alexi and Angela, sailing down the main road of the subdivision, on their bikes, towards Mapleview Road. They were dolled up so cute in their fashionable clothes, styled hair, makeup and whatever perfumes that blew in the wind behind them. They weren't going to the park! The two girls were on the way to downtown Mapleview!

Eileen was a child once. And she recalled the many times of believing to have pulled a "fast one" on her mother. Hopefully, Alexi wasn't going to get into too much trouble. Surely it involved a boy, probably one who lived in town.

Another 10 minutes passed and Eileen was struck with the terrible thought that perhaps her daughter was going to meet that Wayne! But she calmed her worries. Surely Wayne was ancient history. Alexi's phone had been spot-checked, regularly, which showed no communication with the older guy. During those late night bed-checks, the girl was found to be sleeping soundly under the blankets with head on the pillows.

Ironically, at the very moment that Mother convinced herself that all was well, Alexi and Angela pulled their bicycles into the parking of Big Boy's Beef and Ribs. Wayne's midnight-blue Mustang was parked in the back lot, just as shiny as ever. And it was lunchtime as evidenced by the multitude of cars that filled the remaining lot.

The two girls parked their bikes near the front window and entered the noisy establishment. Patrons sat at tables, ripping away at ribs or wolfing down jumbo burgers with all the works.

And famished people stood in one of 3 lines, waiting to give their orders.

Wayne wasn't standing behind one of the cash registers. He couldn't be seen filling drinks or bringing trays of food to tables. Where could he have been? Alexi was deeply disappointed. Her sorely missed ex-boyfriend would be unable to see her sexiness while she stood in line. Still, both girls were hungry and hoped that whatever pooled funds of allowance might get them lunch.

With only one more customer ahead in line, Wayne finally emerged from the back room and took sight of his young and beautiful Eileen who beamed while beckoning for his attention. He missed her so much, but was nearly caught some weeks ago. Wayne halfheartedly smiled and waved while filling a tray of soft drinks.

Finally, the two girls made it to the front of the line with a combined $5.92. The cashier greeted, "Hi, welcome to Big Boy's. Can I interest you in a slab of ribs for $17.89?"

Angela quickly responded, "Do you have bratwurst sausages? I love bratwurst sausages."

Wayne quickly approached the young Eileen and her friend. "Hi girls, how are you doing today?"

Alexi quickly responded, "Good!"

Wayne turned to the cashier, "Get them whatever they want. It's on the house." Then he looked at the two girls, "Lunch is on me, girls." And with that he walked back to the office.

Is this all that Alexi had come for, free lunch? She dressed in her sexiest clothes, wore glossy lipstick and slightly curled her hair. But the best Wayne could do was offer a free lunch? Although generous of Wayne and most appreciated, Alexi was disappointed to say the least.

Seated at the booth with Angela while waiting for their food, Alexi took a deep breath, pulled out her cell phone and selected Wayne from the contacts list. She simply texted, "Hi."

Moments later, Wayne responded. "Wut r u doing here?"

"Came 2 c u. I miss u :-("

But Wayne reminded the young girl of his concerns. "I dnt wnt 2 get in trbl. Parents... cops... jail."

Alexi reassured her boyfriend, "Don't worry, its all cool now."

Soon, the food arrived: Alexi's Works Burger *without* lettuce, tomatoes, onions, mushrooms or cheese; and Angela's bratwurst sausage on a bun with mustard.

Wayne had yet to respond, so Alexi continued the conversation. "I just want 2 c u. Its been long enuf now."

Wayne finally agreed, "Ok fine. Meet 2nite @ spot. But pleeze b careful."

Keep in mind that Alexi was unaware of Mother's regular bed-checks. And they weren't done every night. Eileen wasn't an obsessive, fanatic mother. But she did have a daughter who was sneaking out at night to be with an older man. Do you blame her for the checks that usually happened on Friday or Saturday night?

But on this particular Saturday night, Eileen and her husband opened up a couple bottles of wine, and then retired to the bedroom for one of those eventful evenings behind the closed door. Eileen made a mental note to check on her daughter in the late night hours. But all that wine and before-bed exercise caused Eileen to sleep deeply until the morning hours.

She awoke on Sunday morning, fully rested but disappointed she had missed the Saturday night check. Alexi now lay in her bed, sound asleep. Eileen carefully inspected the curtains and the window sill for any evidence of climbing out. It was October and no reason for the window to be open. It was closed, for now, and the lock was engaged. Still, this didn't satisfy her curiosity.

Eileen went outside below her daughter's window in search of any shoeprints in the dirt garden. And there, a barely discernable print that could have been matched to Alexi was imprinted in the cold ground. The print could have been left over from weeks ago, but Mother knew better. Instincts told her that Alexi had, once again, sneaked out to be with some boy. In fact, she probably went to see that Wayne!

The evidence piled against the sleeping girl. Eileen took the cell phone from her daughter's nightstand and brought it into the kitchen for inspection. Searching the archive of messages, no texts were sent or received from Wayne. And from what Eileen could read, there were no late night activities much less discussions of meeting in the evening. Apparently, Alexi had deleted the evidence.

Mother was cunning. Rather than approach her daughter with her suspicions, it was best to let her believe that all was well. And suddenly there was a little project to be done on that cold, October Sunday. Being that autumn was well under way, winter would soon arrive. There was no reason for windows to be open. On that day, Eileen went through the house and lowered the storm windows for added insulation of heat. On Alexi's window a simple detection device was added: a transparent piece of tape that connected the frame to the window sill outside. If Alexi opened the window; something unnecessary in the cold, autumn air of Mapleview; the undetectable piece of tape would break. Alexi would be busted!

But the tape remained unbroken! Every day when Alexi was in school, Eileen checked her daughter's window and could see no evidence of a late night escape. She continued to check her daughter's phone, but no messages to or from Wayne existed in the archive. Eileen even suspended the practice of checking the phone with the hopes of throwing her daughter off guard. And when seized for a surprise phone check, nothing was found. Alexi was truly a bright girl, indeed!

But it wasn't Alexi's intelligence that kept her one step ahead of Mother. In truth, Wayne was keeping his distance. Sure, a couple text messages may have been sent throughout the week. Wayne's young Eileen would ask how his day was and then mention that she missed him while inquiring of the next night out together. He'd entertain the young girl and make plans to meet the upcoming Friday. But then Wayne would send a "regretful" text late on Friday which mentioned his fictionally, ailing mother that demanded her son's presence. If Wayne's mother wasn't ill, then Wayne, himself, would be ill while claiming to have some nasty stomach flu or a case of mono.

Soon it was November. And perhaps where you live, this month may offer a few warm days here and there. But for Mapleview, these days in the middle of autumn are not had. Halloween is cold and has even offered flurries in recent years. Windows are shut, snow begins to fall and people look forward to the holidays to remain cheerful.

Wayne was a lonely man and not very fond of the winter months. He developed seasonal depression once the weather grew cold and wouldn't pull out until spring returned. And during this time of year, Wayne yearned most for his Eileen, not some teenage girl that reminded him of a love that had been lost. Really, Alexi was the next, best thing to Eileen; and Wayne loved her nearly as much as the original. But seasonal depression caused a tendency to lose value in things important to Wayne.

That would change on a Thursday morning when Wayne awoke much, too early. It wasn't necessary to report to Big Boy's Beef and Ribs until 10:30. Why was he wide awake at 6:30? Depression can sometimes do that, and Wayne had every reason to be depressed. He hated his job, bills stacked up and it was another year without the woman he loved. Months were wasted on some young girl that resembled Eileen. What was he thinking? He could have ended up in jail!

Pointless to try and go back to sleep, Wayne cursed while rising out of bed and peeked outside the apartment window. It looked cold and gray outside; a long day for sure!

The apartment needed cleaning, laundry piled up and there wasn't any milk in the refrigerator for cereal. "Bah, I don't want cereal!" Looking in his wallet, Wayne counted $11.00 which could have afforded him a nice breakfast and coffee at the Mapleview Café.

* * *

Seated at a small table at the Mapleview Café, while waiting for his ham and cheese omelet, Wayne neared the end of a second cup of coffee. He gazed out the window which offered a sight opposite to the warm summer. The caffeine buzz temporarily alleviated the depression as he thought to himself, "I'm sick of this town. What do I have to live for, here? I've wasted nearly 20 years of my life since high school, working the same job and putting up with the cold weather each year."

Suddenly, a sense of freedom provided an urge to pack up and leave his hated life behind. Wayne could have moved to where it's warm year round. Maybe he could have landed another job in construction, return to night school and finally make something of himself.

Life's cruelty took that moment of alleviation and provided a family of tourists who entered the Mapleview Cafe. It was such an unusual time of year for visitors; Thanksgiving wasn't until weeks away. And what do you suppose Wayne noticed of this family? The happy wife and mother who seated her children slightly resembled his long, lost Eileen.

She was probably very, much how Eileen would appear today. The woman was such a nurturing mother and beautiful as ever. Wayne continued to study from a distance as his omelet finally arrived with a refill of coffee. Soon the woman took notice of his watching and occasionally glanced up to lock eyes with the stranger. At some point, her husband rose from the table for a quick trip to the restroom. Such a lucky guy! Why couldn't Wayne have had the same luck?

Although a darker color hair and a slightly different body type; the woman's eyes were so blue, just like the Eileen he once dated and the one who was now a young girl. It wasn't necessary for Wayne to wish! His wish had already come true, and it was better.

Earlier that year, Eileen returned with so many years erased, a young girl just as Wayne remembered when he first met her. And she was texting him, sending little messages during the day of how she missed him. The young Eileen even came to visit one crisp, autumn Saturday. With this realization in mind, Wayne decided it was now time to resume his relationship with the young girl.

He picked up the cell phone and sent her a text, "Hey, miss you!"

Five minutes later, she responded back, "Miss u 2. In class. Must b careful!"

Apparently his young Eileen was in class and unable to use the cell phone. That was okay; text messages store in memory for later. He could still ask her out that upcoming Friday. "I'm feeling better. Wanna go out Fri nite?"

"Sure luv 2."

* * *

Thursday night would be marked as the eve before a weekend of terror that started with a simple conversation by Father, during dinner. "I guess they're closing down the Mapleview Coffeehouse."

Mother rang in, "Awe, that's a shame."

Father continued, "You know, it's amazing how one jerk can screw it up for everyone. That place was there for years. And the owner is the third woman missing."

Mother sighed, "I hope they find whoever is behind the disappearances." Then she looked up at her precious Alexi, "And please be careful out there, Honey."

Father quickly interrupted, "Well the same goes for you!"

There was a moment of silence as the family ate their dinner of mostaccioli and meatballs. Then Father looked up at his daughter, "You going out this weekend? Any plans?"

"Um, I haven't talked to Angela, yet."

"Good; stay home this weekend. It's too cold out there, anyway."

Alexi was disgusted and quietly exclaimed her despise towards Father's harsh decisions.

But Father would only reinforce his order. "Look, it's going to be cold this weekend! There are women disappearing! You want to find out what happens to them? I suggest you stay home. You're too young to be going out Friday and Saturday nights, anyway."

A weekend without friends was going to be a long one, indeed. Really, Father didn't mean that Alexi couldn't go out Saturday morning and afternoon. He only wanted his daughter home before dark. But little did he know that in the darkened hours, Alexi had Friday night plans to sneak out her bedroom window and willingly see a man who was quite dangerous, himself.

The mission would begin on Friday afternoon, just after dark. Alexi carefully opened her bedroom window and slowly raised the storm window. Surely it must have broken the transparent tape, and Mother would find out the following morning. The storm window was terribly noisy as the frame screeched through the tracks. It was best to do this now while Father was in the living room—TV volume up and Mother preparing dinner in the kitchen. Alexi would act her usual self during dinner, appearing to be disappointed that she was confined to the house that night.

Alexi remained in contact with her boyfriend throughout the evening (deleting messages in case mother seized the phone, of course!) 8:00…9:00…10:00: Mother and Father stayed awake in the living room. Surely they would retire after the 10:00 news. All the Alexi could do was watch videos on the web and play games.

"They shud b going 2 bed soon."

"Ok"

"Plez dont leave!"

"I won't. I miss u 2 much!"

10:35, the sound of Father cracking open a can of beer could be heard. Adding to the frustration, Mother placed a bag of popcorn in the microwave. How much longer would Alexi have to wait?

"They're still awake!"

"Its ok I've got all nite."

At 11:06, Alexi could hear the TV turn off and Father stumble to bed. Mother opened the door and peeked her head in her daughter's bedroom. "It's time for bed, Alexi."

"Okay."

While lying in bed, fully dressed, Alexi listened in darkness for the sound of Father's snoring. When heard, she waited until nearly midnight before getting out of bed and putting on her jacket. Now I won't bore the reader with the lengthy technique of slowly opening that bedroom window. It wasn't until 12:20 when her feet touched the ground. Living on ground level, she slowly closed the window behind her. And it took almost as long to close the window as it did to open.

Alexi was a free woman and ran to the forested patch that separated her neighborhood from the other. As she walked across the soccer field towards the playground, she could see the silhouette of Wayne's midnight-blue Mustang. When close, he exited the vehicle and approached the young girl until they embraced.

Years of missing his precious Eileen along with the Thursday morning experience at the Mapleview Café fueled Wayne's desire to hug and caress the young girl. "I missed you so much. I love you."

"I love you, too."

As Wayne gave the young girl a taboo kiss, he enjoyed teeth that hadn't been brushed since 7:00 that morning. Even so, they were probably lightly grazed with a modest amount of toothpaste; backs were most likely neglected. The young girl had the greasy, cafeteria pizza for lunch and Mother's broiled salmon for dinner. While waiting to meet her boyfriend, she snacked on Doritos, candy and soda. These things should have served as a strong repellent against older men like Wayne. But Wayne didn't care. He only combed the young girl's hair with his fingers and could feel how cold she might have been.

Wayne quickly suggested, "Let's get in the warm car."

They drove off together, holding hands.

Wayne further suggested, "What do you say that tonight we go back to my place? I'll put a pizza in the oven and we'll watch a movie."

Alexi agreed, "Sure."

And that's just what they did.

But there was one, small item that Alexi left behind. Being that she changed into a tighter, fitting pair of jeans that evening, the original pair that was worn on Friday afternoon still had Wayne's ring in the pocket. And as I'm quite sure you are aware, this was the same ring that Mother had worn some 15 years ago.

But Mother didn't discover the ring that late, Friday night. She did peek her head in Alexi's bedroom, on her way to the bathroom, and discovered that her teenage daughter was not in bed.

While Wayne and his young Eileen sat on the sofa with a frozen pizza cooking in the oven, the young girl's cell phone sounded the musical ringer. Pulling the noisy device from her pocket, the look on her face turned to that of horror. "Oh no! It's my Mom!"

"Your mom?"

I'm not answering it." She quickly selected the option to ignore the call. But Mother would only try again and again, each time her daughter had ignored the call.

A text message came in, "WHERE ARE YOU?"

Wayne finally spoke up against the rude mother's interruptions from his evening with the young Eileen. "Why don't you just block her?"

"I'd love to right now!"

A second text message came in, "ANSWER ME! YOU ARE IN SO MUCH TROUBLE WHEN YOU GET HOME!"

Wayne continued his urging, "Just block her!"

"I want to, but she's my mom."

"What? You can block me, but you can't block her?" The alarm on the oven sounded, signaling that the pizza was done. Wayne stood up while shaking his head in disgust at the young girl. While he was in the kitchen, Alexi powered down the phone so no further messages would be received.

Moments later, Wayne returned with a large pan of evenly sliced pizza and two plates. "You know, earlier this week I was thinking of how sick I am of Mapleview. I've lived here my whole life and had to put up with everyone's crap." Then he suggested to his young Eileen, "How about you? Aren't you sick of it all?"

The young girl helped herself to a slice of pizza while agreeing, "Yeah!"

Wayne continued, "I mean look at you! You can't even go out on a Friday night with your boyfriend. Your mom is calling you and asking where you are. I bet they come down on you hard because of your grades, grounding you and stuff. I was there, once. I know all about it."

"Mmm-hmm!" She continued to agree while eating her slice of pizza.

Wayne put down his plate and looked at his young Eileen with a serious face. "What do you say that you and I move far away from here, out of state? I was thinking about that. We can go to a place where no one knows us and start a new life, together. We can move where it's always warm and I can probably get a construction job. We'll get an apartment and just tell everyone that you're my daughter. What do you say?"

She was so frustrated with her parents, not to mention dreadful of returning home to face the music. "Seriously? Sure, I'll do it! Yeah, when do you want to go?"

Wayne answered, "Tomorrow morning; we can leave in the morning once I get a good night sleep. I don't feel like going to Big Boy's anymore. I got some money we can live on while traveling to Florida or somewhere warm. It'll be easy for me to get a quick job for some cash and save up for an apartment. In the meantime we can live in a hotel. You sure you're up for this?"

His young Eileen affirmed, "Yeah!"

Don't even think that this was to become another tale of "What to do with Little Lolita"! Wayne wouldn't dare sleep with the young girl! He had more class than that. Although the couple decided to start a new life, together, the young Eileen remained a young girl in Wayne's eyes. When they finally did get that apartment, it would be best if she had her own room and bed. Wayne also realized that he was now responsible for the young girl's education, probably even supporting her through college as she was very bright with promise to be someone great in life. When his young Eileen finally grew into adulthood, Wayne could marry her and start a family. Only then would it be appropriate to sleep together. Tonight, she would sleep on the sofa.

It's interesting how a couple hours of sleep can provide proper insight into life's problems and crises. Originally laying on the sofa with a pillow and blanket that was provided by

Wayne, Alexi breathed in deep and exhaled, imagining all her problems roll off and fade away. Mother and Father no longer had their stranglehold. And although their daughter was still such a young girl, at only 13, Alexi believed herself to be a woman. She needed her independence. Many women (she imagined) crossed this threshold in life which required leaving the safety and comfort of a mother's wing.

But thinking was much different upon awakening in the middle of the night. Suddenly, Alexi could feel her worried mother fret in agony over her missing daughter. She probably thought that Alexi was an addition to the mysterious Mapleview disappearances. And although frustrated with the control of Mother and Father, Alexi realized that life would be very different without her loving parents.

What was she doing? Was this decision realistic and wise? She was so young with still much to experience. Angela and all her friends would no longer be seen. And what about school? Alexi was wise enough to understand that one couldn't go far with only two months of an 8th grade education.

Perhaps it was best to return home. But how? Alexi dreaded angering her boyfriend; but if he truly loved her, he would understand. Returning home would guarantee much music to be faced. It would involve furious parents who scolded along with a harsh sentence of a month or two being grounded. But these things were so small in comparison to a life of hardship and the absence of dear, old friends.

Lying there, a strange clarity overcame Alexi which allowed her to see that Wayne would refuse to understand. He expected her to leave in the morning and follow the decision to start a new life. Perhaps if she tricked him it would be possible to return home, which provided safety from a persistent and angry boyfriend. He would cool down, eventually. But how could he be tricked?

It flashed before her eyes like an answered question: The ring was still at home! Surely Wayne would not want it left behind in Mapleview. It was special and purchased just for her. She crafted a clever lie while imagining, "Wayne, I should return home and get the ring. I'll let my parents yell and ground me. Then when I'm alone, I'll run out to meet you." Of course the real plan would involve staying at home and blocking Wayne's text messages. After some weeks he would cool down and she could call in hopes to make him understand.

And so Alexi slept through the night while awakening every 45 minutes or so. She bounced from having empathy towards her worrisome mother to worrying, herself, about the morning's plan of escape.

In the predawn hour, Wayne awoke with an unsettled feeling brought on by the realization that he had abducted a teenage girl. He also had the peculiar sensation that perhaps the young girl changed her mind, overnight.

Wayne quietly walked into the 2nd bedroom which he often referred to as the computer room. Really it was just a small bedroom with a PC and monitor that sat on an old desk. He opened the bottom drawer and removed a commando knife with blade held in a sheath. When removed, the sharp blade was seven and three quarter inches in length. He tucked half of the undrawn knife inside the waist of his pants and covered the remaining sheath and handle with his coat. Wayne quietly passed the sleeping girl and carefully stepped out of the apartment. From there, he would hide the commando knife under the driver's seat of his midnight-blue Mustang.

The apartment door that closed had awakened Alexi. She assumed he had stepped out to load some luggage or belongings into the car. She arose to use the bathroom. Upon returning she took sight of Wayne's second bedroom with PC seated on the desk. There were pictures of what she originally thought to be family members and loved ones. Curious, the young girl entered to see who they were.

Shock and fright overcame Alexi upon viewing multiple photos of Mother; some alone, some arm-in-arm with Wayne. Mother was much younger in the photos, but it was still Mother none-the-less.

It didn't take long for Alexi to understand the reality. But her reactions were a mixed rush of terror, anger and disappointment that Wayne was in love with Mother, not her. This would certainly explain his insistence of calling her by Mother's name. Just how old was Wayne? How long ago did he date Mother? And was this the same man who Mother claimed to have beaten her with a tire iron?

Alexi must not have heard the sound of the apartment door opening. While she gazed at the photos in horror, Wayne entered the room. "Good morning!" His young Eileen looked seriously disturbed. Surely she had second thoughts. "What's wrong, Honey? Everything okay?"

The young girl pointed at the photos, "Why are you with my Mother?"

Wayne's face turned a shade of white while pausing before speaking. At times he fancied the idea that perhaps the young girl was Eileen's daughter. She looked so much like her, the spitting image! All Wayne could do in that moment was stall the frightening reality. "Are you Eileen's daughter?"

She nodded in near tears. The poor girl was distraught and confused beyond anything Wayne could imagine. This was truly bad. Not only had he abducted a teenage girl, but it was the very daughter of the woman he was in love with.

He heavily sighed, "I loved your mother, once. But she left me for your father and it really hurt. Years later, I found you. I didn't know that you were Eileen's daughter; but you reminded me of her, except better. I'm happier in our relationship than the one I had with your Mother. Please try to understand."

It was a lousy excuse for Alexi. Suddenly, she didn't like him and desired to be as far away as possible. But he wasn't about to set her free; Alexi knew this. And perhaps you, the reader, now call out to Alexi, "Run! Run out of the apartment, Alexi!" But Alexi was a very, bright girl and realized that the captor trusted her. If she ran away in that moment, Wayne would surely seize her. Escape would have to be done out in the streets, maybe flash open the passenger door while at a red light and run to a gas station for help. And what if it was necessary to rely on the ring escape plan? Wayne would no longer trust her and wouldn't allow temporarily returning home. Alexi swallowed her fear in the presence of danger and pretended to love Wayne. He trusted her and that was the best weapon for the moment.

The streets were not as Alexi imagined. It was a dark, cloudy, early-dawn, Saturday morning with no one in sight. She knew how Wayne chased after experiencing those frightening nights of the midnight-blue Mustang that nearly cornered her. Running away in the condo complex was too risky. There wasn't a soul, and the young girl was unfamiliar with the small streets and alleys.

Mapleview Road and the entire downtown of Mapleview were unlike what Alexi imagined. Again, no one was in sight. Surely there were gas stations open, but the traffic lights remained green which allowed Wayne to sail through downtown Mapleview and into the older section of forest.

Perhaps if Wayne hadn't discovered that he now possessed Eileen's daughter, the issue of a ring left behind wouldn't have been so important. Now in the wooded section of Mapleview, Alexi exclaimed, "Oh no! I left the ring back at my house!" The young girl desperately hoped the plan would work.

Little did she know the effect it would have! The ring was more important than imagined. Such an item would immediately be recognized by Mother and provide evidence of who might have abducted the young girl. Wayne shouted, "You left the ring? How could you do that?"

She apologized, "I'm sorry; I'm sorry; I forgot. I don't want to leave it behind. Maybe just drop me off at the park and I'll go home. My mom and dad will yell at me and stuff. Wait a while and I'll come back."

Wayne was furious and panic-stricken. "You're damn right you'll get that ring! You can't leave that alone!"

But his mood suddenly shifted so that the ring was not so important. How many times in life had Wayne lost Eileen? The very town, the very forests of Mapleview symbolized the dead-end scenes and moments of his own life. Freedom was only a drive up Mapleview Road and a left turn onto Creek Highway where the interstate highways would appear some several miles down the road. The only thing that trapped him in Mapleview was his life that had been robbed nearly two decades ago. Now in some reincarnated form, that life had returned and sat beside him. Only now, she was asking to go back home. Although his young Eileen promised the return to be temporary, Wayne wasn't taking any chances.

The midnight-blue Mustang traveled past the entryway to his girlfriend's subdivision and past Vine Road. The young girl carefully looked over, "Aren't you going to drop me off?"

"No."

"What about the ring?"

"I'm not losing you again, Eileen!"

Just like Mother, the young girl's frustration and anger suddenly appeared. "Why do you keep calling me by my mother's name? My name is Alexi, duh! Eileen is in her thirties and is married to a man named Curt. Can't you get it straight?"

These moments of challenge would have to be endured. At times, Wayne would need to play the father. He looked over and calmly spoke, "No, since we're starting a new life together, I think it's best that you have a new name. People will be looking for a girl named Alexi. Your name is no longer Alexi Saulmon, it is Eileen Brockman. It sounds prettier, anyway."

The young Eileen slapped her thigh in disgust while sighing, "Whatever! You know, you can't get away with this; they will find you!"

Girls that age can be rebellious. And they often require reminders of who and what to answer to in life. The girl needed discipline and would thank Wayne later in life. He remained calm, but the tone of anger could still be detected, "You know, years ago I took your mother to a place where I set her straight. It was when I caught her cheating on me. She was just as rebellious as you are, now. I think it's time we pay that place a visit. It's time I establish who's the boss around here."

The car passed Hotlicks Sports Bar and Grill where it stopped at Creek Highway and made a left. Alexi had her cell phone and contemplated calling for help; but Wayne would only seize it when nearby. If there was some way to escape, she could run and then call for help.

"Where are you taking me?"

"That's for me to know and you to find out."

It was a strange moment for Alexi as she realized that this is what it felt like to be abducted. Although not in a trunk, she was still in fear of whatever her captor was about to do.

15 years ago, Eileen was beaten at the entryway of a closed forest preserve on a dark, summer night. 15 years later, it was a cold morning in November. That same entryway was now open and it was best to travel inward to stay out of view of onlookers.

Alexi's anxiety intensified as she found herself traveling on a heavily, forested, narrow road. You could almost imagine how petrified a child would appear in a moment of being trapped, in danger. How she wished she had obeyed Mother and Father. Mother's very words of warning echoed in Alexi's mind of a jealous man who beat in a fit of rage. Little did Alexi know that on that evening of being grounded, Mother had warned of the very man who now sat beside her.

Mother was punished with a tire iron. The young girl would instead experience the fear brought on by the sight of a commando knife with seven and three quarter inch blade. That's what Wayne planned. But the child was quick when the Mustang parked. She never saw the blade as her captor reached under the seat. Instead, Alexi flashed open the door, the way Mother should have done at Grandma and Grandpa's house on that frightening night, 15 years ago. She ran off into the forest, fueled by desperation and a desire to be free.

With the knife in hand, Wayne quickly exited the vehicle and chased after the running girl who was now in the forest. "Eileen, get back here! You're making me mad!"

Alexi continued running while cursing the fallen, decaying leaves of autumn which now crunched under her feet. How could she run and hide? The noise would surely signal her whereabouts.

Back at home, Mother had such a sickening feeling of danger. Mothers can sense when a child is in trouble. Where was her baby? What was happening? She pulled out her own cell phone and tried calling Alexi. No answer as usual! Alexi's phone had been powered down.

Frantically, she rummaged through her daughter's room. Somewhere the answer was in there!

Curt entered, equally frantic. "Eileen, we've got to call the police! She ran away and will get in trouble sooner or later."

But his wife was unresponsive while rummaging through Alexi's belongings.

Curt continued to call out, Eileen...? Eileen...?"

Gripped by instinctive anxiety, the worrisome mother was lost in the sensation of her daughter now in trouble and unable to respond. Somehow she managed to say, "Call 'em; call the police."

Back in the woods, terrified Alexi continued to run and run. Although Wayne remained thin all those years from neurosis and other emotional problems, he was in poor shape and had difficulty keeping up with the young girl. But he had determination and continued behind. And just as he was near giving up, he realized an opportunity to outsmart the young and speedy girl.

There is a wide stream that Alexi needed to cross. The dreaded thought of walking through the cold water was quickly overcome at the sound of Wayne's approaching crunch of fallen leaves.

He called out to disguise his plan and lead the young girl to believe safety was reached. "Eileen! Don't you dare cross that stream!"

It was only ankle high, cold but not terribly deep. Once getting to the other side, Alexi continued running. The fear and state of panic made her numb to the cold and fed her need to push on.

Wayne only watched as she ran uphill. He had been here before on those nights of wild partying many years ago. They used to call this section of forest, "the trippin' woods". It was the place where he and his friends would consume beer and finish pipes filled with cannabis. But there was a rule that partiers would follow that was more of a caution in case police ever raided. If the police came, one should never cross the stream and run up the hill to the other side. Officers would only run along the bank of the stream where a little-known trail would quickly be met. It traveled diagonally and would intersect with the path of one who had fled. Whereas an escaping partier made noise through sticker bushes and fallen leaves, the pursuer had a clear path which made travel easy and faster.

Knowledgeable of this little-known trail, Wayne ran along the bank of the stream until finding it. He crossed it and lightly jogged uphill. Alexi was heard some distance away, fighting through sticker bushes and many obstacles in her way.

Looking behind her, Alexi noticed that Wayne no longer chased. Perhaps he gave up! This was the perfect opportunity to call for help. The cell phone was pulled out of her front pocket, powered up and then watched as the logo flashed on the screen. It felt like an eternity for the home screen to appear. And when it did, she wasted not one second calling Mother.

Back at home, Mother picked up her daughter's used pair of jeans that lay next to her child's dresser. There just had to be something, anything! Do kids pass notes these days? Would there have been a receipt? Reaching into the front pocket, Eileen took hold of a ring and pulled it out. The sight of the piece of cosmetic junk brought on extreme revulsion and an urge to whip it across the room. She recognized that ring; and in a few seconds, the memories pieced together "the whos and the whats" which transformed revulsion into a God-awful fear. The very name that had haunted her daughter's cell phone did not belong to an older boy named Wayne. It was the same Wayne who tormented Eileen years ago. Wayne now had her daughter, Alexi!

At the very moment of Eileen's realization, her cell phone rang. It was Alexi! The teenage girl was truly in danger as Eileen hadn't been called "Mommy" in many years. The voice was choppy and frustrating to comprehend. Even still, Alexi was breathing heavy. From what Mother could make out, Wayne had her daughter in some forest preserve and was chasing her.

"That son-of-a-bitch!" But there was no time for anger, now.

"Alexi, what woods? This is important!"

"I don't know, Mommy! Please help me! It's the same road before we get on the highway!"

Eileen knew exactly where that monster had taken her daughter as her mind went back to that night of 15 years ago. It was such a horrible thing for Alexi to experience; in addition, being chased by the same man who was capable of transforming into a stark-raving maniac.

Mother warned while holding back her tears, "Baby, we're getting help. Just keep away from him, okay?"

Alexi did not respond. Instead, the squeal of a terrified girl shrieked through the receiver. Wayne had finally surprise-intercepted Alexi who thought she was alone and safe to call Mother. Her youthful 20/20 vision was sharp enough to perceive the hand that reached out from the side of a tree, and took a firm hold of her jacket shoulder. It was necessary to drop the cell as she quickly unzipped the jacket with amazing speed, providing an ability to slip out and escape a near capture. Wayne was cunning with his knowledge of that forest and nearly had her. But the Alexi was far more acute than he imagined. Adrenaline now enabled his young Eileen to leap over bushes and logs, youth and fear being the advantage over his older and out-of-shape body.

A young girl has little tolerance for sticker bushes and must leap over in a moment of unexplained power. A grown man who is desperate can tolerate sticker bushes and only runs through while bearing the sharp stings and scratches. She could not escape; Wayne would not allow it! The blade of the commando knife had been withdrawn from the sheath. And when the chase had slowed Wayne remained some distance behind. "Eileen! You can't last! You don't know these woods! I will capture you and I will be very angry!"

Looking back, the sight of the crazed man who wielded a large knife only spelled life's end if captured. Where were Mother and Father? Where were the police? How would they find her out in these woods?

It was in this moment when Alexi realized her mistake. She was deep in the woods which would make it impossible for help to locate her. Needless to say, it was best to be closer to the road. But going the opposite direction was not so easy. Wayne was highly successful in barricading his young Eileen's return to the opposite direction, which forced the young girl to continue running deeper and deeper into the forest.

Cold, without a jacket while growing weaker every moment, the chase had continued for over an hour. In Alexi's favor, thanks to her desperate call to Mother, the Mapleview, Sillmac and State police knew for certain that Wayne Brockman had the young girl out in the untamed forests off Creek Highway. A midnight-blue Mustang was parked some distance from one of the entrances. But the forest was miles and miles of wilderness. Finding the young girl would take some time.

It this was 50 years ago, such a search would end unsuccessful. It might have been days before the body of a young girl was found; perhaps months for an unfortunate hunter to stumble upon human remains, all the while a fugitive on the loose. But this was the 21st century. Helicopter crews, all of whom had much military training, now hovered over a 5 mile radius of deep forest with heat-sensing cameras to detect living creatures and people who were shrouded by towering trees.

After some time through the image of those heat-sensing cameras, the glowing ghosts of two humans danced along the bottom of the forest in a most frightening scene of a girl trapped in a chase. This was when highly trained specialists were lowered from ropes to the forest below. 2, 4, 6 officers were very near the crazed abductor with a knife. Believing the chase to be over and much relieved, Alexi made the mistake of remaining still for help to arrive. This only provided an opportunity for Wayne to seize his young Eileen in a last moment's attempt to freedom.

The knife was to her throat which communicated to officers that Wayne expected to be left alone. But in this part of the country, officers who trained for such missions (that would probably never happen until that Saturday in November) were skilled hunters and very handy with scope rifles. Do you really think that the crazed abductor could slit the young girl's throat upon a rifle's bullet which penetrated his eye?

Detective Tom cursed when the announcement was made over police radio. He and his partner were there that morning, hopeful that they had found the person behind the disappearances. If true, maybe the suspect could have provided information of the three, other missing women. The girl was unharmed, but Wayne Brockman had been killed during the rescue.

Chapter 44

Now towards the end of a second bottle of Halloween Merlot, which included an unusual painting of a half human / half tree, Dana began to question the unbelievable story as she set her empty glass down.

She exclaimed, "But Wayne didn't have anything to do with the previous disappearances of Mapleview! The person behind the disappearances was still out there, right?"

Dana watched as the man she was falling in love with finish his glass of Merlot before pouring the remains of the bottle in his own glass, never offering to fill hers. Considering his often generosity, it was an act very much unlike him. Maybe he exhibited more selfish tendencies while drinking. With a good wine buzz, herself, Dana wasn't going to make a big deal. She probably had enough wine anyway.

Neither Dana nor the wonderful man she was with understood the story as clearly and detailed as you and I. Based on information in the news and mostly hearsay, the story told over a couple bottles of wine was a bit fuzzy and sketchy. There were some moments that were of fine detail, in particular, those moments of Mary's suspicions and frustrations, and the time when Kelly lived in the Trivelli house.

He took a sip of wine before answering her question, "And right you are, Dana! Ironically, there were no further disappearances after Wayne Brockman had been killed by the police. And despite the fact that the Mapleview police announced that he could not have been the person behind the previous disappearances, townspeople, along with the media, concluded that the villain had been caught.

* * *

Thanksgiving had come and gone. Detective Tom sat in his warm and cozy office on the Monday after the holiday weekend, drinking coffee made by Officer Ralph. Although a peaceful weekend with no homicides or disappearances, the veteran detective was disappointed.

Detective Larry entered the office and sat down in front of his partner's desk.

Detective Tom was not in his best form that morning. "What do you want, Larry?"

"Why so down, Tom? Is it rough coming back after a holiday weekend?"

"No, the weekend was fine, but Monday is a little too quiet. It would appear that Coldsworth is no longer abducting women. I bet he's done with that painting. And you know what kills me? Everyone wants to believe that Brockman was behind the other disappearances."

Detective Larry nodded in agreement, "Well if that's what they want to believe, let 'em. I guess people need to feel safe. What if there are no more disappearances and the public just figured we did our job?"

Detective Tom took one final gulp of his coffee before throwing the Styrofoam cup in the wastepaper basket. "Larry, if you want to put another notch on your belt, be my guest. But that would be the difference between you and me. There's a serial killer on the loose, and I won't rest until I've caught my man!"

Chapter 45

As late November transitions into early December; the cold, Mapleview air brings with it fallen snow. Just like everywhere else, the blanket of white is a welcome sight after Thanksgiving while people anticipate the holidays.

The snow put Mary in the mood for Christmas as she had already set up her tree on the Saturday morning which followed the Thanksgiving weekend. Colored lights illuminated the house along with wintery decorations, a beautiful nativity and many holiday candles throughout various rooms. Unfortunately, the radio stations throughout Mapleview and surrounding areas played their idea of holiday music: Twangy ballads that spoke of being lonely and unable to face the cheer, or songs that preached we shouldn't be happy for Christmas because it might sadden those who are less fortunate. Fortunately for Mary, she had a CD collection of real Christmas music to put one in the holiday spirit. The Trivelli house now echoed with those joyful tunes as she worked feverishly, outside, decorating the lawns and exterior with more colored lights, illuminated figures of wintery animals, and of course, an outdoor nativity.

Don't even think that Mary's nativity contained the inflatable Snoopy and Grinch that overlooked the sleeping, infant Jesus! Mary was quite familiar with the story of Christmas as it was told in church each year. Snoopy and the Grinch weren't part of it, at least to her recollection!

Working through lunch, the holiday decorating project was completed by about 1:30 that afternoon. Through experience, Mary knew that it was best to eat light when having a late lunch. And a nice cup of coffee was enjoyed afterwards while sitting near the Christmas tree where, for a brief moment, she dozed off for a quick recharge.

She probably hadn't slept more than a few minutes when the voice of Kelly spoke an alarming phrase, "...when you finally join us..."

Irritated from being awoken so soon, Mary reached over to the side table for another sip of coffee. The dream originated from the people who now lived in the mausoleum: Kelly and her friends who often communicated with Mary.

It was sad, really. Poor Mary was finding herself lonely for the winter months as her husband continued to travel in his job. She was making friends with people who were imaginary and called out from the blasted mausoleum in the backyard!

Married for nearly six months, she hoped to have been pregnant with their first child by then. Daren often argued that he wasn't ready for parenthood, but he went along with Mary's wishes and seemed fully cooperative. But despite the attempts, no children were on the way. Was this the life that Mary had to look forward to?

What Mary needed was a pet, a puppy that would remain small enough to live in the historic house while providing companionship during the cold and lonely, winter months. But would Daren allow a dog? Even if this went against his wishes, Mary recalled a day of returning home to discover the hideous mausoleum in the corner of her backyard. Daren went against Mary's wishes and had the mausoleum constructed. If anything, he owed his wife. Mary should have been allowed to get her own dog, and that's just what she did!

A visit to the pet store on Sunday afternoon resulted in the purchase of the cutest puppy one could ever find: a brown Yorkshire terrier that barked from behind the glass window as-if calling out to Mary as she approached. She immediately named him Muffin, after a stuffed animal dog that she had as a child.

Of course it would require much energy and patience to house train the puppy, but Mary expected this and followed the proper guidelines. She was diligent and observant for those warning signs of when to take the dog outside. And although the saddest thing one could experience, Mary caged Muffin while leaving for work on Monday. The puppy's panicky yelps called out for Momma as Mary closed the door behind. Fortunately her friend and boss, Shelly, allowed Mary to return home during lunch to let the dog out and offer some comfort before, once again, caging it.

The dog was more of a pleasure than it was work. Daren wasn't to return from his business travel until Wednesday evening. Under normal circumstances, Mary would spend the days lonely. But the yorkie offered plenty of companionship as it saw Mary as his Momma that fed him and offered warmth while seated on the sofa. And during playtime, Mary realized there had never been so much activity and excitement in the Trivelli house. She played tug of war with Muffin and bounced the dog's squeaky ball down the hallway in a game of fetch, all the while the puppy would bark in excitement.

One of Mary's most favorite events would happen daily in the early morning hours as she let Muffin out into the snowy backyard. Upon coming in, he would follow Mary back to bed and run through the tunnel of blankets to dry off and get warm.

It was so simple to rid those depressing moments of imaginary friends that called from the mausoleum. This doesn't mean to say that Mary forgot the important messages of her husband and the frightening dreams that pointed out her suspicions. She kept those memories at the edge of her consciousness, waiting for more evidence that might further prove her doubts of Daren.

But for now, she had her baby to take care of and a husband who was soon to return to the surprise addition of the family.

Muffin screamed at the window while watching Daren pull up from the driveway on a late, Wednesday afternoon. It was already dark, and he could see through the illuminated window the spasmodic dog that scratched at the glass with a look of being ferocious. Inside, Mary announced to the dog that, "Daddy is home! Is that Daddy? Are you excited to see your Daddy?"

Daren entered the house that echoed the sounds of the dog's hideous barking. It stood 6 feet away and warned the intruder not to take one step further in the house. After a week of traveling on business and dealing with the commotion at the airport, Daren had hoped for a quiet evening with his wife. Still, he could see that Mary purchased a companion and was sure to appear happy with the addition of Rat Dog, which now declared Daren to be most unwelcome.

He kissed his wife and spoke over the barking, "You got yourself a rat dog?"

Mary playfully slapped her husband's arm, "Stop it! He's a yorkie. Isn't he cute?"

Rat Dog growled and snarled at the man.

Realizing it was best to make friends with the animal, Daren knelt down in an attempt to pet it. But Rat Dog only backed away while producing more ferocious barking.

That's when Mary picked up her puppy. "Oh, it's only Daddy!" She carried her baby over to Daren who tried, again, to pet the dog. Rat Dog nearly snapped at his hand.

Daren quickly pulled away, "Oops! Okay, you just need to get used to me."

Rat Dog followed Daren through the house with its hideous bark while biting at the strange man's feet. It was annoying for Daren, but he maintained his composure and appeared to see humor in the situation. Secretly, he wished for a quiet evening after his travel and wished his wife hadn't purchased Rat Dog.

Mary had a hearty beef stew prepared for dinner. But that night was unlike the previous dinners at the Trivelli house as Rat Dog continued its ferocious barking at Daren. If he tried talking to his wife, the dog would intensify its threats.

Halfway through dinner, Daren kindly suggested, "We're going to have to get a de-barker collar for that dog."

Mary dropped her fork. "A de-barker collar? No, that's cruel! How would you like it if I tied a de-barker collar to your neck?" Of course, the dog screamed along with Mary.

Daren remained calm, "If I had an inch of fur on my neck it might be equal. Come on, they make those for dogs and they're proven to work. We're going to have to do something!" It was now necessary for Daren to shout over the dog's hideous barking. "I mean this is ridiculous!"

Mary shouted in return, "So are you telling me you don't like the dog?"

"I didn't say that, Mary! I just wanted to eat dinner with my wife without shouting over a barky rat dog!"

Mary quickly picked up the dog, "Shhhh! Calm down, calm down! Daddy doesn't like it when you bark. Here, you want something to eat?" She hand fed the dog some pieces of meat from her plate which actually quieted the yorkie.

Daren was appalled, "Don't feed the dog at the table. He's going to expect you to feed it whenever it's meal time."

Mary returned an angry glare, "You know Daren; I'm beginning to realize that you're jealous of Muffin. You're jealous that I get something to keep me company while you're gone. Well he's not going anywhere! Muffin is here to stay. Isn't that right my little baby?"

Rat Dog licked Mary's lips in response to her up-close baby talk.

Bedtime was very much different than the previous nights spent in the Trivelli house. Of course Rat Dog didn't appreciate Daren sleeping in bed and Daren vice-versa.

Daren yelled over the vicious barking, "You let the dog sleep with you? You're not supposed to do that! He'll think he's equal to us!"

Mary was furious, "Daren, if you don't like it then you can sleep on the sofa! He's the one who's with me night-after-night, not you! Muffin will sleep in this bed whether you like it or not!" Then she coaxed the yorkie to lie down, "Shhh! Lie down, lie down. Lie next to momma; go seepies.

And that was the night Daren lost his status in the marital bed. Children couldn't be made, now. Rat Dog slept close to Mary and would become vicious if Daren touched her.

* * *

Eventually, Rat Dog became conditioned to Daren's presence and relaxed it's compulsion to bark at the unwelcomed stranger. Because of the nature of his job, it was necessary for Daren to travel which caused the small dog to lose any memory of the man who fought for Momma's affection. Hideous barking would resume for a day or two upon Daren's return. But the dog became a way of life and Daren simply accepted it.

Romance resumed between husband and wife, provided Mary coaxed Rat Dog to lie down and "go seepies". But the yorkie expected to participate in the exchange of affection so that there would be a third party involved in the loving making. Daren would have to enjoy the sight of Rat Dog licking Mary's arms and legs while often growling at the man who dominated Momma. It was a serious turnoff for Daren! Aside from that, the panting of stinky breath was most unpleasant!

Chapter 46

Dead winter came and went and there were no further dreams or "communications" from the mausoleum. And despite how her husband hated Muffin, Mary realized the importance of the dog. Loneliness was not a good thing, and the yorkie remedied its harmful effects.

On a Sunday afternoon in April, nearly a year since getting married, Mary sat at her desktop PC in the den while browsing for some new recipes to try. Daren sat in the family room while watching the ballgame. Muffin laid on the ground at Mary's feet, somehow aware that the typing was connected to food.

Finding an interesting recipe for pork tenderloin, Mary opened the WordPad with the intention of copying and pasting the text to be printed. In Mary's opinion, the advertisements and pictures just wasted ink. She was only interested in the actual recipe.

Mary wasn't the most skilled in operating a computer. She knew how to "get around"; type up documents, browse the web, etc. And she knew how to highlight text so that Edit could be selected followed by Copy.

But for some reason, Mary only highlighted the text of the recipe and then switched over to the WordPad to select Edit then Paste. Whatever had been copied before Mary sat down, it now appeared on the WordPad. It wasn't her expected recipe for pork tenderloin. Rather, it was the most bone-chilling writing one could ever read.

Mary could feel herself shrink in size and fall deeper into the chair as the blood rushed to her head, heart nearly palpitated and controlled breathing attempted to stabilize her consciousness. It was an obituary, Mary's obituary! Somehow she recognized the writing format to be appropriate for a young woman. Opening by stating her full name, age and of belonging to the town of Mapleview; it soon took a bizarre direction by mentioning that foul play was suspected. In fact, it quickly turned into more of a newspaper article that told a gruesome, story-like confession that was narrated by Daren. Apparently he had written the document and copied and pasted it to be stored on some remote email account, never to be saved on hard drive. Maybe he kept a journal.

The startling text on the PC screen read, "I loved her more than anything, more than anyone could comprehend. She was my wife who lived under the same roof. We were intimate together. I even had the pleasure of observing her naked as she dressed each day. How much more could I have possibly wanted of my wife?

But it wasn't enough! It felt as though there was an invisible veil between myself and her and I couldn't fully touch her as deeply as I wanted. It's normal for a man to want to love his wife. But I wanted to love her in such a crazy way. I mean I just wanted to LOVE her; LOVE the very life from her and keep her mine forever.

Late at night, I followed through with my plan. I grabbed my beautiful wife by the throat and choked her to death! Unable to scream, her eyes spoke of the terror while pleading for my mercy. I watched her lifeless body lie at the foot of the stairs.

Then a great sadness overcame me. I would never hear her voice, hear her laugh or enjoy the many things she does. It was better to enjoy my wife who was alive and wore the imaginary, invisible veil over her body.

Fortunately, this is only fiction. My beautiful wife is still alive. So I now search for a woman who looks just like Mary. Even if she possessed only a few subtle features, I could LOVE the life from her and keep her forever!"

Still in shock, Mary leaned over her chair to verify that Daren was on the sofa. As usual, his eyes were glued to the TV with beer in hand.

For the first time in the marriage, Mary decided to keep her finding and suspicions a secret. She quickly printed Daren's story, folded it up and put it in her pocket. Then she copied the intended recipe and printed that up.

"What are you doing, Mary?" Daren called out across the family room.

"Oh, nothing; just printing a recipe for tonight."

"What's for dinner?"

"Pork tenderloin."

Daren stood up for another beer, "Alright! I can't wait, Babe!" At least he appreciated his wife for one thing or another!

* * *

While alone; Mary often read Daren's short story, pondering its meaning and at least finding comfort that she had been spared strangulation. Perhaps it was only a dark fantasy, a release from his daily frustrations. But what if as the years unfolded, Daren's dark fantasies became overpowering, and his aged mind did follow through with killing Mary? It would certainly be worth considering, maybe prepare for the future.

But there was something even greater that disturbed Mary. The mention of finding a substitute woman to murder along with Daren's vague mention of owning her was troubling. Mary wouldn't dare consider that perhaps the imaginary people living in the mausoleum were a collection of Daren's murdered women! But this dreaded theory was met with the firm belief that the answer was in Daren's mausoleum.

But how could she access this off limits building that remained locked? The last time she requested a tour, Daren had turned frightening and nearly abusive. And the more Mary recalled the tour, the more she remembered how Daren had gone out of his way to open the crypt at the front of the building. On that morning, he and Mary both stood at the deepest wall of the mausoleum with Daren's back towards the wall while Mary faced Daren. It was necessary for him to pass his wife and open one of the crypts at the front of the building.

Dreams and memories distort as time passes. Perhaps she was only filling in the gaps; but Mary recalled the dream of walking out to the mausoleum while being aware of someone in one of the crypts of the far wall (where Daren stood the following morning). No wonder his behavior turned dramatic. The other crypts could not be opened!

Many nights while Daren was home, Mary lay awake and thought of rummaging her husband's pants pockets for the key to the mausoleum. She could learn, once and for all, the answer to the mausoleum's mystery while her husband slept. But what if he awoke with the terrible feeling that something was wrong in the backyard? What if he suddenly appeared just as Mary made a gruesome discovery? Surely, she would become an addition to the mausoleum, or at the very least, receive harsh punishment.

It would take a month after the frightening story was discovered before Mary could have her wish. This took place on a Sunday afternoon in May while Mary did her yearly planting of impatiens, mums and marigolds throughout the backyard. Being the new owner of the historic Trivelli house, Mary could plant however she wished and expanded the yearly gardening so that the entire perimeter of the yard and house were outlined with flowers.

Daren was home that weekend and agreed to help his wife by making an emergency run to the home improvement center for more planting soil. Suddenly, Mary was aware of Muffin missing.

"Muffin?" She really should have had a small fence to separate her yard from the woods. "Muffin?" Now in a panic that the dog had ventured out of the yard, she ran towards the direction of where the yorkie was seen last, in the direction of Daren's mausoleum.

"Muffin?" Mary walked towards the front of the building to discover that for some reason the door had been left unlocked and probably blew open from the wind. The curious dog now stood inside of the mausoleum, poking his nose around.

"Muffin, you're not supposed to be in here." She knew the building was off limits and projected her guilt onto the dog. For the first time, Mary was alone with an opportunity to investigate what was in that crypt nearest the deep wall. The locks didn't look terribly challenging to open. Daren did it with some ease on the morning of Mary's tour.

Suddenly, Muffin began to sound his excited bark while running out of the building. Daren was home which meant an unsuccessful end to Mary satisfying her curiosity. But she left the door undisturbed while quickly leaving with the intention of exploring the inside, later. It wasn't her fault that Daren had left the door open. It was best to leave it alone. As Mary walked out to greet her husband, she could determine that he was unaware of the invasion. Hopefully, Daren would remain off guard for the evening.

Although Muffin was responsible for the discovery, he later destroyed any hope of Mary entering the mausoleum, later. The day's work of planting flowers had been completed. Husband and wife lounged in their chairs while overlooking the beautiful backyard. And the light of sunset bled through the leaves of trees. Muffin was getting braver and able to venture further away from Mary. On evenings like this, he often strolled about the yard, exploring and rolling around, maybe chewing a bone left over from dinner.

Of course the curious dog went beyond the bushes and towards the front of the mausoleum which was hidden from the view of Daren and Mary. Rat Dog was near the front of the building longer than Daren liked. He exclaimed concerned. "What's the dog doing over there? Did he go down into the woods?"

He quickly rose from his seat and ran down the stairs, then nearly flew to the front of the mausoleum.

Mary was aware of what concerned Daren. He didn't care of the dog's safety; wolves could have dragged little Muffin away and this would make the man happy. With only a slight delay, Mary ran down the stairs equally as fast. Maybe her presence at the discovery of the open mausoleum would welcome another tour.

As Mary approached the side of the building, she heard the sound of the door closing. It wasn't a slam shut; it was more of gentle, cautious close as if not to let Mary know that the door had been left open. Then Daren quickly emerged around the corner with Muffin in his arms.

Mary was quick to ask, "What happened?"

Daren was a little more worried about Muffin than what was normal as he replied, "The dog was halfway in the woods. We've got to get a small fence to keep him away from there."

Daren had lied. Mary knew that curious Muffin went into the building. This was her first concrete piece of evidence that something was being hidden from her.

* * *

The following week, Daren was still home and preparing for an upcoming biomedical equipment convention. Mary returned from the flower shop on that Monday afternoon and took notice of subtle tire imprints on the backyard grass. They suggested that Daren's vehicle had been backed up to the mausoleum.

Mary asked her husband, "Did you drive on the backyard lawn?"

"Yeah, I had some electrical equipment to bring to the mausoleum. The AC is on the fritz; had to do an upgrade."

It sounded fishy to Mary. Just what sort of electrical equipment would weigh heavy enough to require backing up on the lawn?

There were no further happenings or unusual phenomenon with the mausoleum that summer. Of course Mary kept watchful eye on the building along with any opportunity to finally enter alone. She would lay awake on the nights that Daren was home, only a split second from rising out of bed to rummage through Daren's pants pockets. How easy it would be to enter the mausoleum while he slept. Still, it was too risky. And aside from that, Mary was worried of making a gruesome discovery in the dead of night, alone.

Chapter 47

The summer had come and gone, and it was nearly a year since the mysterious disappearances of Mapleview.

It was a Saturday night in mid-October with Daren supposedly on his way home from another business trip.

Mary held out the keys to Daren's mausoleum for her best friend, Shelly, to see. "They were lying on the floor, near the edge of the bed. He probably knows they were left behind but afraid to call me and ask about them."

Shelly laughed. For months, Mary had been updating her with the findings of Daren and the Mausoleum. Based on what Shelly heard, Mary was the last person who Daren would have wanted to find the keys!

She commented, "I bet it was a miserable week for him! But what time does he come home?"

"I don't know. Supposedly he left Seattle 4 hours ago. He usually calls once touching down, but then he has to drive up through Robin Creek. It takes him a little over an hour. I think we still have time. I wish I would have vacuumed earlier in the week!"

Shelly tried to lighten up the situation, "Are you sure you don't want to whip up some of your famous margaritas before we go outside? It'll be fun, like a spooky Halloween party!"

Mary remained serious. "No Shelly, I want to be sober for this one. It's time I see the truth of what Daren is hiding. The answer is out there."

The two women put their autumn jackets on and stepped outside. Mary was sensitive to the cold, October air and did her best to contain herself. Instead, she broke down in uncontrollable shivering while exclaiming, "I have so much anxiety right now!"

Her best friend patted Mary on the back. Times like this required much support from a friend. "It's okay; this will all be over, soon. You've always wanted the truth. I've known that about you all these years. Once the truth is known, you'll feel better."

They made it to the edge of the yard where the building stood behind the tall bushes. Suddenly, Mary stopped and pulled out her cell. "I better call Daren and make sure he's not close."

It was dead silent in the cold, night air as Shelly listened to the faint sounds of the callout tone which pinged Daren's own cell. After 4 rings, his voice could be heard, "Hello?"

Shelly could detect the nervousness in Mary's voice. "Hey! Did you touch down, yet?"

"Yeah; you know Mary, I stopped in Robin Creek at some hotel. I'm so exhausted and keep falling asleep behind the wheel. Do you mind if I spend the night?"

Whereas most wives would be disappointed and suspicious of a husband who couldn't drive an hour home, Mary sounded nearly relieved. "No, go on right ahead. I'd rather you be alive."

Daren could be heard over the receiver, "Thanks, Babe! You sure you're not mad?"

"No, Daren; I don't care. You work hard and I'm sure you're exhausted."

"Alright... Oh, hey, I was wondering if..."

The keys for the mausoleum? Was Daren going to ask Mary if she found them? But he stopped short after the word, "if" and then continued, "Nah, never mind! Love you, Babe! See you to-morrow morning!"

"Love you too, Daren!"

The call ended and Shelly couldn't help but add her comment of what was overheard. "He was going to ask about the keys, wasn't he?"

"I think so."

Once at the front of the mausoleum, Mary unlocked and opened the door. The light switch was flipped on; two illuminated sconces on the far wall provided light for the women to inspect to their heart's content. There was a mild smell of bleach in the air that Mary immediately found odd. "He was cleaning in here. I didn't notice bleach back in May."

Mary walked to the far wall where the illuminated sconces were mounted. Shelly followed and they both faced the crypts that were on the left side wall (left if one were entering the building).

And then Mary paused before touching the lock of the crypt that she was most curious of. Her back now faced the far wall as she spoke to her friend. "Daren was standing right here, and I was where you are standing, now." She demonstrated while speaking, "He actually walked around me and went over to the crypts over here!"

Shelly agreed with Mary's suspicion, "That's weird! I think this is the first crypt you should open." She pointed to one that Mary was most curious of."

The two women nearly held their breaths as the simple lock was undone and the crypt open. But to their disappointment, it was empty, waiting for a resident.

There were four crypts on the two sides of walls, giving a total of eight crypts. Both women took turns opening them. Before each lock was undone, hope filled the air that the vault would produce a most gruesome discovery and a mystery solved. They were like children who had been given lottery scratch tickets, waiting for the grand prize! And for extra luck, they didn't open the crypts in the order of their positioning. They would bounce between walls while randomly selecting another lock to undo.

"No, do this one first!"

"But that one's directly below! Do the diagonal one!"

Mary was beginning to feel guilty with the amount of fun, especially after wishing she had, in fact, made that margarita mix for a spooky Halloween party.

Shelly had the last crypt to open. The hope and smiles soon turned to dread as her face became pale. "Mary, there's something in here!"

Mary's hand rose to her mouth in anxiety. How terrible it would be to discover the rotting corpse of her dear cousin, Kelly. But it was only a cooler that Mary soon took hold of and slowly lifted the top. Bottles of beer floated in what was once ice. It perplexed Mary. "Beer? Daren has beer in here? So much for being sacred!"

Shelly had to ask, "Is he an alcoholic or something?"

Mary replied, "Not that I know of. He used to drink heavily before we were engaged. Now he just drinks beer, plenty of it."

Mary remained motionless for a brief moment and then restated her original question. "I mean why does have to hide beer in here? Why can't he just put in the house?"

While closing up the crypt in disgust and exhaling the disappointment along with any remaining anxiety, Mary made a suggestion that would restore the fun in the evening. "Well, what do you say we end this Halloween party with a pitcher of margaritas?"

Shelly perked up, "Oh yeah; now you're talking!"

But before switching the wall sconces off and locking the door, Mary paused at the peculiar condition of the floor. It seemed to bow, particularly at the center. The building had only been up for a little over a year; but through time, the floor would certainly cave in. She commented, "Do you want to know what my brilliant husband did? He went against my wishes and quickly built his mausoleum over the ancient well."

Shelly quickly asked, "Ancient well?"

Mary pointed to the center of the floor. "Shelly, there used to be a large hole over there. It was probably an ancient well. Anyway, when I was growing up, I remember that the hole could never be filled! Apparently, Daren had cemented over the hole, like my grandfather tried to do for years, and then constructed the building. And now, his mausoleum is sinking into the ground! I laugh! It couldn't have happened to a better person!"

Chapter 48

It was a Saturday night in mid-October. Dana sat with an empty wine glass before her while listening to the end of the confusing and unbelievable story. She was beginning to feel a bit queasy, probably brought on by the cheap wine that boasted the Tree Goddess painting. It had a unique taste, but not bad. The ill feeling would probably wear off soon.

Not all Dana's questions had been answered. "Okay, so Mary suspected that her husband was killing women and keeping their bodies in the mausoleum. But that doesn't explain the artist who made the painting on the bottle. Why did he have encounters with them before they disappeared?"

Daren took the final gulp of wine from his glass and set it down on the table. He had been referring to himself as "Mary's husband" throughout the story.

At that very moment, his wife's best friend, Shelly, had entered the Trivelli house. Mary discovered that the keys to the mausoleum were left near the edge of the bed, right where Daren had intentionally left them. Tonight would be a "spooky Halloween party" for the two women. Too bad Mary didn't whip up her famous margarita mix before visiting the mausoleum.

Savoring every last bit of flavor, Daren exhaled. "Ahhhhh, good wine! What did you think?"

Dana didn't want to hurt his feelings, "It was alright."

This was Daren's secret "bachelor pad" that was a good hour from home. Men who make plenty of money can afford such luxuries. Most men only wish for their own private pad where they can drink wine in peace and bring home beautiful women. Of course Mary would be livid if ever discovering Daren's other place.

Would Dana ever have her question answered? "What about the artist? What did he have to do with the disappearances?"

Daren had no idea the very depth of what he played with. He assumed that the few vivid dreams of the artist who had a fascination with his women were only dreams and nothing more. It was necessary to come up with a quick explanation. "The artist served as a scout. He had some kind of psychic connection with Mary's husband and would announce through dreams when the next sacrifice was found." Although trying to sound humorous, Daren had no idea how accurate that statement was.

Dana stood up. "Okay, that's just weird. You're beginning to scare me! And I'm not feeling too well. Can I have a drink of water?"

Daren rose from his seat, "Of course, I'll get one for you right away."

Dana followed him into the kitchen where a tall glass was pulled from the cupboard. He had a water cooler in the kitchen and filled the glass with crisp, clean refreshment. Handing it to Dana he watched as she gulped it down while looking so much like his beloved Mary.

It quickly reminded him that his own wife was due to call any minute. Daren missed the window to call which would have announced his fictional landing at the airport. In reality, he had spent the past few days preparing for his special night out with Dana.

Dana walked over to the sink to set the glass in. While doing so, she noticed that the bottom cupboard doors were all locked. "Why do you..."

Daren's large hands tightly wrapped around Dana's throat as the woman silently fought for dear life. Her eyes spoke of the terror while pleading for his mercy. At one point Daren nearly stopped because she reminded him so much of his dear Mary. But the job needed to be done; mercy could not be given. The weight of Dana's body soon weighed down on Daren's strangling arms and then collapsed into a lifeless shell.

With Dana now dead, Daren straightened out her limbs and carefully removed her clothes. She looked so much like Mary; so much, in fact, that Daren nearly believed he had made a mistake until a call came through the cell phone. It was his wife, thank goodness.

"Hello?"

"Hey! Did you touch down, yet?"

Daren quickly inhaled. Hopefully Mary would believe him. "Yeah; you know Mary, I stopped in Robin Creek at some hotel. I'm so exhausted and keep falling asleep behind the wheel. Do you mind if I spend the night?"

"No, go on right ahead. I'd rather you be alive."

It was too easy; was she on to him? "Thanks, Babe! You sure you're not mad?"

"No, Daren; I don't care. You work hard and I'm sure you're exhausted."

Surely, Mary had found the keys. "Alright... Oh, hey, I was wondering if..."

That might sound suspicious. Keys to the mausoleum should be the last thing on his mind. "Nah, never mind! Love you, Babe! See you tomorrow morning!"

"Love you too, Daren!"

Before beginning his project, Daren took both empty wine bottles and peeled off the Tree Goddess paintings. It was best to print up a couple new ones for the next time he opened a bottle of wine. The dreams of the painter were so vivid that he could actually see the Tree Goddess and remember it. Nearly obsessed with what was seen in the dream, Daren used the PC Paint Pad along with photo shop to copy and paste a frightening tree (found on the Internet) and then embedded various limbs within the image, followed by alteration of color. Orange background with jack-o-lanterns suggested something that of Halloween.

Once the labels had been peeled and discarded, he unlocked two of the bottom cupboard doors. The center frame had been altered so that it could be quickly removed, making it easy to partially pull out a glass tank of dark, red wine. Tonight, Kelly was enjoyed. But next time he drank wine, he might prefer something with a full body. The tank that he dunked the empty bottle of wine in at that moment contained the year-dead, rubenesque body of Sara, late owner of the Mapleview Coffeehouse. If he preferred something more lively and exuberant, he might have chosen wine from the next tank over, Stephanie. And after she's aged about a year, Daren will have a sweet and pleasing wine, made possible by a mock-Mary. Very few people understand the fine fruits of necrophagia, but Daren was a true connoisseur!

Locking up Sara's cabinet and then sealing the two bottles of wine, Daren next turned his attention to the evening's project. Two bottom cupboard doors on the left side had been unlocked, and the center frame was removed. An empty, glass tank was pulled out onto the floor. Keep in mind that the entire bottom row of cupboards had been modified so that all shelving was removed, making room for the 4 flavors of wine.

Finally, Daren could have Mary like never before! It was only a mock-Mary, but would probably taste the same. And it would take a good year for her to age. Her lifeless, naked body was gently laid in the tank. The tank was lifted and pushed back into the cupboard.

Daren next walked out to the parking lot where his red pickup truck sat near the back. Needless to say, Dana wasn't aware of his other vehicle, and neither was Mary. Tonight it sat parked with a hardtop installed on the bed. Inside, cases and cases of red, table wine waited to be unloaded. It was a job that took 15 minutes, carrying stacked cases in the condo two at a time.

Once inside, bottles were opened and the contents dumped into Dana's tank.

Halfway through the job, Daren thought to himself, "Oh my; I believe I've made a hybrid wine. Dana was drinking Kelly tonight."

The End!

Author Biography

Tom Raimbault resides in the Chicago land area with his wife and two daughters. When not writing, he works as a lab technician at a telecommunications company and is self-described on his resume as a "technology professional" who has worked with cellular & IP infrastructure, biomedical equipment, emergency two-way radios and computer hardware.

Tom began to produce weird writings back in 2000 while working the graveyard shift. The nightly edits were emailed to a small collection of coworkers who looked forward to something unusual to keep them awake or humored.

This practice was ended when he was moved to a different shift. Sadly, his enjoyment of writing was forgotten for several years until the autumn of 2007 when old friends received a "blast from the past" email with the recognizable words, "Hello All". The strange writings and short stories had resumed and a personal website was soon to follow.

In autumn of 2009, Tom published his first book, Freaked out Horror (a collection of short stories), through Create Space and was soon available on Amazon and Kindle. The work was revised and republished in 2011 with additional stories.

If you enjoyed the adventures of Mapleview in this book, be sure to get your first installment of the Amber trilogy, The Death Mask. It was released in autumn of 2011. The three books will continue the unfolding Mapleview stories.

Tom stays in contact with his readers by offering free short stories and writings throughout the week. Check out his website that includes the blog at:

http://sites.google.com/site/tomraimbaultwritings/